The Carousel Man

Stephen Paul Sayers

HELLBENDER BOOKS

an imprint of Sunbury Press, Inc.
Mechanicsburg, PA USA

HELLBENDER BOOKS

an imprint of Sunbury Press, Inc.
Mechanicsburg, PA USA

For information about special discounts for bulk purchases, please contact Sunbury Press Orders Dept. at (855) 338-8359 or orders@sunburypress.com.

To request one of our authors for speaking engagements or book signings, please contact Sunbury Press Publicity Dept. at publicity@sunburypress.com.

FIRST HELLBENDER BOOKS EDITION: September 2024

Set in Adobe Garamond Pro | Interior design by Crystal Devine | Cover by Lawrence Knorr | Edited by Sarah Peachey.

Publisher's Cataloging-in-Publication Data
Names: Sayers, Stephen Paul, author.
Title: The carousel man / Stephen Paul Sayers.
Description: First trade paperback edition. | Mechanicsburg, PA : Hellbender Books, 2024.
Summary: Haunted by nightmares and visions, a desperate man returns to the childhood carousel ride that spawned them. There, he uncovers a shocking truth—and a long-forgotten promise he's condemned to fulfill.
Identifiers: ISBN 979-8-88819-249-8 (softcover).
Subjects: FICTION / Horror | FICTION / Occult & Supernatural | FICTION / Thrillers / Supernatural.

Designed in the USA
0 1 1 2 3 5 8 13 21 34 55

For the Love of Books!

PROLOGUE

Twenty-Five Years Earlier
Spring Valley, Missouri

The battered pickup bounded along the dirt road, raising twin dust plumes from the trailer's rear wheels and adding choking grit to the humid breeze. The old man dragged a sleeve across his forehead.

"Bloody heat," he muttered, remembering how a Missouri scorcher could break a man by mid-morning.

Gazing through the bug-stained windshield, he scanned the endless golden farmland glowing under hazy sunshine. Missouri had always been part of his territory, but he hadn't been along these country roads in, what? A year, two maybe. Truth was, he hadn't had a job this far south in over a decade. Not that his memory was slipping; he was still sharp as a tack. But time passed differently for him now.

Sometimes on long journeys, he would do the math in his head to figure out his exact age. He no longer had the knack for adding, subtracting, or carrying the one, but his bandy legs, withered frame, and silver mane told him all he needed to know. He had outlived everyone he had ever known or loved—his precious Zachariah and Rebecca, and of course, Annabelle, his adored. But none of that mattered anymore.

Nothing else mattered but the job.

Thud . . . thud . . . thud . . .

The old man pinched his temples to soothe the pounding in his head. He didn't relish the task awaiting him. He never did. Today, he would meet a client—he liked calling them that—a young man with his whole life ahead of him. Edging the truck to the roadside, he killed the engine and swore under his breath. Bloody heat. He glanced through the passenger-side window at the knee-high corn swaying in the thick breeze.

The young man, Jack, would be here soon.

He slid from the driver's seat and arched his stiffening back. Shuffling to the trailer, he released the straps securing his load. He threw the tarp back halfway, examining the metal poles, platform pieces, and engine components needed for the carousel's assembly. It wouldn't take long to put the machine together, and when he did his client would come. They always came. He figured the swirling carnival music called to them, touching a place inside and reviving memories of a bygone era filled with carefree summer evenings, cotton candy, and first kisses. Or maybe the universe orchestrated happenstance and fate to intersect at some exact moment and time for everyone. The old man couldn't say—the "why" of it was way above his pay grade.

Folding the tarp back further revealed a collection of hand-crafted wooden horses secured to the trailer's deck. They lay side-by-side, adorned with polished leather saddles, and silky manes and tails. When a client mounted one of these five jumpers and the carousel twirled, they experienced something magical, as if heaven had cracked its gates and revealed its bounty. They left the ride changed forever.

A sixth horse lay separate from the others, secured with a much heavier rope.

Like the other five, the sixth horse was hand-crafted and beautifully appointed. The old man hesitated as he approached, his stomach squirming as he settled a tentative hand on the coffee-colored mare's sleek mane. The silky coat twitched beneath his palm, a slurring pulse pounding beneath his fingertips. He yanked his hand away, imagining something dark and festering beneath its skin. When a client dismounted the sixth horse, they also left changed forever—but in a way he didn't like to think about. Once, he tried to douse the coffee-colored mare with kerosene and burn it to ash, but the fluid had no effect. The pounding inside his skull afterward had been a warning to never again attempt such betrayal.

Taking a deep breath, the old man calmed the flutter in his chest. "It will be over soon," he said. But his words brought no comfort.

Before every job, he fought the light and darkness inside himself. He wanted to help his clients make the right decision, but the carousel had a special power over them, one that drew them in and blinded them.

His clients didn't appear to notice his traveling carnival brought with it no Ferris wheel or funhouse, no fried dough or hot dogs—and no other souls to join them on their special ride. He didn't worry about passersby happening along and witnessing a lone carousel spinning in a cornfield. They did all the time, sometimes with a hearty "hello" or "good day." They would stare right at it and see nothing at all.

People see what they want to see.

Thud . . . thud . . . thud . . .

The old man rubbed his temples in slow circles. The pounding in his head always got worse when he had a deadline. He released the straps securing the equipment. The job. Nothing else mattered but the job.

"Time to stop the bloody pounding."

PART ONE

The Awakening

CHAPTER ONE

Present Day
Edgartown, Massachusetts (Martha's Vineyard)

Jack paced the smooth wooden planks running along the back deck, his gaze darting to the cell phone clutched in his grip. *Come on, Hal. Where are you?* He glared at the device again before stuffing it in his back pocket. Hal Bader would be calling soon with an update for sure. Six months ago, a small studio had acquired the screenplay for Jack's latest novel, *Double-Barrel Justice*, and he had been dancing on pins and needles ever since. It had been a while since any Jack Rainne novel had garnered Hollywood attention, but he was confident his agent could broker a deal and get him back on the map.

Time to deliver, Hal, the damn bills are piling up.

He turned his attention to his wife launching bold strokes through the Atlantic surf yards off their beachfront property. He could almost smell the rich Hawaiian Tropic dark tanning oil and sea salt mixture coating Sam's skin. The aromatic blend was a delicacy he had grown to love but didn't partake in much anymore, and not for lack of trying. They were just in another rut. Happens in every marriage. But the cracks had grown deeper and more damaging over the past year. It made sense, given all that had happened. He'd been trying to stay positive and give Sam her space. She needed more time, that's all.

Sam dragged a towel through her dripping blond hair and threw a T-shirt over her head as she crossed the backyard. The shirt fell across her frame and accentuated each curve, as if J.Crew had hand-woven the fabric using her body as the blueprint. Jack, on the other hand, could never find a tee that agreed with his eroding physique. He pressed a hand across his bare midsection, lamenting the dad bod that had formed while he wasn't looking.

He fished in his back pocket again for his cell and glared at the screen. *Goddammit, Hal.*

Leaning his elbows against the deck railing, Jack gazed into the pool below. Such a beautiful day and no sign of Morgan. He glanced over his shoulder at the second-story dormers perched along the sloping Spanish-tiled roof. His daughter's bedroom window rested against the sill with curtains drawn. How long had it been since he'd heard her squeals of laughter, like a favorite song, drifting from the backyard as she scampered through the sprinkler with her friends. Shutting his eyes, he pictured the pint-sized bodies in the pool's shallows, the furious splashing, and intermittent shouts of "Marco" and "Polo" carrying through the neighborhood.

The memory dispersed as the phone buzzed in Jack's hand. He fiddled with the device, swiping a finger across the glass. "Tell me the good news, buddy."

He imagined Hal leaning back in his Boylston Street office, feet on the desk, and one of those obnoxious Cuban cigars plugged between his lips. He'd be getting ready to spit out the numbers any second, film rights dollars, budget percentages, and potential box office take. But Hal's lengthy silence brought a twist to Jack's insides.

"Backstreet Films didn't exercise the option, Jack."

He raked a hand through his shoulder-length coif. "They had it for six months. What happened?"

"Too risky, I think. They got burned on a cop film with Colin Farrell last year, and your screenplay gave them flashbacks."

"Flashbacks?"

"Yeah, like sell-your-assets-to-make-up-the-financial-loss flashbacks. Producers hate those. And speaking of flashbacks, readers hate them, too. Your books use way too many. You should—"

"Thanks for the writing tips, Hal," Jack said. "But you're my agent, not my editor."

"Then you need a better editor."

"Maybe I need a better agent."

"Maybe I need a better writer."

Jack fought a grin but understood once a studio dropped the option on a film, others wouldn't touch it. If one studio couldn't get financing or find an A-list director or actor for a project, the others would peg it as a wounded duck.

Jack repositioned the cell to his other ear. "What do we do now?"

Hal let out a breath. "Well, Netflix and Hulu need content. I know a few smaller production companies that are feeders for streaming services. I'll make a few calls."

"And wait another six months?"

"You understand how this works, Jack. Listen, if they agree to a look, it will put a little money in the bank until things . . . well . . . start looking up. In the meantime, let me see about getting you some appearances. Writing conferences, book signings. That kind of thing."

"Thanks, Hal. Every little bit helps."

"You tell Sam I said 'hi.' And, um . . . get rid of the flashbacks."

Jack disconnected. Pressing his palms against the deck railing, he eyed the pool below. *Now what?* Maybe a swan dive off the balcony and into the shallow end? Another call like that from Hal and he might consider it. He faced the cloudless blue sky, sensing the glowing sun warming his skin. Nope, not today.

Sam bounded up the steps to the deck. "Was that Hal?"

"Yeah." He couldn't hold her gaze. "Backstreet Films didn't come through."

Her jaw hung open. "Damn, Jack. We needed that one."

"I know. Hal's gonna keep working on it, pitch it to other studios."

Sam appeared to deflate, her sagging shoulders a reminder she understood how the Hollywood thing worked. They had met on the set of the film version of Jack's first novel, *Road Rage*, the one with Mel Gibson— before the actor's own road rage incident. After his drunken rant went viral, the film fizzled, but romance bloomed, and Jack returned from LA with more than what he had packed.

She pivoted and gazed at the ocean. "We haven't had a nibble since *Caribou Man*. And that was, what, three years ago?"

"Yeah, don't remind me. We'll be fine. Something will come up. It always does." But it hadn't lately, and Jack wasn't sure he believed himself anymore.

Slipping his shirt over his head, Jack padded across the deck. He pulled the slider and entered the living room, his eyes taking a moment to adjust from midday sunshine to sixty-watt lighting.

Thud . . . thud . . . thud . . .

The headaches had started up again. Stepping into the bathroom, Jack cracked the medicine cabinet above the vanity and fingered the row of vials on the shelf—Valium, Clonazepam, Paxil. Out of Cyclobenzaprine.

"Dammit." He grabbed a handful of Tylenol and swallowed them dry. Dropping onto a barstool, he poured himself a highball to help wash away the chalky remnants. As he brought the glass to his lips, Sam slipped in from the deck. Jack had been married long enough to recognize the urgency in her stride as she moved across the carpet. She would have more to say on the subject.

He rattled his ice-filled glass. "Need a drink?"

She peeked at the clock and shook her head. She had always been one of those after-five drinkers, but Jack never understood how getting tipsy evolved into something more honorable after a certain hour.

She crossed the living room. "Where does that leave me?"

He spun on the seat. "What do you mean?"

"Well, we talked about me getting back into things out there. Maybe getting a part in the film."

Jack gave his shoulders a hitch. "Can't do anything about it now."

"Then I need to make a few calls. I told you I was serious about this."

"Listen, Sam. You haven't done any work out there in years. And parts are harder to get, especially as you get old—" Jack cut himself off, wishing he could have stuffed a sock into his mouth a second earlier.

"Older? Is that it?" She jammed her hands against her hips. "So now I'm old?"

Jack stood and settled his hands on her arms. "Christ, Sam. You're forty-something going on twenty-five, but it's a whole new scene out there. New directors, new favorites."

She twisted from his grasp. "I still have my contacts, you know."

"I'm sure you do, but I thought you wanted to concentrate on being a mom?"

"Don't guilt me, Jack." Sam crossed her arms. "For the last ten years that's all I've done. Don't forget who gave up their career to be a mom."

He pressed a hand to his chest. "I haven't."

Slipping past him, Sam propped herself against the bar. "I guess I'll have that drink."

He poured a Malibu and Coke over ice. She swirled the glass and took a gulp. "I'm worried, Jack."

"You shouldn't be."

She pivoted to face him. "Are you in denial or do you have your head stuck in the sand? I mean, you invested everything we had into *Jigsaw*, and that wasn't the only clunker film with your name on it. The books aren't flying off the shelves anymore, either."

"Tell me something I don't already know."

"I'm just being honest. You haven't written anything in, what? Three years? The last piece I read about you was in a where-are-they-now article."

Ouch.

"We need steady paychecks coming in."

"We're fine," Jack said, his tone rising. "And besides, you go out to LA to act again, and you could be gone for a while."

Sam didn't answer. The silence weighed heavy before she added, "Maybe that wouldn't be so bad."

"What?" Jack sank onto the barstool.

"We've been drifting for a while now. You know this last year hasn't been easy. Maybe we could use a little time apart."

He sensed the heat flush his cheeks.

"I don't know." Leaning her elbows on the bar, she swirled her drink in slow circles. "Maybe I could get out of Martha's Vineyard for a while. You could get back to writing."

He dragged a hand across his stubbled chin. "What am I supposed to say about this?"

"You don't need to say anything." She left her glass on the bar and crossed the room. Before slipping through the patio door, she turned. "We should just think about it."

He slid off the stool and steadied himself against the bar, his numb limbs struggling to support his weight. "What about Morgan? She would want you to stay."

Sam closed her eyes. "This has nothing to do with Morgan. This is about us. Just think about it."

And at that moment, it dawned on him that *she* had been thinking about it. While he had been going about his day, helping with dinner, mowing the lawn, or watching TV beside her in bed, her mind had been somewhere else, planning a different future. Moving on.

How long had she waited to tell me?

He pressed his eyes shut as images of Sam flew at him like snowflakes in a squall, the pieces of their life together flashing before him: the smell of her skin after a shower; the way her tongue danced on her lower lip; her warm breath against his neck on the dance floor; her clothes clinging to her wet skin in the rain. He relived the softness of their first kiss and the warmth of her hand when he held it for the first time. The memories accelerated, picking up speed: her bare feet in the sand; the taste of wine on her lips; her dark hair flowing across the pillow and her body's shape beneath his hands; her smell on his clothes. A million things swirled in his memory, weakening him. Defeating him.

Jack quick-stepped across the living room and out onto the deck, but Sam stood at the ocean's edge, staring at the sea. He glanced over his shoulder at the second-story dormers. Through Morgan's bedroom window, Jack observed his daughter's outline behind the glass.

She drew the curtains and slipped from view.

CHAPTER TWO

Twenty-Five Years Earlier
Spring Valley, Missouri

On the last day of his seventeenth year, Jack Rainne disappeared off the face of the Earth. He couldn't have foreseen the curious turn of events before meeting the stranger in the cornfield perched beside the spinning carousel. The sun glinted off the twirling machine, sending shards of hypnotizing light across the teenager's face. It must have been the numbing glare, or maybe the swirling calliope melody that coaxed him off his bicycle and through the Johnsons' cornfield. He had been riding home from school past the sun-drenched farms and meadows on County Road 4 when he heard the discordant tones. As he reached the top of Prairie Road, he figured the Johnson boy was pecking at the piano keys in the house nestled behind the line of maples. But the sound had come from farther away and with a more hurdy-gurdy tone, like the music Jack heard at those tired Midwest traveling carnivals.

"Fancy a go?" The old man leaned back on a stool, whittling a wood chunk with a gleaming blade pressed into his palm. A scant British lilt hung beside each word.

Jack shielded his eyes from the reflecting glare. "What are you doing in the Johnsons' field?"

"I could ask you the same." The old man stood, securing the knife in his back pocket and pinning his sterling silver hair into a ponytail.

The teen crept closer, inspecting the grizzled carousel operator with his flat-front wool trousers, billowy white cotton shirt, and pocket-watch chain dangling from his vest. He resembled a man lost to history, pulled from a grainy, post-Civil War-era black-and-white photo. He could have been anywhere from fifty to one hundred and fifty years old, but Jack settled on somewhere in the middle.

"Well, what's it going to be, mate?"

Jack gazed at the lone carousel spinning in the corn. He sensed this ride was special, maybe even built with him in mind. The exquisite hand-crafted horses with life-like manes and tails distinguished them-selves from the cheap plastic ones he had ridden at the local carnivals. The horses before him had gemstones embroidered into their bridles and well-tanned, quality leather saddles that would cradle him like a pillow. One horse stood out from the others, beckoning him to grab the reins and climb onto her back. The mare's mane shimmered, and her tail swished back and forth as if she was alive and champing at the bit to gallop across an open field. He could sense the beast's power, how her hooves would pummel the earth as she gathered speed. A pounding swelled in Jack's ears, the dull rhythm pulsing beneath his feet, working its way into his core, and rumbling upward as if the Earth had its own throbbing heartbeat.

Thud . . . thud . . . thud . . .

The bouncy carnival melody droned in Jack's head, drowning out the cicadas' electric buzz sizzling the still air. He hadn't been on a car-ousel in years, but a flash of nostalgic images swirled in his head: the county fairgrounds as a child and the metallic clatter of roller coaster cars banking through a turn; roasted peanuts and fried dough aromas wafting through the air; his hand folded within his mother's palm as they roamed the trampled sod. Even with his eyes closed, Jack could picture the fair-ground carousel: horses bobbing up and down as the platform twirled; his mother standing beside him with one hand on the guide pole and the other against his back, keeping him safe. *Safe and sound*, she would say. Or used to say, anyway.

Jack turned out his pockets. "I don't have a ticket."

"You don't need one for this ride." A vein in the old man's temple throbbed in unison with the pounding in Jack's skull. "Go ahead, pick yourself a jumper."

"A what?"

"A horse, mate." The old man hoisted himself onto the platform and gestured toward the gallopers like a gameshow host showcasing the grand prize.

A tremor rumbled through Jack's gut. He wanted to bolt, but his feet graduated toward the beckoning carny.

Thud . . . thud . . . thud . . .

Jack climbed the carousel's warped wooden steps and swiped a hand across each horse's mane as he passed—one, two, three—searching for the right one—four . . . five . . .

The right fit.

As he touched the coffee-colored sixth horse, the animal's mane twitched, and the Earth's strange pulse ceased pounding in his head. The breeze rustled the field's swaying corn in a welcomed silence.

"You sure that's the one?" The old man gestured to the others.

Jack nodded and mounted the majestic beast.

The old man pressed his lips into a flat line and glanced downward. "Good luck then, mate." He stepped from the platform, the rickety steps groaning under his weight. Grasping the carousel's main lever, the old man jammed it forward. Gears and cogs crunched as the drive mechanism engaged and the platform lurched ahead, gaining momentum.

Jack leaned back, spinning in time with the carousel's waltz-like thrum. Darkness swept across the swaying corn as the sun dropped from the sky. The carousel picked up speed, the machine's blinking lights streaking across the sky's dark canvas like shooting stars.

Faster.

The sixth horse came alive and burst free from the guide pole. The animal thundered across the meadow, leaving the carousel a distant blur behind them. Jack closed his eyes as the coffee-colored mare's massive hooves hammered out a staccato triplet against the dry earth. The charger rumbled forward, gaining speed.

Faster.

The teen drew a deep inhale, his senses heightened as if experiencing the world for the first time. He tasted the rich meadow aroma and shared the steed's power beneath him. Jack breathed from the horse's snorting nostrils, and his legs squeezed and released in time with the pounding hooves as if he and the animal had merged as one. Pictures flashed in Jack's head, and his childlike wonder disappeared. His mind weaved horrific images of the boy he had been with the man he would become: clutching a blood-stained tree branch and grinning with revolting fascination at a dying bird wriggling at his feet; pounding his fists on a pleading classmate's swollen face behind the school bleachers as friends cheered him on; dragging a woman's broken body through the woods and into an earthen pit before showering her with shovelfuls of dirt.

Thick saliva sprayed from the horse's snarling maw as the rifling wind grew colder. Jack pried his eyes open. The meadow had changed to treacherous, rocky terrain. The mare bellowed a piercing scream as she bounded forward through scorching hot canyons hewn into the earth. Stoney outcroppings flew past Jack in a smoldering blur. As the steed charged deeper and deeper into the glowing earth's dank bowels, the fetid rot stench grew stronger. Darkness shrouded the pair as the animal powered forward, a pinpoint of light shimmering far upon the horizon. The mare slowed, and Jack recognized what loomed before them. His vision went snowy, his mind's internal breaker switch tripping to prevent overload. As his consciousness fizzled, he released his grip on the beast and sensed himself fall.

Then, nothing.

CHAPTER THREE

Present Day
Edgartown, Massachusetts (Martha's Vineyard)

After Sam's bombshell, Jack padded the steps to his second-floor office and shut the door. He dropped onto his desk chair as if he had taken a gut punch.

He scanned the office with its oak desk, matching chairs, and tasteful art adorning the walls, a cozy space paid for with profits from the written word. He had his first short story published as a student at Northeastern. Not long after, he submitted *Road Rage* to his first agent and ended up on the *New York Times* best-seller list. Everything he touched had turned to gold.

He inspected the bookshelf opposite the bay window, stopping at the first edition hardcovers: *Road Rage,* followed by *Cold Steel* and *The Following.* God, he had hit the ground running with those books, foreign-language translations, screenplays, and two Hollywood blockbusters. Could have been three, but thanks again, Mr. Gibson. In a few short years, he had established himself as a hot commodity in entertainment. But it didn't last long. He blew his Hollywood earnings backing *Jigsaw* and *Back to Dead,* both of which tanked. Then *Caribou Man* didn't find any takers. Sam had been right. He had been living in denial. But now that *Blood on the Sabbath* and *Double-Barrel Justice* had barely found homes with publishers, he had to face the music. His career was in free fall. And his marriage had followed suit.

Even before Sam mentioned a separation, Jack had sensed it in that quiet place in the back of his mind. It had hurt too much to think about, so he ignored it. He had never been in love with anyone until he met Sam.

She seemed to love him back, maybe not as much as he did, but whatever she could give had been enough for him. She had always had one foot in LA, and a chunk of her heart, too—the part he could never claim.

When they first married, she adapted well to Martha's Vineyard and East Coast island life, requiring nothing more than gourmet coffee in the morning and a beach outside her door. When she needed pampering, she would take a week or two in the Berkshires for spa treatments at Canyon Ranch. He hadn't grasped how much she missed the LA lifestyle and red-carpet gala events they attended. How long had she been going through the motions?

He squeezed his eyes shut. Complacency, the siren luring him into the rocky shallows. It had kept him living in an alternate reality, a place where everything would be okay between them, where he would recapture the early career success, where she still loved him. He had been living in a dream world, and it all slowly unraveled as he stood watching.

His mind cycled to Morgan. Did she sense the change in her parents? Maybe that's why she spent so much time in her room lately. Jack stepped down the hallway to check on her. He tapped on the door.

"Who's there?"

"Dumbledore," Jack said.

"How do I know you're not a Death Eater who drank Polyjuice Potion? Maybe you're only pretending to be Dumbledore."

"You're about to find out." Cracking the door, he peeked inside to find Morgan lounging in bed. "Expelliarmus." Jack grinned, waving an imaginary wand as he stepped into the room. "What are you still doing in your PJs?"

"That wasn't the right spell," she said, swirling a pencil across a sketch pad. "And they're comfy, that's why."

Can't argue with that logic. Jack crossed the carpet and lowered himself onto the mattress. Blue sky and sunshine beyond her window contrasted the bedroom's gloomy interior. "What do you say we do something today, get out of your room for a while."

"I should probably stay here, don't you think?"

"Why? We have a whole island out there."

"It might be easier to stay here. People might stare."

"No one would stare at you. Why would you think—"

"Not at me," Morgan said. "At you."

"The only reason anyone would stare at either of us is because we are such a great father and daughter team, and they're jealous." He planted a kiss on top of her head. "If you could go anywhere on the island, where would it be?"

Morgan's tongue probed the edge of her lip. "Hmm . . . what are my choices?"

"Anywhere."

She closed her sketch pad. "I guess it would be the big merry-go-round. The one near all the boats." She scrunched her face in thought. "The Fly . . . Flying . . ."

"Flying Horses," Jack finished, picturing the Oak Bluffs landmark, one of the country's oldest carousels. He and Sam had once taken Morgan there on her birthday, but he couldn't recall which. "What made you think of that place?"

She grabbed his hand. "It's my favorite place in the whole world."

Jack tilted his head. "Since when?"

"Since forever." Morgan peered into her father's eyes. "You see, you have to pick the right horse, or everything goes bad."

Jack's vision dimmed as he pictured the Missouri cornfield and the ponytailed carousel operator. *Go ahead. Pick yourself a jumper . . .*

Morgan continued. "And when the carousel spins, it feels like it takes you someplace far away."

The air caught in Jack's throat. "What do you mean?"

"Somewhere beautiful."

He pressed his fingers to his temples as heated blood thrummed through his veins.

Thud . . . thud . . . thud . . .

"I want to go back and ride my horse again." She dropped her head against the pillow.

Jack sensed the tremors building in his legs, ascending into his core. Images flickered behind his vision and bloomed. He perched astride the coffee-colored horse, its powerful body bucking beneath him. The frigid wind braised his skin as the brute thundered across the alien landscape.

Faster.

The mare's hooves punished the rocky tundra as it descended farther and farther into the earth, deeper and deeper into the glowing, fetid depths. Jack shook away the vision and sprung from the bed. Struggling to remain upright, he reached for Morgan's dresser to steady himself. The pounding amplified beneath his temples.

THUD . . . THUD . . . THUD . . .

"Dad, what's wrong?"

"Huh?" He pressed his palms against the sides of his head. "Nothing, Morgan. Everything's fine."

"You don't look fine."

I didn't choose the right horse. "I am, honey. I promise." Jack tested a smile but couldn't tell if she believed him.

He wasn't sure he did, either.

CHAPTER FOUR

Twenty-Five Years Earlier
Fulton, Missouri (Fulton State Hospital)

"How are you feeling today, Jack?"

The teenager slumped on the doctor's faux-leather sofa, scheming how he would answer the question Dr. Lang posed each session. Jack Rainne made it a point to answer differently each time, just to keep the doc on his toes.

"I feel like shit."

Dr. Lang glanced from his notebook. "Tell me why."

Jack scanned the doctor's miserable little office in Fulton's crazy house, Missouri's homage to primitive mental health treatment. He almost expected Nurse Ratched to come in any minute with his meds in a paper cup.

"Because I don't belong here."

Dr. Lang leaned back in his chair, appearing to reflect on his patient's response. Jack sensed the man wasn't aware of the imperceptible head nod accompanying his silence. As a Black man living in rural Missouri, maybe the man could relate in some way.

"Why do you think you don't belong here?"

Jack pressed his fingernails into his palms. "Because there's nothing wrong with me."

Lang cleared his throat but remained silent.

"What?"

"Do I need to remind you about the nightmares and hallucinations? These are signs of something." Lang leaned forward. "And if we're gonna get you to a better place, we need to find out where they're coming from."

Jack stood and spun toward the window. "Just crack this looney bin's front door and I'll get to a better place right quick. There's nothing wrong with me."

"Listen to me, Jack. You're right. There's nothing wrong with you, but something happened to you. There's a difference, and we need to talk about it."

"Okay. Let's talk." Jack glanced at the clock. "What do you want to talk about?"

"How about the carousel." Lang eyed him as if waiting for a reaction. Jack didn't give him anything. "You're drawn to the carousel in your dreams, correct?"

"It pulls me in, I've told you before. But before I ever had the dreams, I rode the carousel . . . for real, and something happened. Something bad."

Lang scribbled on a notepad. "You mentioned before you sometimes black out and—"

"I don't black out." Jack folded his arms. *Yes, you do.* "It's like I have the dream in the middle of the day when I'm awake. The carousel horse comes alive and takes me somewhere."

Lang peeked above his glasses. "Where?"

"I'm not sure," Jack whispered. "But it's somewhere bad, and that's where the dream ends."

"Well, we need to find out why the dream ends there."

"Be my guest. I'm not going anywhere."

For the rest of the session, Jack dodged Lang's questions until the man closed his notepad and directed the conversation to the St. Louis Cardinals' and Rams' playoff chances. Jack chuckled, having bested him, at least for the moment. He hadn't made much progress with Dr. Lang, but he liked him well enough and didn't mind the sessions. They sure beat the hospital's rubber walls and real-life nut jobs wandering the hallways.

With a few minutes left in the hour, Lang rose from his seat and opened the venetian blinds, inviting the late-afternoon sun's final bloom. He eyed the clock. "We have a few more minutes, and I wanted to get you thinking about something for our next session."

Jack had risen halfway off the couch before letting out a deep groan and sinking back onto the cushions. Maybe he hadn't bested him after all.

Lang nibbled the end of his pen. "Can we talk about your father a little bit?"

"What about him?"

The doc ventured back to his seat. "Anything."

Jack checked the clock. Too much time to stall, not enough time to talk. "I don't miss him."

"How come?"

"He was a mean bastard."

"I'm sorry." Lang sighed. "I can't imagine what that must be like."

"You're lucky, then." Jack shifted in his seat. "I guess you have a nice dad."

Lang paused a beat. "He was a good man."

Jack leaned forward. "Was?"

Rolling his pen between his fingers, Lang said, "Lost him when I was about your age."

"What happened?"

"We're here to talk about you, Jack. Not me."

"But I want to know. Aren't we supposed to build rapport and shit like that?"

Lang grinned. "Okay." He rested his elbows on his knees. "The world has a lot of misdirected hatred, especially in places where people don't look the same. My father happened to be in the wrong place at the wrong time."

He sensed a numb resignation behind the doctor's eyes, from an experience someone like Jack could never truly relate to. "I'm sorry, Dr. Lang. Really."

Lang nodded and clicked his pen. "Ancient history. Now, is there anything at all you miss about your father?"

"Nothing." Jack raked a hand through his hair. "I only remember one time when he made my mom laugh." He held up his index finger. "Once."

"How about you? How did he make you feel?"

Jack considered the question. "Scared."

Lang made a note. "I want you to think for a minute. Back to a time before you had the carousel dreams." Lang gestured about the room. "Before all this. If I asked you the first thing that popped into your mind when you thought about a carousel, what would it be?"

Jack hesitated. "I don't know."

"Come on, Jack. Picture a carousel and tell me what comes to mind. First thing."

"Okay . . . my mom?"

"So, what do you suppose the carousel in your dream might represent?"

Jack rubbed his chin. The minute hand hung way past the twelve. The session should have ended. "It doesn't represent anything. It just is."

Lang checked the clock. "Okay, I want you to reflect on something before our next visit. You're seventeen now, almost a man. You'll be out in the world soon, right?"

"Only if you tell the people who run this place I'm not crazy."

"You mean lie my ass off?"

Jack grinned. *Chalk up a zinger for the doc.*

Lang leaned in; the doctor hadn't finished with him yet. "Do you ever feel as if you're not ready to head out into the real world yet?"

"Like . . . every day."

"When you dream about carnivals and carousels, do you think it might represent the thing you can't return to?" Lang didn't say anything for a while. Jack sensed the doctor was going for effect. "Maybe the carousel is something you long for because it brings you peace, in a way. Thinking about a time when adulthood and responsibility weren't staring you in the face. A time when you still felt like a kid."

Jack glanced at the clock.

"And in the dream, the horse runs away from the carousel . . . in effect, taking you away from that safety."

"I don't know. Maybe."

"Can I ask you another question?" Dr. Lang closed his notebook and tossed it onto the desk.

Isn't that all you do? "Shoot."

"How did your father die?"

Jack chewed his fingernails. "He broke his neck working on the farm."

"What happened?"

Jack spit a nail onto the carpet. "He fell off a horse."

CHAPTER FIVE

Excerpt from *Double-Barrel Justice*, by Jack Rainne:

"How're we doing?" the dentist asked as he removed the bloody forceps, another tooth clutched between its tongs.

The patient didn't answer. She had been in and out for a while now. Glen Hamilton flipped the operating light away from the girl's face and dropped the instrument onto the steel tray. The dripping tooth skittered across the metal, joining the others with a gentle plink. He loosened his mask and squeezed his numb forearm. The discomfort hadn't been that bad while loosening each tooth from its socket with the hand-held elevator. But the twisting and tugging with the forceps during extraction had caused his forearm muscles to cramp.

So many teeth to remove.

As he massaged his limb, Dr. Hamilton paused to inspect the girl reclining in the dental unit. Despite a swollen jaw and crimson-streaked saliva oozing from her mouth, she maintained a certain beauty.

The dentist leaned forward and whispered in the girl's ear. "Are you ready for another, Missy?"

"Please . . ." she mumbled, keeping her eyes squeezed shut.

"Well, in that case. Let's get 'er done." Hamilton chuckled as he imagined Larry the Cable Guy dressed in scrubs, holding bloody forceps and reciting his trademark phrase. "Whatever happened to that guy? God, he was funny."

The dentist loved it when his patients said please. He instructed them to do so. Although this please came across more like a plea than an affirmation.

Poor Missy.

"Beverly," Dr. Hamilton shouted. "You'll need to cancel my three-thirty. This is going to take a while." He cocked his head, listening for his dental assistant's reply from the front desk.

He waited. But there was no front desk and no Beverly.

Hamilton scanned the room where the naked girl lay strapped . . . well, duct-taped to the chair. Depriving his patients of their clothing kept them more compliant and made the hours of work a bit more enjoyable. The blood leaching from Missy's mouth had soaked through the powder blue dental bib and sent soupy rivulets along her chest and stomach. The white, glistening office walls the dentist pictured in his mind were nothing more than dark, rotting basement wood covered in soundproofing to muffle the screams. He kept the doors bolted from the outside, on a timer. That way both he and his patient remained trapped.

It was best to keep the Ugly inside.

He had discovered the Ugly as a teenager in the woods behind his house. He had passed his thirteen-year-old neighbor, Peggy Fishman, taking the shortcut home. He didn't remember much about what happened. Although, he remembered pleading with the Ugly to let her go and not hurt her anymore, to make her stop screaming. He recalled watching her return home after dark from the upstairs window across the street. She had stumbled along the street like a zombie, wearing her patterned dress inside out with stippled mud stains and blood splashed across the fabric. She had hidden in the backyard tool shed and refused to come out for two days. Peggy never told anyone about what happened in the woods behind the house, and she was never the same afterward. She didn't smile or play outside anymore. The family moved away soon after.

The good part of Hamilton sometimes wondered what happened to her.

Hamilton gazed at the girl beneath the lights. Missy hadn't been his first patient, but she was his most important by far. The others had simply been practice for the real thing. The plan had been formulating in his mind over the past year but had been set into motion the day after his disciplinary hearing. His supervising attending, Dr. Ben Pruitt, had assured him the hospital board would view the incident with the teenage patient as a misunderstanding. Everyone knows how conscious sedation can affect a patient's memory. She must have imagined the things she accused Hamilton of doing.

"The hospital's disciplinary board will take into consideration all your extraordinary accomplishments during your residency," Dr. Pruitt had told him. Hamilton had published academic papers, performed complicated oral surgeries, mentored students, and was the leading candidate for next year's chief resident. "And I'll stand beside you at the hearing to support you."

Due to the nature of the allegations, the hospital hadn't allowed Hamilton to continue with his residency or set foot in the building until the hearing. Instead, he remained in his apartment, pacing the floors alone with his thoughts.

Alone with the Ugly.

When the story hit the local news—and when detailed allegations came to light—things changed for Hamilton. The other pediatric dental residents and supervisors stopped reaching out to offer their support. After a while, even Dr. Pruitt stopped returning his calls. Okay, maybe his hand had brushed against the patient and lingered in places. Was that all that happened? Hamilton couldn't remember. The teen had been so beautiful. He had tried to control himself. He hadn't slipped up with any other pediatric patient until then. Shouldn't he get credit for that? No one could possibly understand the restraint it took each day to keep the Ugly under control.

When he reached the hospital's eighth-floor conference room the day of the hearing, he had expected Dr. Pruitt to be waiting. Hamilton lingered in the hallway until the committee called him into the room. He took a seat at the enormous mahogany table.

"Dr. Hamilton," the hospital's president addressed him in a somber voice, "that we must meet under these circumstances is disturbing, to say the least. The panel will—"

"Please. If I may," Hamilton said. "Can we wait to start the hearing until my advocate arrives?"

"Dr. Pruitt informed us this morning we should continue without him. He has withdrawn his support and won't be attending..."

The president's words ran together, muffled in Hamilton's ears as though filtered through a wet cloth. His fingers curled into fists beneath the table, and a vein in his temple throbbed in tempo with his pounding heartbeat. Pruitt had abandoned him, the man who had recruited him into the residency program, introduced him to his family, and invited him to his house to grill burgers and dogs beside the pool. He had treated him like one of the family, like a son. But now, Hamilton awaited his fate alone.

He barely listened as the board laid out the complaint's details. Had he truly done what they said he did? He thought about what dwelled beneath his pressed white shirt, the hidden thing squirming deep inside himself.

The committee reached their decision and wrapped the hearing, dismissing Hamilton from his residency. When the panel revealed their intent to petition the board of dental examiners to revoke his medical license, Hamilton barely flinched. He even allowed a grin to spread across his cheeks.

That's when the plan took root in his mind.

A moan escaped Missy's lips, drawing Hamilton back from his reverie.

The dentist scanned the steel tray with over a dozen teeth scattered across the surface. He had capped and polished them the way he had perfected during his residency. In certain teeth, he had drilled cavity-like holes straight through to the nerve, but he filled and repaired them flawlessly. Artistically. As soon as he had finished the remaining extractions, Hamilton would force Missy to consume each tooth. All but one. He already knew the one he would keep as a souvenir. The tooth on the top row angled slightly inward. The one that caught his eye the first time he met her. The one he would fix his gaze upon when he visited the house, when the family invited him to grill burgers and dogs beside the pool and treated him like one of the family, like a son. And when they found Missy's body and examined her stomach contents, they would see what amazing work her dentist had done.

Hamilton leaned closer to Missy Pruitt and whispered in her ear. "By the way. How's your dad?"

CHAPTER SIX

Boston, Massachusetts

Jack stood beside the fabric-draped table at the Boylston Street Barnes and Noble. He checked his watch. Fifteen minutes until they let the public swarm the table. Each of his novels rested on display stands, extra copies stacked a foot high on the table. A cup sprouting ballpoint pens and an assortment of fliers, cards, bookmarks, and other freebies in acrylic table-top displays rested within arm's reach. Five-foot-tall banners for his biggest film adaptations, *Cold Steel* and *The Following*, dangled behind the table on retractable stands.

He hadn't done a signing in years, but Hal had arranged a steady string over the next few months. He had caught the promos on WZLX and Magic 106.7 during the traffic-clogged Friday afternoon trudge along Route 3 to Boston. Now all he had to do was smile for the public and make sure his pens didn't run dry. Hal had further arranged speaking gigs up and down the East Coast for the remainder of the summer, including keynotes at several top-notch writing conferences and masterclasses in New York City and Washington, DC. The work wasn't glamorous, but it would put a little money in his pocket.

Hal had set him up at the Copley Square Hotel after the signing. He would make the short trip along the south shore to bookstores in Hingham and Hyannis the following day. Other trips would come in the following weeks. Maybe Jack's being away might help Sam recognize she needed him as much as he needed her. They hadn't talked much about the separation since Sam brought it up. Life had resumed its normal flow. But her admission hung like a weight on Jack's shoulders, driving him toward the ground with each step he took.

"Can I get you a water or anything?"

"Huh?" Jack spun around to find the store manager, Julie something, hovering beside the table. He should have studied Hal's itinerary. "I'd love one. Thanks."

"If you want to have a seat, I'll let you get started." Moments later, Julie reappeared with a lukewarm Dasani and welcomed the patrons to the table.

Jack sold and signed a respectable number of books, softening the where-are-they-now barb Sam had stung him with earlier. But by 9:30, the steady gathering had trickled to a handful of gawkers, none of whom appeared willing to pony up for an overpriced book and a complementary bookmark. One boy had been eyeing him from the indoor café, gripping a magazine and weaving in and out among the latte zombies. But he hadn't ventured to Jack's table yet. Each time Jack glanced over and made eye contact, the boy would drop his head and pretend to read his magazine.

With fifteen minutes remaining, the crowd had dispersed, leaving Jack alone at the table. He stretched, preparing to collect his things and return to the hotel. The boy sauntered toward him and slapped the journal onto the table.

Jack pressed his fingers against his temples as the pounding flared inside his head.

Thud . . . thud . . . thud . . .

"Mr. Rainne, would you sign this?"

Jack forced a grin through the searing pain. "Sure thing, buddy." He estimated the boy's age as a year or two older than Morgan. "What's your name?"

"Jack."

He grinned and tousled the boy's hair. "That's an easy one to remember. Last name?"

"Morgan."

Jack let his jaw drop for effect. "No way! My daughter's name is Morgan. You and I have a lot in common. Let me guess. You're going to be . . . what, eleven this year?"

A grin creased the boy's lips. "I'm supposed to be eleven in November."

Jack chuckled at the boy's phrasing.

"How did you know how old I am?" The boy leaned forward and whispered, "Did the old man tell you?"

"Old man?" Jack glanced about the store for someone the boy might belong to. "You mean your father?"

The boy shook his head. "My father's not here."

"Okay." Jack sensed a miscommunication. "Well, nobody told me how old you are. You just remind me of myself when I was your age. You like books?"

"Yeah, but I don't get to read them much anymore."

Jack took a moment to inspect the boy. Maybe his family couldn't afford books. He appeared a bit ragged: his shirt and pants had hand-me-down written all over them, and Jack had never observed the kid's sneaker style before. Everything he wore must have been a thrift store find. *Poor little guy.*

Jack sighed. "Okay, pal, what do you want me to sign?"

The boy slid the journal forward.

Jack rotated the mag and squinted at the title, the familiar cover sending a warm flush through his skin. *The American Short Story.*

"The story's called 'The Nefarious Spinster.'"

Jack leaned back in his chair. "Do you know that's the first short story I ever wrote?" He grimaced. *God, what an awful title!*

"It's kind of scary, but I liked it a lot. That's why I want you to sign it."

Jack leafed through the journal until he came to his entry. He grabbed a pen. "To my friend Jack." His hand flew across the page. "Read . . . imagine . . . dream." He signed his name.

Young Jack gaped at the signature. "That's so cool! Thank you, Mr. Rainne."

"You can call me Jack." He stood and tried a fist bump, but the boy simply gawked at him. Then the youngster extended his hand.

Ah, old school. They shook hands, and Jack set about assembling his belongings. But the boy remained standing at the table.

Jack stopped loading his gear. "You a horror fan?"

"Those are my favorite books, but my mom stopped letting me read them. She said they were too scary."

Unacceptable. Jack reached under the table and grabbed a copy of *The Following*, his only semi-supernatural thriller but without as much violence and R-rated language as his signature crime novels. "Take a look at this." He wrote a quick inscription on the title page. "Read the back cover. If you like it, you can take it home with you."

The boy's eyes lit up. "No way! Really?"

"If you think it will be okay with your mom."

Flipping the book over, the boy scanned the blurb on the back flap with his tongue glued to the corner of his mouth.

As Jack waited, he dropped into his seat and leafed through *The American Short Story*. When Jack first published his story, he had been so excited he never bothered to peruse the other submissions. Locating the table of contents, he scrolled through the list of authors and titles. He cracked a smile when he reached "The Nefarious Spinster" by Jacoby Rainne. Jacoby. He forgot he'd used his real name as his byline. Hal had suggested he use "Jack" when he came on board. He glanced at the boy. Pretty smart kid to figure out the author.

Jack frowned as he scrolled the table of contents.

"The Carousel Man" by Graham Carver. The title triggered something inside. Jack had a doozy of a nightmare with spinning carousels and horses coming alive just the other night. Same intensity. Same reaction upon waking.

He fanned the journal's pages until he reached the story.

"Fancy a go?" The old man leaned back on a stool, whittling a wood chunk with a gleaming blade pressed into his palm. A scant British lilt hung beside each word.

Jack shielded his eyes from the reflecting glare. "What are you doing in the Johnsons' field?"

"I could ask you the same." The old man stood, securing the knife in his back pocket and pinning his sterling silver hair into a ponytail.

"What the fuck . . . ?" Jack muttered.

The boy raised his head.

Jack squinted at the text. A sweat bead formed at his hairline and dripped toward his eyebrow. He tried to swallow, but his mouth had filled with sand.

Jack gazed at the lone carousel spinning in the corn. He sensed this ride was special, maybe even built with him in mind. The exquisite hand-crafted horses with life-like manes and tails distinguished themselves from the cheap plastic ones he had ridden at the local carnivals. The horses before him had gemstones embroidered into their bridles, and well-tanned quality leather saddles that would cradle him like a pillow. One horse stood out from the others, beckoning him to grab the reins and climb onto her back.

Jack bolted to his feet, sending his chair skittering across the floor behind him. The lively bookstore's bustling clatter filtered to silence. Pressing his hands to the table, Jack lowered his head and scanned the pages with furious speed. The words provoked images, not from the writer's pen but from a hidden place inside his own memory.

This is my story. He squeezed his eyes shut as the thudding rose in his head. "Somebody wrote about what happened to me."

When he opened his eyes, Jack Morgan stood before him, mouth agape and gazing upward.

"Are you okay, Mr. Rainne?" the boy asked. "You look sick."

Jack drew a palm across his forehead, pulling it back damp. "Yeah, I'm fine."

"Can I have my magazine back?"

Jack slid the journal across the table and dropped into his chair before realizing the seat no longer rested beneath him. He scored a direct hit on the floor with his tailbone, his body crumpling into a heap. The store manager—Jack had no idea what either of her names were at this point—and a flock of patrons hurried over. Reaching beneath Jack's armpits, a burly man eased him to his feet.

Jack's legs shook like those of a newborn fawn as he steadied himself against the table.

The manager held out a bottle of water. "I'm dialing 9-1-1."

"No, I'm fine." Jack grabbed the bottle and poured half down his throat before he could stand on his own. "I must have gotten up too quickly. Head rush."

He took a deep pull of air and flashed a forced grin at the gawking patrons. As they shuffled away, Jack searched the crowd.

The boy had disappeared.

———

Jack stumbled onto Boylston Street, pulling rapid sips of air. Julie something-or-other agreed to hold onto his belongings until he came back to retrieve them. But books and banners were the farthest thing from his mind. He had to find *The American Short Story*. In all the excitement, Jack had completely forgotten who the author of "The Carousel Man" was. He had to track this guy down, find out what he knew and how he knew it.

Graham something-or-other. He thought about Julie something-or-other. "I've got to get better with last names."

Jack trekked gingerly along Huntington Avenue toward the hotel, his tailbone screaming with each step. Pulling out his cell, he tapped the starred favorites button and pressed Hal's name.

His agent picked up before Jack raised the cell to his ear.

"Hey, buddy. I don't have anything for you yet. I've been playing phone tag with—"

"Never mind all that," Jack shouted. "I need your help with something."

A pause. "I thought you were at the Boston signing."

"I am . . . I mean, I was." Jack checked left and right and hobbled across the street to the hotel. "I'm heading over to the hotel now."

"How did it go? Did Julie Miller take good care of you?"

Miller, that's it. "Yeah, and she has a great story now about a writer whose ass missed his chair and ended up leaving twin cheek impressions on the hardwood flooring."

"Do we have time for that story?"

Jack rubbed his tailbone. "Not a chance. Listen, I need you to track down my *American Short Story* submission. The first thing I ever published, like twenty-plus years ago."

"'Nefarious Spinster?'"

Jack rested a hand over his heart. "Hal, I'm touched. You remembered?"

"Yeah, I remembered how bad the thing was. Dreadful title, too."

"Never mind that. There's another short story in that journal. It's called 'The Carousel Man,' by someone named Graham something. I can't remember the last name. I need you to find the journal and tell me the author's name."

"Why? Did he plagiarize you or something?"

"Huh?"

"Well, I'd love an excuse to sue somebody. You're not exactly contributing to my income anymore."

"I just need you to help find the guy's name."

"You're about a block from Boston Public Library. They'll have it there. Why don't you head down Boylston Street."

Jack pressed a hand against his ear as a line of cars whizzed past. "Because it's probably closed, and I pay you to do shit like this."

"Pay me? Since when?"

"Check's in the mail." Jack approached the hotel and handed his ticket to the valet.

"Story of my life." Hal blew out a breath. "Well, you're lucky enough to have an agent who keeps everything their once-successful clients ever wrote. I'll have to find my where-are-they-now box, though."

First Sam, now Hal. "Kiss my ass."

"I love you, too. I'll call you back when I have something."

After Hal disconnected, Jack scrounged through his pocket and grabbed a handful of crumpled bills. Pressing them into the valet's palm, he eased himself into the driver's seat, using the door and roof to lighten the load on his backside. He squirmed to get comfortable, then backtracked up Huntington Avenue. He pulled in front of Barnes and Noble, where Julie—*Miller, goddammit*—met him to retrieve his gear. Ten minutes later, he had loaded everything into the trunk and thrown the neon-orange parking ticket onto the passenger seat. As he weaved through traffic back to the hotel, his cell phone buzzed.

"You got something?" A clicking sound filtered through the line. He pictured Hal's thumb pressing his pen's plunger up and down, a nervous habit Jack knew well.

"I'm not sure."

"What does that mean? Were you able to dig up the journal?"

"Yeah, I found your story, but I didn't see anything called 'The Carousel Man.'"

Jack spotted a traffic opening and shifted lanes. "I'm sure you missed it. Look again."

"I have the damn thing open right in front of me. The story isn't there."

"Impossible. This kid had me sign 'Spinster' for him. I flipped through the journal and read the story."

"Had to have been a different journal."

Jack kept his voice from rising. "Hal, the kid and I were the only people at the table, and we only had one journal."

"Well, that doesn't make any sense."

"You're not gaslighting me here, are you? Making me sweat a little before you tell me you're joking?"

"If I had the chance to fuck with you, Jack, believe me, I would. I did a quick internet search for 'The Carousel Man' and an author named Graham something. There were a couple of novels on Amazon called *The Carousel*, but no short stories, and no Graham anything."

"What the hell?" Jack rubbed his forehead.

Hal cleared his throat. "You sure you're okay, buddy?"

Jack gripped the steering wheel as he sat motionless behind a line of cars on Huntington Avenue. "Come on, you know me. I'm fine. It sounds crazy, but I don't make things up."

"Jack, you're a writer—you make things up for a living."

"Good point. Just . . . never mind. I'll figure this thing out."

"Sorry, my friend. I'll keep looking around for you."

"Thanks." Jack disconnected and tossed his cell on the passenger side floor hard enough to dislodge the protective case. "Fuck!" He pounded the steering wheel and leaned on the horn, drawing raised fingers and mouthed expletives from the other friendly Boston motorists packed together like salmon swimming upstream.

While stuck in traffic, Jack's mind wandered through the evening and tried to make sense of it. Maybe he had drifted into a fugue state and had a particularly realistic daydream. Can't say it hasn't happened before. *No, goddammit!* The kid handed him the journal with "The Carousel Man" in it. He had seen it with his own eyes. Twice. Once in the table of contents, and once in the text. He had read it. End of story. But how could Hal, as logical and meticulous as he was, search the same journal and not find anything?

The kid. He would have the journal. The kid would let him have a peek at it again.

"Jack Morgan," he muttered, picturing the unkempt waif. "If I can't find Graham something-or-other, I'll settle for Jack Morgan."

CHAPTER SEVEN

Twenty-Five Years Earlier
Fulton, Missouri (Fulton State Hospital)

"How are you feeling today, Jack?" Dr. Lang straightened his glasses.

Jack snaked a hand through his hair. Same question, different day. "Peachy." *Let's see what he does with that.*

"Well, that's encouraging. You starting to get something out of our talks?"

"Isn't that for you to analyze in your little book?"

"Hmm." Lang leaned forward with hands together, tapping his lips with his index fingers. "Okay, then. Remember I asked you about carousels and carnivals and what they represent? Did you give it any more thought?"

"I forgot to do my homework." Jack straightened in his seat. "But I can tell you carousels don't represent anything to me."

Lang stood. "In our last session, we talked about the carousel representing safety, a return to your childhood. But there's another part of your past that might be contributing to this dream you have. It's something we've danced around a little, but we don't really talk about. You have any idea what I'm referring to?"

Jack remained silent.

Lang glanced out the window. "Each day, I ask you how you're doing because I think maybe you'll surprise me and be ready to talk about it."

"Let me guess, you want me to talk about my father?"

"Only if you're ready to."

Jack pictured the man, elbows propped on the kitchen table with a calloused hand around a half-empty Wild Turkey bottle. The Cardinals game squawked from the battered transistor radio as "Big Bobby" Rainne slurred his words and lashed out at him or his mother, whoever was closest when one of the Red Birds struck out or made an error. Big Bobby hated the world and everyone in it starting the day Jack turned seven— the day the Jefferson City bank foreclosed on the farm and his tongue discovered bourbon whiskey.

Jack picked at the sofa's armrest. "I don't think it's going to help to talk about him."

"We can talk all day about sports and the weather, but that won't get us to a better place. It's the things we *don't* want to talk about that will."

There's that better place again. "Nowhere to go but up, I guess."

Lang folded his hands behind his back. "You told me your father died falling off a horse. Do you think it's just a coincidence that the horse in your nightmare comes to life and takes you away from the carousel, the object you associate with childhood and comfort?"

Jack's downward gaze bore holes into the floor. "So, what? My father's a horse now?"

Lang chuckled. "Not the way you're thinking."

"If my father's death took me away from my childhood, why is it that when the horse first takes me away it's beautiful, and I feel alive?"

Lang leaned his head back in thought. "For someone growing up with an indifferent father, even a cruel father, you may have experienced some relief after his death. Maybe even joy."

Jack leaned forward, holding his head in his hands.

"What are you thinking?"

He glanced at the doctor. "None of this talking matters because you've never believed me. It doesn't matter who the horse is or what it represents. You believe what's happening is in my head, and I know what happened is real. We'll never get past that."

"Doesn't matter what I believe. If something happened to you in a field . . . or in your head . . . it still happened to you. It's real." Shuffling to the coffee maker, Lang poured himself a steaming mug. He filled a paper cup with water and handed it to Jack.

"What, I don't get coffee?" He glared at the flimsy cone.

"Do you drink coffee?"

"No, but it's nice to be asked."

Lang rolled his eyes and took a seat. "Let's get back on track here. You're on the horse, flying through the meadows. Part of your dream is this amazing experience, but things change. You start to see yourself in a different light. You witness terrible things you've done and things you haven't had a chance to do yet. Violent things."

"Those are things I would have done, for sure."

"Like pounding a classmate with your fists or burying a body out in the woods? That doesn't sound like the Jack Rainne I know."

"Does anyone really know anybody, Doc? That was me. I saw myself doing it."

Lang stirred sugar into his java. "I don't think we can see with our minds what hasn't happened yet. Maybe your mind put those images there for a reason?"

"Like what?"

"Maybe to make you feel a certain way?" He took a short sip and added another sugar packet to his mug. "How did those violent images make you feel?"

Jack shrugged as the silence stretched.

"Come on, Jack. You know."

"Okay. Maybe a little bit guilty?"

Lang gave a quick head bow in agreement. "When we harbor guilt, our mind doesn't always show us exactly what we feel guilty about."

"You think I have guilty feelings. What about?"

"I think you know."

"This sounds like twenty questions." Jack laced his fingers together and rested them on his head. "Can you just get to the point?"

Lang sighed. "Part of this process is to help you get there yourself, but I'll throw you a bone here." He joined Jack on the sofa. "If you're busy feeling guilty about things you haven't even done yet, you remove your guilt about not being there to help your father. You were supposed to help work on the farm that day after school, weren't you?"

"I was late. I didn't get there before . . ."

"His accident, right? And no one was there to help him or call an ambulance."

Jack slumped in his seat.

"And in your dream, you see yourself riding this beautiful horse."

Jack blinked as his eyes filled up.

The doctor continued. "And where did the horse go? Deep into the earth as if taking you straight to hell, where any church-going kid like yourself, carrying all that guilt, would imagine himself going. Sound accurate?"

"Former church-going kid," Jack insisted.

"Do you think it's possible your father's accident led you to create a terrible, new experience in your mind? Something worse than the accident itself?"

"I didn't imagine it, Dr. Lang, and I didn't create anything in my mind. It happened. I'm never going to admit it didn't happen."

"Well, whatever happened to you in that Spring Valley cornfield distracts you from your true feelings. Maybe so you don't have to come to terms with your father's passing or the guilt that goes along with it."

Jack stared straight ahead. *My father's passing was a blessing.*

Lang shifted into his chair and gazed at the ceiling. "What do you say we go back to Spring Valley and get us some answers."

Jack straightened. "What, Johnson Farm? You mean, like, leave the hospital and go there?"

"In a sense." The doctor grinned. "But we'll do it from here."

CHAPTER EIGHT

Present Day
Hyannis, Massachusetts (Cape Cod)

On Sunday morning, Jack rolled out of bed at the Sea View Bed & Breakfast in downtown Hyannis. He had finished his final book signing at the local Barnes and Noble the previous evening, too late to catch the last ferry to the Vineyard. Swinging his legs over the bed, he pressed his bare feet onto the hardwood floor, his tailbone still aching from the ass-plant he suffered at the Boston bookstore. He rubbed his temples to help shake off the nightmare clinging like a parasite. The dream didn't have a carousel, but it still left him unsettled.

"Jesus Christ."

He rose on weary legs, his midsection still twisted in bedsheets. In the dream, he held hands with Sam and Morgan as they proceeded along a church aisle. Family and friends filled the polished wooden pews flanking both sides of the church. He gazed at the familiar stations of the cross textured into the stained-glass windows and the wood-beam rafters high above the altar. He was back at Lady of the Lord, his old parish in Spring Valley. He inspected the faces in the pews. They hadn't aged since he'd left the Valley, and he sensed he hadn't either, despite having Sam and Morgan beside him. His father knelt beside his mother with his head bowed, but Jack knew his father was already dead. His high school friends blinked away tears and wiped their eyes as Jack advanced along the aisle. A mahogany casket resting on a draped bier lay before him on the flower-laden altar. Jack's heart hammered against his ribcage, recognizing that the coffin belonged to him and his life had ended.

He dropped Sam and Morgan's hands as they approached the altar. Reaching to open the casket, he jolted awake.

You're dead, Jack. You never left Spring Valley.

Having shaken off the dream, Jack crept from the Bed & Breakfast, careful not to disturb the guests sleeping off the weekend revelry. A haze shrouded the empty streets, giving Hyannis an abandoned, ghost town quality. Get up early enough on Cape Cod, and the day might appear a total loss. But before long, the mist burns off, the sun breaks through, and the crowds arrive, packing the beaches and tiny downtowns from Falmouth to Truro. With an hour's drive to catch the Woods Hole ferry and another forty-five minutes across Nantucket Sound to the Vineyard, Jack and his bruised tailbone faced a long, painful trip home. He checked his watch and opted for a short jaunt along Main Street to work out the kinks.

Trudging to his car, Jack tossed his overnight bag into the trunk and locked the vehicle. He took a deep breath, inhaling the misty salt air as he trekked toward the deserted downtown. Quaint storefronts with weather-beaten shingles and colorful shutters lined the main street. He glanced into the darkened T-shirt and gift shop windows, bistros, and ice cream shops, lost in silent thought.

Jack checked his watch. *Where the hell is everyone?*

As he meandered along the sidewalk, a shopkeeper's bell split the silence. A smartly dressed woman struggled to pull a display table through her boutique's doorway, EM Designer Jewelry & Gifts stenciled on the storefront window. She gave the table another tug, its silver stem glides beneath the legs screeching against the cement sidewalk. Tabletop jewelry trees teetered atop the surface as she fought the heavy piece.

Approaching the woman, Jack cleared his throat. "Morning, ma'am. Need help?"

She glanced at Jack limping toward her. "Looks like you're the one who needs help."

She appeared to be about his age, mid-forties, but maybe a few years older.

"Took a tumble onto my backside the other day."

"Haven't we all."

Jack chuckled. "Need a hand?"

The woman rested her palms against the tabletop. "Thanks. These are heavier than I remember."

Jack stepped through the doorway, marveling at the shop's tasteful handmade crafts and jewelry. He positioned himself opposite the woman, lifting the table while she dragged it along the concrete with a teeth-rattling screech. Despite leaving deep pavement grooves, they managed to maneuver the table onto the sidewalk parallel to the storefront. Jack lifted each end until the table lay flush against the shingles below the store window.

He wiped his hands on his pants. "That ought to do it."

She straightened the tabletop displays with meticulous care. "Have we met? You look familiar."

Jack cocked his head. "I don't think so."

"Well, either way, I'm glad you came along. Thank you, Mr. . . . ?"

"Rainne. It's Jack, and you're very welcome." He tipped an imaginary cap.

"I once had a son named Jack."

"Oh . . ." Jack shifted his weight from one foot to the other. "I'm sorry."

She forced a half-hearted smile. "It was a long time ago."

He switched gears. "You have a beautiful shop." He perused the display trees on the table, each with the same storefront logo etched into it. "EM Designer Jewelry & Gifts." He pointed to the stenciled window. "Is that you?"

"I'm Ellen. That's the 'E' in 'EM.'"

"Well, it was nice to meet you, Ellen. Hope you have a good day." Jack scanned the empty street. *What a ghost town today. She'll be lucky to break even.*

"Hang on a minute. Before you go." She rummaged through the gold and silver bracelets dangling from their display trees, turning them over as if searching for a particular one.

He raised a hand. "You don't need to—"

"I won't take no for an answer," she said. "A gift for your wife."

He grinned and narrowed his eyes. "How do you know I'm married?"

She pointed to the gold band on his finger. "Dead giveaway." Over her palm, she draped a silver chain with a horse pendant. Her slightest hand movement caught the light and appeared to coax the horse into a gallop.

Jack squinted at the piece from different angles to recreate the illusion. "That's incredible. Your workmanship is amazing." *Sam will love this!*

"Thank you, Jack." The woman dropped the pendant in a mini felt sack, cinched the drawstrings, and handed it to him.

Jack closed his palm around the pouch. "My wife, Sam, would have chosen the exact one."

"I thought so." Her lips stretched into a grin. "Tell her to wear it."

"When she sees it, I won't need to. But I insist on paying you." Jack fished through his pockets before leaning his head back with a grunt. "Damn, I left my wallet in the car."

As he faced Ellen, he swooned. He pressed a palm against his forehead as black and white dots raced toward the center of his visual field like a closing curtain. He sensed the blood drain from his head, pulling away layers of consciousness. Steadying himself against the display table, Jack sucked in deep breaths to keep himself upright as the world's sounds muffled. He dropped to the pavement, raising his head to glimpse Ellen hurrying toward him. His vision blurred and doubled as her advancing shape split into two, one-half mimicking its slightly off-center shadowy twin. But what approached wasn't exactly Ellen anymore. One of her moved differently, out of sync with the other, hobbling as if injured. Ellen gazed at him with concern, but the other's face appeared crushed, like it had been beaten with a hammer. Blood leaked from the cracked skull, forming ropy clots in her hair, and its left eye dangled from its shattered socket, like a gristly pendulum. Jack backpedaled and dropped to the cement, crab-walking with limbs akimbo before crashing into the shingled storefront.

"Is something wrong, Jack?"

He covered his eyes with both hands, feet still scrambling.

"Jack, what's the matter?" He sensed a gentle hand on his shoulder.

He dragged his hands along his face, forcing his eyelids open. Ellen stood before him as the strange vision dissipated. *What the fuck?* He struggled to gain his feet, balancing on stiff legs before letting go of the table. "Everything's fine, but I gotta go now." He stumbled away, laboring to place one foot in front of the other.

"Don't forget, Jack." She stood beside the jewelry table, but her grin had receded. "Tell her to wear it."

Jack hurried in retreat along the sidewalk.

When he arrived at his car, he dropped into the front seat and held his head in his hands, attempting to dispel the troubling vision embedded in his skull. *You're crazy, Jack.* He rested a moment before firing the engine and steering the vehicle along Main Street. The morning finally had the sun's commitment, drawing people from their hiding places and filling the sidewalks and roadways. He would pass EM Designer Jewelry & Gifts on his way from town to the ferry, but he would just have to keep his eyes focused straight ahead and fight the gnawing urge to gawk at Ellen and see if the monster from his vision still lingered. But as he approached, he weakened, his curiosity like a hand reaching out and grabbing his chin, forcing him to look. The breath caught in his throat as he rolled to the curb, gaping through the passenger side window.

This can't be right.

An ancient "For Lease" sign rested against the window's lower inside panel, and broken shingles lay scattered about the sidewalk. A dented gutter and downspout hung precariously from the moldy roof, and rotting wood outlined the front door's frame. Stepping from the car, Jack cupped his hands against the grimy window to observe a dilapidated room filled with cobwebs, broken shelving, and discarded boxes, as if the space had sat unoccupied for years. The floorboards lay pitted with holes, and cockroaches scuttled about the dim room. As he pushed back from the glass, his eyes drifted to a set of grooves embedded in the sidewalk cement. He recalled the metallic screech as Ellen yanked the girthy display table from the store. Dropping to a knee, he swiped a hand along the fissures. They could have been there for years.

Or not.

He must have gotten confused when he returned for the car. Maybe he passed the store already or hadn't gone far enough yet. He hopped into the car and circled back around Main Street. When he completed the loop, he peered toward the building where the store should have been. Where the store *was* thirty minutes ago.

You're crazy, Jack, and you always were.

He snapped on the radio and sped off toward Route 28. If he didn't make up for lost time, he would never get home to the Vineyard. He opened the window and hit the gas, hoping the wind in his hair might dispel thoughts of recurring nightmares, bizarre visions, and vanishing gift shops.

By the time he disembarked the ferry and wound his way through Vineyard Haven toward Edgartown, his knuckles glowed white. He wiggled his fingers, unaware of the death grip he had imposed on the steering wheel since Hyannis.

Driving home, Jack pictured Morgan and checked the dashboard clock. She would still be in her pajamas early on a Sunday morning, her blond ringlets bouncing on her shoulders as she played in her room. After the crazy morning he'd had, he couldn't wait to scoop her into his arms.

Sam would be a different story.

He couldn't predict the reception he would get, but he would understand the moment he glimpsed her eyes—they had a way of welcoming him. Her eyes would soften and glow when she gazed at him, as if an indescribable light erupted from her soul and leaked into her irises. Maybe they always possessed such magic, but he only sensed their fiery aura after they had been apart.

He rolled into the driveway and killed the engine. Reaching into his pocket, he produced the felt bag and emptied the contents into his palm. *Maybe a gift will bring the light to her eyes again.* A patch of sunlight had worked itself through the cloud cover, casting shadows inside Jack's vehicle. Squinting, he aimed the pendant into a sunbeam and wiggled his fingers.

The reflected light flashed across his face, forcing his eyes shut.

Images took root behind his vision and merged into moving pictures. When he opened his eyes, he could see nothing but the coffee-colored horse's powerful body beneath him—the sixth horse—thundering across a meadow. Its hooves pounded against the rocky ground as it veered through fissures and canyons and descended into the earth, deeper into the depths—

Jack startled, pushing his arm forward like a piston against the steering column. The car horn's blare pierced the calm.

He swiped a hand across his damp brow. "Jesus Christ, what is happening to me?" Popping the door handle, he stood and steadied himself against the car door and vehicle's roof. The house resumed in his vision, shimmering like a mirage before settling into its proper geometry. Reaching into the cupholder, he grabbed a Dasani bottle from last night, or was it the night before? Didn't matter. He gulped the warm fluid until he had emptied the contents.

Lugging his bag through the front door, he dropped it at the foot of the stairs. A door creaked on the landing above.

"Daddy?"

Jack sprinted the steps to the landing. From her bedroom doorway, Morgan held her arms wide.

He padded along the carpeted hallway. "Hey, baby girl." He kissed her cheek as he spun her around. "Did you miss me?"

"Nope." Morgan flashed a toothy grin.

"What?" Jack dropped her onto the bed and tickled her. "Are you sure?"

"Okay, okay," she squealed. "Maybe a little. Did you miss me?"

"That's a silly question." Jack held out his arms as wide as they would go. "That's as far as I can stretch, and it's not anywhere close to how much I missed you."

"That's a lot of missing."

Damn right. "It's a nice pool day. Want to invite friends over?"

Morgan craned her neck and gazed out the window. "I don't like the pool anymore."

"Why not?" This week, the pool. Next week, something else. *Just when you think you got your kid figured out.* "You're a regular water bug out there."

"Not anymore, I'm not." A slight tremor hugged her voice. "I sink."

Jack put his hand on hers and squeezed. "Well, we can use the bicycle pump to fill you up with air next time. That will keep you afloat."

"That's not funny."

Jack glanced at the sketch pad and colored pencils on the floor beside the bed. "What have you been drawing?"

Morgan grabbed the pad of paper. "Pictures."

Jack grinned as he viewed the pages. She must have used every colored pencil in the set. She had captured the backyard in vivid hues—the grass and flowers in neon green, reds, and purples, and the ocean swells in electric blues, aquas, and whites. He flipped the sketchbook's pages, each entry featuring the swimming pool front and center. In picture after picture, Morgan had drawn her friends playing in the crystal-clear water. They leaped from the diving board and barreled down the slide with ear-to-ear grins. The bright yellow sun beamed in the sizzling blue sky. Then the pictures changed, growing darker. Jack leaned closer to inspect the drab, lifeless images. Morgan had drawn the backyard in charcoal black, with the sun blotted out. No children splashed in the water or sprang from the diving board. Morgan had swapped the pool's calm, clear water with a churning vortex black as night. Page after page. In the sketchbook's final entry, Morgan lay in the grass beside the turbid water, wearing her pajamas, her eyes marked with an "X."

Jesus Christ. Jack closed the sketch pad and gave Morgan a weak smile. "No wonder you haven't been out swimming lately. Looks like an ocean storm in the middle of the pool."

"That's why I stay up here."

"Why did you draw those sad pictures, Morgan?"

She gave a quick shrug. "I don't know. I didn't have fun the last time I went out there." She peeked out the window toward the pool.

"What happened?"

Morgan's face twisted into a pout. "You mean, you don't remember?"

Jack's mind went blank. He couldn't recall any skinned knees or squabbles with friends. He sensed a shiver tremble her tiny frame and pulled her close. "You're cold."

"That's why I don't like to swim anymore. The pool is like ice water."

"I miss you running around outside, playing with friends. Seems like you spend more and more time in here." Jack played with her ringlets. "What's going on?"

"Nothing," Morgan said, hugging herself. "Will you promise me something?"

"Anything."

"If I ever sink, you'll rescue me."

"You're not gonna sink." He brushed the hair from her eyes. "Not on my watch."

"Promise me."

"I promise. Cross my heart." Jack turned Morgan's words over in his mind, but they didn't make sense. She had never feared the water before. And those drawings. Jack's heart squeezed in his ribcage. She was here beside him, safe and sound, and he wouldn't let himself think about such an unimaginable scenario.

Jack caught Sam peeking from the doorway, her eyes lacking the softness or the light he had hoped for.

"What are you doing?" Sam asked.

Jack stood. "Spending a little time with Morgan."

She pressed her lips together as if trying to remember how to smile. "Okay. You tell her all about your trip. I'm going downstairs to make some coffee."

"Hang on." Jack followed her into the hallway. "I have something for you." He fished through his pants pocket and dropped the pendant into her palm.

Sam gazed into her cupped hand, turning the chain's centerpiece over. She raised her head. "It's beautiful."

Grabbing the chain, Jack clasped it behind her and balanced the horse in the tiny indentation of her neck. He pulled out his cell and snapped a picture as Sam feigned protest. She peeked at the image but said nothing, offering her tacit approval. She could never resist a camera.

"Did you miss me while I was away?"

Sam pivoted. "You just got home, and you want to start in with me?"

His hands dropped to his sides. "All I did was ask the question."

"I haven't had enough caffeine for this conversation." Sam breezed along the staircase to the first floor.

Jack glanced over his shoulder at Morgan peeking from her bedroom. She frowned and shut the door. By the time he reached the kitchen, Sam leaned against the counter, cradling a steaming mug in her hands.

"Why did you walk away from me?"

"You're looking for an answer I can't give you. You want to check a box that says 'we're okay' so you can continue living life as usual. Well, we're not 'as usual' right now, and we're not okay."

Jack dropped onto a high-back chair beside the center island. "Well, excuse me for not accepting the bomb you dropped on me last week. I haven't had the time to process all this. You've been thinking about this separation thing a lot longer than I have."

"Listen." She leaned her head back and sighed. "I've made some calls. I've booked a flight to LA next week, and I'm going to talk to my people out there."

Jack folded his arms. "When will you be back?"

Sam grabbed a coffee cup from the drainer and placed it beside him. "Depends on how things are going. I have a lot to do—"

"Oh, I see. If things go well, maybe you stay?" Jack pushed the cup away. "If not, you come back to your shitty Martha's Vineyard life?"

Sam waved a hand. "Just stop."

"When are you coming back?"

"I'm not sure yet."

"What's the return date on the ticket?"

Sam hesitated. "I don't have one."

"You're traveling one-way?"

"Open-ended. In case I need a few extra days, that's all." She threw her arms up. "Don't get all accusatory."

"This is where our life is." Jack gestured about the room. "Morgan, too."

"This isn't about Morgan anymore. This is about me. Why don't I have the right to satisfy the needs in my life?" She stared through the kitchen window toward the ocean. "When's the last time I spent time away from Massachusetts? I can't even remember. I need to see the West Coast again. I need time with my friends. I'll have answers when I return. If that isn't good enough for you, I don't know what is."

"I love you, Sam."

"Jack . . ." She spun from the window with her hands clenched.

"I'm not sure how my saying 'I love you' can get you so angry, but I won't apologize for it." He stomped from the kitchen and through the entryway. Grabbing his bag, he pounded the steps to the second-floor landing. He hoped to hear Sam call his name from the kitchen or voice a plea for him to return, anything to show she gave a damn.

He waited, then advanced along the hallway to the bedroom.

———

Once Jack had unpacked his things, he shuffled to his office and shut the door. His marriage was falling apart, but maybe he could salvage his sanity. He sank into his desk chair and rubbed his eyes, trying to piece together the bizarre weekend. "The Carousel Man" and its strange similarities to his life left him unsettled. The fact that Hal couldn't find the piece made Jack question whether he had officially lost his marbles. And what about the crazy funeral dream, or the bizarre hallucination at the jewelry store, a place that may or may not even exist?

You've always been crazy, Jack. That's what everyone thinks.

After Fulton State Hospital and all the psychiatrists he had tried on like department store pants over the years, he vowed to bury whatever happened to him in that Missouri cornfield. Dreams or no dreams, he'd had to move on from it.

But in the past few days, Jack wondered whether it had moved on from him.

At least he could call the book signings a success. When he discovered people still read his books and were excited for more, the motivation to write stirred inside him again. Despite the optimism, Jack had constantly checked his phone throughout the day Saturday, hoping for an update from Hal on the story, the journal, or the author—Graham something-or-other—but it never came. He sympathized with those who waited patiently at the Hyannis signing, as they must have sensed his distraction. Now he couldn't focus on anything else until he found answers. And the only way to get them would be to find the one corroborating piece of evidence he had.

The boy, Jack Morgan.

He powered up his laptop and opened the browser. Against his better judgment, he googled the boy's name. He didn't expect a ten-year-old to have an extensive online profile, but what else could he do? Call every greater Boston area Morgan family and hope one had a ten-year-old son, Jack, who happened to be alone at Barnes and Noble last Friday? A mountainous effort with a mole hill's possibility of success. *And who the fuck still had a landline anyway?* Might as well start with the internet.

After entering the name "Jack Morgan," he stared at page one of over a billion listings. *Well, this shouldn't take long.*

Jack Morgan, the actor . . .

Jack Morgan, the porn star . . .

J.P. Morgan, the philanthropist—*didn't know his nickname was Jack.*

Jack-O Blast Captain Morgan Rum . . .

Captain Jack will get you high tonight lyrics.

Google had lost its focus. Or maybe he had.

He tried "Jack Morgan images" to see if the boy had his picture in the local paper after a spelling bee or pizza-eating contest. He found a close-up image of the *one* Jack Morgan he most definitely did *not* want to see: page after page of headshots and mugshots and mid-west Jack Morgans posing with shotguns, deer carcasses, and four-wheel-drive vehicles for their dating websites. An hour later, Jack dropped his head in his hands. Okay, now what?

He wanted to slam his laptop closed and take a break from the Jack Morgan thing, but he also had to turn off the weird-o-meter beeping at him all day. He googled EM Designer Jewelry & Gifts.

He immediately spotted the storefront with its Cape-style, weathered shingles and black shutters and clicked the images tab. A half-dozen storefront pictures populated the screen. Jack peered at the images, noting the pixelation. They appeared to be early digital photos taken years ago, judging from the boxy older-model cars parked out front. Jack exited the page and clicked the news tab. Pages of local *Cape Cod Times* headlines from decades ago popped up, features about the store's grand opening, holiday sales and discounts, and the nineties pop-star diva who happened by one day to buy jewelry. But one headline grabbed his attention.

Local Hyannis Businesswoman and Son Still Missing

Two years after disappearing without a trace from the Barnstable County Fair, local and federal authorities have little to go on. Ellen Morgan, 46, and her son, Jackson, 10, were last seen by her husband, Brad Morgan, on Saturday evening when he dropped them at the fairgrounds on Route 151 in East Falmouth. He returned to pick them up several hours later, but the pair never arrived.

In a bizarre coincidence, Marsha Mason, a local *Falmouth Enterprise* reporter, photographed the pair in what may be the last known picture of the two (photo featured below). Mr. Morgan remained the prime suspect in their disappearance until the Morris photograph surfaced a year later, establishing the two were alive when his whereabouts could not be verified. Falmouth Police chief Hank Silva told the *Times*, "Every day, we work tirelessly with local, state, and federal law enforcement to bring Mrs. Morgan and her son, Jack, back home. We will not rest until we find them and give the family closure."

Ellen Morgan was the owner of EM Designer Jewelry & Gifts, once a popular gift shop on Main Street in Hyannis, and Jackson was to enter the sixth grade at Barnstable Middle School.

Jack scrolled to the beginning and re-read the article. When he reached the last sentence, he mumbled, "Ellen Morgan *was* the owner of EM Designer Jewelry & Gifts, *once* a popular gift shop . . ."

What the fuck?

Clicking the images tab, Jack spotted the abandoned storefront in a more recent photo. He scrolled back to the eerie photograph of Ellen and Jack Morgan from the *Cape Cod Times* article. The two shared snocones and traipsed through the ring of bright lights blazing from the illuminated rides. They remained blissfully unaware of their impending fate, as if that night was just another Saturday on the Cape. He had a hazy recollection of the Barnstable County Fair disappearance and the national coverage that followed, but he couldn't recall the victims' names until now. Jack rubbed his eyes, then zoomed in on the image. He couldn't distinguish the boy's face clearly enough to recognize whether he was *the* Jack Morgan he sought or whether the name proved a bizarre coincidence. But with her head tilted toward her son, Jack did get a good look at Ellen Morgan—and he had seen her today in Hyannis, in a gift shop that no longer existed. And if the Jack Morgan in the photo was her son, he had seen him in Boston on Friday night. He leaned back in his chair and raked both hands through his hair.

Now I'm seeing ghosts.

CHAPTER NINE

Excerpt from *Jigsaw*, by Jack Rainne:

Detective Sal Molinaro aimed the Crown Vic toward the road-side, hugging the crumbling curb. He gaped through the windshield at the uniforms huddled behind the yellow crime scene tape. The patrol vehicles' flashing strobes threw electric light off the rain-soaked buildings and pavement, adding the familiar cobalt-blue hue of murder to the steamy August night. Shimmying his generous hindquarters off the car seat, the detective stepped onto the damp grass and ducked under the hastily strung police tape.

"Hiya doing, partner."

"Hey, Sal." Detective Carlo Fiano clapped the portly man's shoulder and shook his head. "We have a mess, my friend."

Molinaro jammed a thumb toward the uniforms. "How many of our boys tramped through the crime scene?"

"A few, but most just peeked from the doorway. You don't see something like this every day."

"Forensic guys here yet?"

"On another call. Busy night."

"Didn't know we needed to take a number." Molinaro scratched his ear. "All right, show me the way."

The detectives stepped through the brownstone's double glass doors and mounted the creaky wooden steps to the upper floors. Curious neighbors tracked their movements through chain-locked apartment doors but asked no questions. Cops and crime scene tape in the middle of the night rendered the unspoken answer.

Molinaro hauled his frame upward, grabbing the banister halfway through the second flight. "Anyone see anything?"

Fiano paused on the landing. "The tenant beneath the victim's apartment. A Mrs. Gibbs. She noticed a stain spreading across her ceiling and went to have a look upstairs."

"Let's get her out here and ask—"

"Paramedics took her to the hospital," Fiano said, pressing his hands against his hips. "After what she saw, she may need a little time."

Molinaro nodded and proceeded to the third-floor landing, where his partner led him to an open door. The overhead light spilled from the apartment, illuminating a blood trail seeping into the hallway. Ducking beneath the yellow tape, the detectives circled the body splayed out upon the wooden floorboards.

The dead woman appeared to float in the blood pool beneath her, a red moat surrounding a flesh castle. Molinaro dropped to a knee and leaned over the body, squinting through his glasses. He scanned the blood-soaked flooring visible through the woman's gruesome injuries.

"Jesus Christ." Snapping on a pair of latex gloves, he pressed a finger against the deceased's upper arm. It rolled away from the body, detached at the joint.

He waved his partner to the floor. "Look at the incisions, Carlo. Each body segment . . . the forearm, the fingers . . . cut away from the next. Right through the joint." The two detectives examined the woman's lower body. Each body part had been separated from the adjoining segment, mirroring the home surgery performed on the upper body.

Fiano drew a heavy breath. "This guy must have studied his anatomy."

Molinaro lifted his gaze. "He took his time." Rising to his feet, he inspected the body from above. "Wait a minute, Carlo. Something ain't right."

"You can say that again." He turned away from the mutilated corpse.

"No, look over here." Molinaro whipped out a flashlight and directed a steady beam across the upper and lower left arm, then the upper and lower right arm.

Fiano knelt beside the victim. "What is it, Sal?"

"Check out the size and shapes of each body segment. The coloring. Look at the forearms."

The detective focused his gaze on the opposing body parts. "I'm not sure what you're—"

"They're not the same," Molinaro said.

"What?"

"Each body segment is different." Molinaro inspected the lower limbs, feet, and joints of each hand, then raised his head. "They belong to different people. Assembled like a human jigsaw puzzle."

Fiano swallowed and rose on shaky legs. "Holy Christ!" He pressed a hand across his mouth.

Molinaro's cell phone chirped from his back pocket. "Hey, Chief. Yeah, we're at Trinity Court right now. Where's the forensic team? We have a major problem." The detective switched the cell to his other ear. "What? They're where?"

Fiano tilted his head. "What is it?"

The detective raised his index finger. "Well, we need them over here. We've got a dismembered—" Molinaro leaned his head back and remained silent for a spell. "I see." Ending the call, he lumbered to the window and stared off into the night.

"What's up, Sal?"

"Across town. They have another one."

"Another body?"

Molinaro rubbed the back of his neck. "Another jigsaw puzzle."

CHAPTER TEN

Twenty-Five Years Earlier
Fulton, Missouri (Fulton State Hospital)

Jack shifted in his seat and glared at Dr. Lang. "So, you want to take me to Johnson Farm, but you don't want to leave the office. That doesn't make any fucking sense."

"Does anything I say to you make any fucking sense?"

Jack scratched his head. "Not really."

"Then just go with it. Have you heard about hypnotherapy?" Lang slid his chair beside the sofa. "I wouldn't usually suggest it, but I think it's worth a try. We put you in a relaxed state and help you relive an experience. But because we do it from the safety of the office, we can make the experience more positive. Or we can stop it and discuss it. We can make it anything you want it to be."

"But you don't believe I was ever there."

"I believe that *you* believe you were there. That's all that matters."

Jack considered Lang's rebuttal. "You said you usually don't suggest that type of therapy. Why not?"

"It's typically used for behavior change," Lang said, removing his glasses and wiping them on a tissue. "You know, to stop smoking or lose weight, that kind of thing, not for a traumatic experience. But I think we can take a negative and make it a positive, relieve the guilt you're carrying inside. Get you to a better place. What do you say?"

"A better place sounds good." Jack's fingernails dug into his palms as he gazed about the office. "Can anything . . . happen to me?"

"Nope. You're in full control."

Jack plodded across the room to the window. "At my high school assembly, they brought in a hypnotist and made people do embarrassing stuff in front of everyone. I don't want you to make me do something—"

"No one can make you do anything you wouldn't ordinarily do. I'm guessing your classmates were highly suggestible and got caught up in the moment. Have you ever been working on the farm, maybe you're mowing the grass, and you find yourself done and you don't even remember doing it? Or where the time went?"

Jack nodded. "Happens a lot, actually."

"Just means you were in a hypnotic state. Happens to me all the time when I'm driving. I'll arrive home and can't remember diddlysquat about the trip. I'll help put you in a state like that, and we can see what's behind those walls you've put up."

"What if something happens to me when I'm out there?"

Dr. Lang dropped a hand on his shoulder. "Then I'll be right here to get you out."

"All right, Doc, but I'm not going to sing 'Macarena' standing on one foot like Johnny Merrill did last year."

Lang barked out a laugh. "Don't worry, Jack. I wouldn't do that to you. I've heard you sing before."

Doc made another joke. Jack raised an eyebrow. "Nice one."

Lang acknowledged with a nod. "What do you say we get started?" He rummaged through his desk drawer, producing a wooden metronome. Positioning it on the coffee table, he twisted the knob, generating a repetitive chirping sound and flashing green light. He approached the door and dimmed the overhead lights.

"Okay, Jack. I want you to focus on the light and the gentle clicking in your ears."

Jack bathed in the flashing light's calming effect.

"I want you to remember getting on your bicycle and riding home from school that day. Remember how the sun felt on your skin. School's over and you're going home. Your world is good. I want you to remember coming over the hill beside Johnson Farm."

Jack closed his eyes, feeling the burn in his legs as he churned the bicycle up the hill. He could sense Dr. Lang beside him through the flashing green haze as well as the heat from the heavy sun blanketing the back of his neck. His perception of peace shattered as his body exploded into darkness, ripping him from Lang's sofa. As he reached for the doctor, his flailing arms couldn't latch onto him. His brain flooded with curious images and memories that didn't belong to him, fear gripping him like a set of hands pulling at his insides. As the light rose in his eyes, Jack found himself beside an old man in the passenger seat of a battered pickup bounding along a dirt road. Jack recognized the man in an instant.

The old man swiped a sleeve across his forehead. "Bloody heat," he muttered. Through the windshield, Dr. Lang appeared in his dimly lit office, perched in the chair beside the sofa. Jack pounded on the truck's glass to get his attention, but the doctor didn't respond. He considered throwing the door open and jumping out to remove himself from whatever dream state he'd entered, but the road sped past his window in a fevered blur. He might escape the vision, but he might break his neck as well.

Jack glanced toward the driver's seat and sensed his heart squeeze as the old man reflected on his lonely years. Dr. Lang had not only put him in the passenger seat, but inside the man's head. He would be meeting a client today, one for whom happenstance and fate had intersected.

Jack shivered. *He's meeting me today. I'm the client.*

Edging the pickup to the roadside, the old man pulled the key from the ignition and peered out the passenger-side window. Jack couldn't understand why the old man didn't spot him, stop the car and yell at him, or ask him what the hell he was doing plopped in his passenger seat.

Because you're not really here.

"Bloody heat." The old man eased himself from the driver's seat and arched his back, his boots crunching the gravel as he twisted to the left and right. Jack slid out, too, his stiffened joints aching like those of the old man. Shuffling to the trailer, the man released the bungee cords securing his load. He yanked the tarp back, exposing metal poles, platform pieces, and engine components. Folding the tarp back further revealed hand-crafted wooden horses tethered to the trailer's deck. Five horses lay side-by-side. A sixth horse lay separate from the others, secured with a much heavier rope.

The coffee-colored one. My horse.

The man touched the mare's coat before yanking his hand back and massaging it with the other. Jack pressed a hand over his chest, experiencing the same adrenaline surge as the old man. Releasing the straps and bungee cords securing the equipment, the old man filled his lungs and shut his eyes. Jack's jaw swung as the pieces assembled themselves on the golden cornfield. When the old man blinked his eyes open, the carousel and its six horses spun slowly as the droning hurdy-gurdy carnival jangle floated across the still air.

The man spat on the ground. "Bloody heat." For the first time, the old man acknowledged Jack's presence. He glared at him and snapped his fingers. "Wake up!"

Jack exploded into Dr. Lang's office as if launched from a slingshot, bouncing from the couch into the coffee table. The metronome flew across the room, shattering against Lang's desk. The doctor sprung from his chair as Jack rose on wobbly legs. Lang eased him onto the couch.

"What the . . . ?" Jack held his head.

"Jesus, Jack. You okay?"

He raised his head. "I'm not sure?"

"I snap my fingers to bring you around," Lang said, glancing about the office, "and you go and destroy all my cheap-ass furniture."

"Wait . . . I was here the whole time?"

Lang chuckled. "Of course, Jack. I said you wouldn't be going anywhere."

You were wrong.

Jack fixed his gaze on a portable fan on the floor, its blades swirling air in his direction. "Where did that come from?"

"Oh, the fan? I set it out for you. You were sweating and rubbing your forehead. You were getting more uncomfortable, mumbling a bit. So I ended the session, told you to wake up."

Mumbling? Jack straightened in his seat. "What was I saying?"

"Just muttering things.

"About what? Tell me exactly what I said."

"Nothing important," Lang said. "Just 'bloody heat' over and over."

PART TWO

Revelation

CHAPTER ELEVEN

Present Day
Woods Hole, Massachusetts (Cape Cod)

On Monday morning, Jack called the *Falmouth Enterprise* to locate Marsha Mason, the newspaper's photographer who had captured Ellen and Jack Morgan's image at the Barnstable County Fair. He had expected to hear "I don't know . . ." or "You might try . . ." along with a day's worth of wrong numbers and goose-chase leads. To his surprise, Marsha had answered the phone. Not only did she still work there, but she had a hand in just about everything involved in small newspaper publishing, from photography, to feature article writing, to editing. Even taking out the trash. She agreed to meet him during lunch to discuss the Morgans' disappearance.

After rolling off the ferry in Woods Hole, Jack weathered the ten-minute jaunt to Falmouth Center, maneuvering through congestion at Locust Street until he escaped with a left onto Depot Road. He parked beside the refurbished rail trail and followed the sidewalk to the building's front entrance. He squinted through the screen door at the empty front desk.

"Hello." He rapped on the wood frame.

"Come on in," the woman's voice called.

Jack entered and strode along the carpeted hallway. He popped his head into an open office door. "Ms. Mason?"

The woman behind the desk lowered her sandwich and dragged a napkin across her mouth. "You must be Jack. Come on in and have a seat." She rose and shook his hand, moving with the confidence of someone much younger than the age her graying locks betrayed. "I'm a big fan of your work. I thought *Double-Barrel Justice* was your best yet."

Jack liked her already. "I appreciate your saying that, Ms. Mason. Thank you."

"It's Marsha. You know, I've reviewed each of your books for the *Enterprise*. It's great you're considering writing a book about the Morgan disappearance. I assume this one will be more of a true crime novel?"

"Not sure yet." Jack had hated to lie about his true intentions over the phone. But if he had discussed meeting Ellen Morgan and possibly her son, Jack, over the weekend, the entire Cape Cod police force would have been waiting in her office to introduce themselves. "I'm only gathering information at this point. I remember when it happened. It's a fascinating case."

"Oh, without a doubt. The Barnstable County Fair is one of the biggest family attractions on the Cape each year. For two people to simply disappear . . ." Marsha shook her head. "Anyway, the incident sort of marred the event for a lot of people." She raised a straw to her lips and sucked down the remaining soda with a slurp. "Are you native to these parts?"

Jack leaned back. "I don't know if Edgartown counts."

She unveiled a youthful smile. "It doesn't, but we'll let it slide."

"Fair enough. That was quite a photo of Ellen and Jack Morgan you snapped at the fair the night they disappeared."

She crumpled her sandwich wrapper and tossed it into the trash. "Dumb luck, really. Didn't find the photo until a year later. It hadn't occurred to me I shot an entire roll of film that night, and it might provide evidence for the investigation. When I saw the Morgan photo, I couldn't believe it."

"Talk about being at the right place at the right time."

"I'll say. As a journalist, I should have been more excited about it. Here I was in my twenties, and overnight every news organization in the country was publishing my photo and asking me questions about it."

Jack tilted his head. "That didn't excite you?"

"A good journalist shouldn't be the story." She paused a beat, running a hand through her shoulder-length hair. "But there's more to it than that. I sometimes think about where I was during that fateful moment when I snapped the shutter. You look back and wish you had known something you couldn't possibly know. I wish I could have said, 'Go! Get the hell out of here.' Anything to change what happened."

"Whatever happened to the jewelry shop she owned?" Jack didn't want to change the subject, but his Sunday weird-o-meter had started beeping again, and he wasn't ready to pull the plug on it.

"Ellen Morgan basically ran the place. When she disappeared, no one was there to take over. Her husband didn't understand much about jewelry and crafts, so he shut the doors and boxed the inventory. I'm sure it's still sitting up in his attic somewhere."

"How come he never rented out the space again? It's like a storefront in a ghost town."

"The Morgans owned the building. I suspect he kept it for her, in a way. In case she ever returned. But he got older, couldn't keep up with the maintenance, and it fell into disrepair. Now he couldn't rent it out if it were the last place in Hyannis."

"Whatever happened to him?"

"Still living there. Rumor has it he goes by from time to time to clean the place. Every now and then, he'll have a microphone shoved in his face on the fateful anniversary." She clicked her tongue. "Poor son of a gun. Guy loses his wife and kid, and on top of that, the police pegged him as the prime suspect."

"Can you blame them? It's always the husband. At least on *Forensic Files*, it is."

"Not if the wife gets him first." Marsha chuckled and extracted a folder from a file cabinet. She sifted through the contents, pulling the Morgan photo. "As much as this picture haunts me, it helped establish that Mr. Morgan dropped off his family, and they were alive during a time when he had no alibi. It settled the investigation on him. Of course, with police focusing on only one suspect, the trail turned as cold as a Cape Cod winter."

Jack eyed the folder. "Are those the pictures from the fair?"

She raised the manila folder. "A whole file. The police went through them but didn't find anything, and there were no more images of the Morgans."

"Can I take a peek through them?"

"Be my guest." She passed the folder across the desk.

"Thanks."

Marsha nodded toward the phone jangling at the front desk. "Gotta get that. I'm head secretary around here as well."

"They call them administrative assistants now."

She rolled her eyes. "Not on the Cape, they don't. Back in a minute." She hustled out into the hallway.

Jack leaned forward and cracked the folder. He found a stack of eight-by-ten glossy color photos developed old-school, the darkroom chemicals' aroma still lingering. Marsha must have put them in order according to the time of day, as each series of pictures darkened with the day's waning light.

He leafed through the photos. He had already deduced Ellen Morgan was long gone, despite having seen her yesterday in a store, vacant and boarded up for the past twenty years. This alone meant his hallucinations, or whatever they were, had spiraled out of control. But Jack would have to find out whether the Jack Morgan who visited him on Saturday was Ellen's son as well. Now, if that proved true . . . well, he might need to book another room at Fulton State Hospital. Better not to dwell on that possibility.

Jack examined each print as Marsha Mason put out fires at the front desk. He could tell she had a knack for photography, especially the use of existing light. She had captured the essence of fairground Americana drenched in golden sunset hues: giggling children in blurred momentum on twirling suspended swings; families trekking across trampled grass, arms around shoulders and melted ice cream trickling through fingers; teenagers in sandals and tank tops holding hands as the setting sunlight framed faces in pollen-rich halos.

Marsha must have taken the final photos long after sundown to contrast the carnival lights against a dark background. Again, the work was artistic. Jack flipped through the series until he reached the last picture. She had taken the image from a distance, capturing the entire fairgrounds shrouded in electric light, every ride, tent, and booth framed within the shot as night fell. Jack peered closer, scanning the frame.

Something didn't look right, the symmetry, maybe?

Organizers had laid out the fairgrounds with rides and attractions in the middle and food and prize tents surrounding the perimeter. But

Jack observed a set of distant lights between two tents, positioned outside the fair's boundaries. He held the print closer to his eyes, the resolution at such distance—or his forty-something-year-old vision—affecting the photo's clarity.

Jack stood and set the photo on the desk. Grabbing his cell, he accessed the Magnifier app. He toggled the slider until the distant object filled the entire screen.

He stopped breathing.

Jack tried to swallow, but his tongue felt like a swollen, wet sponge. He staggered as the dream exploded. Familiar scenes flickered inside his head until they clouded his vision and rendered his world black. Jack rode the coffee-colored sixth horse with the shimmering mane. He jammed his heels into the mare's side to spur it onward through the golden Missouri farmland, driving it to its breaking point. The mighty animal's thumping hooves beat the dusty earth as Jack inhaled the fertile meadow's sweet scent.

"Mr. Rainne? Jack!"

The woman's distant shout rumbled like a tinny voice from an old transistor radio as Jack urged the horse forward. *Faster.* He sensed the hands poking at him, tapping at his face as a wind blew in through the lush valley and rustled his hair. *Faster.*

"Wake up!"

Jack's eyes flew open as an open hand stung his cheek. He lay on his back in Marsha Mason's office as she knelt before him, her face inches from his own.

"Jack! Are you okay?"

He blinked his eyes into focus and rose to the seated position. "What . . . happened?"

She dashed to the bubbler and returned with a paper cone topped with water. "Here," she said, transfering it to Jack with shaky hands. "Take a sip."

You're losing your mind, Jack.

He chugged the fluid. "I was looking closer at your final photo, and the next thing I knew, I hit the floor." Jack struggled to his feet, steadying himself against Marsha's arm.

"Please, sit." She led Jack to his chair and helped ease him onto the seat. She reached to the floor and returned his cell phone, then picked up the photo from her desk and inspected the image. They locked gazes as Jack raised his head.

Her eyes widened, flicking back and forth between Jack and the print. She steadied herself against the desk as her hand slowly opened, and the photo tumbled onto the floor.

"Oh my God," she mumbled.

CHAPTER TWELVE

Falmouth, Massachusetts (Cape Cod)

Jack settled into the front seat and rested his hands on the steering wheel as he worked to control his breathing. A breeze filtering through the window cooled his forehead.

He recognized the carousel in the photograph and the old man on the stool beside it, archaic and out of place among the modern carnival rides and attractions. Marsha Mason must have sensed something about it, judging from her reaction. She had ushered him from the office so fast he didn't have a chance to ask.

Jack leaned his head against the headrest. *You were wrong, Dr. Lang!* After twenty years of recurring nightmares involving the old man and the carousel, he discovered they both existed. Now he was sure he hadn't imagined the dream; he had lived it. The image brought comfort that he wasn't completely out of his mind.

But he would still need to find young Jack Morgan.

The boy had sent him a message with "The Carousel Man": someone else understood what he experienced in that Missouri field. Could it be Jack wasn't the only person having nightmares? Had another author reached out through his prose to find others with similar experiences? If he could only remember the author's damn name—*Gregory? Grant? Sonofabitch!* He still needed the boy to help him understand what was happening. He prayed that Barnes-and-Noble-Jack was not Ellen's son, because if he was, then Jack had seen a ghost and would never find the answers he needed. Unless Jack Morgan sought him out again.

With a couple of hours to kill before the next Vineyard ferry, Jack sped north along Route 28 to Hyannis. He figured he could gather information about the Morgan family and find out whether any neighboring shopkeepers knew Ellen or her son. With any luck, someone might have a picture of the family or could provide the boy's description. He didn't have anywhere else to start.

When he reached Hyannis, Jack eased into a pay lot near the JFK museum. Swiping his card, he bought himself a couple of hours. He hoofed along the strip as the midday heat descended. He entered the candy stores, ice cream parlors, T-shirt shops, and bistros surrounding Ellen Morgan's old storefront, searching for anyone with information to share on the family. Repeating the lie about writing a book on the case instantly spurred people to talk, especially if he asked them how to spell their names. Somehow the lie didn't bother Jack much the second, third, sixth, or fourteenth time he told it. He subscribed to the Lance Armstrong rule of lying: If you only have one lie, it doesn't matter how often you tell it, it's still only one lie. He could live with that.

But no Main Street proprietor had ever met Ellen Morgan or her son. It had been twenty years since they disappeared. Businesses had come and gone. To most downtown Hyannis shopkeepers, the old EM Designer Jewelry & Gifts was nothing more than an abandoned eyesore they bitched about at city council meetings.

Crossing Main Street, Jack peered inside the vacant storefront's cloudy windows. He stepped back and scanned the facade, the store name etched on the foggy glass barely visible. His trip had been for nothing, but at least no ghosts were handing out jewelry today.

Checking his watch, he still had time to drown his sorrows in a Sam Adams. He found a shady sidewalk taqueria and an outdoor table. Blue, flowering hydrangea bloomed from behind white picket fences along the tidy avenue as an aromatic mix of seafood and sunscreen wafted from the crowded street. After ordering a Summer Ale, he rested his heavy eyelids. A balmy midday breeze ruffled his locks.

He took a pull from his beer and leaned his chair back, eyes unfocused in a blank stare across the intersection. A man ambled along the sidewalk running beside Ellen Morgan's deserted storefront. His clothes appeared well-worn and dated, as if he had grown old inside them. He met Jack's gaze from across the street before pulling out a set of keys and jangling them inside the front door lock.

Jack burst from the table, banging his knee against the metal underside and upending his beer. Dropping a ten onto the table, he secured it beneath the frothing beer bottle and raced across the road. He clutched his knee as he shimmied around the line of cars inching through the Hyannis downtown.

"Hang on a minute." Jack waved from the middle of the street. "Wait!"

The man glanced in Jack's direction as he unlocked the door, nudging the doorframe with his shoulder.

Jack caught up with him at the entrance. "I'm sorry to bother you," he said, sucking in air. "Are you Mr. Morgan?"

The man pivoted and narrowed his eyes. "Depends."

"On what?"

"On whether I know you." He stepped into the store. "So, I guess that makes me someone else."

"Please, wait." He pressed his hand against the door. "I'm Jack Rainne. I'm a writer, and—"

"*Double-Barrel Justice?*"

"Huh?"

The man cracked the door a few inches. "The book. Did you write it?"

Jack grinned. "It's my latest—"

"An absolute piece of shit, that one."

Jack's face fell. *Ouch.*

Propping the door open with his right arm, the man waved him in with the other. "The guy who wrote that turd can't be the same fella who wrote *Road Rage.*"

Jack emptied his lungs as he stepped over the sill, massaging his throbbing limb. "One and the same, unfortunately."

The man scratched his forehead beneath a tattered Red Sox cap. "What's a has-been like you want with me?"

Ouch, again. Jack resurrected his inner Lance Armstrong. "I'm here because I'm interested in writing a book about what happened to Mrs. Morgan and your son. I'd love to talk to you about it."

Brad Morgan's eyes clouded over. "What good would it do?"

Jack combed his fingers through his hair. "Maybe stir up memories or recollections from people who might have seen something. Could generate new leads. People want to know what happened to them."

"No one knows what happened to them, and no one ever will." Brad dropped his keys on what appeared to be the former store's front desk. "And I'm not interested in satisfying people's morbid curiosity or helping you profit off my loss."

"I wouldn't do that. Usually, the proceeds on these things go to a nonprofit foundation or a charity—"

"Even nonprofits make money." He waved his hand. "Someone always profits."

"Fair enough." Jack held up his hands. "I understand. I wouldn't consider doing something like this without your cooperation." Now he could stop lying, at least. Well, lying about the book. He couldn't promise himself he wouldn't lie to find out more about Ellen and Jack Morgan.

Brad tramped across the floor and opened the door. "Looks like you wasted your time."

Jack eyed the red spider-web veins in Brad Morgan's bulbous nose. "Maybe. But has-been writers don't have anything else to do but waste time."

Brad let loose a grin. "I'll bet."

"I still have at least an hour to kill. Can I buy you a beer?"

Brad Morgan smacked his lips and swallowed. "I don't frequent the kind of places yuppies like you tend to gather in, but I wouldn't say no to a six-pack."

Yuppies?

Brad reached into his tattered shirt pocket and dropped a roach motel in each corner of the store. "A cold one . . . or two, maybe . . . would make the work go by faster."

Jack took the cue and hiked across the intersection to the convenience store on the corner. Brad didn't fit the microbrewery demographic. He would need to choose his suds wisely from the walk-in cooler if he planned to make any progress with the guy. Upon his return to the jewelry store, he slung a frosty six-pack of Pabst Blue Ribbon onto the front desk. Lowering himself onto a stool, Jack removed his cell from his back pocket.

Brad grinned and popped open the tab, a frothy spray spitting from the can. He took two voluminous gulps before letting out a beer-drenched breath. "Hits the spot."

Jack cracked a can and choked down a swig, trying not to grimace. "Sure does." He scanned the room. "You mind if I still ask you a few questions about your wife and son?"

"For what?"

"For me. Got some time to kill. Besides, I'm a local, Mr. Morgan. I remember when it happened."

Brad took a chug and dragged a sleeve across his lips. "Local? Like Cape Cod local?"

"Edgartown."

"Doesn't count." Dropping the empty can onto the counter, Brad disappeared into the back room. He emerged with a wide push broom, the bristles so old and worn they curled at the ends like a dead spider's legs.

"Doesn't seem right to watch you work while I'm drinking beer." Jack stood. "You need a hand cleaning up?"

Brad popped another can. "Wouldn't mind none."

"What can I do?"

Brad handed him the broom and took Jack's seat. "You can start by sweeping up."

Jack sighed and grabbed the Libman. He pushed the broom around the room in circles like a Zamboni while Brad finished his beer. In minutes, the dust shavings had formed mini mountains on the creaky hardwood. "You fixing up the store for a rental or something?"

Brad shook his head. "Can't do that."

"How come?" Jack gazed through the glass onto the busy street. "You have a good location."

"I had a dream. Ellen . . . my wife . . . She was getting the store ready for another workday. She was dragging tables out on the sidewalk like she used to, setting up her displays. Leaving grooves in the pavement again." He chuckled, but his vacant gaze drilled holes into the tabletop. "I think it's a sign she's coming back."

Jack swallowed. *Or she's back already.*

"I've never had such a realistic dream like that before." He traced the frost streaks running along the can with his finger. "I want the place ready for her, just in case. Is that crazy?"

"I don't think so." Jack took another gulp. "What about your son? Was he in the dream, too?"

Brad stood and grabbed a dust rag from beneath the counter. "I don't dream about Jackson anymore."

"You don't?"

"When someone abducts a child. Well . . ." Brad's gaze dropped to the floor. "I don't suspect I'll be seeing him again."

Jack gripped a dustpan and scooped the debris from the floor. For a guy who didn't want to answer questions, Brad Morgan sure wanted to talk now. Maybe he had no one to talk to anymore. Or maybe the beer had lubricated his vocal cords just enough.

"What was he like, your son?" Jack folded his hands over the top of the broom handle.

"He was ten when . . . it happened." Pulling off his cap, Brad dragged a palm across his thinning hair. "Would have been eleven that Thanksgiving."

Jack recalled his conversation with the boy at the bookstore. *I'm supposed to be eleven in November . . .*

"I always wanted a son," Brad said, blinking his eyes in succession. "You hope they'll like the same things you do. End up just like you." He snorted out a laugh. "But Jack didn't take to fishing or hunting so much. Worse yet, he didn't give a damn about the Red Sox."

"That's rough." Jack leaned the broom against the wall. "What did he like to do?"

"He liked to read." He emptied the third can down his throat. "Spooky stuff, mostly. Never figured out where he got it from. His mother didn't like it none, either. She figured those scary ones would keep him up at night."

Jack's heartbeat rattled against his ribcage. Too many coincidences. Ten-year-old kid, November birthday, reader, and horror fan. He had heard the same story from the boy himself on Friday night. Jack sensed heat building behind his cheeks.

Brad Morgan's eyes glistened. "Boy woulda been thirty-one this year. Been gone nearly twice as long as I ever knew him." His grin morphed into a flat, quivering line. "Funny, I remember everything from each of his ten years but nothing from the twenty since."

"You got a picture?"

Lowering his can, Brad rustled through a back pocket for his wallet.

Jack gazed at the aged Polaroid with a tightening in his chest, as if someone had reached through his ribs and squeezed his heart. Coincidences over. The boy in the picture was *his* Barnes-and-Noble-Jack, after all. He *was* seeing ghosts.

"Good-looking kid." The words struggled from Jack's sandpaper-dry tongue. He took a welcomed gulp from his Blue Ribbon.

"And here's a picture of Ellen." Brad's lip quivered as he peered at the photo. "She's getting a plaque from the town council. Something about commitment to the Hyannis community."

"She was very beautiful, Mr. Morgan."

"It ain't the best picture of her, but you can see how proud she was to be honored. This store meant a lot to her," he said, gazing about the decaying space. "Ever see it in its heyday?"

"Unfortunately, not. Never made it down here."

"She had a talent with jewelry. See this?" He beamed at the gold band as he flipped his hand over. "She made our wedding rings. See how the two pieces of gold wind around each other like rope? She used to say we were like that. Bound together."

"Amazing work." Jack beamed.

"You a married man?" Brad slurred his words as he grabbed the plastic beer ring and tugged at another can.

Jack repositioned his cell on the front desk, aiming it toward the tipsy Brad Morgan. "This is Sam." He tapped the glass, and her image filled the screen.

Brad glanced at the device. "She's one beautiful woman, son." Popping open a fresh can, he took another slug and returned his gaze to the cell. "Looks like some kind of movie star." As he gave the image a lengthy inspection, his Adam's apple bounced in his throat. In an instant, his face changed, as if his dead wife had brushed past him and touched his shoulder. He glowered at Jack as a vein in his temple pulsed.

"You okay, Mr. Morgan?"

"Where did she get that?" Brad pointed to the screen and folded his arms.

Jack's gaze lingered on his wife's picture before he lifted his head. "Get what?"

He picked up Jack's cell. "That jewelry. Where did she get it?"

Jack took the phone and examined the picture more closely. He winced at Ellen Morgan's pendant necklace fashioned around Sam's neck. *Fuck!* "Um, I don't know. It's just a piece of jewelry I bought for her."

Brad Morgan turned instantly sober. "Ellen made it. That was one of her last designs before she . . ."

Think, Jack. "Of course, I remember now." Jack bumped the heel of his palm into his forehead. "Duh, I bought it here. Long ago. Mrs. Morgan said it would be a great gift for my wife."

"How long you been married?"

"Close to sixteen years."

Brad's head tilted upward as if contemplating a riddle. "Ellen disappeared twenty years ago. Your math don't add up."

Jack backpedaled. "I wasn't married yet. She said it would be a wonderful gift for a wife someday. That's what I meant to say."

"Is it?" He pointed to the image. "You just told me you've never been in the store before. Then how the hell did you buy it here? I'm gonna ask you again. Where the hell did you get it?"

Jack stood and cleared his throat, stuffing his cell into his pocket. "I didn't get it in the store. I got it on the sidewalk out front—"

"You're lying!" He stepped forward, his face twitching.

Jack backed toward the door. "I'm not lying. Why would I—"

"I don't fucking know, but nothing coming out of your mouth sounds like the truth right now. Last chance, asshole." Reaching beneath the counter, Brad gripped a hammer and smashed the remaining beer cans, sending sticky foam shooting across the room. He wiped the beer from his eyes and tapped the hammer in his open palm. "Where did you get that pendant?"

Jack's mouth opened, but no words formed.

Brad's lip curled into a sneer as he reared back and hurled the hammer straight at Jack's head.

Jack ducked, but the tool nicked his forehead as it whizzed past him and shattered the front door's glass. Liquid warmth trickled into his eyes as he hurled himself through the door and rolled across the biting glass shards covering the sidewalk.

As a bloodied Jack Rainne sprinted down the street, he could sense the passersby's bewildered stares boring into him like lasers. But all he could hear was Brad Morgan inside his store, shouting "liar" at the top of his lungs.

CHAPTER THIRTEEN

Excerpt from *Cold Steel* by Jack Rainne:

The medical examiner inspected the lifeless form prone on the metal gurney. After twenty-five years in the profession, he understood everyone eventually ended up naked on a cold, stainless-steel slab, vulnerable and exposed. It didn't matter if you were rich, poor, unknown, or famous. Life subjected the living to humiliating moments, but death dealt the final blow.

As the city's chief medical examiner, Fred Valli had witnessed his share of the dead—celebrities, politicians, the unwashed masses—grace his autopsy tables. Only weeks ago, he determined the cause of death for that up-and-coming YouTube influencer with the bullet hole where his eye used to be. Don't believe the social media rumors about government forces silencing Gen Z's newest messiah. With powder residue on the young man's hand, bullet trajectory analysis from the scene, and eyewitnesses recounting his showing off a new .38 caliber toy, connecting the dots wasn't much of a challenge. In the end, the kid might have deserved the bullet lodged in his brain—and maybe a Darwin Award.

The man on the steel slab appeared to be in his early fifties, a few ticks younger than Dr. Valli. Usually, the youngish bodies beneath the doctor's meticulous gaze weren't as pristine as this one. Too often, they bore the indications of a hard death—ragged piercings from knife wounds, crushed skulls from windshields, or shattered limbs from swan dives off highway overpasses or high-rise balconies. He leaned in closer. Even in death, the man possessed handsome features. No bulging eyes or tongue lolling from a gaping mouth. A tinge of blue around the lips, but otherwise, he had cheated death's final indignity. He looked as if he might wake up any moment and hop off the table.

Valli's gaze darted to the medical chart on the table beside the gurney. William Mann. Prying the man's left eyelid open, he said, "How ya doing, Bill? Looks like you've seen better days."

Valli strapped on his gloves, inspecting the deceased's muscular frame while sensing the soft goo around his own midsection resign itself to gravity's pull. Although Mann's family hadn't requested an autopsy, Valli had to determine the cause of death. He had reviewed the man's medical chart but would need to take blood and urine samples to run the usual panels. He would obtain X-rays and CT scans, especially in the coronary arteries. At Mann's age, a cardiac issue wouldn't be out of the question. Most enter heart attack country somewhere in their fifties. And with a history of high cholesterol, Mann would have been a prime candidate.

"Maybe there's a reason for everything, eh, Bill," Valli mumbled, acknowledging such a serendipitous finding.

In the late hour, Dr. Valli worked alone. He had promised Mann's widow, Kate, he would have an answer soon. He already knew what killed William Mann, but he wouldn't be putting it into his report.

Valli leaned across the table, drumming his fingers against Mann's thick chest. He recalled the hospital's black-tie fundraiser he and his wife, Joanne—Jo-Jo to her friends—attended, what, ten years ago? That's when they first set eyes on the dead man. He had been very much alive at the time, a big shot at the Pharma giant Valli's hospital did business with. And while hospital fundraisers are usually forgettable affairs, something about the charismatic William Mann left an indelible impression. He drew people like groupies to a rock star.

Especially Jo-Jo.

As the state's youngest chief medical examiner and high-profile physician at Northeast Medical Center, Dr. Valli had responsibilities at these fundraisers—pressing palms and pro-moting the facility. And Jo-Jo was a powerhouse partner, more than simply eye candy on the doctor's arm. Subtle and seductive, she could chat up a potential donor and pry open a checkbook with the best of them. But that night, Valli kept catching Jo-Jo and Mann together from the corner of his eye. He didn't think twice about it—just Jo-Jo working her magic again.

But in the weeks following the fundraiser, she appeared dis-tracted. Distant. Valli worked long hours but would come home to an empty house and a "working late" text message. Her business trips took her away from home more often. He sensed dread in his gut when he spotted an unfamiliar cell phone peeking from her purse, by the looks of it, a pay-by-the-minute burner. Valli didn't question her at the time, figuring he would explore her handbag one night after she had fallen asleep. But when he crept through the house long after midnight and spilled the purse's contents onto the basement floor, the cell wasn't there. He never saw it again.

Lying in bed one night, he turned to her in the dark. "What's going on, Jo? With us?"

She shifted onto her back and gazed at the ceiling.

"Do you still love me?"

"Don't ask me that right now, Fred."

"Why not right now? Aren't I entitled to know if my wife—"

"It's not about love right now," she said. "You used to take my breath away, but . . ." A long pause. "I guess I need to accept things the way they are now."

She hadn't answered his question. But she had told him all he didn't want to know.

On the following Thursday, he waited at Jo-Jo's building after work. She had left him a message about a get-together with co-workers in the Irish pub downtown to celebrate a new client. Desperation had fed his desire for the truth as he waited out-side her building, but he still sensed the humiliation as he darted behind light poles and parked vehicles to remain undetected. When she bypassed the pub and entered her car, Valli sprinted to fetch his ride. Staying hidden among the traffic, Valli followed her through the grid-like city streets.

Jo-Jo's vehicle continued past the steel and glass structures away from town. As the city streets yielded to grassy lawns and hedgerows, she parked before a stately townhouse and strolled along its brick walkway. Reaching above the side door's transom, she snatched a key and let herself in. Valli crept after her, inching across the yard until he reached the house. Raising himself on his tiptoes, he cupped his hands against the first-floor windows but only viewed his reflection staring back from the darkened pane. Circling the house, he spotted a light halo illuminating a patch of lawn. He slunk through the hedge beneath the window and peeked through a slit in the curtains. His legs quivered and dropped from under him. Burying his face in the dirt, Valli shook his head to dispel the image of his wife wrapped in William Mann's embrace.

The air pulled from his lungs as he stumbled from the bushes. He braced his hands against his knees, his lungs crying out for air, suffocating right there on the grass. When the episode subsided, he staggered to his car and sped home, clutching his aching ribs from the wrenching sobs. That night, in a dream, he pictured himself trapped beneath the earth, smothered in the darkness. He woke with his face in a pillow, gasping for air.

Sometime in the following months, Valli sensed Jo-Jo's re-engagement in their marriage. The affair had ended, but he couldn't stop picturing her with Mann. Each day, as painful images scrolled through his memory—groping hands and impassioned bliss etched upon her features—he would double over, hands against his knees, struggling to fill his lungs. Suffocating in that place beneath the earth.

In time, the pair resumed raising their two children and living as a family again. But a deep pain gnawed at Valli's core as if parasites were eating him alive. And when the pictures played in his mind, he found himself buried beneath the earth again, pulling at the air that wouldn't come.

Valli shook the images from his head and continued with Mann's autopsy. He scribbled notes on his charts from which he would assemble a report.

But the report would be incomplete.

The report wouldn't describe how he had visited Mann's home only a few days earlier, reaching above the side door transom to find the spare key. In the report, he left out details of how he had crept up the stairs to the main bedroom, knelt beside the snoring adulterer, and smothered his face with a cloth drenched with chloroform. He failed to recount how he had pried open Mann's jaws, inspected the veins underneath his tongue, and injected one hundred milligrams of the paralytic drug, succinylcholine, into the bastard's bloodstream.

Valli's report did not describe how he had dropped onto the bed beside Mann as the sux took effect. The text omitted how Mann's respiratory muscles failed to pull the precious air into his lungs and how his eyes widened as if he understood exactly what was happening to him. Dr. Valli didn't mention how he grinned as Mann slowly suffocated while fully conscious and how the light in his eyes faded.

Dr. Valli glanced at the wall clock opposite the gurney supporting the late William Mann. The test results would be in soon, and since sux was virtually undetectable, the doctor's dull and straightforward conclusion would be in keeping with the unremarkable findings.

He leaned across the corpse on the metal slab and whispered in Mann's ear. "Definitely a heart attack, Bill. You should have done more cardio."

And soon Jo-Jo would be on the slab. Six months from now, maybe a year. Who knows? He hadn't decided yet. She had been to the doctor for palpitations recently, most likely related to work stress. Another serendipitous finding. That and her family history of heart disease wouldn't raise much suspicion. He would have the dimwit Simons lead the autopsy, but Valli would be there to guide him through the procedures. What to look for—and what not to look for. And the night before the autopsy, when Jo-Jo's eyes widened and darted back and forth, pleading with her husband as her body went slack, Valli would show her the shriveled testicles he had extracted from William Mann's corpse. He would dangle them before her, and she would understand why she couldn't breathe anymore and why he hadn't been able to for the past ten years.

"I don't take your breath away anymore, eh, Jo-Jo?" Valli would say, staring at the hypodermic needle. He would be damn sure he was the last man who did.

CHAPTER FOURTEEN

Edgartown, Massachusetts (Martha's Vineyard)

By the time Jack departed the ferry and drove the eight miles from Vineyard Haven to Edgartown, the blood had dried on his shirt, and the gauze hastily taped to his forehead had stanched the blood rivulets streaking his face. Lucky for him, Brad Morgan's hammer only nicked him. It could have been much worse. He still resembled a character from a horror movie, but he had avoided the townsfolk's pitchforks and torches by spending the ferry ride hidden away in his vehicle.

He eased into the driveway, hoping Sam might be doing errands. He didn't want her to see him like this. But sooner or later he would have to confide in her about what was happening. And it might as well be sooner, as she would be leaving for LA in a few days.

Jack steered the car into the garage. He killed the engine and entered the house through the mudroom. Lumbering into the kitchen, he found Sam loading dishes. As she glimpsed him in the doorway, she fumbled a plate onto the floor.

"Jesus, Jack!" She tiptoed to his side through the porcelain shards. "What the hell—?"

"I'm fine. Head wounds tend to bleed."

"Wait right there." She scampered down the hall to the bathroom, returning with the first aid kit. "How in God's name did you get a head wound? I thought you were gathering information for a book today."

Jack chewed on his lip. "I was . . . but that was only half true."

She grabbed an antiseptic wipe. "How about you forget the half-truths and give me the full truth." Dabbing at his wound, she exacted a groaning wince.

Jack pointed. "Oh, and you're bleeding, too."

She examined her foot where the broken plate had pierced the skin. "I'll live."

As she tended to his lacerations, Jack detected concern in her eyes, something he hadn't expected. "Okay, here's the truth. I didn't want to worry you with your trip coming up. But the dreams started again."

She froze. "The carousel stuff?"

"It's okay, it's good news. Well, good news and bad news."

"I'll bite." She refreshed the gauze on Jack's forehead and stepped back. "What's the good news?"

"It's all real. The carousel and the old man." Jack beamed. "I swear, I found out today."

Sam's shoulders dropped. "When's the last time you talked with Dr. Lang?"

"What does that matter?"

"Answer me."

Jack rubbed his chin. "It's been a couple of years. I haven't had to. All that stuff was behind me."

"Behind you until the dreams start again. They always do." She grabbed a wipe and washed the dried blood from his face. "Are the dreams only at night?"

"I have daydreams, too."

"Those are hallucinations, Jack, not daydreams. That was why they hospitalized you all those years ago."

Jack pictured Fulton State Hospital's polished floors and bleached-white rooms speckled with blood, sweat, and feces. He hadn't forgotten the pungent odor of anxiety and desperation permeating the place, as well as the hollow wails disrupting his sleep each night. Dr. Lang had made it tolerable during his multiple stays. What had he called it? Jack's Missouri vacation destination. That one never failed to draw a laugh. And the doctor had continued to stay in touch and help him through repeated crises over the years.

"I've told you about all this, Sam. When I was seventeen, something happened to me that couldn't possibly be true. I didn't handle it well, and I had to spend time at Fulton. I've spent the last twenty-five years coming to terms with it, convinced my experience was something irrational from a part of my brain that didn't work as well as the other parts." Jack reached out and grabbed her upper arms. "But now I know everything that happened was real. And there's more."

Jack told her about the strange happenings at the Barnes and Noble with the missing-and-presumed-dead Jack Morgan and the carousel piece appearing in *The American Short Story*; the meeting with the boy's mother, Ellen Morgan, in her beautiful Hyannis store that no longer existed; his trip to Falmouth to meet with Marsha Mason, and the presence of a familiar carousel at the Barnstable County Fair at the time the Morgan family disappeared; and running into a less than reasonable Brad Morgan in Hyannis, who didn't take too kindly to his presence.

"I also have photographic proof."

"Where?"

"I don't have it with me, but—"

"Oh, Jack."

"No, I can get it for you." Jack fumbled through his pockets for Marsha Mason's business card. Maybe she would snap a picture of that final print and send it to him. He punched in her cell number and waited. *Come on, come on.* No answer.

"You need to listen to me." She put a hand on his cheek. "If you could only listen to how this all sounds."

"I know how it sounds." Jack eased her hand away. "But I'm not crazy. Even when I was at Fulton, I knew I wasn't crazy. Everyone tried to convince me I was, but I knew what happened to me *really* happened. And now I know for sure it *did* happen." He shuffled to the sink and pressed his hands against the countertop. "As for the other stuff with the Morgans, that I can't explain."

Sam threw her hands up. "Then you need to get back on your meds, and you need to talk to someone about it."

"I am. I'm talking to you about it."

"I mean someone with expertise in these matters." She dropped the remaining wipe onto the bloody gauze pile and brushed them into the garbage. Then she tended to her foot wound, leaking blood droplets onto the cement tiles. "You need to get help with this. And it can't just be a phone call to Dr. Lang. You need—"

"I know what I need," Jack said. "I need you to believe me."

"I want to, Jack." Sam curled a lock of blond hair behind her ear. "You told me a long time ago stress can bring on these . . . events. We're under a lot of stress right now, both personally and financially, but medications can control it."

"It's not stress, Sam." Jack folded his arms. "And I'm done with meds. I won't live my life like a zombie."

"Only for a little while, until you get this thing . . . whatever is happening to you, under control."

"Please believe me."

Sam pressed her hands against her temples as if fitting her head in a vice. "It's hard to believe something that can't possibly make any sense. Years ago, Dr. Lang made you see that things were happening in your head. Things that weren't your fault. You trusted him, and he put you on medication. You've been fine ever since. A few hiccups here and there, but nothing we couldn't handle. But now you're seeing ghosts and things that simply can't be."

"What I've seen is real—"

"Listen to yourself!" Sam grabbed his face. "What's more likely, Jack? The ghost of a mother and child visited you over the weekend?" She forced a deep breath. "Or someone who's off their meds and not getting professional help is imagining things again?"

"But there's a picture. The old man and the carousel. I can show you." Jack punched in Marsha Mason's phone number again. It kept ringing. *Where the hell is she?*

He disconnected and raised his head, but Sam had left the room.

Jack reclined on the bed as Morgan hummed to herself and peered out the window. Daylight had faded, and the moon's reflection on the sea left a shimmering trail to the horizon. He let his eyes linger on his daughter longer than usual, content to lie beside her until she drifted off to sleep.

"You look like you got into a fight." She pressed a gentle finger against his forehead bandage.

He sneered. "You should see the other guy."

Morgan raised her head. "What other guy?"

"Never mind, honey."

Morgan pushed her pajama sleeve to her elbow and held out her arm—part of their bedtime routine. Jack caressed her forearm with his fingernails.

"I don't think I want Mom to go," Morgan said. "I want her to stay here."

Me, too. Jack brushed the hair from her forehead. "She's not going out to LA to live. Just for a visit."

"I heard Mommy on the phone last night talking to someone about maybe living out there someday."

"She said that?"

"Do you want to move away from here?"

"Not really." He pressed his lips together. "But remember, Mom used to live out there. That's where all her old friends are. When we married, she moved all the way across the country for me. I suppose it's only fair she gets to spend time back there, right?"

Morgan yawned. "I guess. I just don't want to ever leave my ocean."

Jack grinned at how she described her backyard's border. "Yeah, well, they have an ocean out there, too."

"But it's someone else's ocean." Morgan exposed her forearm on the opposite side.

"That's true." He combed a gentle hand across her skin, grinning at how both sides had to be even. "But you'll never have to leave your ocean. I promise."

She lifted her head to peek out the window at the waves lapping the sand at the property's edge. "Hey, Dad? Why didn't Mom ask us all to go with her?"

Jack had been lying to too many people lately, and he never wanted to mislead Morgan. But now wasn't the time for the truth. "Well, I wanted to go, but I have work to do this week. Mom's trip came at a busy time. Uncle Hal has me teaching a writing class in Boston this weekend. I couldn't go anyway."

"But why didn't Mom want me to go with her?"

Jack stroked her cheek. "Like I said, she might just need some time to herself."

Morgan deflated. "Mom doesn't love me like she used to."

"That's not true."

"She always used to come in and lay down with me, read me books, brush my hair. She never has time for me anymore."

Jack's heart twisted in his chest, sensing his daughter's feelings of abandonment. Truth was, he sensed the same thing, but he hadn't been paying attention to how Sam treated Morgan lately. "Your mom loves you more than anything in the world, but she's having a tough time right now. When she gets back from her trip, she'll be her old self again. I promise."

Morgan took his hand and set it on her forehead. Jack caressed her face with gentle circles around her eyes, nose, mouth, and cheeks. A shiver trembled through her.

"I'm cold, Daddy."

Jack rose to a seated position and hoisted the window open. "What do you say we let in a little warm air, and you can snuggle up against me?"

She leaned against him. "I wish we could all be a family again."

"What do you mean, honey? We'll be a family forever. No matter what happens."

As Morgan rubbed her eyes, her lips pressed into a Mona Lisa grin. Jack's breath caught in his throat. Somehow her smile pried open a place inside him few ever witnessed, including himself. She left him vulnerable to the unbearable weight of life's unpredictability. What if something happened to her, and he wasn't there to protect her? He had never grasped the illusion of control as acutely as he did until Morgan came along. He chalked it up to an innate instinct associated with fatherhood, maybe a psychological shift occurring in response to offspring. *I'll have to ask Dr. Lang about it.* But whatever it might be, he recognized the feeling wasn't going away anytime soon. Probably never. He would always be there to protect her. The more pressing question involved Sam. What if she wanted to move to LA? What would he do? He would fight the move any way he could. And if he couldn't fight it, he would move to LA, too, though he would hate it. The bottom line was he would do anything to keep the family together.

Jack arranged the pillow behind his head and leaned back. The overhead fan's blades drew a gentle breeze across the bed. He closed his eyes and stayed with Morgan until she fell asleep. Sensing the heaviness in her breath, he crept from the bedroom. He lingered for a moment in the hallway before shutting the door. The hall fixture's glow pierced the room's darkness, casting a slender light beam across Morgan's face.

"Goodnight, sweetie," he whispered.

Padding along the hallway, he ducked his head into the main bedroom now serving as Sam's bedroom. Since she dropped her bombshell, Jack had spent his nights on his office couch, sparing them any pre-separation, sleeping-in-the-same-bed awkwardness. But nothing could have left them in a place more awkward than where they were after Jack's confession today.

"I'm heading down the hall. I'll see you in the morning." He lingered for a moment and tapped the doorframe, holding out the decaying hope that one night he might glimpse something in her eyes, an invitation to join her and forget this whole thing. She reclined against the headboard, reading her book, her long legs crossed at the ankles and a mountain of decorative pillows surrounding her. God, how he hated those damn things. But he would bury himself under an Everest-sized collection to curl up beside her again. She looked amazing, tanned and toned, and the horse pendant sparkled against her skin. Ready for her return to Tinseltown.

"I'll be up early tomorrow to do some shopping around Oak Bluffs." She kept her eyes on her book. "I need a few things for the trip and probably won't be back until afternoon."

So much for forgetting the whole thing. "Okay."

Sam closed the book. "I haven't been back there in a long time. I was thinking about Morgan and the birthday we spent at the Flying Horses." She flashed one of her old smiles, but it wasn't for him.

Was she planning her final goodbye to the Vineyard? To Morgan and me? Jack pressed a hand against his forehead. *Thud . . . thud . . . thud . . .*

"What's the matter, Jack?"

"Nothing." He rubbed his hand along his face. "I just have a lot on my mind."

"That's why you need to talk to someone. Tomorrow."

"I will. Hal set me up at the writing conference in Boston this weekend, but once it's over, I'm going to call Dr. Lang and see if he knows any good therapists out here."

"Call him tomorrow and get someone's name. It's the only way we can move past this." She returned to her book, the discussion over.

"I know." He retreated from the room and shut the door. *We?* He was getting tired of dissecting everything she said as if it were the Zapruder film, searching for hidden clues. But he couldn't help wondering whether "we" meant the two of them together, or only him.

Jack trudged along the hallway to his office bedroom.

CHAPTER FIFTEEN

Edgartown, Massachusetts (Martha's Vineyard)

Jack tossed and turned, unable to find the sofa's sweet spot. Too many thoughts swirled in his head, and he remained torn between seeking the help Sam insisted on and pursuing what his mind held to be true. The Barnstable County Fair photo kept flashing in his head as if it proved the lynchpin in this entire mystery. He needed to get a copy. But that would only happen if Marsha Mason would return his calls and texts, and he was beginning to lose hope. He had encountered the same carousel in the Missouri cornfield, and he teetered on the cusp of proving to Sam, Dr. Lang—and, most importantly, himself—that his dreams and visions were real and not his mind's invention. He might even figure out what really happened to him in that cornfield.

Where are you, Marsha?

In the meantime, he would have to find something on the old man, anything connecting him to a carousel. Throwing back the comforter, he shuffled to his desk and fired up the laptop. He hovered above the keyboard, his fingers unable to conjure the terms to initiate a web search. He didn't have much to go on. Jack puffed his cheeks with air, letting them deflate like a leaky tire. He googled "history of carousels."

"Might as well start there."

He pored over web pages related to early rocking horses, spring horses, and toy carriages and their evolution into modern carousels. The names of European and American inventors, patent holders, and early steam-powered platform carousel builders came up again and again, wedging themselves in his brain: Gustav Dentzel, Thomas Bradshaw, Andrew Christian, and Charles W.F. Dare. The Flying Horses Carousel in Oak Bluffs and the Watch Hill Flying Horses in Rhode Island had prominent roles in his search as the country's two oldest carousels. He also learned the carousel originated as a jousting exercise for medieval knights, and the British carousel spun in a clockwise direction, opposite the American carousel.

Jack glanced upward, considering why America did everything in direct opposition to the mother country—carousel direction, steering wheels on the wrong side, and driving on different sides of the road. *Still angry with King George, are we?* Interesting, but not much he could use.

He checked the clock on the laptop's screen. 10:15 p.m. Rubbing his eyes, he leaned the desk chair back and propped his head against the headrest.

When in doubt, check the obvious.

Jack huddled over the keyboard and typed in "Flying Horses Carousel, Oak Bluffs." The information placard on the Oak Bluffs attraction's wall loaded onto the screen. He had passed it once or twice on his visits but never bothered to read it. The Charles W.F. Dare company had built the Flying Horses Carousel in New York City in the 1870s, and the leadership in Oak Bluffs—or Cottage City at the time—had the carousel shipped from Coney Island in 1884. When he saw the Flying Horses image, he zoomed in and squinted at the screen. His heartbeat pulsed in his throat. The carousel was a replica of the one he stumbled upon in the Johnsons' cornfield all those years ago. The guide poles, suspension cables and struts supporting the roof, and even the color were identical. He had never recognized the similarities before during his rare visits, probably because he concentrated on navigating the crowds and keeping an eye on Morgan. Maybe he hadn't studied the carousel up close to avoid dredging up the past. But with the similarities staring at him online, he couldn't deny it. There had to be a connection between the two.

He continued to dig into the Dare company. He scrolled through page after page of historical text and an extensive history of the owner's legal and monetary troubles—attempts at burning down the business, insurance fraud, insolvency, labor strikes, and an inability to pay and retain engineers. He discovered Dare carousel horses distinguished themselves from earlier ones because of their genuine horsehair manes and tails and their life-like eyes. A headache sprouted in the center of his skull. He was about to take a break when he glanced at the carousel horse images along the website border.

Jack's jaw tensed. He gaped at the horse as its eye locked onto his. The coffee-colored mare.

His vision went cloudy, but he fought the urge to let the horse take him away on a gallop along the barren Missouri tundra and into the earth. Bolting from his chair, Jack pressed his palms against his temples.

Thud . . . thud . . . thud . . .

"Not this time! Not now!"

The hooves pounded a steady rhythm as the wind whistled through his hair. He could sense the powerful beast rumbling beneath him.

"Not now!" He fell to his knees. "Get out of my head!"

The thundering gallop sound retreated, as if his brain had snatched the volume knob and cranked it to the left. He stood in the middle of the field as the sixth horse charged ahead without him, disappearing in a dust cloud. The vision flickered on and off before fading out.

Jack's second-floor office shimmered back into existence as he gained his feet. Shuffling to the desk, he dropped into his seat and cradled his head. "Don't let a little run-of-the-mill hallucination stop you now, Jack."

His eyes fluttered, and he was moments away from laying his head against the keyboard, but he vowed to find something useful before calling it a night. He dug into the archives for the Vineyard Preservation Trust. The organization had acquired the century-old Flying Horses Carousel as a historic landmark in 1986 and kept meticulous records on it as well as other endangered historic Martha's Vineyard properties. Deep within the archives, Jack discovered a single sentence about a Brit hired as the Charles W.F. Dare Company's head engineer and platform carousel builder in New York City.

Graham Carver.

The name reverberated in his head like a silver ball chiming off a pinball bumper. Jack's eyes sprung open, an adrenaline surge pounding through his veins. He pictured Jack Morgan sliding the journal toward him for his signature. He recalled "The Carousel Man" and the author's name below it.

Graham Carver. "How is that possible?" Jack mumbled.

He attacked the keyboard as if he had downed a handful of Vivarin, his muscles brimming with vigor. He searched the Trust's leadership page, where a list of Trustee names, office phone numbers, and emails populated the screen. Judy Van Dorn, executive director. He googled her name but found no personal contact information.

Fuck me.

He shuffled to the couch and sank into its cushions. No one would be in the office to answer the phone; nothing more he could do tonight. He slid beneath the comforter and snapped off the lamp, but his eyes remained saucers. He fumbled for his cell on the end table. Maybe one more option. He had no idea about Judy Van Dorn's social media presence, but most people tended to be careless with their personal information, especially phone numbers and emails. A professional woman of her stature most likely wasn't posting on Snapchat or TikTok. But Instagram, Twitter, or Facebook? More likely. On each platform, he typed her name into the search box and scrolled through the scores of Judy Van Dorn profiles populating the screen. He ignored the photos since he had no idea what she looked like, instead searching bios for a Judy Van Dorn who lived on the Vineyard or mentioned the Trust. He struck out with Instagram and Twitter, considering for the first time there might be someone alive today surviving in the world with no online presence. He opened the Facebook app and found another sixty-seven Judy Van Dorn profiles. His eyes fluttered. *Do I even have this in me tonight?* But within the first ten profiles he had located a Van Dorn from the Vineyard with a phone number and email that differed from those on the Vineyard Preservation Trust website.

"It's got to be her." He gazed at the clock. 12:15 a.m. *It's already tomorrow . . . this is crazy.*

He tapped out the number and held his breath. After a lengthy wait, a sleepy voice filtered through the line.

Jack bolted to his feet. "Is this the Judy Van Dorn from Vineyard Preservation Trust?"

"Do you have any idea what time it is?"

"I do, and I'm sorry. I wouldn't call anyone this late unless it was important. My name is—"

"How did you get this number?"

Just come clean. "I searched you on Facebook. You might think about removing your personal information—"

The line disconnected.

"Fuck me." Jack ran a hand through his hair and punched in a text message:

> **Trust me I'm not a stalker - any chance I can talk with you about the Flying Horses - I apologize for the urgency**

Jack hit send and waited. The minutes ticked by. He dialed her number, but the call went to voicemail. He glanced at the clock, mulling over his options. "Fortune favors the bold," he mumbled, tapping the phone icon. He figured he was already on her shit list, anyway. He might as well keep calling until she picked up and talked to him or cursed at him to stop calling. Either way, he would have her on the line. He tapped out the number and waited. Voicemail. He tried again. Another voicemail. On the fifth attempt, Van Dorn answered.

"I'm not going to get rid of you, am I?"

"I wish I could say you could, but I really need your help, Ms. Van Dorn. My name is Jack Rainne, and I found you on the Vineyard Preservation Trust website. I—"

"*Double-Barrel Justice?*"

"Pardon?" Jack switched the phone to his other ear.

"Are you the writer Jack Rainne?"

"Yes, ma'am."

"I have a copy of one of your books."

"Thank you. I appreciate your support."

"Oh, don't thank me. I found it the other day at the Edgartown Books bargain bin. They were practically giving it away."

Ouch. "Well, I'm glad you could get it at a discount." *Hal will be so pleased.*

"I'm sure you have a reason for calling at such a late hour."

"I do, and my apologies. I need an expert on Martha's Vineyard history, and you might be the only person who can help me. I'm searching for anything you may know about an engineer from England who built the Flying Horses Carousel. I didn't see much historical information or anything about the engineer besides his name on the Vineyard Preservation Trust website. And nothing about him comes up on any search engine."

No response.

Jack checked his phone. "Ms. Van Dorn?"

"What is so important about him that you wake me up in the middle of the night?"

"A long time ago . . . something happened . . . um, it's hard to explain. I wondered if you had any historical information about the engineer. Like what happened to him when he came to Cottage City in the eighteen hundreds. A photograph . . . anything. His name is—"

"I know who he is, Mr. Rainne," she said. Covers rustled through the line, and he pictured the woman rising from her bed. "You're looking for Graham Carver."

Jack's jaw swung on its hinge.

"You're not the first person who has inquired about him."

There are others . . .

She let out a breath. "I need to ask you a question."

"Of course."

"Why do you want to know about him?"

Jack dipped into his Lance Armstrong playbook. "I've been considering writing a book about the carousel, and—"

"I don't believe that's true, Mr. Rainne. Desperation pushes people to do desperate things, like search a perfect stranger's social media accounts and call them out of the blue in the middle of the night. I hear desperation in your voice, so I'm going to ask you again. Why do you want to know about him?"

He lowered his head. "You wouldn't believe me if I told you."

She paused. "Well, here's the deal. I'll tell you about Graham Carver if you tell me what's so important about him."

Jack opened his mouth to speak but caught himself. If he tried telling his tale to a stranger over the phone, he would get a dial tone before he finished his first sentence, and she would never pick up again. She might even get a restraining order. He had told the story to Dr. Lang for years, and even he didn't believe him. "I'll tell you, but we need to meet in person. Tonight. I understand it's late, but I have a story the Vineyard Preservation Trust might be interested in."

"It's after midnight, Mr. Rainne. Can't this wait—"

"I wish it could. I just . . . I can't wait. It's been twenty-five years, and I'm on the verge of finding out about something that has haunted me my entire adult life." Jack paced his office, ignoring the torture in his voice. "Please. Please meet with me."

He waited. He considered another round of pleading but didn't want to appear any more desperate than he already had, or worse, come across as someone she should be afraid of. He would let her deliberate on her own. The fact she hadn't disconnected by now convinced him the lore surrounding Graham Carver held her interest.

The silence stretched before Judy said, "I can't believe I'm agreeing to this. Are you familiar with Isaac's Pub?"

"The place on the dock behind the boatyard?" *Christ, she can't want to meet there.*

"That's it." The change in her voice indicated she sensed his hesitancy. "They're open late. Meet me there in fifteen minutes." She disconnected.

Jack tossed on jeans and a clean shirt and tiptoed along the hallway. He poked his head through Sam's bedroom door. She didn't stir. He descended the staircase and fished his car keys from the porcelain bowl on the hallway table.

Jack needed answers, and he finally had someone who could provide them.

CHAPTER SIXTEEN

Edgartown, Massachusetts (Martha's Vineyard)

In a shadowed corner of Isaac's Pub, Judy Van Dorn and Jack sat across from each other. A wobbly oak table with napkins bunched beneath a stem glide kept their drinks from sliding off the surface. Jack nursed a Sam Adams while Judy spooned a teabag from steaming water and pressed the fluid into her mug with practiced hands before setting it on her saucer. She stuck out like a sore thumb in a bar like Isaac's with its hard-drinking, working-class Joes. And though she had picked the venue, her attire appeared more appropriate for a business meeting at the Vineyard Preservation Trust.

"I appreciate your meeting me tonight," Jack began, glancing about the place. "If you end up feeling uncomfortable here, we can always go someplace else."

The place resembled a living museum to old-school drinking, a relic among Edgartown's upscale piano and wine bars. The scent of skunked beer wafted from the scuffed, hardwood floors, and neon lights cele-brating time-honored suds like Busch and Miller buzzed like beehives from above the bar. He doubted the owner had made any upgrades or renovations during the pub's lengthy tenure on the island. Big screen TVs, Wi-Fi, or any connection to the outside world were conspicuously absent, replaced with the crack of pool cues against ivory and four-letter words even the most hardened Edgartown salts might not think to use.

"I wonder if it might be you who feels uncomfortable." Judy pursed her lips. "Believe it or not, when I first moved to the Vineyard in my twenties, I worked here at Isaac's tending bar." She pressed a napkin to the corners of her mouth with a delicate hand. "When I wasn't slinging drinks, I threw back more than I care to admit." She leaned across the table and gestured toward the pool sharks in the bar's back corner. "Don't worry, I've heard all those words before."

Jack leaned back against the booth's tattered cushion, attempting to visually chip away the woman's years to reveal a wild child from, what . . . the seventies? But her genteel aura and conservative dress foiled his efforts.

"If you ever run into old Isaac, don't get him going. He holds a few secrets about me that could get me kicked off the Vineyard Preservation Trust." Judy chuckled and removed a manila folder from her shoulder bag, placing it on the table. "But we're not here to talk about my sordid past, thank God."

Jack gripped his beer. "Tell me about Carver."

Judy sifted through a stack of newspaper articles. "Graham Carver worked for the St. Nichols Ironworks Company in King's Lynn, England, building platform gallopers."

"Precursors to modern-day carousels, right?"

She nodded. "The English were true craftsmen, way ahead of their time in the art and science of carousel building. Graham Carver learned his craft well, and because the industry was growing, people in the states sought his expertise." She slipped on her glasses. "In the spring of 1874, St. Nichols Ironworks provided four tickets for Carver, his wife, Annabelle, and two children, Rebecca and Zachariah, on the Hamburg-American Steamship line from Southampton to Hoboken, New Jersey. The Charles W.F. Dare company had hired Carver as their primary engineer and carousel builder in New York City."

"How did he end up on the Vineyard?"

"Carver led the Dare Company team, reassembling the machine in Cottage City a decade later. By the time the operation was over, Carver had fallen in love with the island, quit the Dare Company, and settled in Cottage City with his family."

Jack sipped at his beer. "How long did he live out here? Did he ever move to the Midwest? Missouri, maybe?"

"Not likely. Tragedy struck the family soon after Carver left Dare. Here's a short article about it from the *Vineyard Gazette*."

"Wow, 1885." He scanned the story. "Carver's family vanished?"

"Police questioned Carver about it, but no one knows what happened to them. After the interrogation, no one ever saw him again. The local gossip was that Carver must have jumped into the ocean and kept swimming."

"What do you believe? Did he kill his family?"

Judy sipped her tea. "I can't imagine another plausible scenario."

A shaggy-haired man from behind the bar strode to the table and set a red napkin folded in the shape of a rose beside Judy's tea. "Cousrtesy of the management." He flashed her a grin despite a missing front tooth. Jack pictured a well-aimed punch at closing time as a likely culprit.

"Thanks, Scotty." Her smile lit up the place. "Please thank *the management* for me."

Jack leaned forward. "They still remember you here?"

"It's like a family," she said, inspecting the hand-crafted rose.

Jack took a swig from his Sam Adams. "Do you have anything . . . police reports or documents with a photo of the guy?

"There may be something buried somewhere in this file." She dabbed a finger with her tongue and leafed through her pages. "Why the interest in him?"

"Like I've said before, you wouldn't believe me if I told you."

"Try me."

Jack rested his bottle on the table. "I've met Graham Carver before," he said. "In a Missouri cornfield when I was seventeen. I rode on an exact replica of the Flying Horses Carousel." Jack dropped his gaze and picked at his beer label. "The experience . . . changed me."

Judy remained quiet.

He hitched his shoulders and took a pull from his bottle. "You asked."

"And you truly believe this happened?"

"I wouldn't be here if I didn't."

"May I say something?" Judy positioned her elbows on the table but didn't wait for an answer. "You come off as someone . . . quite normal. But what you're telling me makes me wonder if you might be—"

"Crazy?" Jack said.

She chuckled. "I guess. So, which is it: normal or crazy?"

"You'll have to decide. Hopefully I won't say anything else that will convince you of the latter." He chuckled. "But the night's young."

She plucked a photo from the folder. "You must know it's not possible to have met Graham Carver."

"I understand how it sounds, Ms. Van Dorn. But . . ." Jack's thought train derailed as he inspected the grainy nineteenth-century black and white photo. The Dare Company team assembled the Flying Horses Carousel under the Vineyard's crisp autumn sky. Jack's eye drifted to the team's leader standing in the middle of the throng and pointing to his men as he barked out directions. A man with shoulder-length hair pinned back in a tight ponytail. Despite the man's youthful appearance, Jack had no doubt.

"That's him."

Jack considered what Dr. Lang would say about Carver's resemblance to the old carousel operator. *Wouldn't mean diddlysquat*, the shrink would have squawked from behind his desk. Dr. Lang would have leaned back in his chair and insisted Jack had come across this information before. He had somehow subconsciously incorporated it into his dreams and visions and invented the older version of Graham Carver. Jack racked his brain, trying to thwart Lang's presumed logic. When he lived in Spring Valley as a child, he had no access to the information revealed during his recent web searches or in Van Dorn's photos and newspaper clippings. Only a rudimentary internet existed at the time, and he had never used it, for school or the farm. Plus, the local library was a thousand-square-foot house with nothing but books on farming and animal husbandry.

"Ms. Van Dorn, who came to you asking about Carver?"

Judy took a sip from her cup. "A young woman sought me out, oh, maybe forty years ago, give or take. Much like you did. She asked me who built the carousel. She told me she had been drawn to it and a man she met there. A man with a ponytail. I showed her the same pictures of Graham Carver I showed you. She thought he was . . ."

"What?"

"It's hard for me to even say this." She swallowed her tea and composed herself. "She thought Carver was . . . the Savior."

"You mean *the* Savior? In a rose-from-the-dead-on-the-third-day sort of way?"

Judy nodded. "She told me she had witnessed something . . . divine, and she had to find out more about him."

Divine? Which fucking horse did she ride?

"I sort of chalked it up to someone who was—"

"Crazy, like me?"

"Maybe."

Jack drained his beer. "Did she seem crazy when you talked with her?"

"Not at the time. She was more manic than anything, like one of those born-again hippie types. It's only when I recall our encounter that I convince myself she must have been a little . . . off."

"Do you have any idea where I can find her?'"

Judy worked her jaw. "What you're thinking is probably not a good idea."

Jack leaned forward, balancing on his elbows. "I've been living with this thing for twenty-five years. If there's a possibility someone else may have experienced something similar . . ." Jack lowered his head, his voice trailing off. Van Dorn's hand slipped across the table and covered his. When he raised his head and met her gaze, she pressed her lips together, as if weighing the wisdom of playing matchmaker to two people living within arm's length of madness.

"I'm not sure this is the right thing to do, but I'm doing this to help you find some peace." She opened her folder and sorted through her papers. "Can't say for sure why I kept this," she said, handing a folded slip of paper across the table. "Maybe I figured one day I could help her . . . or someone else. She once lived in Hartford, but who knows if she's still there anymore."

Jack glanced at the faded paper with the woman's name and address. *Melanie Pastula.* "I can't convince you I'm not crazy. The jury may still be out on that one." He paused, returning her grin. "But with all the sanity I have left, I'm thanking you for your help tonight." Jack folded the paper and slipped it into his pocket.

"I'm sorry you've suffered with all this, but please . . ." Judy waved her hand. "Never mind."

"What is it?"

"It's not my place to say this but . . . please try to get help."

Jack glanced at the floor before pressing his hands against the table and gaining his feet. "I've taken enough of your time tonight, Ms. Van Dorn. Can I walk you out?"

Judy smiled at someone behind him. Jack glanced over his shoulder at a man leaning against the bar. He had to have been thirty years Jack's senior, but the chiseled frame beneath his tattooed exterior belied his age. He beamed at Judy. Beside him, Scotty no-tooth grinned at her as he threw a towel over his shoulder and whispered to the man. Jack noted the resemblance between the two men despite a notable age difference. In fact, side-by-side, the two men could have passed as father and son.

"No thanks, Jack. I'm well taken care of. As I said, it's like a family."

CHAPTER SEVENTEEN

Wilton, Maine

Jack came to a stop before the aged ranch-style home on Hidden Hollow Road and silenced the engine. Glancing at his phone, he confirmed the location. He had spent days searching Melanie Pastula's name, hoping Google would gift him with an easy search. It had not. He had hunted through twenty years of New England newspapers, land records, and police reports to follow the woman's meandering tracks. Her post-Vineyard journey took her from jails to psychiatric hospitals, one after another, year after year. When the money had run out, she ended up on the streets. After her mother's death, she inherited the dismal plot of land before him. According to records, she had lived in Wilton for more than twenty years.

He scanned the property, searching for signs of life. Weeds infiltrated the front yard, and discarded junk peeked out from knee-high grass. The house listed forward and rested in eternal shade, heavy foliage blocking any hope of daylight. Spongy moss spread across warped and discolored roof tiles like a rash. Easing himself from the driver's seat, Jack stepped onto the moist gravel road. He leaned back, pressing his hands against his spine to relieve the lower back kinks.

He straightened when the screen door slammed.

The stooped woman shuffled onto the porch. Pulling a shotgun from behind her back, she fired a shot over his car roof.

Jesus Christ! Jack dropped onto all fours.

"Get away from my property or I'll dump you at the bottom of Wilson Pond."

He raised a hand above the car's hood. "Wait. It's Jack Rainne. I called the other day."

"Show me your face and I'll blow it to hell!" She fired another shot.

Jack clamped his hands over his ears before venturing a peek above the quarter panel. "Don't you remember? We talked about the carousel."

The woman lowered the gun. "Jack Rainne?"

He half-stood, ready to drop if necessary. "From Martha's Vineyard."

Dropping the shotgun, she stepped from the porch. "Oh, I've been waiting for you." She approached in a ratty nightgown, opening her arms wide in an anticipated welcome. She wore nothing underneath.

Jack stood and brushed wet muck from his pants. Stepping from behind the car, he accepted her stranglehold hug.

"You've seen it, too, haven't you? The eternal." A sulfur odor clung to her clothing.

"I'm not sure what I've seen," Jack said, disengaging from her clinch. "That's why I came to see you. I wanted to hear your story."

"I'm sorry if I startled you. Crooks try to steal my property all the time. Driving up in their fancy cars, trying to move me off my land. When I send buckshot at 'em, they don't hang around." A smile creased her lips. "You did, though. You got some balls on you." She glanced over a shoulder, her stringy, silver-gray hair pressed flat against her head in the humid air. "Come on inside."

Jack escorted her to the porch, grabbing her hand as she reached for the shotgun. "How about we leave this on the porch for now? I'll make sure no one comes for your land."

Melanie grinned. "Well, aren't you a gentleman?"

She led him through a tattered screen door. The smell hit him first, an overpowering urine stench combined with rotting food. Cats roamed a broken floorboard maze, navigating the stacks of boxes and refuse piled floor to ceiling. Feces littered the walking space and discarded trash-filled rooms off the main living area. Jack had watched shows about hoarders on A&E, but this lady could have had an entire season dedicated to her.

She directed him to the only space in the house free from debris—two wooden chairs beside a vintage 1960s TV dinner table. She shooed away the cats and gestured to the seat.

Jack winced as he lowered himself onto a moistened seat cushion streaked with stains. "Thank you, Melanie." He gazed at the crucifixes and religious artifacts adorning the water-stained walls and crumbling mantel.

"Do you want to know something?" She positioned her chair facing Jack and leaned across the table, glancing left, then right. "I've seen God."

Batshit crazy, Van Dorn was right. "I want to hear about that. But do you remember our phone call, when I asked you about a man you met at a carousel on Martha's Vineyard?"

Her face went blank. "Oh, where are my manners." She wandered into the kitchen, pulling a cloudy drinking glass from the sink. "You must be thirsty after your trip."

"Please," Jack began. "Don't trouble yourself."

Jack endured the house's fetid stench as Melanie reappeared with a glass filled with discolored water and set it on the dinner tray. He winced as he took a courtesy sip. "Thank you, Melanie." He sensed a bloom of self-awareness and embarrassment reflecting in her eyes.

"It's been a long time since I've had a visitor." Melanie knelt beside a box on the floor, pulling out a floral patterned, kiss-lock purse. Twisting it open, she clutched a metal lipstick tube and smeared a dark red line across her mouth. She grinned, revealing a crimson streak across her teeth. Digging through the bag, she produced a brush and dusted her cheeks with a moldy skin-toned powder. She stood and ran a hand through her hair. "That should do it. You know, you're the only person who's called me in a long time. How do I look?"

Despite her sending buckshot his way minutes earlier, Jack sensed a growing compassion for her. He stood. "Well, you haven't forgotten how to be a wonderful host. And you look beautiful."

Her face flushed.

Jack took her hand and helped her into her seat. "Do you remember what we talked about yesterday?"

She scrunched her eyebrows. "I can't say that I do." A black tabby pounced onto the rickety table. Melanie scooped it into her arms and cradled it against her chest. "I call this one Cleopatra because of her dark hair. I've named all my babies. The one over there is Rascal, and the one in the window is Barnaby." She rattled off a list.

Amid her rambling, Jack redirected her. "So, Melanie. We talked about a man yesterday. Does that ring a bell?"

Her tongue poked at the corner of her painted mouth. "The carousel man?"

"That's who I want to talk about." Jack edged forward, elbows against the table. "A woman told me you came to see her a long time ago because you wanted to learn about the man who built the Flying Horses."

"Such a wonderful carousel. I remember she showed me pictures of a beautiful man with a ponytail."

"I saw the man once when I was a boy." Jack described meeting the old man in the Missouri cornfield, riding the coffee-colored horse, and how he couldn't remember anything afterward. He told her he believed something horrible had happened to him. "Did you experience anything like that?"

Melanie pressed her eyes shut. She kept them sealed so long Jack wasn't sure if she had fallen asleep.

"I met him, too," she said after a long hesitation. "But he wasn't an old man. He was young like you." She spoke with a clarity Jack hadn't expected. "The night I saw him, I was at the beach with some people I met. We all fell asleep, but the tide came in during the night and woke me up. Everyone had left me there, and I ended up soaked to the skin. I searched for them in Oak Bluffs, but I might as well have wandered into a ghost town. I couldn't find a soul anywhere. And the crazy thing was, the whole town looked like something from an antique photo. Like I had stepped back in time."

Melanie reached for a cat, gripping it against her chest like a security blanket.

She continued. "I can't explain it, but something called me to that old carousel building. The door was open, and I went inside. I saw the ponytailed man sitting on a stool beside the carousel. He eyed me for a long time. Then, he took my hand and helped me onto a horse."

Jack dropped a hand over Melanie's. "Do you remember the horse's color, what it looked like?"

She shook her head. "I don't know. I remember its eyes. They were so lifelike and followed me wherever I went. When the carousel picked up speed, that's when the colors exploded in my mind and God came to me. Then I remember waking on the beach as the sun rose." A fat tear slipped

from her eye and smudged her powdered cheek. "I think the man with
the ponytail helped me see God."

"Did he ever tell you his name?"

"I never asked. I'm sure the woman told me, but I can't remember."

"Your friends. Did they go to the carousel?"

"Well, they weren't really friends. I was only at the beach for the
Lucy. I don't know what happened to them."

Jack tilted his head. "The Lucy?"

"You know. Lucy . . . in the sky. With diamonds?"

Jack frowned. "You mean LSD?"

"Oh, don't be such a prude."

For Chrissake, she was tripping.

Melanie stroked a tabby as it padded across the table. "The next day,
I went to the carousel to find the ponytailed man. So many people were
riding the horses, but he wasn't there." Another tear tumbled along her
cheek. "I searched everywhere, but I couldn't find him."

Jack leaned back in his chair, unsure what to believe. "Do you think
you could have been feeling the drugs' effects when you . . . saw God?"

"The ponytailed man showed me. I'm sure of it. He was Jesus Christ,
revealing his Father's kingdom. When I went to see the woman, she showed
me his picture. She told me he built the carousel." She leaned across the
table, her face inches from Jack's. "The carousel is the gateway to heaven."

"Did you ever go back?" Jack glanced at the religious trinkets dangling from her neck and wrists.

Melanie let out a breath. "I used to go back the first few years after
it happened. I'd sleep on the beach and wander into town in the middle
of the night, hoping it looked like it did the night I saw God. Each time
I tried to find the ponytailed man. I broke into the carousel building a
couple times, but he was never there."

She had spent more than her share of nights in Oak Bluffs' jail because
of it. Jack had read the police reports. "You got in trouble for that. Is that
why you stopped."

"Jail never bothered me," she said, waving a hand. "But it came to
me one night. A realization. We're not supposed to see God. Whatever I
saw, whatever happened to me wasn't meant to be. I tried to forget about

it. I tried everything I could . . . and I mean everything . . . to forget, to escape from what I knew." Tears rimmed her eyes as she twirled the cross around her neck. "But when you've seen the eternal gift, it's hard to live life on this earth."

"I bet."

She may have believed her story, but Jack wasn't convinced. Her drug-fueled evening had him doubting whether she had imagined the entire event. She was either tripping, truthful, or flat-out crazy. Still, her demeanor had changed as she recounted her story, a mental clarity unveiling itself in her words and emotion. It reminded him of someone with dementia who forgets their family's names but can sing every line of a favorite song. Jack sensed a kernel of truth, or at least something so deeply ingrained she believed it. But how could her magical experience be so different from his? The carousel a gateway to heaven? He played the conversation over in his head, considering that their experiences may not have been that different after all. They faced different outcomes at the carousel, but both encounters had haunted them their entire lives. They had something in common.

"Thank you, Melanie." Jack stood, sensing a wetness on his pants. *Damn felines.* "Thank you for letting me into your home and telling me your story. It is only a story, isn't it?"

"Wait. Are you leaving?" She smoothed her nightgown and surveyed her surroundings. "Will you visit me again sometime?"

"I will." He flashed a wan smile he suspected betrayed his intentions.

She led him through the garbage maze to the door. Cats scurried outside and into the long grass as she cracked the screen door. Sweet air rushed into his lungs.

Jack leaned in and hugged her. Bending over, he picked up the shotgun off the deck and handed it to her. "I'm gonna make a few calls. Make sure you get to stay on your land and keep living here. Don't shoot anybody in the meantime."

"I won't." Her distant stare had returned. "I wouldn't want to miss out on my chance to see God again."

Jack stepped from the porch and over to his car. Opening the door, he glanced over his shoulder. "Hey, Melanie. Was that just a story, or did it really happen?"

She tilted her head as a grin played at her lips. She cocked the shotgun and fired a shot over his car's rooftop. "And stay off my property or I'll kneecap you."

Jesus Christ. Ducking into the front seat, Jack keyed the ignition and slammed on the gas, fishtailing gravel chunks as he slung a U-turn on Hidden Hollow Road. He gazed through the rearview at Melanie Pastula, staring across her front lawn, shotgun in hand, as if she couldn't remember what she was doing there.

CHAPTER EIGHTEEN

Excerpt from *Caribou Man*, by Jack Rainne:

The man in the late-model sedan tracked the SUV through the slushy snow, far enough behind to blend in with the slow-moving traffic. Blending in, a skill the man had mastered. He understood the human eye hungered for arousal, something on which to attach and linger. Most gazes moved quickly past him in search of greater stimulation. But that never bothered him. Such a quality had served him well.

The man's own eyes hungered for arousal the moment he arrived at the mall, and it didn't take long before he spotted the woman. She had the bouncy gait and demeanor of someone shopping for that special someone, carefree and oblivious to the world around her. Like an unsuspecting deer in the woods wandering too close to a hunter's blind. He loved the mall at Christmastime. Its hallowed halls teemed with life, and its buffed floors and glass storefronts glittered with holiday cheer. Here, he would spot his quarry. He imagined himself a great predator, tasked with weeding out the herd's weak and vulnerable. Unlike predators in the wild, the man honored a social contract, remained loyal to his female mate, supported his offspring, and held down a job. But on certain days of the year, he allowed his inner beast to emerge.

The Caribou Man.

The creature had been born during the Christmas season. The man had loved the holiday as a child: cartoons on television, glowing tree lights peeking through frosty living room windows, and the festive downtown shop displays. Each holiday season portended a time of hope. He had adored Santa's reindeer and written a book report on caribou in the fourth grade. But when the time arrived to present his report before Mrs. Watson's class, his hands trembled. His voice fluttered so much it didn't come out right, and his cheeks stung as if on fire. He remembered Sandie Ray and her friends snickering, and he wondered why they covered their mouths and pointed at him. Sometimes he would sit with Sandie on the school bus. Each morning, his stomach would tingle in anticipation, hoping the seat beside her would be free. He imagined one day he would get the nerve to talk with her and ask her about her favorite teacher. Maybe their favorite teacher was the same one, and she would smile at him. Then, she would save a seat for him every morning and ask him to walk her to class.

When he took his eyes off Sandie and her friends and glanced to where they pointed, he discovered a growing stain extending along his leg.

After that, he never sat with her on the bus, but he could feel her laughter's sting each time he trudged along the aisle to the seats in the back. When he passed her in the hallways, he would relive the humiliating chortles coming from the far row of desks in Mrs. Watson's class and the wet sensation spreading from his crotch.

That day proved to be the moment everything changed for him, his mounting failures blossoming after that painful Christmas season. But he still loved the caribou. How fierce they were as fighters, establishing dominance in their herds, using their huge antlers to battle and subdue their rivals. Each year, the males would lose their weapon-like horns, only to grow them back bigger and better than before, with a greater number of tines. At times during the year, their antlers appeared red from the hardened blood forming them.

Antlers and blood. What a wonderful combination.

He followed the woman's SUV from the mall's slushy parking lot to the grocery store across town. The snow had picked up, blanketing the store's lot in muffled silence. She took her time picking the freshest produce and checking the nutrition labels before placing her comestibles into her cart. With such healthy choices, she must have expected to live a long and wonderful life.

The man had managed to do some shopping of his own as he stalked her, killing two birds with one stone. Keeping one eye on the woman, he filled his hand-held shopping basket with the sugary snacks his sedentary offspring devoured before the TV and the boxed meals his lazy mate warmed for him in the microwave.

The woman had parked beneath a flickering light pole in the parking lot's far corner, no doubt to maximize her step count. The man scanned the nearly empty lot as he followed her outside, his footfalls muffled on the fluffy, loose snow. She had opened the SUV's hatchback and methodically loaded her groceries.

"Sandie? Sandie Ray?"

The woman pivoted. She took an instinctive step backward, bumping against her vehicle.

"Do you remember me? We went to Hunter Elementary together."

The woman softened a moment at the man before her, grocery bag clutched to his chest. No threat, she must have figured. Pressing her eyebrows together, she flattened her lips. "I'm sorry. You must have the wrong person. I didn't go to school around here—"

"Of course, you did." The man stepped closer. "We rode the school bus together. You used to save a seat for me every morning. We would talk about our favorite teachers, and I would walk you to class. Don't you remember?"

"I don't think so. I guess I have a doppelgänger out there somewhere." She gave a polite smile as she dropped her last grocery bag into the trunk and lowered the hatchback.

As she reached the driver's side door, the man inched toward her, just enough to block her escape route. "That's strange," he said, leaning forward. "You look so much like her."

The woman swallowed, her eyes darting left and right. He had cornered her. Like prey.

"Listen. I need to go. Please. I'm sorry I wasn't the person you were looking for—"

"Oh, but you are." He reached deep into his grocery bag until his hand wrapped around the familiar object. It accompanied him on each of his excursions during the killing season. He imagined her snickering and pointing from the far row of desks in Mrs. Watson's class and whispering to friends as he made the lonely journey along the school bus's center aisle. He sensed his face flush with heat.

"Maybe you're not her exactly." The Caribou Man raised the spiked antler above his head, its tines honed to razor-sharp points. "But you'll do."

CHAPTER NINETEEN

Oak Bluffs, Massachusetts (Martha's Vineyard)

Darkness shrouded the highways and backroads by the time Jack rolled into Woods Hole to catch the last ferry across Nantucket Sound. Turning over the mysteries and facts coalescing in his mind, he disembarked at Vineyard Haven and sped through the quiet town toward home. He had connected Graham Carver to his Missouri carousel adventure, and Judy Van Dorn had confirmed it. Although Melanie Pastula had crazy written all over her, the woman's tale had gone a long way to verifying the Graham Carver angle. Their similar experiences with the carousel operator were difficult to dismiss. She had included several farfetched details, like Oak Bluffs resembling an old-time photo, the carousel calling to her, and a young Carver as Jesus Christ. Could those details, or the entire story, be related to the drugs? He didn't know what to believe.

As Jack sped along Edgartown Vineyard Haven Road, he detoured onto County Road and wound through the narrow streets leading into a slumbering Oak Bluffs. Swinging the car into a space on Lake Avenue, Jack hopped out and approached the Flying Horses. He gazed at the ancient building, a living, breathing dinosaur surviving among the town's modern structures. He had never witnessed the old barn in absolute silence, bereft of children's joyous shouts and carnival sounds pumping from the Wurlitzer Band Organ. For the first time, he appreciated how odd the building appeared, the way it stood out like a sore thumb as if pretending to be part of the peaceful little town. The boisterous livelihood surrounding it each day proved the perfect distraction and served to mask its true identity, keeping it camouflaged in plain sight.

Jack reached to touch the wood building. A buzzing charge thrummed inside him as if he stood beside an electric grid radiating a pulsing hum from its transformers and power lines. As he touched the door, a static detonation rocked him, expelling him from his perch onto all fours. He raised a heavy head as the world settled into focus. On Lake Avenue, a man and woman strolled toward him along the empty street.

The man clutched the woman's palm as two children zipped about them like moths orbiting a streetlamp. The little girl and boy raced from storefront to storefront, pressing their faces against the waterfront's shop windows and glancing back at the adults. But their beseeching gazes did nothing to accelerate the couple's deliberate stroll. Their voices flitted across the still night air, clear as a bell, as if broadcast inside Jack's skull.

"We lived too long in New York City's hustle and chaos for me to quicken my step for anything. Cottage City's milder pace suits my constitution."

Cottage City? Jack struggled to his feet and inspected the silent town. Wood and clapboard storefronts and cobblestone roads had replaced the familiar concrete, masonry, steel construction, and asphalt roadways. Nothing resembled the modern world, no T-shirt shops or bustling restaurants, smoothie stores, or gift shops.

Like something from an old-time photo.

The full moon illuminated the man and woman emerging from the shadows. "Do you remember my old team? How they couldn't wait to get back to that dirty old city once they finished rebuilding the Flying Horses? I still can't figure it out."

The woman squeezed the man's arm. "Well, darling. I could point out how much younger they were than you and without families. More skirts to chase in the big city."

The man grinned and rubbed the woman's hand.

"You've finally found a place that speaks to your soul, a place you can call home. As I have." She leaned her head on his shoulder. "And the children."

"These strolls, my dear. These are the payoff to my busy days at the carousel." He pointed to the water. "Look how you can see the moon reflecting off Lake Anthony." He grabbed her hand as they approached the waterfront and a monstrous dwelling resting on the water's edge.

"Children, come. Rest your eyes on this wondrous place." The family gazed upward at the finely arranged four-story structure with its ornate piazzas, tiered balconies, and mansard roof looming above the ocean's skyline like a modern-day castle.

"When we first moved out here, the Wesley House was nothing more than an ice cream saloon. But look at it now."

The woman rolled her eyes. "I don't care how many wealthy vacationers stay here each summer; the Wesley is the best place on the island for ice cream."

As the family ambled along Lake Avenue in Jack's direction, the children appeared content to hold hands and keep pace with their parents' lazy gait.

The man gestured toward the water. "The scuttlebutt is that Cottage City might be planning to cut a channel through Lake Anthony and into the Sound to make a proper harbor."

Jack rubbed his eyes, gazing at where the harbor should have been. No vessels sat moored in its waters. No access point allowed vessels into or out of Nantucket Sound.

"It will assuredly help the fishermen trying to make a living out there on the sea."

"I only hope it's a few years away," the man said. "Keep this place to ourselves for a while longer."

The family's route took them past the barn-like structure housing the Flying Horses Carousel. They came within arm's length of Jack, but they didn't acknowledge his presence. The boy tugged at his mother's sleeve.

"What is it?" The woman dropped to a knee.

The boy pointed.

"You want to go in?" She peeked at her husband.

The man groaned. "No more than a quick visit," he said, fumbling through his coat's pockets and extracting a keychain. He led his family up the steps. "We're not supposed to be inside after customer hours."

He twisted the key into the door lock and pushed open the heavy double doors. The rusty hinge's squeak split the late hour's silence. As the family strolled past, Jack glimpsed the man's hair pinned back into a tight ponytail.

It's gotta be Carver. Who else would have a key? Jack followed them into the barn.

The children raced past their parents and jumped onto the silent platform, running their hands across the horsehair manes and tales.

"Go ahead, children. Climb on," the man said.

The girl stopped at a coffee-colored mare, jammed her foot into the metal stirrup, and dropped into the saddle. She gazed at her little brother, who stood beside her horse, raising his arms toward her.

The man grinned. "Annabelle, look. Out of all the jumpers Zachariah could choose, he wants to sit with Rebecca."

Annabelle, Zachariah, and Rebecca . . . the whole family.

The woman reached beneath the boy's arms and hoisted him into the saddle with his sister, who wrapped an arm around her brother's waist. The woman grabbed the guide pole.

"Okay, now you guys hold on tight." The man retreated from the platform, patting the mare's mane. Yanking his hand back, he stumbled and nearly lost his balance.

"Graham?" his wife asked.

The man inspected his hand, curling his fingers into a fist and releasing. He swallowed and crept toward the horse. Sliding his hand beneath the mane, he pressed his fingers against the coat. "Did you feel that?"

The woman cocked her head.

He reached toward the mane and caressed the hair. "When I touched its neck, I felt some sort of . . . shock. An electrical charge."

"Perhaps the horsehair had a buildup of static electricity," Annabelle offered.

"Could be."

He seated himself on a stool beside the carousel. Jamming a control lever forward, he gazed at his wife and children twirling with the carousel's jangly carnival-style music. They grinned and waved, the children reaching for the brass ring with each turn of the platform.

The man leaped from his stool as a whirring sound erupted from the carousel's engine like a controlled explosion. The platform accelerated to a fever pitch, spinning out of control. The smiles faded from the children's faces as they gripped the guide pole with both hands, eyes darting to their mother. The woman wrapped both arms around the children, widening her stance to fight the growing centrifugal force scheming to toss her from the platform. The man's stricken features betrayed a sickly horror as he spun knobs and dials, pulling back on the lever to slow the machine. Instead, the carousel picked up its tempo until the horses melted into a twirling blur.

He jumped to the spinning platform's edge, ready to time a bold leap and join his family on the whirling carousel, but no opening afforded his feet a solid purchase. To jump on now would surely tear a limb from his body.

"Annabelle. Hold on!" he shouted, yanking the emergency stop. Nothing. He fell to his knees as his wife and children's muffled screams filled the room. They rose in tone, then descended, now seeming to originate from miles away. The man pressed his hands to his ears as the chaotic, discordant music ascended in volume, reaching a crescendo in one solid, screaming note. The machine slowed and ground to a halt, the coffee-colored horse perched inches from his face as he lowered his hands.

He stood and faced the mare, now empty of riders. Sprinting about the building, the man whipped his head back and forth, calling for his wife and children. The coffee-colored horse shook its mane as an electric charge sizzled across the platform. Stepping to the machine, the man threw the lever forward, igniting the jangly music and resuming the carousel's counterclockwise spin. As the platform picked up speed, he grabbed a support pole and hoisted himself onto the machine. Dashing to the coffee-colored horse, he jammed his foot into the stirrup and swung the other over the saddle. The carousel's speed shimmied upward as he gripped the guide pole. In moments, the man was a blur as the carousel spun.

The room's light imploded to a pinpoint before going dark. In the blackness, the horse had shifted into a living, breathing charger standing many hands above the man's head. The carousel had fallen away, and the mare had escaped the guide pole's confines. The ponytailed man jerked the reins and pumped his heels into the animal's ribs. The beast thundered across a vast meadow, ripping through the knee-high wheat and scrub brush. The night wrapped them in a smothering darkness, the sliver of moon and a scattering of desperate stars providing the only light. In moments, the terrain changed, and the mare rumbled across rocky outcroppings and into a gorge, flying further and further into dank staleness.

Then downward, downward . . .

The animal jerked and bucked, and the man guided it no longer, but held on with desperate intent as it roared through red, rocky fissures and deep into the glowing earth.

The room went dark. The kind of pitch black where Jack couldn't see his hand before him. When the light came up, the carousel slowed, and the music stopped.

The carousel man had disappeared.

CHAPTER TWENTY

Edgartown, Massachusetts (Martha's Vineyard)

The sunlight streamed through Jack's office window, sending magnified heat across his face. Extending a palm, he shielded his eyes from the blinding assault. He mumbled to himself as he swung his legs off the couch, still grappling with the strange vision involving the nineteenth-century man and his family the previous night in Oak Bluffs. He had somehow witnessed the same thing that had happened to himself twenty-five years ago, the coffee-colored horse thundering across the valley and deep into the earth, but this time with a different rider aboard. Despite the man's youth, Jack had no doubt the man he encountered in the wee hours could be none other than his carousel operator, Graham Carver.

He stumbled into the hallway, shaking off the morning fog. After ducking his head into Sam's bedroom, he descended the steps to the first floor, expecting to find her in the kitchen, cup in hand, cradling her mug of high-end coffee. Since moving to the Vineyard, Sam had thrown herself onto the gourmet java altar. Her morning revolved around imported high-altitude Columbian beans painstakingly ground to fine dust and brewed with Amazon-supplied Canadian iceberg water. Jack usually finished his first Keurig-prepared cup of Dunkin Original before she assembled her gear for the task. But today, the kitchen sat empty. His bare feet slapped against the tile as he approached the kitchen island and reached for the note wedged between the brown-speckled bananas:

Shopping in Oak Bluffs for trip, then to Flying Horses. Been thinking about Morgan—

Jack sensed the heat flush his face as he read the last sentence:

Feels like carousel is calling to me

The note fluttered to the floor. *Something called me to that old carousel building.* Melanie Pastula's chilling words echoed in his head. If the carousel called to her, who says it couldn't call to someone else?

Jack raced to the second floor to check on Morgan.

He cracked the bedroom door. Empty.

Jack's heart hammered in his chest as he searched the room, throwing open the closet doors and scanning the yard through the open window. Advancing along the hallway door by door, Jack shouted Morgan's name, checking bathrooms, closets, and her favorite hiding places. He descended the stairs two steps at a time until he reached the foyer.

"Morgan, where are you?" *Please be here.*

He searched the house but could already tell she was gone. Maybe the eerie stillness or the buzzing silence in his ears that only comes with the complete absence of sound betrayed the fact. They were both heading to the Flying Horses, and Graham Carver would be there to usher them onto the cursed carousel.

"Holy Christ." His worst nightmare had come to fruition. He couldn't protect Morgan. Or Sam.

Jack raced upstairs to his office to retrieve his cell. He had to warn Sam to stay away from Oak Bluffs. No telling who would disappear next on that fucked up ride. Whatever had happened to Graham Carver and his family, Melanie Pastula, and Jack in that Missouri cornfield was poised to happen again. He could feel it.

Rumbling to his office couch, he scattered the comforter and pillows to search for his cell. He yanked the cushions back but found nothing, only a solitary cord attached to the charging block. Bolting downstairs, Jack scoured the rooms. He flung open the door to the garage and checked the car, cupping his hands against the glass to peer through the window. *Thank God.* Jack snatched the cell from the center console and tapped the screen, waiting for it to light up, but the battery had drained overnight.

"Fuck me!"

Jack stormed to his office and plugged the adapter into the cell. Pacing the floor, he dragged a forearm across his damp forehead, waiting for the phone to build sufficient charge.

The doorbell's shrill chime interrupted his office laps.

Now what?

He dashed into the hallway and descended the staircase. Two imposing shapes peered through the front door's opaque glass. The chime rang again as Jack threw the door open. Inspecting the two men on the stoop, Jack pegged them as police officers before they withdrew their badges, their threadbare sports jackets likely thrown off and on more often than the material could withstand.

"I'm Detective Mike Stahl, and this is Detective Chris Daniels from the Cape Cod Bureau of Criminal Investigations." Stahl pressed his thumb and index finger along his mustache but kept his eyes trained on him. "Are you Jack Rainne?"

Despite the detectives' youthful appearances, they had a grizzled edge only veteran cops possessed. Especially Stahl, who looked as if he had witnessed a few things in his day.

"Is there something I can help you with?" Jack swiped at his moist forehead.

"May we come in?" Stahl asked. He had kind eyes, unlike the more suspicious ones of his partner, Daniels. The shorter man remained rigid beside Stahl, Ray-Bans resting atop his blond brush cut.

Jack escorted the detectives into the living room and offered them a seat. Daniels removed the sunglasses and slipped them into his jacket pocket before dropping onto the sofa. Jack stood, tapping his foot against the carpet and rubbing his hands.

"You okay, Mr. Rainne?" Stahl asked. "You seem a bit nervous."

"No, it's not that . . . it's just . . . hold on." Jack raced up the steps to his office and checked his cell. Still no signal. He grabbed the charging block and cord and carried them to the living room. After plugging in the device, Jack resumed his pacing. "Sorry. I'm expecting a call. Can I get you something to drink?"

"No thanks, Mr. Rainne. We don't want to take too much of your time." Stahl appeared to be in charge.

"Call me Jack." He checked the cell. No charge yet.

"Before we start," Daniels interjected, "both Detective Stahl and I really enjoyed *Double-Barrel Justice*. Very realistic portrayal of police life. You did your homework."

"Thanks, I appreciate it." *And I can't get a movie deal? What the fuck?*

Stahl worked his jaw. "Jack, as part of BCI, Detective Daniels and I lead a team of Cape Cod detectives who work cold cases throughout New England. One case we've been working on for the past few years is the Morgan family's disappearance. Are you familiar with it?"

"I remember it well."

Daniels leaned forward. "We haven't had a single lead in years, Mr. Rainne. But in the past two days, people have come forward to talk with us." He pointed at Jack's chest. "And they all mention you."

Jack held up his hands. "I know. I've been asking around a bit. I've been doing a little research for a true crime novel." *Let the lies begin.* "And to be honest, I had a minor problem with Brad Morgan—"

"Minor problem?" Daniels said. "He threw a hammer at you through a glass window. Witnesses reported a bloodied man with shoulder-length hair running from his store. I assume that was you?"

"Hang on, Chris." Stahl put a hand on the detective's forearm. "Mr. Rainne . . . Jack. We've got two problems here. First, Mr. Morgan says you possess something belonging to his wife before she disappeared. A pendant with a horse. Is that true?"

Good luck explaining that one.

"I bought it, like, twenty years ago when his wife would sell jewelry on the sidewalk," he lied, making sure to maintain eye contact. "My wife has it now."

"You gave it to your wife twenty years ago?" Daniels asked.

"Not exactly. I got it twenty years ago, but only gave it to her recently."

"Second thing, Jack." Stahl raked his thick brown hair. "Mr. Morgan claims you told him you had never been to the store before." He consulted a notepad to refresh his memory. "Then, when he saw your cell phone and the pendant around your wife's neck, you said you *had* been to the store. I give up, which is it?"

Jack's cell phone lit up as it attained its minimum charge. He snatched it off the bar. "Hang on." He pressed Sam's number, but she didn't answer. He held up a finger as he sent a text, punching the words out with his thumb.

Don't go to carousel not safe. Call me NOW

Jack grabbed a Sprite from the can cooler beneath the bar and popped the tab. He took two monstrous gulps, sensing a sweet, fizzy blood-sugar spike. "He misunderstood. Listen, I brought him a six-pack, and he was four beers into it when all this happened. I was helping him sweep up the place, and he asked me if I'd ever been inside the store during its heyday. I told him no. But I *had* bought the piece *outside* the store. Semantics. Just a misunderstanding." Jack checked his phone. Nothing.

"Do you have the pendant here, Mr. Rainne?" Daniels asked.

"I'm not sure where it is right now."

"Is there anyone else in the house that would know?" Stahl asked.

"Well, my wife is out shopping right now, but she could tell you."

"Can I see the picture of the pendant, Mr. Rainne?"

Jack scrolled through his cell phone and showed Daniels the image. The detective pecked at the screen.

"Gonna send myself a copy so we can do a closer inspection later. Is that all right with you?"

"Sure, whatever you need."

"When Mr. Morgan spoke with us the other day, he said those horse pendants were one of the last pieces of jewelry Ellen Morgan ever made." Stahl flipped his notebook closed. "They weren't even for sale yet. In fact, Mr. Morgan said she was wearing one on the night she disappeared."

"Turns out she never had the chance to sell them. Do you know anything about jewelry finishing, Mr. Rainne?" Daniels asked.

Jack shook his head.

"Ellen Morgan had a type of enameling she applied to the back of her pendants, which gave them a signature appearance. That was her last step in the process. And she never sold anything that didn't have her signature enameling." Daniels checked the image on his cell. "Can't see it on this picture, though. Mr. Morgan showed us a box full of horse pendants that Ellen Morgan hadn't gotten around to enameling yet."

"And?"

"Jack." Stahl leaned forward and rested his elbows on his knees. "If the pendant in your possession wasn't enameled, then someone could ask the question, how does this piece of jewelry that hasn't been sold come into your possession?"

"You see where we're going?" Daniels added.

"I told you. I bought it years ago." Jack's cell lit up with a text message. "Hang on a sec." He squinted to read the message.

Enough Jack!

He pressed a button to call, but she didn't pick up. He held up a finger again as he pecked out a text.

Please call!

"Listen, Detectives. I'm in a hurry to get to Oak Bluffs. I think my wife . . ." *What? She's going to visit a carousel and might disappear? They'll love that one.* "I think she's expecting me," he mumbled.

"We won't be too much longer," Stahl assured him. "You can join her in a few minutes."

"Mr. Rainne, how long have you lived in New England?" Daniels folded his arms. "I read on the back cover of your book that you're from Missouri."

"Spring Valley. A little place south of Jefferson City. I came to Boston to go to school. Twenty-three . . . wait, twenty-four years ago."

Daniels checked his notebook. "Northeastern, wasn't it? School of Journalism?"

They came prepared. "That's right."

"I heard Mizzou has a good journalism school. Why not stay in Missouri?"

Jack scrunched his eyebrows. "Where would you rather live, Boston or Missouri?"

"I guess you have a point." Daniels scratched his head. "Nothing in Missouri you might have wanted to run away from, is there?"

Jack rolled his eyes and didn't answer.

"What I can't figure," Daniels continued, "is, what's a college guy from Missouri doing in Hyannis buying jewelry for a wife he doesn't have yet?"

"I spent every summer during and after college on the Cape." He jammed his hands against his hips. "One day, I bought a piece of jewelry that spoke to me, that's all. I figured I would keep it and give it to someone special someday."

Stahl stood and approached Jack. "It would be helpful if you could bring us the pendant and let us examine it."

"You know," Daniels added, "for the enameling. I'm sure we'll find it since she never sold anything without it."

"You shouldn't have anything to worry about," Stahl added.

"Or maybe you should . . ." Daniels let the statement hang.

Jack flushed. "Is there anything else, gentlemen, because I should—"

"One more thing," Daniels said. He stood and extracted an envelope from his jacket pocket. "We had a call from a Marsha Mason at the *Falmouth Enterprise*. She told us you examined her pictures from the night the Morgans disappeared."

"Yes, I did. Again, I've been exploring the book angle. She let me have a look through her portfolio."

"Where were you the summer the Morgans disappeared?" Stahl asked. "Massachusetts or Missouri?"

"I'm sure I was on the Cape." Jack deliberated for a moment. "I'm guessing Harwich Port, one of those mini cottages across from the little pizza place on Route 28."

"I know that area." Daniels tilted his head. "George's Pizza?"

Jack pointed at him. "Yeah, that's right."

"Good pies," Stahl mumbled, glancing at his partner.

Daniels resumed. "You ever been to the Barnstable County Fair?"

"If there were girls and beer," Jack replied with a grin, "you can bet my friends and I were there."

"Ms. Mason said something happened to you at her office." Stahl leaned an elbow against the bar. "You wound up on the floor. You want to tell us more about that?"

Jack sighed. "It's hard to explain. You see, when I was a teenager, I was hospitalized for something that happened to me after my father's death. I had—"

"Hallucinations?" Daniels offered.

Jack's jaw dropped.

"We spoke to your doctor out in Missouri, Jack." Stahl checked his book. "A Marcus Lang at Fulton State Hospital. He wouldn't give us any records without a court order and refused to provide any specifics, but he did mention you were admitted for hallucinations. That was the gist of it."

Daniels stepped forward. "You were seeing things, right?"

"At the time. I was seventeen. But they treated me, and I haven't had any problems since."

You sure about that, Jack?

"You weren't running away from anything when you came to Boston, were you? Like spending time in a nut house?"

Jack's jaw clenched as he dug his fingernails into his palms.

"That's enough, Chris." Stahl removed a pair of glasses from his front shirt pocket and checked his notebook. "We still need to understand what happened in Ms. Mason's office. She said you were eyeing a photograph and then she found you on the floor. Does that sound about right?"

"I thought I saw something. It triggered old memories, that's all."

Daniels set the envelope on the bar and extracted a photograph enlarged many times its original size. Jack's eyes widened as he identified the Dare carousel in the distance and the old man perched on the stool.

"That's it." Jack pointed. "This is what I saw in the picture. You see the old man sitting beside the carousel?"

Stahl and Daniels hesitated as they met each other's gaze.

"What's the matter?" Jack asked.

"That triggered your episode?" Stahl asked. "A carnival ride?"

"Wouldn't you expect something like that," Daniels said, hesitating as if for effect, "at a carnival?"

"It's not your normal carousel—"

"Doesn't matter," Daniels said, waving a hand. "Because that's not what Ms. Mason called us about."

"She saw something else, Jack." Stahl pointed at the photograph. "Look over here."

At the photo's border, a man in a college T-shirt stood alone with his hands in his pockets, the lights from a food truck illuminating his face. Jack examined the face he hadn't seen in over twenty years. *What the . . . ?*

"Look familiar?" Daniels inspected Jack's face.

Jack raised his head and opened his mouth, but nothing came out.

"Northeastern T-shirt, shoulder-length hair." Detective Stahl folded his arms. "Mr. Rainne, that's you in the picture. You were at the Barnstable County Fair the night Ellen and Jack Morgan disappeared."

CHAPTER TWENTY-ONE

Twenty-Five Years Earlier
Spring Valley, Missouri

Jack urged the Schwinn along County Road 4 toward home. His father had mumbled something over breakfast about the Millers having to corral some of the Rainnes' livestock after finding them wandering along Burnham Farms Road. Jack understood he would be riding fences with the old man after school, scouting for breaches, and making repairs. To make matters worse, Mr. Fowler had kept him after seventh-period science to discuss his most recent exam disaster and slipping grade. Jack pedaled harder, praying that by some miracle, time would stretch and he wouldn't bear the brunt of Bobby Rainne's wrath.

The old man rejoiced in lashing out. The punch, kick, slap, or beating wouldn't happen right away, but it would happen. Simply a matter of when. The old man would seethe in silence while they worked, leaving Jack on pins and needles as night fell. They say the night brings out the demons, but demons were nothing compared to a cruel man with a bottle of Wild Turkey.

As Jack rumbled past Dowling Farm along Prairie Road, he sensed the urgency, dormant pain sensors in his face, ribs, and jaw throbbing in anticipation of the evening's main event. He had grown accustomed to the beatdowns over the years. He had even gone toe-to-toe with the old man several months back, matching him punch for punch and asserting destiny would soon award the elder Rainne's heavyweight belt to the challenger. But standing up to the old man that day had a downside. The following morning, his mother had slathered on rouge and cover-up to hide her swollen face.

The next time, Jack took the beating. As he would tonight.

He pumped the pedals along River Road until he reached the family farm. Bobby Rainne bounced along the property's boundary, perched in his work horse's saddle.

Fuck me. Jack veered the bicycle across the grass and joined his father at the property's northwest corner.

"This is a two-man job, Jack."

"I know. Mr. Fowler kept me after class—"

"You fucking up again in school?"

"Only a bad science grade. I gotta do a make-up test next—"

The fist descended in an arc, catching Jack's temple and driving him into the dirt. As he struggled to his feet, he grasped the fence to keep his legs under him. His head throbbed, the farm swimming before his eyes. The punch had caught him unawares, the consequences commencing sooner than expected.

Bobby spat brown chaw onto Jack's pants leg. "I left a piece of tape at the fence sections needing attention. Go get the tool belt in the barn and get to work."

The heat simmered in Jack's core, sending the blood whooshing through his veins. He couldn't stop the words that flew from his mouth. "Fuck yourself, asshole!"

In the silence that followed, Jack figured he had cost his mother a beating. He wasn't about to let it happen again.

"What did you say, boy?"

"You heard me, you pathetic sonofabitch! It all stops now. Everything."

Bobby Rainne threw a leg over the saddle, his lip curled in a grimace and the light extinguished from his eyes. "We'll see about that."

Jack shouted as he rushed at his father's horse, arms thrust above his head. The spooked animal reared back on his haunches, throwing the old man over its back and into the drainage culvert beside the road. Bobby Rainne fell awkwardly, his arms flailing to regain control. He landed on his neck against the culvert's rocky bank. The impact ripped the silence, reverberating like a branch cracking in a high wind. Bobby's glassy eyes darted back and forth as he faced his son standing above him.

"Can't . . . move . . ." he said, gasping for air. "Go on now, boy . . . call for help . . ."

Stepping into the culvert, Jack knelt beside his father. He raised the man's lifeless arm, dropping it against the rocks with a sickening slap. "Can you feel anything?"

"I said . . . I can't . . . move." Fear grew in the elder Rainne's eyes as the struggle to fill his lungs intensified. A muddled wheeze rattled from his throat as he pulled at the air.

"I'm sorry, Dad."

"Get your ass . . . moving . . . you worthless fuck . . . call 911!" Bobby Rainne barked, spittle flying from his mouth. "You got . . . a job . . . to do."

"Yeah, I guess I do." Jack stood and scanned the horizon, east to west, searching for cars, horses, and dust plumes along the distant gravel roads. Anything with a human attached. He listened for the sound of machinery, mowers, and combines. He heard nothing but cicadas buzzing in the afternoon heat. They were the only two people in the world on Burnham Farms Road in Spring Valley, Missouri.

He knelt beside his father.

CHAPTER TWENTY-TWO

Present Day
Edgartown, Massachusetts (Martha's Vineyard)

After Detectives Stahl and Daniels left, Jack hurried through the kitchen and into the garage. He stabbed the automatic door opener and jumped into his vehicle, a dust cloud rising from the spinning wheels as he fishtailed across the gravel driveway. Accelerating through the tight streets of his picturesque hometown, he silently willed the tourists and vacationers to hug the sidewalks' white picket fences and stay close to the curb. Jack floored it when he reached Beach Road, weaving in and out of traffic on the narrow roadway hugging Nantucket Sound.

Graham Carver and his goddamn carousel.

With any luck, he would intercept Sam and Morgan before they wandered into the man's clutches. But their radio silence and unknown whereabouts ratcheted his stress level into overdrive. On top of that, Jack had wandered into a legal pickle. Marsha Mason had photographic evidence that he had visited the Barnstable County Fair the night the Morgan family disappeared, and Stahl and Daniels knew he had jewelry belonging to Ellen Morgan, which she had never sold. Jack racked his brain, trying to understand how he didn't recall being at the County Fair that night. He would be the first to admit he enjoyed boisterous nights of revelry during those Cape Cod summers, but had he gotten so drunk he had no recollection he had been there? Jack would also need to hand over Sam's pendant or the detectives would get a warrant. Either way, they wouldn't find the enameling they expected. And then what?

Well, you're fucked.

The evidence may have been circumstantial, but it pointed directly at him with laser precision. In a cold case without a substantial lead in years, Jack understood the detectives would shift their focus to him. And once law enforcement zeroed in on a suspect, you might as well phone in the orange jumpsuit order. Jack had watched too many late-night, true crime shows not to figure that one out. He attempted to clear his mind and focus on his rescue plan at the carousel, but his anxiety kept his thoughts spinning.

Jack grabbed his cell and dialed Hal.

"Hey Jack, what's doing?"

He hesitated, considering how to kick off this conversation. "Quick question. How open is your mind right now?"

"Well, I'm getting used to opening it a bit wider for you lately. How open does it need to be this time?"

"Probably more open than before you answered my call." Jack zoomed past a slower-moving vehicle across the "*Jaws* Bridge," sliding back into his lane moments ahead of oncoming traffic. "Listen, I need your help. I had detectives at my door this morning, asking questions about a twenty-year-old disappearance on Cape Cod."

"What the fuck, Jack? Why are they asking you?"

Jack transferred the cell to his other hand. "Thing is, I've been asking around, and it's gotten me into a bit of trouble."

"What kind of trouble?"

"Long story, not enough time."

"You're not good at telling long stories anyway. As your agent, I should know." Hal appeared to be waiting for the chuckle Jack wasn't about to grant him. "What's your interest in this twenty-year-old disappearance?"

"I don't know. Book idea, maybe." The road had emptied ahead of him. Jack tested the gas pedal. "Either way, I may need a lawyer soon."

"Criminal?"

"Looks that way."

"Jesus, Jack," Hal mumbled. "Okay, I know a couple good ones out your way. Let me see what I can do."

"Thanks, Hal. I appreciate it."

"You know, Jack. Going to jail might not be the worst thing for you. It would do wonders for your writing. Twenty-three-and-a-half hours a day in a cell might help you produce something good. And I might start getting paid again. You gotta look on the bright side—"

"Bye, Hal." Jack disconnected as he crossed into Oak Bluffs, refocusing his attention on the task at hand. He had to get to the Flying Horses Carousel before Sam and Morgan did. He checked his phone for messages, but Sam hadn't called back. He tried her one more time, but the call went straight to voicemail.

"Sonofabitch!"

Before long, Jack's weird-o-meter went off again, the needle burying itself in the red. Not a single soul inhabited the side streets, inns, and restaurant decks along Seaview Avenue. Ocean Park to his left appeared abandoned, along with Town Beach to his right.

What the fuck?

He hung a left onto Lake Avenue, expecting to join the bumper-to-bumper parade through the center of town, but no cars filled the deserted street. The city still appeared like a sepia-toned photograph from a history book. Horses and buggies stood secured to wooden posts beside the dry goods and feed store, the general store and apothecary, and the butcher shop. Flat wooden planks created a maze of walkways about the city, keeping the townsfolk's shoes dry along the muddy streets. Women in ankle-length dresses strolled along Lake Avenue, warding off the summer sun beneath lace parasols, their men beside them adorned in wool trousers, collared shirts, and bowlers atop their heads. Jack trained his eyes toward the harbor, but no ferry bobbed in the water, waiting to transport travelers back and forth to the mainland. With no significant access point to the open sea, the harbor resembled nothing more than a lake. Jack aimed his car toward the Flying Horses, passing a sign announcing the Cottage City Town Hall to his right.

He had returned to nineteenth-century Oak Bluffs.

Jack stepped from the vehicle to the shrill squawk of seagulls floating overhead. The town's residents passed but paid no attention, as if the interloper invading Cottage City's resuscitated past didn't yet exist. He longed for the comfort of the familiar, cars jamming the narrow streets, crowds packed around Giordano's busy take-out window, or the pleasant ice cream and coffee shop aromas on Kennebec. But everything familiar had vanished from this freakish time warp.

Except for the carousel.

Jack swung the car door shut, the vacuum-like whump sounding shockingly out of place in the pre-Oak Bluffs time warp. Mounting the wooden steps to the carousel's entrance, Jack sensed the electric thrum pulsing from the archaic structure. He slid through the open door, careful not to touch the sides and risk any more unprescribed electroshock therapy. He gazed at the carousel's polished green flooring, rust-colored suspension cables, and struts supporting the horses' guide poles, as shiny and bright as the day Graham Carver assembled them in 1884. From behind, the Wurlitzer's swirling carnival music grew from the silence as the carousel initiated its gradual counterclockwise rotation.

Beside the carousel, a young, ponytailed man rose from a stool and brushed the lint from his wool slacks.

Jack took a tentative step toward the man he recognized from the previous night. "You're Graham Carver." It wasn't a question.

The man flashed a welcoming smile. "Hello, Jack."

He scanned the empty building. "Where are they, you sonofabitch?"

Carver cocked his head. "You mean your family? Same place as mine."

"I don't give a shit about yours." Jack's voice rose in tenor. "Where is my wife and daughter?"

He winced. "That smarts, Jack. I lost everything the day they disappeared."

Jack's jaw muscles clenched. "It's gonna hurt a lot more unless you start talking." His arms shot forward like pistons toward the man's throat but halted in midair, as if hitting an invisible wall. He dropped to his knees and pressed his hands against his ears. A sharp thud reverberated in his head as if someone had let loose a wrecking ball against his skull.

THUD . . . THUD . . . THUD . . .

Carver shook his head. "None too pleasant, is it?"

Jack thought he had experienced the crushing head discomfort before, but the current pain stabbing at his skull scored off the charts.

"What's happening?" Jack raised his head. "Make it stop!"

"I'm not doing anything, Jack. But if you stand down, you'll be okay."

Jack groaned and stumbled to his feet. As he stepped back, he sensed the pressure release in his head. "Jesus Christ."

"My boss is very protective. Sorry, mate."

Jack leaned forward, resting his hands on his knees. "Who's your boss?"

"Someone who expects people to honor their commitments. Something you didn't do."

"What are you talking about?" Jack straightened.

Carver stuffed his hands in his pockets and paced the barn's floor. "Jack, we have a slight problem. When you were seventeen, you had an arrangement with my employer, a gentlemen's agreement, you might say. But you didn't honor it."

"What agreement?"

"Tsk, tsk, tsk. It's getting more and more difficult to remember, isn't it?" Carver circled behind Jack, dropping a hand on his shoulder. "You've been away a long time, and you're not sure what happened, or if anything happened at all. I imagine all those doctors got you thinking and messed you up pretty good in there."

Jack pushed away the finger tapping his head. "Where's my family? Put me on the carousel, Carver." He jumped onto the platform. "Let me go with them."

"I can't do that." Carver gestured toward the machine. "This isn't your carousel. Yours is somewhere else—I'm sure you know where to find it."

Jack pictured Johnson Farm and its golden cornfield. "What did you do to them?"

"I did my job." Carver held up his hands.

"Your *job*?"

"Sometimes the universe has plans we don't understand." Carver scratched his chin. "You might say I'm a delivery man. One of many. Each has different skills, but we all deliver the same thing."

"And what's that?"

"People, where they're destined to go."

Jack opened his mouth but couldn't string words together. He dropped from the platform and advanced toward Carver but hesitated, recalling the earlier skull thudding. "And you delivered me somewhere, didn't you? Where did I go, Carver? Tell me."

"I think you know where."

A sickening lump expanded in Jack's stomach. As he slumped forward, his vision narrowed. Carver reached out to steady him, lowering him onto the stool beside the carousel.

"Who are you, Carver?"

"Just a carousel builder who uses his talent differently now."

Jack cradled his head in his hands. "The horse that took me into the earth . . . took me to hell, didn't it?"

"It took you to the Underground. But . . . yeah, same thing, mate."

Jack fell to the floor and retched, his stomach clenching in waves, but nothing expelled from his empty gut.

Carver stepped back. "Don't worry, it's a natural reaction. Just let it all go."

Jack wiped the saliva from his mouth. "The Underground?"

"Your 'hell,' Jack."

"And you work for the devil?"

"In the Underground, he is Tartareus. 'The Tar' for short." Carver dropped to a knee and wrapped an arm across Jack's shoulder. "He is the darkness from your Bible, mythology, ancient lore, or anything else humanity has woven into stories or parables. That's why you can't remember him, or your trip to the Underground. The human brain can only take so much before it shuts down or shatters."

"Like Melanie Pastula?"

"Just like her and others."

"But I'm not dead. Why did I go to hell?"

"Forget the playbook, Jack. You don't have to die to go to the Underground. The Tar takes what he wants when he wants. There are no rules. No rhyme or reason." Carver helped Jack back onto the stool. "It's a lot to take in, I know."

"Why me?"

Carver shook his head, staring at the ground. "There's no *why*, Jack. There just *is*. This was your fate, your fork in the road. You changed it temporarily, but our meeting again was inevitable. Unfortunately, I need to make things right."

"So you arranged all this?"

"As I said, it's my job, and you were my charge. I had a responsibility to come get you."

Jack stood and leaned on Carver's shoulder. "You sent me the boy, Jack Morgan, to show me the story in the journal, didn't you? To show me the author's name, Graham Carver, and that he knew everything about what happened to me in Spring Valley. Once I had your name, I'd learn you were the carousel maker, and I would come find you."

"Well, the boy was The Tar's idea." Carver folded his arms and chuckled. "But you couldn't remember my last name."

"Story of my life."

"Jack Morgan liked the book you gave him, by the way."

Jack rolled his eyes. *Good to know my fans are overzealous cops or the dead.* "You sent me his mother, Ellen, didn't you?"

"Again, The Tar. He had to get the pendant into Sam's possession."

Jack tilted his head.

"To facilitate her journey. It wasn't Sam's time to go, and if it isn't your time to go, you need an object to get you there." Carver strolled to the carousel and raked a hand across a jumper's mane. "Ellen Morgan's pendant served as Sam's passage to the Underground."

Like a first-class ticket on a doomed steamship. "But why Sam? She had nothing to do with all this."

"I know." Carver pressed his eyes shut. "The Tar needed to get serious with you so you would find me. It's been a long time, and he's grown impatient."

"And what about Morgan, did you take her, too?"

"Certain families go together. Like mine all those years ago. But Morgan's a different story altogether, Jack. You should know that."

"What do you mean?"

Carver hesitated and bit his lip. "It doesn't matter, Jack. The point is, you have little choice but to honor your agreement."

He rubbed his temples. "Jack and Ellen Morgan rode your carousel all those years ago, didn't they?"

Carver shrugged.

"I know it's true. I saw you in a picture. You were there. How come I didn't see you there that night?"

"Because the carousel wasn't yours to see."

"People see what they want to see, right?" Jack scuffed his foot against the floor. "I never should have given Sam the pendant."

"You never should have visited Mr. Morgan, either. After he saw the jewelry on Sam, he put two and two together. The police don't seem happy with you, either."

"Yeah, thanks for that!" Jack threw his arms in the air.

Carver held his palms up. "This isn't my doing, Jack. But regardless, now you have nothing in your world to return to. If you ignore your responsibility to my employer and leave your loved ones to serve the penance, you're going to prison. Too many fingers pointing at you."

"Leave my family in hell?" Jack worked his jaw. "How could you think I'd do that?"

"I don't." Carver waved his hand. "But the pendant gives you no choice but to go back with me."

"Will going with you save my family?"

Carver hesitated. "That's not up to me."

Jack stood and paced the barn's wooden floors. He pressed his face against a window, gazing at the past world and its long-dead participants going about their business.

"Listen, Carver, what happened—"

"Call me Graham," he chimed in. "We should really be on a first-name basis after all this time."

Great. Just what I need. Getting chummy with the River Styx ferryman.

"You see, we're connected." Carver moved to the window and leaned a hand against the wooden pane. "It's why you see me sometimes. It's the reason you can spy on my family and me. It's the reason I see you."

"Connected, huh?" Jack's gaze dropped to his feet.

"Why do you suppose you live here? Just a few miles from Cottage City."

Jack spun from the window, deep fissures fanning out between his eyebrows.

"Of all the world's places you could have lived, you chose to live just miles from the country's oldest carousel. The machine I designed and built."

"Then it's not a coincidence?"

Carver shook his head. "You're drawn to carousels, always have been. But you never understood why?"

"My doctor would say it's a psychological desire to return to my childhood or to avoid dealing with the guilt of my father's death. Maybe you're not real at all."

Carver smirked. "You don't believe that, though, do you?"

Jack shifted his weight from one foot to the other. "What happened to me, Carver . . . when I was with . . ."

"The Tar?"

"God, even the name is disgusting."

"I'm not sure, Jack. I don't really talk to him." Carver dug his thumbnail into the sill's soft wood, carving out a tiny half-moon. "He tells me what he needs, and I do it for him. We haven't been on the best terms since you got away. He's been angry I haven't been able to get you back."

"Why didn't he just come for me?"

Carver pushed himself from the window and strolled to the carousel, hoisting himself onto the platform. "The Tar can't come here. There are rules. He's stuck in his place, and we're stuck in ours. But he can still tell me what he wants."

"Wait. . . you don't see him, and you don't talk to him. How does he tell you what he wants?"

Carver pressed his hands to his temples. "The pounding against my skull. You've sensed it for years. You sensed it when you came at me. The pounding tells you The Tar wants something from you."

As a young man, Jack figured he had a clot in his head, an aneurysm, or some malignancy nestled in his gray matter pulsing in time with his heartbeat. What else could it be? Nothing else could explain the pain. The throbbing. Day after day. If only it could have been that simple. Something the docs could have gone in and yanked out, snipped, or tied off, giving him instant relief from the constant pounding. Instead, The Tar had been reaching out the only way he could.

"For me, the pounding tells me it's time to meet a client. So I drive, and I let my car take me where it's supposed to go. Sometimes I go to sleep and my car takes me there. And when I get there, the client shows up. Don't ask me to explain."

"And what does the pounding tell me?"

"That's for The Tar to reveal."

"Why don't you walk away from all this?"

Carver waved a hand. "I have a territory I work as part of my nego-tiation with The Tar. If I meet my quota, I take one more step closer to satisfying my agreement. Come, let's take a walk." Carver jumped from the platform. He led Jack by the elbow and swung open the barn door.

As Jack descended the steps, the roar of Oak Bluffs swelled in his head. Cottage City melted before his eyes. The Island Queen ferry's horn blasted as island hoppers waved from the upper decks at the tourists promenading about the harbor. Cars filled the streets in a desperate crawl as pedestrians dashed from shop to shop along Oak Bluffs Avenue. Engine exhaust and fried food aromas filled the pungent air as music blared from the taverns and bars. Jack glanced at the suddenly aged man beside him, silver hair pulled back in a tight ponytail. Carver lowered himself down the wooden stairs, holding the rail for support. He treaded on unsteady legs with short, choppy strides to keep his balance.

Carver gazed about the town and frowned. "Mercy, what's become of this place? A wasteland of excess, overconsumption, and all those goddamn T-shirt shops. How I miss the place I once called home. The downside to living forever."

The men strode along Lake Avenue toward the harbor.

"Tell me how I escaped The Tar."

Carver shook his head. "I don't know the specifics of your agreement, but you must not have followed through, or The Tar wouldn't be after you. He may have let you go, expecting you to keep up your end of the bargain, but you must have decided to take your chances. As time passed, the trauma of meeting him and witnessing the Underground blocked out your memories and left a void filled with—"

"Carousel nightmares and hallucinations," Jack said. "Visions of me galloping into the Underground."

"You had doctors telling you everything happening to you was all in your head. But deep down, you knew everything happening was real."

Jack swiped the moisture from his forehead. "It's time to pay the piper, is that it?"

"You don't have any more wiggle room. It isn't pleasant for anyone's loved ones in the Underground. And you can't stay in your world unless you want to end up in a jail cell. The Tar has you by the short-and-curl-ies, as they say across the pond."

Jack folded his arms. "What do I do?"

"You need to go home. Back to the cornfield in Spring Valley. That's your carousel. That's where you enter. I can meet you there."

"Why can't I jump on the one here?" He pointed toward the Flying Horses.

"That's not how it works. Your carousel is in a cornfield in Missouri, and as long as it's functioning, that's your ride."

Jack dropped onto a bench facing the harbor, a salty breeze cooling the sweat on his heated brow. "Tell me about your arrangement with The Tar."

Carver eased himself onto the bench beside Jack. "Work for him, and I get to be with Anna and the children one day. I keep doing the job, holding out hope to meet my quota and reunite with my Anna, and with Zachariah and Rebecca, in a better place." He blinked and turned away. "That's why I do this."

"A better place?" *How many times am I going to hear that phrase?* "You mean heaven?"

Carver hitched his shoulders. "Anywhere but the Underground is a better place."

The Tar had Carver between a rock and a hard place as well. Had him by the balls. Still, his just-following-orders excuse didn't sit too well with Jack when it came to Sam and Morgan. "I feel like punching you in the face, but at the same time, I'm sorry about your family."

"I don't blame you." Carver stood on rickety legs. "Let's get you back to your car. You need to go home. Take some time and get yourself ready."

Jack rose from the bench, a sense of urgency pulling at him as he pictured his family stuck in the Underground. "Let's go. I'm ready now."

"Patience, Jack," Carver said. "I have other clients to meet, and it takes a few days' travel. I can meet you at the cornfield within the week. But listen to me. You need to get yourself ready, and not just for the trip. You only have a few days to finalize things, get your affairs in order."

"My affairs—?" Jack paused. He glanced at Carver, who gave him a weak grin. The weight of his simple action stooped Jack's shoulders and left him as deflated as a New England Patriots football on game day.

Reality set in. Carver had just told him he wouldn't be returning from the Underground.

PART THREE

the Descent

CHAPTER TWENTY-THREE

Edgartown, Massachusetts (Martha's Vineyard)

By the following afternoon, Jack had done all he could do to get his affairs in order. Of course, Jack's definition of affairs differed from Carver's. He hadn't been sorting documents, putting his financial papers in order, or providing instructions on his final wishes. Instead, Jack had initiated a detailed inventory of his liquor cabinet, starting with his best scotch whiskies as he watched *Predators & Prey* on Animal Planet.

He didn't give a damn about his worldly affairs anymore. Fuck it—let Hal sort it all out. Jack's time was up, and fate would soon snuff out his natural life the way the slow-motion crocodiles on TV picked off the weak and old river crossers.

"Wildebeests," Jack muttered, shaking his head and pouring another burning scotch down his throat. "The Spam of the Serengeti."

Jack chuckled at the idea of his agent and friend trying to locate anything in his packrat record-keeping style. Or attempting to decipher anything he might locate in oddly labeled computer files only Jack understood, or in shoe boxes filled with papers, receipts, and major appliance instructions and warranty cards.

Pouring himself another two fingers of Glenfiddich—fuck it, make it three fingers—Jack picked up his cell. He had a habit of calling Sam when he drank too much at Hal's or one of his old college buddy's houses and wouldn't be driving home. He would ramble on and on, and she would listen for as long as he would talk. She had always been his ear, and even if she couldn't hear him tonight, Jack needed to believe she could. He needed normalcy in an abnormal situation. He tapped her name on the phone icon as he gazed at the wildlife slaughter happening on his big screen. The call went to voicemail, but Jack still went along with the charade.

"Hiya, Sam." He glanced at his glass. "It's been a three-finger day, many times over. I've been thinking about something, how unfair it is to know when your last days of life are upon you. Like, remember on our drive up to Nova Scotia right before Morgan was born, we had that long talk about if you could find out the exact date of your death, would you want to know?" Listening to his voice, Jack noted the pronounced slur in his words. "You wanted to know, but I always thought no one should know that. There would be too much to do to get ready. But do you know what really happens? What you actually do to prepare? Nothing. You don't phone anyone to say goodbye, leave behind notes or explanations, or eat every Double Stuf Oreo cookie in the bag. You do the same goddamn things you did when you figured you had another forty years. You eat breakfast, watch nature shows, brush your teeth, load the dishwasher, and separate the paper and plastic recycling . . . as if it mattered anymore." Jack swirled the caramel-colored fluid in his glass and took a sizeable gulp. "The only thing different is the eighty-proof liquid analgesic makes its appearance earlier in the day with no guilt attached."

As Jack contemplated the mundane response to his approaching demise, his cell phone buzzed with another call. For a moment, his heart twitched, thinking Sam had called to argue her point again, like she had from the passenger seat all those years ago. He still remembered the trip, how he couldn't find his license at the border and was in danger of having to turn around until one of the Border Service Officers recognized him from the back flap of the paperback in his hand. He and Sam joked that he could be a real asset to any terrorist organization. Just sign books and pose for a Polaroid at any border and he was in. They got into one of those laughing fits that lasted all the way to Nova Scotia.

Jack swiped the screen to answer the call.

"Hi, Jack? This is Sasha . . . Sasha Kohl?"

Jack squeezed his eyes shut, trying to place the name or the voice. It wasn't just the last name he couldn't remember this time. "Hi, Sasha, how are you?"

"I'm freaking out a bit, Jack. Sam gave me your number in case I couldn't get hold of her."

He still had no idea. "What did you need to get hold of her for?"

"For the trip. To pick her up at LAX."

Oh, shit! Now he remembered. "Of course, sorry."

Sasha Kohl. Hollywood. Sam had only introduced her to Jack once before, during *Road Rage* filming. But he didn't remember much about her. He had been in vigorous pursuit of Sam at the time. Every other face and name from the period blended into a nondescript, featureless amalgam he labeled "Sam's friends" and stored in a place he didn't often unpack.

"Sam texted the other night with the itinerary. When I went to pick her up at the airport today and she never arrived, I got concerned. I tried to call her, but her phone keeps going to voicemail." An urgency rose in Sasha's voice. "Tell me you know what happened to her. Tell me she missed the plane and she's home."

"She's here . . . I was . . . just talking to her." In the chaos, Jack had completely forgotten people were waiting for Sam in LA. He wasn't prepared for a phone call demanding an explanation. He concentrated on un-slurring his words. "My apologies, Sasha. I should have called you. Sam's sick. She asked me to tell you, but it slipped my mind."

Silence on the line. "That's okay, Jack, but what happened?"

"Um . . ." *Think!* "Food poisoning. No way she could have made the trip."

"Oh my God! I just talked to her yesterday. When did she get sick?"

Jack paused a beat, backtracking to construct a plausible timeline. "Yesterday at lunch, I think. She'll be fine. The doctor said for her to stay in bed and get rest. The usual. These things turn around in time."

"Can you put her on? I want to give her my best."

"She's been asleep for a while. I really don't want to wake her up. She needs all the rest she can get right now."

"I understand. Food poisoning is a bitch. I got it a few years ago in this brand-new boujie LA restaurant. What strain was it?"

The wheels spun inside his head, picking up speed. "Um . . . I'm guessing E. coli. That's the one with meat, right?"

"It can be . . . didn't the doctor tell you anything?"

Jack rubbed his forehead. "Yeah. I'm sure he said something about E. coli." *Is she buying this?*

Another lengthy hesitation. "Did they give her antibiotics?"

"Um . . . I can't remember exactly what the doctor gave us. She's fine, though. If you call her back tomorrow, I'm sure she'll tell you all about it."

"Okay . . . thanks, Jack. I'm sorry about all this. I was looking forward to seeing her."

"She wanted to see you, too, and I know she doesn't want you to worry. Call back in the morning. Good talking to you, Sasha." Jack disconnected.

That was fucked up.

He leaned back on the sofa and grabbed the remote, raising the volume. One clearly doomed wildebeest leaped over a crocodile's gnashing maw and somehow made it across the river, giving him hope.

He poured himself another Glenfiddich. He didn't worry about the fingers.

CHAPTER TWENTY-FOUR

Edgartown, Massachusetts (Martha's Vineyard)

Jack had little trouble getting to sleep that night. Truth was, he didn't remember getting into bed at all. The spirits had left his body relaxed and his brain a bit fuzzy, but his recurring dream remained vivid and detailed.

He was back at Lady of the Lord church in Spring Valley, holding hands with Sam and Morgan as their footfalls echoed along the tile leading to the somber altar. Jack set the pace, slowing his steps to avoid reaching the altar too quickly and having to open the casket. He understood he had to, but he didn't want to witness his younger self flushed with embalming fluid in a suit he had never worn before. He glanced at Morgan beside him, her tiny hand folded gently in his own. His heart swelled with love for her in a way he hadn't expected, as if she had been away for a long time. He peeked at Sam, hoping she might know where Morgan had been. But she didn't acknowledge him, pulling her dark veil over her face and continuing toward the altar.

By now, the cries of mourners filled the church. He could smell the aromatic incense rising from the metal censer as the priest swung the silver sphere back and forth against a chain. The sun streamed through the stained-glass windows, leaving a multicolored light pattern on the opposite wall. As he strolled past his dead father kneeling in a pew, Jack turned, keeping the man in his vision and hoping he would glance at him just once. But the old man didn't acknowledge him. Jack wanted to say he was sorry for what happened on the farm that day. But he wasn't sorry at all.

Sam, Jack, and Morgan approached the casket. He tried to halt his steps, but his feet kept moving, inching him closer and closer toward his casket. He released Morgan's hand and reached for the lid, throwing it open and gazing inside. As he lifted Morgan into his arms, she began to cry, wrapping her arms around him and burying her face in his neck.

Jack jerked awake on Sam's side of the bed as the dream splintered, giving way to daylight streaming through the window. He clutched her pillow against his chest. Despite the grog-induced throbbing in his temples, Jack relished a moment of peace, Sam's lingering presence, and a faint whiff of her scent on the pillow. But when he rolled over, he sensed an unbearable heaviness pressing against him. A foreboding that life as he knew it had ended. In a few hours, he would get on a plane and take what would most likely be his final trip to Missouri. And then on to the Underground. He would be meeting The Tar, on whose agreement he had reneged, and who he had pissed off for a quarter century.

Probably wouldn't be a very friendly meet and greet.

A low groan escaped his lips as he imagined his family in that hellish place. Sam and Morgan now served a sentence for the twenty-five additional years he'd stolen, paying the price for the extra serving of gravy poured over a life that should have ended back in a Missouri field. Jack squeezed his eyes shut, unable to shake the images of Sam in the bed beside him and the way they used to be. Talking, making plans, sleeping with limbs entwined and hands clasped while the salt air filtered through the open window. Sometimes, when Jack woke early, he would watch her sleep from the safety of his pillow, sending his heart on a jazz-filled riff. He would take in all her familiar details at once: the curl of her fingers on the bedsheets, her blond hair tickling her shoulders, and the rhythmic pull of air into her lungs until Morgan's precious off-key warble penetrated the bedroom wall and forced a foggy stroll along the dawn-lit hallway.

Jack sensed the maelstrom erupting inside him moments before he bolted from the bed and tore the sheets and comforter off the mattress. "This can't be happening."

He balled up the bedding and hurled it against the wall, then upended the mattress and bed frame. Dropping to his knees, he sensed the dizziness creep over him, a hint of scotch-flavored bile rising in his throat.

He glanced about the room. This place was his life, goddammit, not some stinking underground firepit. This was *his* better place, and now he would have to go to hell to either give it up or get it back. He needed a plan, and he only had a few days to come up with something. Soon he would face Carver in the Johnsons' cornfield. There would be little time for questions, but he had to tap the man's brain and find a way to escape the Underground with his family intact. If The Tar had a weakness, only Carver could help him find it.

Jack stumbled to the bathroom and vomited until pinpricks of light danced around his head. He leaned under the sink faucet and rinsed his mouth, his abdominal muscles aching from the violent spasms. As he straightened and gained his equilibrium, the doorbell chimed.

Jack checked himself in the mirror, noting how the bathroom fixtures highlighted the silver flecks peppering the growth on his face. His hair stuck out at various angles, and the rumpled clothes he had slept in gave him a desperate man's appearance.

A man at the end of his rope.

Jack used his hands to rub the wrinkles from his clothes. As he picked up a hairbrush, the doorbell rang a second time. He inspected himself again and tossed it back into the drawer. "Fuck it."

Trudging down the steps, Jack gripped the banister for support. He peeked through the peephole at the three men outside the door, unsure whether the pit forming in his stomach was another round of nausea from last night or because he recognized them.

"Detectives Stahl and Daniels," Jack announced as he swung the door open. "It's a pleasure to see you again."

"You look like you had a rough night," Stahl said.

"And morning." Even Jack could smell the alcohol leaching from his pores.

A heavyset man stepped forward, hiking his uniform pants above a generous belly. "Mr. Rainne, I'm Brad Maxwell, Edgartown police chief." He pressed a palm against his head, straightening a meticulous combover starting inches above his left ear. "I see you're already acquainted with our BCI detectives."

"We go back aways," Jack said with a smirk. "What is it? A few days now?"

Stahl set his jaw. "Detective Daniels and I are here to serve a warrant for the piece of jewelry we discussed with you earlier. Chief Maxwell is here because this is his jurisdiction." Stahl handed Jack a document.

"Since you have not produced the piece, this warrant, signed by the Barnstable County Superior Court Judge, gives us the right to search the premises."

The three stepped into the foyer.

"Listen, detectives." Jack held his hands up. "The piece isn't here. My wife has it, and she's gone."

"That's strange." Daniels fixed Jack with a lengthy glare. "She wasn't here the other day either."

Jack worked his jaw. "And?"

"Well, that's another problem we have, Mr. Rainne," Maxwell began. "We received a troubling call late last night from a woman in Los Angeles." He checked his notepad. "A Ms. Sasha Kohl. She was supposed to meet your wife yesterday at the airport. She never showed up."

Jack stood silent.

"Can we talk about it while the detectives perform their search?"

Jack folded his arms. "What do you want to know?"

Maxwell gestured to Stahl and Daniels, who fanned out in opposite directions. Stahl entered the kitchen while Daniels mounted the steps to the upper floors.

Maxwell hoisted his sagging trousers. "Well, for starters, where she is."

Jack shifted his weight from one foot to the other. "Truth is, I don't know."

"Ms. Kohl told me you said your wife had food poisoning. I suspect if that were true, she would be upstairs right now?"

"Listen, my wife . . . Sam . . . she left me. I didn't want to air my dirty laundry to someone over the phone."

"Ms. Kohl was aware of your dirty laundry. She told me your wife was planning to initiate divorce proceedings."

Jack lowered his head. *Oh, Sam.*

"Was that news to you, Mr. Rainne? Or did she tell you and you didn't like how it sounded?"

The veins pulsed in Jack's neck. "What the hell is that supposed to mean?"

"Hey, Chief." Stahl's voice echoed from the kitchen.

Maxwell raised his index finger and advanced toward the kitchen. "Don't move." He eyed Jack as Stahl spoke to him in hushed tones.

When they finished their discussion, Maxwell joined Jack in the foyer. "Mr. Rainne. Detective Stahl may have found possible evidence of blood in the back area of the house." He pointed. "We're treating this finding as if a crime occurred here."

"What crime?"

Maxwell ignored him. "In addition to the search detailed in the warrant, we're expanding our search under what we call exigent circumstances. That's when—"

"I know what it is," Jack said. "I'm a crime writer, remember? You believe evidence could be destroyed if you leave the premises."

"We can expand the search as well if we believe there's a risk of danger for anyone who might still be in the house."

"You mean my wife and daughter? They're definitely not in the house."

Maxwell used his fingers to run a spot check on his hair. "Well, we're gonna take a good look around anyway."

Daniels appeared on the landing. "Hey, Chief. You wanna come up here a minute?"

Maxwell fixed a hand on Jack's elbow and led him to the stairs. When they reached the bedroom, Daniels stepped in front of Jack and blocked his way. "Got a bit of a temper, don't you, Mr. Rainne?"

Jack glanced through the doorway at the overturned mattress and bedding flung about the bedroom.

"What happened in here?" Maxwell asked.

"My wife and daughter are gone, and I'm a little upset. Is that a crime?"

"Depends," Daniels said.

"Am I under arrest?"

"Not at the moment," Maxwell began, "but blood traces in the kitchen and hallway leading to the bathroom might change that soon."

"Jesus Christ! That's my blood. Sam patched me up there when I went through the glass at the Morgans' Hyannis store. Stahl must have told you all about it."

"I've been briefed, Mr. Rainne."

"Well, I was pretty bloody when I got home!"

"Well then, you shouldn't have anything to worry about," Daniels offered. "As long as it's your blood."

Jack's face fell as he recalled Sam stepping on the broken plate before scampering down the hall to scrub his wounds.

I'm fucked.

"Let's head back downstairs, let Stahl and Daniels do their job up here." Maxwell guided Jack from the room to the staircase. "They're not only first-rate detectives, but they do forensic work as part of their duties with BCI. They'll be collecting biological samples and possible DNA sources from hairbrushes, toothbrushes, those types of things. Then they'll continue their house search for any, um . . . additional evidence."

You mean bodies, don't you?

The pair descended the stairs. "Once they finish here, we can take a trip down to the station and make your statement. We'll ask you not to leave town in case we have any additional questions. You're not under arrest, and you are free to have an attorney present during your statement if you'd like."

Jack grabbed his cell, then pictured Graham Carver waiting for him in the Missouri cornfield beside Johnson Farm. "I don't think I'll be needing a lawyer."

CHAPTER TWENTY-FIVE

Excerpt from *Blood on the Sabbath*, by Jack Rainne:

Father Mike Bishop strode down St. Thomas Parish's center aisle past the rows of wooden pews as his sermon reached a crescendo. He wasn't the type of priest who hid behind a lectern, whispering into a microphone. He exercised the booming voice God had gifted him.

"Just as Jesus was tempted by Satan in Matthew 4:8, offering all the kingdoms of the world if he renounced his faith in God"—he paused for effect—"your faith will be tested in this life."

Father Mike retreated toward the altar. "Temptation will come in many forms." He counted off on his fingers. "The seduction of power, fame, money, sex. Worldly desires for which we end up relinquishing God and ultimately our souls."

The priest snatched the Bible from the lectern and raised it above his head, gazing about the church at his rapt parishioners. "When you are faced with this choice, will you stay committed to your faith? Only when the tempter comes will you understand your devotion to God."

After the service ended and Father Mike had shaken hands and bid farewell to his congregation, he retreated to the sacristy to remove his vestments and reflect on his sermon. Satan had dangled much before him to test his faith, and it showed on his face. But at every turn, the priest had stayed true to his sacred vows. He glanced in the mirror and inspected the man he had become. Grooves zig-zagged through the sagging skin, and his forehead assumed more real estate than he remembered. He muttered a curse as he combed his hair forward with his fingers.

Leaving the sacristy, Father Mike stood before the altar. He marveled at the exposed wooden beams running the church ceiling's entire length and the Stations of the Cross embedded within the stained-glass windows. He missed the old wooden confessionals that once graced the walls along each aisle. The Catholic church had gentrified Confession with the term Reconciliation, deciding that meeting face to face with each sinner rather than behind a screen upgraded the church's stodgy image. But Mike preferred the latter instead of having to provide the obligatory head nod or hand on the shoulder thing. Father Mike loved being a priest, but no doubt was an old-school Catholic. He was an "and also with you," not an "and with your spirit" kind of guy. But don't get him started on that.

He glanced toward the Reconciliation Room and spotted a young man seated in the adjacent pew. He appeared to be in his twenties, long hair swept behind his ears. Father Mike didn't recognize him, either from parish services or earlier Reconciliation sessions. The man had one arm over the seat back while he scrolled through his phone with the other. Father Mike shook his head. Back when St. Thomas Parish had kneelers, people waiting for confession would rest on their knees in contrition. He had to remind today's sinners that trolling for prayer emojis on Facebook wasn't a step in the process.

"I'm afraid you've gotten the days mixed up, my friend. Reconciliation is on Saturday."

"I know." The man's eyes remained glued to his phone.

Father Mike waited.

After a moment, the man slipped the device into his pocket and stood. "I need to make a confession."

The priest checked his watch. "Well, I was about to—"

"It's an emergency."

Father Mike recognized the pain behind the young man's eyes and waved him into the room. He gestured toward the sofa. "What's your name, son?"

The man took a seat, his gaze flitting about the room.

The priest waited. "I'm Father Mike."

"I know who you are." The man raked a hand through his hair. He dropped into his chair. "That leaves me at a disadvantage. I don't know who you—"

"My name's Frankie," he said. "My family used to come here a long time ago."

Father Mike inspected the man, but he couldn't find the resemblance to the father or mother he might have belonged to.

"Bless me, Father, for I have sinned." Frankie made the sign of the cross. "In a big fucking way."

Father Mike frowned. "Please use the appropriate Reconciliation words. If you're not familiar with them, I can help—"

"He's dead, Father," Frankie said.

"Wait." Father Mike leaned forward. "Who's dead?"

"Your friend Danny."

Father Mike scrunched his eyebrows together.

"Guevero?" The young man grinned.

The room darkened at the edge of Father Mike's vision. His labored breath came in gasps as if he had sprinted up a flight of stairs. "Daniel's . . . dead?"

"Had a tough time of it ever since he was a kid, Danny did. This morning, we called it a day."

The priest winced. "Called it a day? What does that mean?"

"I heard you've been helping him out over the years. Helping him get a place to live, buying him things. Sending him money from time to time."

"How do you know all this?"

Frankie stood and paced the floor. "Because I've been watching you."

Father Mike rose to his feet and teetered before steadying himself against the chair. "He's really dead?"

"As a doornail." Frankie shrugged. "And Danny has wanted to die since he was thirteen years old. I just helped him along."

"You did what?"

"Come on, Father." Frankie sprung to his feet. "He had problems he couldn't overcome. Dropped out of school as a teenager. Fell on hard times. He lived in his car, for Chrissake. All I did was ease his suffering. It's like what that guy Kevorkian used to do out in Oregon."

"Daniel wasn't suffering anymore. He was making a life for himself."

"He's been suffering his whole life," Frankie said, pointing his finger. "Ever since my family came to this church twenty years ago."

"I recognize Daniel had it hard. But I tried to help him."

"You? help him?" The muscles in Frankie's jaw rippled as he clenched his teeth. "Don't even . . ."

"Where is he?"

"He didn't show up at work today. Pretty soon the cops are gonna question why one of your gifts is stuck in his chest. You remember, the gold embossed crucifix, tiny jewels along the handle."

A swirling dizziness forced Father Mike into his chair. He stared at the floor, unseeing.

"I whittled the handle. Made it sharp."

Father Mike raised his head. "Why . . . ?"

The grin fell from the young man's face. "Because you saw what happened to my brother. And you didn't say anything."

Father Mike swallowed. "Daniel's your brother? You killed your own–"

"He's been dead for two decades," Frankie said. "No thanks to you. I couldn't stand it anymore, seeing what he had become. He couldn't stand it, either."

Father Mike pressed his eyes shut and fought the images flying at him: little Danny Guevero grinning ear to ear as he donned altar boy robes for his first Sunday mass; Father Stan tousling the boy's thick, blond hair and giving him a big hug after the service; a bespectacled Danny perched in Father Stan's front passenger seat late one evening as the two returned from the church team's basketball practice; Father Stan helping Danny remove his robes after Saturday evening mass, his hands lingering too long on the boy's neck and shoulders; then one day, the sounds coming from behind Father Stan's quarters on the rectory's upper floor, and afterward, a dazed Danny Guevero descending the stairs like a wounded animal; Father Stan's icy glare as he passed the younger priest on the landing. That's when Father Mike knew, but he said nothing. He never said anything.

"I was listening to your sermon today," Frankie said, pacing the floor. "You spoke about how our faith will be tested. Well, I'm gonna find out about your commitment to your faith."

Father Mike rose on unsteady legs. "Let's not worry about my faith right now. You have more to worry about."

"I don't have anything to worry about, Father."

"You killed a man. You've confessed your crime. We need to get you the help—"

"I don't need help." The young man chuckled and folded his arms. "You're the one who's gonna need help. What did you tell the police when they came asking questions twenty years ago?"

Father Mike shuffled to the window. "I don't remember."

"Funny. In the police report, you said you didn't see anything. You didn't hear anything. You had no reason to suspect anything. But your eyes tell a different story. I know those statements weren't true. Your guilt kept you connected with my brother. You needed to help him, justify your silence." Frankie dropped into his chair and crossed his legs at the ankles. "Worked out well for you, it looks like. The church moved Father Stan somewhere else. They promoted you to pastor."

"It never worked out well for me. What happened to Daniel tore me up inside."

"Truth is, we both did something to Danny. You tried to make it up to him over the years. I put him out of his misery."

"Listen, son." Father Mike knelt beside the man's chair and rested his hand on his forearm. "You need to go to the police and tell them what you've done. God will forgive your sins if you are truly sorry—"

"I didn't come here to save my soul, Father." Frankie swatted the priest's hand away.

Father Mike struggled to his feet. "Well, you came here for a reason. You've confessed your sin to me, and I can help you."

"You want to talk about sin? Danny was thirteen years old, for Chrissake. You're the one who needs to confess."

The wall clock ticked behind Father Mike like a hammer, time slowing before his eyes.

"Here's how it's going to play out, Father. Won't be long before the cops show up here. Lots of signs pointing in your direction."

Father Mike pressed his hands to his temples to slow the spinning room. "What signs? I've done nothing but help him over the years."

"Yeah, well, sometimes things don't look that way on paper. You know, things like giving him money, gifts, setting him up in an apartment. Might appear as if he was a kept man." A grin spread across Frankie's face as he circled Father Mike. "Turns out Danny had a journal he kept on his computer, one Danny himself didn't even know about. Tells about how you've helped him for all those years. How you stepped in after Father Stan left and picked up where that pedophile left off."

"That's a lie, and you know it. You need to tell them what you've done, or I'll have to."

Frankie shook his head. "Oh, no. That's not how it works. I've confessed something to you in confidence, and you can't tell anyone. It's like you're my lawyer and we have attorney-client privilege, right?"

Father Mike worked his jaw. "A priest can never reveal what a person confesses. Even if he admits to murder."

"You betray my trust and you've broken the sacred seal of confession. Your bishops and cardinals and all those other guys in long robes would defrock you, kick you out." He gestured about the room. "Danny told me how much this all means to you."

Father Mike said nothing.

"But you have a choice." Frankie pivoted and moved to the window. "The way I see it, there's enough circumstantial evidence to put you away for his murder. Danny's journal has some rather vivid descriptions of your relationship, even if they're not true. I'm sure the cops are reading about it as we speak. I'm sure you left fingerprints over there, too. No doubt, they'll track credit card receipts for the gifts, helping with the rent, even the ornate crucifix sticking out of his chest. Maybe the cops will wonder if you guys had a falling out. Whether Danny was gonna talk. Who knows how they'll play it?"

Father Mike bowed his head. "What do you want from me?"

"You can tell the police I did this and break your vow. Or you can keep quiet and rely on your faith to get you through this. You said it yourself. Your faith will be tested. Well, this is the test. If you turn me in, you're in the clear. But you'll never run a parish or say mass again." After a moment, he faced the priest. "If you stay true to your faith, you take your chances with the criminal justice system. Maybe you're arrested and charged with a crime, maybe you're not. I imagine people will assume you did it, even if you're acquitted. Where there's smoke, there's fire, right? Especially in the Catholic church. The long robes will take you out of commission for a while and move you somewhere remote. But at least you still get to be a priest."

As the young man strode across the room and pushed the door open, spinning blue and red lights bounced across St. Thomas Parish's inner walls. Footsteps grew in volume along the buffed floor as a blue uniformed mass advanced along the center aisle, hands hovering above their weapons.

Frankie grinned. "Your choice, Father."

CHAPTER TWENTY-SIX

St. Louis, Missouri

He hadn't been back to Missouri in a quarter century, but the moment Jack stepped off the plane at St. Louis Lambert International, he remembered why. A stagnant humidity pressed against him and amplified the stifling heat shimmering off the blacktop. Each step advanced him further and further into a furnace, a preview of hell before he even arrived at the carousel. Maybe he would already be acclimated to the heat by the time he made it to the Underground.

Not funny, Jack . . .

As he waited outside the terminal for the shuttle bus to the rental lot, Jack shifted the backpack from his right shoulder to his left, leaving a moist stain. He was sure alarm bells were sounding on the East Coast, alerting all that public enemy number one had left town. But Jack didn't have time to worry about this world's justice. He would face a different type soon enough; one he had never written about in his books but suspected would be worse than he could imagine.

Sweat trickled along his spine and settled along the beltline. Some things about Missouri he would never miss. Living on the East Coast had spoiled him with mild summers, brilliant fall foliage, and cool springs. But he would trade the harsh New England winters for the Show-Me State's milder version any day. That didn't mean he'd had any interest in visiting during the past two decades. Nothing drew him here anymore. Not even the home that held tight his mother's dear memories. When Jack pictured the place, he fought the urge to spiral downward, his father's hellish temper casting a thick shadow across his recollections. He had contemplated burning the place to the ground at one time but had never gotten around to it. He hadn't even bothered to sell. Instead, he took the path of least resistance and abandoned it. By now, the place was either in a colossal state of disrepair, or someone had made it a meth lab. Could be both. He would know for sure soon enough.

Twenty minutes later, Jack manned the diminutive Hyundai—*mid-size, my ass*—and zipped along I-70 west toward Columbia. He had a good hour before the Kingdom City exit. He would stop at Ozarkland for a little fudge—okay, a lot of fudge—before dropping in on his old friend Dr. Lang at Fulton State Hospital. Even after all this time, a final goodbye was in order. Then he would take Route 54 south through Jeff City until he reached home.

Spring Valley, Misery.

That one never failed to get a laugh from the Vineyard folks when he would tell them where he was from, but now it would be truer than ever. As he sped along the highway, Jack scanned the landscape. Things hadn't changed much. More big box stores had moved on, and far too many cell phone outlets, RV dealerships, and gun shops had popped up between the endless miles of cornfields.

Jack grinned at the bumper sticker on the SUV in front of him. *Missouri . . . it's not that bad!* Not exactly the confidence of New Hampshire's *Live Free or Die*, but what can you do?

Veering off Route 54 and onto the business loop, Jack lightened his touch on the gas as he approached Fulton. He checked his watch. Ten minutes until quitting time. His old friend would be expecting him.

He drove along East Fifth, took a left, and eased into Fulton State Hospital's circular drive. Jack gaped at his once temporary home. They had upgraded the exterior with an impressive pavilion-type entranceway, making it appear like a shopping mall from the right angle if you squinted a bit. But the razor wire along the chain-link fence surrounding the perimeter couldn't hide the obvious. The place was a prison for the insane and dangerous, plain and simple. Or a place people went when they had visited hell, and no one believed them. Even the name, Fulton State Hospital, was a euphemism. Pulling out his cell phone, he dialed Lang's number.

A tired voice filtered through the line. "Marcus Lang."

"Dr. Lang. It's Jack . . ." Silence followed, and for a moment he wasn't sure Lang recognized his voice. "Jack Rainne."

"Of course, my most famous ex-patient. I'm sorry, it's been a hectic day. Heading out now. Where are you?"

Jack could picture Lang's shoes moving along the sterile hallways' tiled floors, mirroring the echoing footfalls filtering through the phone's speaker. "I'm in the parking lot checking out the place."

"A stroll down memory lane," Lang said with a chuckle. "I'm honored you would include our humble Missouri vacation destination on your travel itinerary."

"I didn't come back to see the hospital, trust me."

Lang stepped through the facility's front door and shuffled along the sidewalk hugging the building's exterior. Jack swung the Hyundai around and intercepted him as he hit the parking lot. He lowered the passenger side window and flashed the doctor a wide grin.

Lang leaned forward and rested his elbows across the open window. "It's been a long time, my friend." He reached a hand to Jack, who grabbed it. "Time has been good to you."

"You too, Doc." Jack wasn't sure he believed it. A quarter century could be good to you at age seventeen, but a similar period wasn't as forgiving as you aged. Lang must have been in his forties when Jack first met him. Now, the man's frame had the shape and stoop of someone whose prime was a distant view in life's rearview mirror, something even Lang's new suit couldn't camouflage. His scalp showed through his graying, cropped mane, and the mottled skin beneath his neck hung from his jaw like frosting off the edge of a cake.

Turtles and bullfrogs.

Lang used to joke that with age, every man eventually resembled either a turtle or a bullfrog. The two had once laughed together at Lang's theory, but the man had clearly moved into lily pad territory.

"You wanna grab a beer?" Jack asked. "Do you have time before you need to get home to the missus?"

Lang forced a partial grin. "I don't have to worry about time anymore, Jack. Angie passed about a year ago."

Shit. "I'm sorry." Jack cursed himself for being out of touch.

He patted Jack's arm. "It's okay. I'm happy to put off going home to an empty house. Even if it means spending time with you."

"I'll take that as a compliment."

"Get out of the car, Jack. There's a place on Fifth and Market just a couple blocks up. We can walk." Lang tapped the window frame with an open hand. "Come on, it's a nice evening."

Fifteen minutes later, Jack and Lang nursed a pair of sweating lagers in the Fulton Tap & Grill's high-back wooden booth. With a chorus of hellos and waves as he arrived, the doctor had a small following. It dawned on Jack he had never witnessed the doctor outside the confines of his office. It could be he had always been popular at the places he frequented. But the months of therapy had taught Jack the doctor's solitary nature. He suspected Lang only spent time here to distract him from the empty home he would return to each day. At 5:00 p.m., the bar's lights had already dimmed above the sparse crowd, and Al Green's honey-sweet vocals oozed from an old-fashioned Wurlitzer.

"I'm sorry about Angie, Dr. Lang. I remember the photo of her on your desk. Seemed like she was in the room with us during all our sessions."

Lang smirked. "You're lucky she wasn't. You think I was a hard ass? She wouldn't have let you get away with half the shit you pulled with me."

"So, if she was my doctor, I'd have been cured and out of there sooner?"

"Nah." Lang scrunched his face. "We'd have slowed her down. More billable hours that way."

Jack smiled and took a pull from his bottle. "Can I ask what happened?"

"We got older, Jack." He lifted the bottle to his lips but didn't drink. "Shit happens to older people."

"Isn't that why people retire? Enjoy life a bit."

"Some people, I guess."

Jack tilted his head. "Why do you keep at it?"

Lang dropped his shoulders. "There isn't much else for me to do now. Angie and me, we planned to buy one of those motorhomes. Sell the house and hit the road, you know?" Lang took a sip from his Beck's and swirled the bottle with his fingers. "Had the make and model all picked out. We were heading to Camping World in Columbia to pick it up when she felt the lump underneath her arm. We ended up at Columbia Hospital instead. She went pretty quick afterward."

Jack recognized the two had at least one thing in common. The life they had expected, they no longer had. Unfortunately for both, one wouldn't be alive much longer and the other would. "That's a tough break. I'm sorry."

Lang forced another grin.

The server came by and dropped a basket of chips and a salsa carafe onto the table before darting off to relieve her tray's burden at the next booth. Lang poured a salsa glop into a bowl and scooped a dripping tortilla chip into his mouth.

"Hadn't heard much from you in a couple years. I assumed things were okay until I received a call from a Cape Cod detective."

Jack pressed his lips together. "Yeah. Sorry they had to bother you with all that. They have some hair-brained idea I might know about a cold case from twenty years ago. A woman and her son disappeared from a county fair. They haven't had any new direction to pursue since they took over the file." Jack took a pull from his bottle. "They're reaching for anything."

Lang assumed his doctorly manner. "Tell me more about it."

"A bunch of coincidences, that's all. I had been asking around, inquiring about the case. By dumb luck, someone had a photo showing I was there the night it happened."

Lang raised an eyebrow and leaned back against the booth cushion.

"It's nothing, Dr. Lang. I was a college kid on the Cape, hanging out with friends and looking for girls at the fair. Hundreds of people on the Cape were there that night. Just circumstantial stuff they needed to ask me about."

"County fair? Would this have anything to do with—"

"Carousels?" Jack offered.

"Sounds like we might be right back where we were twenty-five years ago."

"No offense, Doc, but that's where I've always been. I can't seem to shake the past."

Lang flagged down the server. "Jack?" He pointed to his bottle.

"I'll have another. Thanks."

Lang held up two fingers. She returned with two sweating bottles and retrieved the empties from the table.

"The detective told me something else, Jack. Something about a piece of jewelry you had that belonged to the missing woman. Is that true?"

"It's another one of those coincidences that looks bad, but it doesn't mean I killed anybody."

"Then what are you doing in Missouri? Not running from anything, are you?"

Jack held up his hands. "Can't I come back to my hometown if I want?"

"Of course, you can. But the timing seems a bit odd." Lang pushed away the basket of chips and wiped his hands. "I mean, when's the last time you were here?"

"The day I left for college. But it's time to see about the property. Maybe sell it."

Lang leaned back. "You could have done that with a phone call."

Jack sighed. "I came home to take care of some business I should have taken care of a long time ago. And maybe I wanted to say hello to an old friend."

Lang hesitated. "Sounds more like you might be saying goodbye."

"Maybe."

Jack gazed at the man across the table. This meeting, this beer, *would* be his farewell to his friend. Jack was about to disappear off the Earth, and he wanted Lang to know whatever he heard about him wasn't true. He didn't care about what anyone else suspected, but for some reason, Lang's opinion still mattered. And if he couldn't bring his family back, their disappearance at the hands of a crime writer would make the news, especially one implicated in the disappearance of a mother and son twenty years earlier. That part would give it legs. *Unsolved Mysteries, Dateline, 20/20.* No doubt it would end up a nine-part series on Hulu or Netflix. Jack had to tell Lang that, as a doctor, the man had done everything he could. But more importantly, he had to tell Lang that, as a friend, the man hadn't failed him, either.

He also had to come clean.

"Listen, Doc." Jack leaned forward on his elbows. "I wanted to see you and let you know I'm okay. No matter what people tell you or how things appear. What I'm going to tell you might seem to erase all the progress I made with you throughout the years. But I've never been saner in my entire life."

Jack detailed the extraordinary occurrences that had happened to him: meeting the missing Jack and Ellen Morgan, finding Graham Carver in Marsha Mason's photographs, meeting the young Carver at the carousel in nineteenth-century Oak Bluffs, and losing Sam and Morgan to the Underground as ransom for his debt to The Tar. Jack explained that he had come to Missouri to rescue his family, and the only way to get them back was to hitch a ride on his carousel at Johnson Farm.

"Morgan's there, too?"

"She's waiting for me." He paused, anticipating Lang's response, but the man only sipped his beer. "You didn't believe me twenty-five years ago, and you don't believe me now."

Lang drained the last of his beer and set the empty on the table. "Remember what I told you when you were a teenager? It doesn't matter what I believe. It matters what you believe."

Lang waved the server over and pressed a wad of cash into her palm. He gave her a wink as he rose from his seat. "Come on, Jack. I want to show you something in my office."

Jack emptied his beer and slid from the booth. "I spent a lifetime trying to get away from that place. Are you really gonna make me go back?"

"It'll only take a minute."

Jack squinted and grabbed his sunglasses as the two stepped into daylight. Fulton State Hospital loomed before him like a haunted mansion from a horror film. His gut screamed at him to turn around, and he could picture people shouting, "Don't go in there!" as they threw their Milk Duds at the screen. But if Lang had something to show him, he would go.

As they entered the building, Lang directed Jack through the labyrinthine network of double doors, checkpoints, corridors, and stairwells until they reached his office. When Lang opened the door, Jack stood face to face with his past. The room hadn't changed much, and he could have sworn he had traveled back through time.

"Have a seat, Jack."

Jack glanced about the office. Everything from the faux-leather sofa to the massive oak desk to the venetian blinds remained exactly as he had last seen them. "I see you've kept up with the times. Going for a retro look by pure laziness?"

"State budgets." Lang threw his keys on the desk. "What can you do?"

Jack lowered himself onto the sofa.

Lang seated himself on the edge of his desk. "I won't lie, Jack. I'm worried about you."

"Don't be."

"Whenever you have great stress or guilt about things, you start seeing carousels again."

"But now I know it's real. I have a picture of it."

Lang rubbed his chin. "And where is this photographic evidence?"

Jack shrugged. "I don't have it with me, but I can show it to you. When I get back from where I'm going."

"Do you remember when we first met?"

Jack raised his eyebrows. "You think I could forget being committed to this place?"

"Your father had just died. You were behaving irrationally. Even you admitted that. You were carrying an incredible burden of guilt over his death. We spent hours uncovering the truth behind your visions and hallucinations. And you got better, didn't you?"

"I did." Jack glanced at his friend. "I had a good doctor."

"Sam got in touch with me last year." Lang circled his desk. "Told me you weren't adjusting well to . . . things."

"She did?" Jack pressed his fingertips into his palms.

"She said you had grown distant and even stopped writing. She told me you spent most days sleeping." Lang seated himself in his desk chair. "She promised to have you call me, maybe even fly out to see me. But I never heard from you."

"We've been trying to work things out between us."

Lang leaned forward, resting his elbows on the desk. "It's understandable. Considering the circumstances."

"Sam and I had been on autopilot for too long, focusing on Morgan and not keeping each other front and center. You need to do that in a marriage."

"Why do you suppose Morgan became the focus?"

Jack shook his head. "She demands a lot of attention. She's a little firebrand."

"Like her mom, right?"

"Gonna look exactly like her when she grows up." Jack swallowed the emotion rising in his voice.

"Well, thank God for that. Can you imagine the alternative?"

Jack chuckled. "You never failed to get a laugh from me, Doc. You haven't changed at all."

"You must not be looking at me too closely." Lang combed his fingers through his thinning mane. "Tell me more about Morgan."

"Well, she stays in her room a lot, doesn't see her friends as much as she used to. She may sense something's wrong with Sam and me. She also thinks her mother doesn't have time for her anymore." Jack squeezed his eyes shut. "It bothers her."

"But you give her time, right?"

"All the time. I'm always in her room."

"Do you agree with Morgan? Is Sam pulling away from her somehow?"

"I do, I guess. She wants to go back to Hollywood and get back into the scene." Jack raked both hands through his hair. "I don't understand how she could do that right now."

Lang stood and paced the carpet. "Well, Sam has a life to live, doesn't she?"

"I guess so."

"And what about you?"

Jack waved his hand. "Look at this—you have me spilling my guts like I'm still your patient."

"Bet you didn't see that coming." Lang gave Jack a wink. "Let me ask you a question, though. It's about a dream you were having. Sam told me about it. Do you know the one?"

"You're familiar with all my dreams, Dr. Lang. I've been telling them to you for over twenty-five years."

"That's true, but this one you never had the chance to talk to me about. It started a little over a year ago." Lang glanced upward as if trying to remember. "You're walking with Sam and Morgan down the aisle of a church . . ."

"I know the one," Jack said, wagging a finger. "But I can never get to the end of it. I wake up every time."

"Sam told me you *did* get to the end of it. The first time you had the dream, you told her about it."

"Doc, I just told you I've come back to Missouri to ride the carousel again. To go back to hell to pay my debt to the devil and hopefully rescue my family." Jack stood. "Why are we talking about a dream Sam mentioned a year ago?"

"Because it's important. And I told you I had something to show you."

"Then show me!"

Lang held out his palms. "I will, I will. After you answer my question."

"Tell you about the dream, huh?" Jack moved to the window and gazed out across the walled compound. "Well, I'm walking toward the front of a church. It's my old parish in Spring Valley. I'm holding hands with Sam and Morgan. I'm attending my own funeral, Doc. That's all the dream is. There's a casket up near the altar, and my high school friends are crying in the pews. Even my father is there. When I get to the casket, I let go of Morgan's hand and I open the casket. I pick her up and she starts to cry." Jack spun from the window. "That's all I remember. No big deal. Don't people dream of their own funeral sometimes? Especially if they've already been to hell?"

"What happens, Jack? Do you see yourself in the casket?"

He scratched his head. "I don't remember."

"Yeah, you do. Think."

Jack squeezed his eyes shut, trying to roll the film in his mind. "I got nothing."

Lang stepped behind his desk and rifled through his lower desk drawer. "Jack, I want you to read something," he said, handing Jack a newspaper. Leading him back to the sofa, Lang lowered himself onto the seat beside him.

Jack focused his eyes on the *Cape Cod Times* article dated over a year ago. His author headshot graced the newspaper's front page. His mouth moved as he read the opening sentence.

"Read it to me, Jack."

Jack cleared his throat. "*In what Edgartown police are calling a 'tragic accident,' writer Jack Rainne's daughter, Morgan, 10, died yesterday—*"

Jack burst to his feet. "What is this?" His breathing labored as his voice trailed off. The newspaper clipping slipped from his hand and fluttered to the ground.

Lang picked it up. ". . . *Jack Rainne's daughter, Morgan, 10, died yesterday after drowning in the family's swimming pool. It is believed she was sleepwalking when the incident occurred.*"

Jack's heart lurched in his chest and his vision darkened, as if someone had reached out and snapped off the lights. The air thickened like a rag smothering his face. He wobbled and fell to his knees. In an instant, the dream played out in his head. He pictured the altar and the mahogany casket resting on the fabric-draped bier. But it couldn't be his casket; he would never fit inside. Jack rubbed his eyes to stop the images from coming, but to no avail. He had released Morgan's hand as he reached to open the lid. He expected to find himself inside, but the casket lay empty. He picked up his crying daughter and trudged to the child-size casket, his numb legs weighing him down. He kissed her on the cheek and lowered her onto the velvet-soft cushions. She struggled against him and screamed, "I don't want to go, Daddy! I want to stay with you!" He held her down with one hand as he closed the coffin, careful not to catch her squirming limbs beneath the heavy lid.

Jack rested his forehead against Dr. Lang's carpet, tears dampening the fabric. Howls escaped his throat, low and guttural, as if a wounded animal had merged with him.

"I'm sorry, Jack." Lang knelt on the carpet beside him, an arm draped across his shoulders. "It's time to face the truth. The truth about Morgan, the truth about everything."

Lang helped Jack onto the sofa. His chest heaved as the air went out of his lungs. Leaning forward, he buried his head in his hands. "My girl . . ."

"She's gone, Jack, and you weren't ready for it. But you are now. If you want to move on in your life, you must be."

"The pool . . ." Jack sobbed. "I was supposed to drain the pool." Jack dragged his hands along his face.

"It's not your fault, Jack. Sometimes things happen—"

"Sam couldn't forgive me. That's why she's leaving, that's why she moved on—" He stopped and rose from the sofa. Hobbling to the bubbler, he concentrated on the task at hand, putting one foot in front of the other, pulling air into his lungs. But his body dragged with each step as if cement blocks encased his feet. He filled paper cone after paper cone, gulping the contents until a cold headache pulsed between his eyes. He gazed at Dr. Lang. "There's no carousel, is there?"

"There never was, Jack. Not then, not now. Your carousel became a symbol of comfort and guilt all at the same time. It sent you back to your childhood, the time when your mother was alive. The one person who loved you and protected you."

Jack buried his face in his hands as the sobs burst forth. Composing himself, Jack pressed his palms against moist eyes. "In the dream, when I walked to the casket, I looked at my father, hoping to see a tear. Hoping he would glance up at me. Hoping he gave a damn!"

"Even when a father is cruel to a child, the child still needs his love. You still carried the guilt of his death. Just as you carry guilt over Morgan's death. That's why the carousel's horse takes you into hell. Your writer's imagination created a different type of hell, but it was hell nonetheless."

Jack leaned his back against the office's far wall, sliding down until he rested on the floor. "What do I do now?"

"You go home, Jack. You wait for Sam to come home. You face your demons together. You get help." Lang crossed the floor and knelt beside him. "And you start over."

"I'm not sure where she is."

"This may be the hardest thing I've ever had to ask you." Lang rubbed the back of his neck. "Did you do anything to her?"

Jack laced his fingers together and rested them on his head. "Never. She's all I have. I'd never hurt her."

"And those people at the county fair twenty years ago. Did you do anything to them?"

Jack shook his head. "But no one's gonna believe me. They're gonna put me in jail."

Lang slung an arm beneath Jack and hoisted him to his feet. "I'll say it again like I have for twenty-five years. It doesn't matter what I think. It doesn't matter what the outside world thinks. It only matters what you think." Lang tapped Jack's head. "And if this space up here is clean and free of clutter, then your mind is free. And when your mind is free, you're going to be okay. No matter what happens."

Jack dragged a sleeve across his eyes.

Lang fixed Jack with his gaze. "And I won't ever abandon you."

Jack wrapped his arms around Lang, holding him in an embrace. Wishing just once his father would have done the same. He held onto Lang, for the seventeen years he lived without a father's love, for the twenty-five years he lived without the ability to face the truth, and for the pain of loss and regret. And for Morgan.

Jack let his arms go slack, releasing his grip. "I don't have anywhere to go."

"You're coming with me. I always have room for a friend. Tomorrow, we'll go to breakfast and get you on a plane home. I'll go with you. The rest of your life, your new life, begins tomorrow."

CHAPTER TWENTY-SEVEN

Fulton, Missouri

Jack woke the following morning with a heavy weight excised from his soul. He had spent his whole life running from the truth, caught in an unreliable mind's clever maneuverings and falling for its seduction. From his father's death to his daughter's, he had never managed the guilt or pain associated with either, carousels and other imaginings clouding his forward progress. But yesterday, in Dr. Lang's office, he had finally faced the trauma and taken the first tentative steps in the healing process.

Propping the pillows behind his back, Jack faced his first day without Morgan. He had always understood his daughter was no longer with him, that she had only existed in his memory. But he had needed her to be alive, and he had made her so. His emptiness after her death had been all-consuming. His life's only joy came in the moments he drifted into her empty room—the place where remnants of her life's energy still clung to the Minions bedsheets; the drawings of horses and princesses, bullfrogs, and an octopus in top-hat and tails, taped to the wall; her Taylor Swift backpack; and the toys: her beloved Barbie dolls, Watermelon Butter Slime kit, and Capybara Warmies, arranged, just so, on top of her dresser. At first, he would stand in her doorway, gazing at what had been, wondering whether any part of her still lingered. He had graduated to sitting on her bed and leafing through her favorite books. Then one night, she appeared beside him. He had found this arrangement could help him claim bits and pieces of happiness, five to ten minutes at a time throughout his day. But he couldn't let go until yesterday. He had finally accepted her loss, although it didn't mean he was over her. His stomach lurched when he contemplated having to move forward without her. Jack knew if he pressed his eyes shut right now, she would be right beside him again when he opened them. But he wouldn't do that anymore. From now on, he would focus on living life and salvaging what he could from it.

The tears surprised him, erupting from a place way down deep where he had kept Morgan all to himself. His reaction forced him to bury his face into the pillow to muffle the anguished cries. Dr. Lang had warned him the emotions would be sudden and unexpected. After a time, the spasms twisting his core had subsided.

Dr. Lang assured him every explosive emotional burst was therapeutic, like cutting out a tumor he carried inside him. The radiating sunlight streamed through the second-floor bedroom window, warming Jack's face and evaporating his tears. He grinned, a sense of renewal and optimism melting his core's icy armor plating, leaving a hint of hope blooming inside him.

He snatched his cell phone off the nightstand and pressed Sam's number. He didn't know where she would be. Had to be LA by now. He hoped she could sense the urgency in his ringtone. "Pick up, babe."

The phone went to voicemail. He hesitated, not sure where to begin. "Sam . . . call me when you get this. Please. I'm in Missouri. I'm with Dr. Lang. I'm ready to drop the past and begin my future. I . . . I just want you in it. And I'm ready to be in it with you. Just . . . call me."

He disconnected. "Please call me."

———

After an artery-clogging breakfast of eggs, bacon, and hashbrowns at Waffle House, Jack bounded along Route 54 toward Jefferson City. Despite Lang's opposition, Jack had insisted upon traveling to the farm before heading back to St. Louis Lambert Airport. He had found closure with Morgan, but the healing wasn't over. Lang discouraged Jack from making the trip alone and agreed to join him to ensure he had the support he needed.

After Jack took the US-50 west exit off Route 54 toward Sedalia, Lang cleared his throat. "We're getting close. How you feeling?"

"I'm good. Really." Jack glanced over his shoulder as he switched lanes. "I appreciate what you did yesterday, helping me come to terms with things, giving me a place to stay. I even appreciate you advancing my artery plaque with breakfast today."

Lang smirked.

"But you didn't need to come to Spring Valley with me. I'm just checking out the property. Getting a sense of its state of disrepair."

"It's more than that. You're gonna see things and feel things you haven't confronted in years. Sometimes it can be overwhelming."

Easing into the right lane, Jack tapped the directional with his pinky and took the Spring Valley exit. "The only overwhelming thing will be thinking about how much money I threw away not selling the place earlier." He glanced toward the passenger seat. "I'm a little frightened of what I'm gonna see when I get there."

"You've done nothing with the place for twenty-five years?"

Jack shook his head.

"No one's been checking on it?"

Jack leaked air from his puffed cheeks.

"You'll be lucky if—"

"Yeah, I get it," Jack said. "I'll be lucky if there isn't someone cooking up something in the kitchen."

"And not something your mama ever prepared, either."

Jack wound the rental car through downtown and past the elementary and high schools' overgrown playing fields. Rusted playground equipment baked under the late morning sun, and ripped netting hung off soccer goalposts and basketball hoops like nylon cobwebs. The town hall, once looming tall and powerful over the main square, appeared hunched and frail, as if it had aged along with the town's remaining residents. These were the folks shuffling along Main Street in their farmer's overalls and flower-patterned dresses, resting on the bench facing the hardware store or sipping lemonade on Merle's coffee shop patio. The bakery on the corner of Second Street hadn't changed at all, but the diner across the intersection had closed. The weeds sprouted through the concrete, nearly obscuring the Pete's Downtown Diner logo emblazoned on the empty storefront window. The town looked like a doctored photograph of the place where he had once lived, like a faded jigsaw puzzle with pieces missing.

"Did you ever reach Sam?"

Dr. Lang's question jolted Jack from his trance. "No luck yet. But I won't stop until she hears me out. This might be my last chance to salvage the rest of my life."

Jack hung a right off Main Street and followed Spring Street until he reached County Road 4, the route he bicycled back and forth to school. The dust roiled from behind the car as he advanced along the dirt road. At Dowling Farm, he took a left and followed Prairie Road until he approached the embankment leading to Johnson Farm. Jack could barely make out the farmhouse peeking from behind the soaring maple trees along the hilltop.

He stopped the vehicle.

"Jack?" Lang glanced toward the driver's seat.

Jack sensed the weightlessness of freefall as he gazed through the windshield. A boy's outline in shadow appeared against the blinding sun. The teen stood on the bicycle pedals, alternate thrusts encouraging him up the hill. Jack sensed a familiar burning in his thighs, and his chest grew and fell as he sucked oxygen into his lungs. As the boy reached the top of the hill, a faint melody tickled Jack's ear.

This isn't happening. He isn't there.

Jack's hands gripped the steering wheel with clenched fingers as the swirling carnival music swelled in his ears.

There isn't a carousel. There never was.

"Jack?" Dr. Lang's voice reached his ear from what seemed a mile away, the music in his head muffling all other sounds.

He closed his eyes and envisioned the carousel spinning slowly in the cornfield. An old man rested beside it, pulling his silver hair into a ponytail.

"Jack!" Lang reached and grasped his arm. "Wake up."

His eyes snapped open, pupils darting back and forth as the world swam in his vision. He leaned his head against the steering wheel. "That's it. Up ahead." He pointed through the glass. "That's the spot where I saw the carousel. The Johnsons' house at the top of the hill. I still sense its presence."

"It's okay. Simply acknowledge it . . . and let it go. There is no carousel. You understand that now."

"I do." Jack took deep breaths, calming his soaring heart rate.

Lang shifted in his seat. "This is the hard part. It's going to feel like returning to the scene of the crime, except no crime occurred. You're okay. Nothing happened here."

"There is no carousel," Jack repeated. "But why is it in my head? Why am I feeling compelled to go toward it?"

"It's normal. The surroundings. Your hometown. It's all triggering your child's mind. The way you used to think back then. But we're here, and we can put it all to bed right now."

"How?"

"You're compelled to move toward the carousel, right? Well then, let's have a look."

"You mean—"

"Let's go." Lang grinned. "You're in the Show-Me State now, right?"

Jack took his foot off the brake and eased the car to the top of the hill. The carnival music filled his head, growing louder as they graduated along the hill toward the farmhouse. He glanced at his passenger beside him. Lang stared through the windshield.

How can he not hear the music?

Jack rolled onto the shoulder, wheels flattening the soft grass beside the Johnsons' farmhouse. He flipped the door open and advanced on foot toward the crest of the hill. The golden cornfield shimmered in the heat below. The music had reached a discordant crescendo as the metallic carousel spun in the field's vast emptiness. Graham Carver perched on a stool beside the machine but stood when Jack appeared, as if he had been waiting for him.

Lang opened his door and joined Jack.

"Do you hear the music, Dr. Lang?"

Lang gaped at the field below him. He rested both hands against his hips. The sunshine reflecting off the spinning carousel deflected piercing light shards across the men's faces.

Jack could sense the heat of Lang's penetrating gaze as if expecting him to explain what he was experiencing, what was happening. How could he reveal to his friend that nothing had changed after all this time? He was right back where he was twenty-five years ago, gazing at the same sight that had changed his life for the worse. The carousel. It wouldn't go away, no matter how much he wanted it to. It would never go away.

People see what they want to see, right?

Jack opened his mouth to speak but hesitated as Lang squinted against the sunlight flashing across his face. Lang's jaw hung from its hinge.

"You see something, don't you, Doc?"

Lang rubbed his eyes and blinked. He stepped forward and pointed a shaking finger toward the field. "It's a trick of my eyes," he said, mumbling.

"You see it, don't you?" Jack grabbed his shoulders. "Tell me you see the goddamn carousel!"

"Gotta be a trick of my eyes," Lang said, voice cracking. He steadied himself against Jack's arm. "It's gotta be . . ."

CHAPTER TWENTY-EIGHT

Excerpt from *Road Rage*, by Jack Rainne:

The crowd at the bar had gotten loud.

Mark Finn pressed the straw against his lips and sipped the sizzling ginger ale in the dark tavern's corner booth. He'd been eyeing the revelers since they arrived. A celebration for sure.

But for Finn, the day marked an anniversary.

The rowdy group of friends ordered another round of shots. Bourbon. The heavy stuff. The man in the glasses with the slight build raised his shooter, poured the amber liquid down his throat, and smashed the glass onto the floor. Following their friend's lead, the group tossed their shot glasses at their feet and covered the dirty floor with the crunchy remnants. Before the bartender had waved a hand, two barrel-chested doormen arrived to escort the unruly bunch into the parking lot. Mark Finn took one final sip of his soda and followed the party from the tavern.

The scrawny, bespectacled man threw high-fives and man-hugs to his friends to celebrate their liquid bravery before jumping into the battered Olds Cutlass. It still had the hood and quarter panel dents Finn had viewed in the accident photos. He sensed the pull from a twitching lower eyelid as he headed to the Crown Vic. Firing the engine, Finn stalked the Cutlass as it departed the gravel lot and accelerated along Mountain Pass Road.

Finn kept the weaving vehicle in view as he navigated the winding hillside road to the scene of the tragedy. Opening his window, he pressed the magnetic beacon onto the roof. The balmy breeze filtering through the vehicle smelled like summer, the way it used to, easing his lips into a reminiscent grin. He pictured the beach and his sun-bronzed "sea-boy," as Linda would call him. Bobby Finn would have frolicked on the sand all day long if he had his way, wading into the surf with his father or hauling around his seahorse bucket brimming with snails and hermit crabs. The boy would fall asleep on the short ride back to the cottage, the salty air ruffling his tangled hair through the open window. When Finn would gaze into the rearview mirror, his sleeping boy loomed in his vision like some heavenly angel.

A year later, Finn would pull back a sheet to identify his boy at the morgue. Whatever he had once viewed in the rearview no longer existed on the steel gurney, three thousand pounds of metal knocking the angelic divine right out of him.

Finn's smile retreated as he followed the battered Cutlass through the winding curves. When he approached the spot, he activated the beacon and grill flashers, illuminating the night with a blue and red light show. Lowering his window, he reached for the spotlight mounted outside the driver's side door and aimed the heavy beam through the man's back window. In the rearview, the man's eyes darted back and forth as if trying to escape their sockets. Scanning his surroundings, Finn exited the Crown Vic and approached the man's vehicle.

He tapped on the driver's side window. "Step out of the car, sir."

The man swung the door open, using the vehicle's frame to hoist himself onto unsteady legs. "What's the problem, Officer?" he slurred.

Finn flipped his badge. "License, please."

The man fished through his pockets before pulling out a worn wallet. Balancing against the car door, he handed over his identification.

"Walter Dailey." Finn noted the man's weight listed on the card. That would help with the calculation. "Do you know why I'm pulling you over?"

"No sir, Officer. Was I speeding?"

Finn could smell the booze on his breath. "I pulled you over on suspicion of driving while intoxicated. The nature of the charge will depend on the breathalyzer results." Finn reached into his pocket and extracted the device. "If you'll step over here—"

"I'm not fucking blowing into that thing. I'm calling my lawyer." Dailey pulled out his cell and tapped out a number on the screen. He glanced at Finn with a smirk, but his confidence faded when Finn unholstered his gun.

"Hang up the phone, Mr. Dailey."

The man swallowed and disconnected, dropping the cell onto the roadside.

"You have any idea what happened thirteen years ago today?"

Dailey shook his head.

"You should. It's your anniversary."

"I don't . . . get it."

"Let me give you a little hint. You were sitting on the barrier right over there." He pointed his firearm toward the overgrown vegetation beside the road. "You had handcuffs on, and for some reason, you couldn't stop laughing. They were scraping little Melanie Wilson's body off the asphalt, and you couldn't stop laughing. Does that jog your memory at all?"

Dailey pointed at Finn. "I served my time for that offense, Officer."

"You don't understand what it's like to lose a child, Mr. Dailey."

"Listen, I don't need a lecture." He puffed out his chest. "I lost ten years of my life in prison because of that girl. Jumped right in front of my car."

Finn sensed the blood catching fire in his veins. "You dragged the girl and her bicycle over a mile-and-a-half underneath your car. Her parents didn't have a body to bury. Only pieces. And you're complaining your sentence was too long?"

"I guess I got lucky."

Finn raised the gun to Walter Dailey, fingers turning white in his grip. "I keep tabs on people like you when an anniversary is getting close."

Dailey raised his hands. "Now wait a minute. You're a cop. You can't just shoot me in the middle of the road."

"Why not?" Finn pictured his son's battered body after a drunken mother of four in a Chevy Tahoe knocked him out of his sneakers at seventy-five miles an hour. "No one would miss you."

The man's ragged gasps intensified. "Please ... just think about what you're doing."

"I was in court the day the judge sentenced you." Finn stepped closer, placing the gun in the center of Dailey's forehead. "I watched you cry to the judge, beg for leniency, and promise you would never drink again. You would spend your life atoning for your mistake, blah, blah, blah."

Dailey's chest heaved as the sweat dripped from his face.

"The Wilsons never recovered from little Melanie's loss. The couple stopped communicating. They couldn't feel any joy. Ended up divorced. Happens all the time after the loss of a child." Finn pictured his ex-wife, Linda, but could only imagine how she had endured their unbearable burden.

"Take me in. Arrest me, for Chrissake." Dailey pressed his wrists together. "But put the gun down."

"Tell you what, Mr. Dailey." Finn lowered his firearm. "I'm gonna give you a choice. I can arrest you and send you back to prison, or you can drive away from this. What do you think?"

"You're saying I can just drive away?" He dropped his arms to his sides. "What's the catch?"

"You just need to make the right decision." Finn holstered his weapon. "Have a seat before you fall and hurt yourself."

Dailey dropped into the Cutlass's front seat. Finn slid into the passenger seat and removed the breathalyzer from his jacket.

"Here. Blow into this. I need a number from you."

"I do this, and I can go?"

"It gets you one step closer." Finn attached the mouthpiece to the device. "I need a four-second count."

Dailey eyed Finn as he positioned the mouthpiece and blew out a slow breath. Finn checked the output on the screen. "Point zero-seven-one percent."

"Ha! I'm under the legal limit."

"Technically not intoxicated, but no doubt impaired." Finn reached into his pocket for his cell phone. "Let's see. You're 160 pounds according to your license. You were drinking Southern Comfort at the tavern, the one-hundred-proof stuff. That's fifty percent alcohol." He entered the numbers into his phone app. "It's been roughly"–he checked his watch–"let's say two hours since your first drink. A zero point seven-one blood alcohol number means you had roughly three drinks in that time."

Dailey gazed at him with a blank expression.

"Here's what I'm gonna do." Finn extracted his backup snub-nose revolver and rested it in his lap. "Thirteen years ago tonight, you mangled and killed a ten-year-old girl while driving drunk. You promised you would never drink again. Tonight, you've violated your promise to that little girl. I'm gonna see to it you honor her memory."

"Let me out of here," Dailey pleaded. "Just arrest me and take me–"

Finn pressed the revolver against Dailey's temple. "Not until you understand your options."

The man's hands shook. "Please . . . don't shoot."

"The thing wasn't even loaded." Finn chuckled and lowered the piece. "The way I see it, you have two choices." He opened the cylinder and extracted a single bullet from his pocket. He slid it into an open chamber and snapped the cylinder closed.

"You're fucking insane."

"I just believe in keeping promises. Here are your choices. Three drinks tonight equals three bullets. Now, we can chamber three rounds in this thing"–he raised the gun–"leaving three chambers empty. When you pull the trigger, that's a fifty-fifty shot at making it out of here tonight."

"When I pull the trigger? Are you talking Russian Roulette?" A single bead of sweat slid along Dailey's temple.

Finn smiled. "Or we can chamber one round, leaving five chambers empty. That's roughly an eighty-three-percent chance of survival, but you need to play the game three times to make up for the three bullets."

A line of saliva dripped from the drunk's mouth. "I can't do this. Please . . . just take me in."

Finn heaved the firearm from his shoulder holster and pressed it against the man's cheek. "It's gonna be you, or it's gonna be me. And your chances significantly improve if you do this yourself."

"Okay, okay." A pulse throbbed in Dailey's temple.

"What's it going to be? One round in the chamber three times, or three rounds in the chamber once?"

Dailey leaned out the car door and vomited.

"Well?"

The bespectacled man wiped his mouth with the back of his hand. "One bullet . . ."

"Three times."

Dailey nodded as the drool escaped his open mouth.

Finn held his firearm against the man's head and dropped the thirty-eight-caliber revolver into Dailey's moist hand. The man closed his eyes, the corners of his mouth trembling. "Now press the muzzle against your throat. Aim it up toward the brain. If I even think your gonna try something funny, I'll open a big fucking hole in the side of your head."

"How can I be sure you won't shoot me anyway?"

"If I was gonna shoot you, you'd be dead already."

Dailey positioned the thirty-eight's muzzle against the underside of his jaw. "Eighty-three-percent chance each time, right?"

"If my math is right."

The man licked his lips. "And I can drive away from here."

"Scout's honor."

"Are you even a cop?"

Finn smirked.

Dailey fingered the trigger. "Okay. Here goes."

The explosion reverberated in the enclosed space as Bailey's head exploded against the ceiling curtain. Finn wiped the blood spray from his face as the corpse slumped against the car door, hand locked around the revolver in a death grip.

Finn didn't have the heart to tell Dailey he had chambered the revolver with five bullets long before he slipped the final one into the lone slot. Of course, this wasn't very sporting of him and eliminated the man's chances of survival. But the result would satisfy the narrative, another grief-stricken drunken driver committing suicide at the site of their earlier crime. A whole string of suicides during the past few years. The true-crime shows had played on the couldn't-live-with-the-guilt angle. This tragedy would add one more grieving killer to the growing list. Plus, little Melanie Wilson's parents might sleep a little better tonight.

Mark Finn slid from the passenger seat and scanned the empty road carved into the hillside. Not a single car. Another stroke of good luck. Dropping into the Crown Vic's front seat, he removed the black notebook from his coat pocket. He clicked the pen's plunger, crossed Dailey's name off the list, and circled the next one.

He keyed the ignition and accelerated along Mountain Pass Road.

CHAPTER TWENTY-NINE

Spring Valley, Missouri

Jack and the doctor hiked across the Johnsons' field. Knee-high grass undulated like ocean waves beneath the humid breeze. Lang trudged across the meadow as if the gravitational force holding him against the earth had quadrupled. Jack helped him along, sensing everything Lang had interpreted as folly for the past twenty-five years was waging an internal battle with the truth unfolding before him. The men continued down the hill, advancing toward the spinning carousel. Its music grew louder and more dissonant as they closed the distance. Graham Carver stood to greet them, pulling back on the gears to slow the machine.

"Hello, Jack," Carver said, checking his pocket watch. "Wondered if you were ever gonna show."

"Yeah, well. I didn't really expect to see you here, if you can believe that."

Carver pointed. "Who's the bloke?"

"My doc—" Jack stopped himself. "My friend, Marcus Lang."

Carver tilted his head. "Only room for one on this ride, mate."

"Who are you?" Lang's jaw hung open.

"Graham Carver, my good man." He extended his hand.

"I know your name, Mr. Carver," Lang said, waving him off. "I've been hearing about you for twenty-five years. I guess I'm asking . . . what are you?"

Carver withdrew his hand and rubbed his chin, acknowledging the snub. "I'm sure Jack has explained what I do."

Lang pointed at the carousel. "Is this really the gateway to . . . hell?"

Carver sighed. "It's one gateway."

"And there are others?" Lang folded his arms. "Others like you?"

"Lots of others."

"You say that like you're proud of it."

"Simply stating facts, mate. You know, thousands of people go missing in this country every day." Carver glanced toward the carousel. "Most turn up. But for the ones who don't, well, it's a pretty good bet one of my colleagues had something to do with it."

"You're vile." Lang wagged a finger in Carver's face. "Tearing up people's lives, leaving families lost and wondering." Lang gestured toward Jack. "Leaving people like this damaged their whole life."

"It could have been worse," Carver said, picking at a fingernail. "He was never supposed to escape the Underground, but he did. And he had a nice, long reprieve."

"But now you're sending him back."

"That's my job." Carver stepped onto the platform and dragged a hand along a horse's mane. "I have no choice."

"Just following orders, eh? That excuse doesn't fly anymore, old man. You're nothing more than a pimp."

Carver jumped from the carousel. "You know, I could make an exception to my one-rider rule."

Jack stepped between the men. "That's enough, Carver."

The old man pointed at Lang. "Your problem is you think life matters. Let me clue you in on a little secret. It doesn't. You're here . . . *poof* . . . you're gone. Like Angie."

"What do you know about my wife?" Lang's hands shook as he curled them into fists. He advanced toward Carver. "Did you or one of your *colleagues* have anything to do with—"

The doctor fell to his knees as if he had run into a wall. He cradled his head between his palms.

Jack winced, imagining the pounding rhythm reverberating in his friend's skull. He knelt beside him. "It'll stop, Doc. You just need to back off."

The doctor shook out the cobwebs as he perched on all fours. Jack helped him to his feet, glowering at the carousel operator.

"Jesus, Carver. Enough." Jack headed over to the machine, the creaky wooden steps groaning under his weight. "You're here for me. Let's get this over with."

Carver tightened his ponytail. "Just to let you know, Dr. Lang, she went naturally. You don't need to worry about her—she's in a better place now."

Lang's hands remained pressed against his thighs, but he raised his head in acknowledgment.

"All right then, Jack. You remember which jumper, don't you?"

"How could I forget?"

Carver approached Lang and dropped a hand on his shoulder. "My apologies, sir. Please excuse my insensitive comments. But it's his time to go. There's nothing else you can do for him."

"Jack. I'm sorry." Lang took tentative steps toward the carousel, trudging forward on shaking legs. "I didn't believe you."

"Nothing to be sorry about, Doc." Jack raised his hand. "You didn't know."

"I'll find a way to clear your name. People won't remember you as a killer."

"No worries. Carver is right. This"—he gestured about the meadow with his hands—"doesn't matter. It's where we're going that matters. You always said you'd help me get to a better place." He glanced at the blue sky and scanned the landscape for what could be the last time. "You did."

Lang glanced at the coffee-colored horse. "It doesn't feel like it."

"I made the choice. I'm giving up my better place to bring Sam to hers."

Lang extended his hand. "Safe travels, my friend."

"A handshake?" Jack hopped from the platform and pulled his friend into an embrace. "If I can get Sam back, she's gonna need you. Like I did after my first trip to the Underground. Promise me you'll—"

"I'll take care of her. For as long as it takes."

Jack slapped his friend on the back and returned to the coffee-colored mare. Reaching into his pocket, he threw Lang the car keys. "You can keep the Hyundai. I'm sure no one will ever find out."

Lang smirked, bouncing the keys in his hand. "I'm a Black man in Missouri. You think I'd be caught dead in a piece of shit like that? I'd lose all my street cred."

Jack shook his head. "Like you had any."

Lang backed to the edge of the clearing. He must have sensed he shouldn't stand too close to the gates of hell when they opened. Who knows what might happen?

Jack filled his lungs and threw a leg over the sixth horse. "I'm ready."

Carver crossed the platform, slaloming through the horse's guide poles until he stood beside Jack. "Listen, mate. I'm sorry. You know that, don't you?"

Jack acknowledged him, sensing the beast's mounting energy surge beneath its frame. The horse would soon take flight and thunder across the meadow and into the Underground. But this time, he wouldn't wake from the dream. This time, he would end up before The Tar.

Carver shuffled to the control lever.

"Wait a minute!" Jack shouted. "You must know something that can help me."

Carver dropped his gaze. "Jack, if I could do anything for you, believe me, I would. The Tar has my family, too. For a hundred years, I've racked my brain thinking about how to get them back."

"He must have a weakness, something I can negotiate."

"The Tar has no weakness, and he's been waiting for you a long time. You might be able to negotiate something for Sam, but I don't see a way out for you. Sorry to be blunt."

His cheeks puffed with air, any chance to gain an edge disappearing down the drain along with his life's last moments. "It's okay. It was a Hail Mary anyway." Jack pressed his eyes shut as a warm breeze drifted across his face. He took in the familiar farmland aromas and the faint, sweet scent of something baked. Cookies, maybe? Or a pie left to cool on a windowsill.

He would never know.

Jack scanned the Missouri cornfield and the picture-perfect blue sky draped above it. He struggled to hold in his mind the world's beautiful things, memories he could grab and take with him from this world to the Earth's dungeon, something to comfort him. But nothing surfaced, darkness sweeping across his vision as if a veil had dropped behind his eyes. The last show performed, a final curtain call. He concentrated on the things he could control, pulling the air into his lungs, keeping his muscles tensed so he wouldn't lose his grip on the guide pole, and calming his mind. And soon, the memories flooded back, overwhelming him. His life swirled around him in images, pictures dancing in his mind like a favorite film played on fast-forward. Peace surrounded him like a bittersweet euphoria.

Jack gave Carver the thumbs-up and grabbed the guide pole. Carver busied himself with the control panel, turning switches and pressing buttons before jamming the lever forward to initiate his rider's journey. Expecting momentum to drag him rearward as the carousel accelerated, Jack leaned forward to counter the anticipation. But the platform jerked backward with an ear-splitting shriek, driving his face into the guide pole and knocking him from the horse.

"Christ!" Jack grabbed his nose as bright red blood leached from his nostrils.

Carver hit the kill switch and hopped onto the platform. He hurried to Jack's side and pressed a handkerchief against his face.

"Ouch!" Jack pushed Carver's hand away from his rapidly swelling nose. "As if going to the Underground wasn't bad enough today."

"What the hell was that?" Lang barked from the edge of the field.

Carver held up a hand. "Technical glitch. Here you go, Jack." He relinquished the cloth, and Jack pressed it gingerly against his face. "Sorry about that."

"Jesus Christ." Jack pushed a finger against his beak, the piercing sting bringing water to his eyes. "Goddamn, that hurts!"

"You got a gusher, mate."

"What the fuck happened?"

"I must have set the damn machine in the wrong direction."

Jack rose to his feet, pressing the handkerchief against his throbbing nose. "Obviously. Wait a minute, don't these things only go in one direction?"

"They do. It just depends."

"On what? Didn't that New York carousel company hire you because you were this whiz-kid engineer?"

"They did. I was."

"Then why did I have to pay for it with my nose?" Jack reflected a moment. *British carousels.* "Ah, let me guess. You Brits are used to them going the wrong way."

"Not the wrong way, mate, just a different way. Clockwise instead of counterclockwise." Carver leaned against a support pole. "I used one of my old British motor designs for the Flying Horses. Had to make a few adjustments to make it go counterclockwise the way you Yankees like. But it still goes clockwise if you're not careful."

"Like just now?" Jack dabbed at his nose.

"Unfortunately."

"And you used the same dumbass design on this carousel?"

"Your carousel is a replica of the Flying Horses, dumbass design and all."

"Just my luck." Jack snorted out a bloody clot and mounted the horse. He tossed the crimson handkerchief to Carver, who held it dangling with two fingers.

"Let's get this thing over with."

"Grab hold." Carver shuffled to the control panel. Adjusting the knobs and buttons, he grabbed the main lever and rammed it forward. The carousel lurched in the forward direction this time, gears and cogs crunching as the platform spun and gained momentum. He gave a final nod to Lang, still perched at the field's edge like a sentry.

The ride picked up speed and snuffed out the daylight as Jack's world turned midnight black. The coffee-colored mare disengaged from the guide pole and leaped off the platform, quickening its gait and thundering across the grassy meadow. Electricity exploded from its hooves as they pounded against the dusty ground.

Faster.

Jack fell into a trance as the recollection of this event—meted out in dreams and hallucinations for the past twenty-five years—finally met reality. He tasted the night's scent in his throat and shared the horse's power as it roared beneath him. He held on for dear life as the wind tousled his hair, terrified the beast would shake him from his perch.

Jack scanned his surroundings. A chill descended deep into his viscera as the mare bounded through deep canyons and rocky terrain, then down into the Earth.

Faster.

The dank, hollow cavern's stench hit him first, then the ascending warmth. The glowing walls throbbed with burning heat as the horse rumbled forward, sparks from its hooves igniting the stony ground and adding to the conflagration.

Fire and brimstone. Everything he had ever imagined about hell coming to life before him. And what he witnessed sent a shockwave through his core. A flame wall danced at the glowing cavern's end, hell's scorching gates awaiting Jack's fiery entrance. He squeezed his eyes shut and muttered a prayer to minimize the upcoming inferno's searing pain. He almost smiled at the irony, praying to God as he approached the Underground. He hadn't thrown Him a shout-out in . . . well, it had been too long. But if there ever was a time to get on a first-name basis again, now would be it.

He kept his eyes shut, assured he would soon understand how it felt to be trapped in a burning building, fall into an erupting volcano, or dropped into boiling water like all those Vineyard lobsters he had eaten. He waited for the scorching pain. But instead, the carousel horse materialized beneath him as the machine slowed and the daylight rose around him, piercing his eyelids. He blinked his eyes open to find himself squeezing the carousel's guide pole as the machine slowed to a stop in the middle of the Johnsons' cornfield.

What the . . . ?

"Carver!" Jack dismounted the jumper and circled the carousel in search of his ferryman, but the old Brit no longer manned his station. Lang no longer stood guard at the field's border. Scanning the horizon, Jack understood his missing compatriots weren't the only things that had changed. He may not have been in the Underground, but he wasn't exactly in the Johnsons' cornfield either. The color was off somehow, faded like a photograph that hadn't had enough time to develop. He gazed to the hilltop where he and Lang had descended the field. The ground had hardened, the decaying turf festering under the simmering heat. The Johnsons' farmhouse lay in ruins, partially collapsed, the other half burned to the ground. The towering maple trees bent at impossible angles or lay uprooted. And a rancid, bitter odor replaced the sweet home-baked scent hanging in the air, as if the Earth had rotted beneath his feet.

What the hell happened here?

Jack wandered through the field until his feet crunched Prairie Road's gravel shoulder. With no clue what to do or where to go, he followed the dusty road south. In about a half mile, he would reach the fork in the road leading to the family farm.

A wretched odor assaulted him in waves.

If Jack had wanted to pen a novel about the last man standing in a post-apocalyptic world, his imagination couldn't have conjured a better picture. Birds and animals lay scattered before him. In the fields beside the road, livestock lay dead on their sides, some bloated from gases built up inside their guts, others having burst in the intense heat. Marauding scavengers fell upon them, ripping flesh chunks from the carcasses. Others hung back, circling above.

As Jack trudged along the road, his vision flickered, and a brief flash of scorched stone and flames blanketed the ground. He backtracked and stumbled rearward, landing on his recently healed tailbone. Scrambling on all fours to escape the conflagration, Jack pressed his eyes shut in anticipation of the Underground's searing pain he had been anticipating.

Here it comes. He waited.

Jack hesitated before prying open a wary eye. The fiery vision had cleared, but the heat approached in continual waves like an immense energy surge. Jack sensed something lay hidden just beyond what he could see, as if he had wandered into a three-dimensional stage show replete with props and special effects swirling around him. He stood and held out his arms, hands grasping to throw back the curtain. But with each clawing swat, whatever physical world lay hidden beyond his senses scampered away from his grasp.

Jack spun in a complete circle to take in his surroundings, but the fiery visions had dispersed along with the withering heat burst. Continuing forward, he moved with tentative steps toward the farm. At the fork in the road, he veered left onto River Road. He could make out the distant shape of his old farmhouse. It had not fared much better than the Johnsons' mangled shack. The roof had been torn away, and the structure pitched ominously to the left. Time and neglect had left the fences and smaller structures razed. The barren field's sheep and cattle lay exposed and rotting. He tugged his shirt over his mouth and nose to ward off the death stench.

Jack cracked the rickety gait and legged along the walkway leading to the house. He glanced at the A-frame roof. Its rafters remained intact, but scattered shingles and plywood littered the yard. The wraparound porch hung at a dying angle, and the rotting trellis work beneath the front steps had crumbled into the patchy dirt. Resting in the field beside the porch, the rusted John Deere had resigned itself to the elements, the untamed growth assimilating the machine as its own, obscuring the tractor's massive rear tires. He stepped across the crumbling pathway's debris and climbed the porch's creaky stairs.

The door hung askew, knocked from its hinges. Jack stepped over its lower corner and shimmied sideways through the open space into the house.

The dwelling hadn't changed much since he last set eyes upon it. The house had no need for the types of updates Jack was accustomed to as part of the Vineyard community—tile backsplash, stainless steel appliances, cellular shades, and recessed lighting. His mother's practical furnishings, rugged chairs and sofas, thick rugs, and sturdy wood floors had been more fitting for a farming family. The home's innards had survived relatively intact compared with the exterior. As he scanned the familiar room, a heat burst blew across his neck and a voice called out from behind him.

"Hello, Jack. It's been a while."

CHAPTER THIRTY

Jack recognized the voice.

The sound brought immediate despair from a place buried deep inside him. It flooded his heart with anguish, reminding him of all that had ever caused him to surrender and lose hope: all the failure and shame hidden inside his mind's secret places, the things he tried to bury and seal away but never could. He squeezed his eyes shut as forgotten passages from his wretched life flew at him in high def, a collage of disquieting still frames and moving images. Jack relived them all in an endless instant, dropping to the floor as if his legs had lost their bones. And at that moment, he understood the carousel had worked. He had come back to hell. Where else but hell would the weight of hopelessness and humiliation drive you to your knees? Where else but Spring Valley, Missouri? Maybe that's why The Tar had waited for him as long as he had. Jack's childhood had given him considerable experience living in hell.

As he labored to his feet, a wave of heat drifted from the voice's direction. Jack's vision shimmered again as he faced its source. He glimpsed scorched stone and burning cave walls outlining the figure's shape in his living room. Jack rubbed his eyes to dispel the hallucination. But as he glimpsed the scene before him, it struck him that his surroundings—his home, the walls, and the furnishings—appeared like a mirage compared to the vivid, fiery image he had witnessed behind it.

The figure stepped from the kitchen. "The prodigal son returns."

Jack inspected the Underground sovereign standing before him. He had encountered books and films depicting the devil as physically striking or decked out in the finest garb. The Tar had not gotten the memo. His ill-fitting clothing and slovenly appearance conveyed something of a homeless vibe, as if the daily pretenses on which humans fixate had no place in the Underground.

The Tar wiped his nose on his sleeve and drew in a quick snort. He gurgled the nasal mucus in his throat before he swallowed. The beast's face didn't offend, but he possessed no outstanding features. If Jack had to describe him, he would have said The Tar resembled everyone he had ever known from every angle all at once, making him indistinguishable and impossible to define. Maybe this was why Jack couldn't recall meeting him all those years ago. He had nothing rememberable about him.

He circled Jack with deliberate steps. An aroma wafted from his moving form, a combined body odor and fecal scent. "I don't imagine I need to introduce myself."

"Carver told me I'd run into you."

"Ah, Mr. Carver. Such a loyal servant. Although not the most efficient anymore. But it's you I prefer to talk about."

Heat radiated from The Tar as if a smoldering core simmered inside him. The beast narrowed his eyes. "You have a lot of nerve welching on our deal."

"What deal?" Jack spread his hands. "How could I welch on a deal I have no recollection of making?"

The Tar rubbed his stubbled chin. "You have a point. I'll grant you that. The trauma you suffered after our first encounter might have contributed. Rumor has it I'm big and scary." The Tar air-quoted the descriptors. "And I know you had doctors disabusing you of the truth you understood in your heart, telling you everything was in your head. But you must accept responsibility here. If you had simply done your job as we agreed, we wouldn't be in the pickle we're in right now."

Jack swallowed. "What do you want from me?"

The Tar draped a heated limb across Jack's shoulders. An overpowering stench drifted from his armpit. "I want what's owed me."

"You owe me something, too."

The Tar chortled. "What could I possibly owe you?"

Jack wriggled from The Tar's grip. "My wife, Sam. I want to see her now."

The Tar threw a hand over his mouth as he yawned. "I'll get right on that."

Jack folded his arms. "I'm not doing anything for you until I see her and she's released."

"Oh, you're making demands now, is that it?" A grin flashed across his face. "You've watched too many movies."

The Tar squeezed his fist. A dull throb swelled in Jack's head . . . *thud . . . thud . . . thud . . .* reaching a crescendo and driving him to his knees.

THUD . . . THUD . . . THUD . . .

Jack wrapped his arms around his skull, trying to keep it from breaking apart. "Stop! Please!"

"*Please* and *thank you* don't work down here, Jack."

The assault continued, the thrumming building in his head like a series of swelling waves crashing against his skull. His body jerked with each pulsing throb.

The pounding subsided as The Tar opened his fist. "Get up!"

Jack rose to a knee, then pushed himself to his feet, his legs wobbling. Stars shot across his vision as his brain struggled to recover from the auditory battering.

The Tar reached out to steady him. "We don't need to be adversaries. We're going to be working together from now on."

Jack tore himself away, stumbling backward. He grabbed the sofa to keep from falling. "I'm not going to be part of anything you do here."

The Tar rolled his eyes. "You seem to think you're cut from a different cloth than me, but you're not. It's the reason I've wanted you here for so long." The Tar folded his hands and tapped his index fingers against his chin. "Come, Jack, I want to show you something."

The Tar led Jack through the living room and out the front door. They stepped across trampled vegetation, careful to avoid the mangled and dying wildlife scattered about the farm. At one time, the farm had reeked of a persistent manure odor, but now it just smelled of death. Still, the death odor was a relief compared to The Tar's rankness inside the house's closed space.

Jack peered across the familiar landscape. "This isn't Spring Valley, is it?"

"It isn't?" The Tar's mouth quivered as if trying not to break into a grin. "It sure looks like it to me."

"I keep catching a glimpse of something . . . behind it. Raging fire and glowing caves. Then it flips back to this." Jack gestured across the field. "This dead, colorless backdrop."

The Tar's grin faded. "I made a mistake revealing my domain to you years ago. You were more sensitive than most. If I showed you again, your mind is liable to switch off completely. Then I'd never get you back again."

As Jack glanced at The Tar, his vision failed him once more. The grayscale images shimmered like a fragile illusion. The Tar's bargain-rack duds appeared to burn away from his body, leaving a blackened, gyrating husk. It leaked a sour fluid, bathing his limbs and torso in a thick slime. The curtain had fallen away and revealed the soulless life form behind it, a creature devoid of anything resembling humanity. Jack spun away, forgetting how to breathe. His heart rattled against its bony cage, trying to signal the lungs to inflate. He fell forward, gulping at the air like a guppy pulled from a fish tank. When he raised his head, The Tar had resumed his staged form. Twenty-first-century clearance-sale mufti covering the smelly skin suit he had appropriated from some unlucky Underground guest.

"You're not equipped to see me, either." He helped Jack to his feet. "Stop trying, it won't help you."

Jack massaged his temples. "If this is the Underground, why am I the only one here?"

"You're not. Your kind is all around you. They're just not part of your adventure."

"All this," Jack said, raising his arms. "Spring Valley. The farmhouse. My own personal hell?"

The Tar tilted his head as if considering the analogy. "Most people's lives are a personal hell. Why should this place be any different?"

When they had reached the fence line along the farm's border, The Tar pointed. "Over there. This is what I wanted to show you. Watch carefully."

Jack waited, gazing at the familiar section of the property. "What am I looking at?"

"Shadows, Jack," The Tar whispered. "The things you do in life leave vivid shadows down here. Things you can see again, people you've wronged. I get to show them to you."

Distant images moved before his eyes, the sequence playing out like a fuzzy memory but from a new and different vantage point. Before him, the farm radiated in a brilliant verdant hue. Instead of his hell-muted surroundings, Jack viewed a virtual Oz from Dorothy's black-and-white Kansas farmhouse door. The images before him blazed in vivid color, as if The Tar had amplified the living memory's contrast and saturation. Bob Rainne perched high in a horse's saddle beside a fence as the sun beat down upon his leathery skin. Beside him, a seventeen-year-old Jack Rainne, about to catch a father's fist across his temple. The day of his father's death, the memory cued up as if The Tar had Jack's life on DVR and pressed play.

Shadows.

Jack flinched as knuckles connected and knocked the boy against the fence. In another moment, young Jack had rushed at his father's horse. It reared back and threw the elder Rainne into the culvert.

Jack stepped forward, advancing toward the sequence playing out before him. But The Tar plunked a smoldering hand on his shoulder. "Don't bother. Your old man dies, and there's nothing you can do about it now."

Like a movie Jack had watched a thousand times, the boy dropped to his knees beside his father.

The Tar grinned. "You never told anyone about it, did you?"

Jack shook his head.

"In fact, you never admitted you were with your father when he died. You told everyone you found him dead. You didn't mention it to your mother, your doctors, not even the police. No one ever knew." The Tar scratched his head. "Why is that?"

"I don't know," Jack mumbled, casting his gaze to the dirt.

"I think you do." The Tar rose behind him and grabbed his hair, yanking his head upward. "You're gonna want to see this."

The teenaged Jack lifted his father's arm and let it drop with a smack against the culvert's heavy stones. He sprung to his feet and whipped his head back and forth as if desperate to flag down anyone along the dusty roads who could help.

The boy waited, peering at his father lying motionless on the ground.

"Why isn't he . . . I mean, me . . ." Jack mumbled. "Why aren't I going for help?"

The Tar smirked.

Then the boy dropped to his knees beside his father. He hesitated for a moment and brushed the strands of hair from Big Bobby Rainne's eyes.

"Get your ass . . . moving . . . you worthless fuck . . ." As he recalled his father's words, Jack's arm muscles tensed, and his hands curled into fists.

The boy's head swiveled one last time to the left and right.

Jack squeezed his eyes shut as he watched the boy cover his father's mouth with his hand. With his other, he pinched the man's nostrils shut.

"Oh, God," Jack cried.

"God can't help him now." The Tar chuckled and pried Jack's eyes open. "You can't either."

The man lay silent, unable to move anything below his neck. The teenage Jack thwarted his efforts to thrash his head from side to side as he pressed his weight against his father's face, his straining arms rigid.

Jack's jaw dropped as he viewed his father's murder at the hands of his younger self. He sunk to the ground, burying his face in his palms.

"I killed him?" Jack whispered, staring into the dirt.

"And quite effectively, I might add. No one suspected anything. That's the best kind of murder."

When Jack glanced up, the boy and his father had disappeared.

The Tar knelt beside him on the patchy ground. "Now do you see why I've been waiting for you all these years?"

Jack shook his head to dislodge the imagery replaying in his mind. "No, no . . ."

"A man who would kill his father . . . he would be a great asset."

The Barnstable County Fair flashed through his mind, a young man in a Northeastern T-shirt following a mother and child through the carnival. And there were other places, forgotten people, and terrified faces.

"You're a killer, Jack, and you didn't even know it."

CHAPTER THIRTY-ONE

Jack clutched The Tar as he rose from the dirt, but it took time for him to gain his feet. Shuffling through the weeds back to the house, the two slipped through the front door and into the living room before Jack collapsed onto the sofa.

"When someone under my charge kills for me, I get the soul," The Tar said, jamming a thumb toward his chest. "Bottom line, I need a killer like you to speed up my operation."

"I can't . . . do that," Jack said.

"You've done it for me before. You killed your father and others."

Jack froze. "How many others?"

The Tar smirked. "You'd be surprised."

Jack's throat tightened as the twitching grew in his stomach and spread into his limbs. *I'm a killer.* "How could I kill and not remember anything?"

"You have a history of forgetting things. Especially when I needed your skills and sent the pounding into your head. You operated on autopilot. Your killings were few and far between, I'll admit. But that's why you're here. I need more from you now."

"I can't."

The Tar ground his teeth together, the veins sticking out on his temples. "Why would you refuse now? I need you to stop fighting your true nature and give in to it. This is your calling. The killings you wrote about in your books. Did you assume you magically plucked all those scenarios from thin air?"

"Whatever you think I am . . . whatever you think you know about me is wrong. I killed my father because he was a tyrant. As for the others . . . I didn't do it alone. *You* made me kill for you, and I won't do it again."

"Then you can watch Sam die in front of you. Slowly." The Tar snorted and hocked a wad of phlegm onto the floor. "It won't be pretty, I assure you. And in the end, it will be for nothing. You can help her live or help her die."

Jack worked his jaw, trying not to show his vulnerability. But when it came to Sam, he couldn't hide it.

"Either way, you *will* kill for me." The Tar's gaze locked onto Jack's for an uncomfortable, lingering moment. "It's in your blood."

He expected the beast to break the linkage, but he didn't, and Jack couldn't look away. His vision grew dim as the color bled from his eyes, resembling the breathless moment before losing consciousness. But instead of blacking out, pictures moved inside his mind, as if The Tar had transferred them through his piercing stare. They picked up speed until they fused together like a film.

Jack trudged through the flattened ground at the Barnstable County Fair, his Northeastern T-shirt clinging to a fitter, younger body. The crowds had thinned as darkness fell, but he still had to weave through the patrons zigzagging through the field to grab their last fried dough or catch one final ride. Ahead, Jack spotted a mother and her son heading away from the grounds toward the woods, as though investigating something that caught their attention. A dull throb pulsed in his head, increasing in intensity as he followed the pair. A whirring click caught his attention as someone snapped a burst of pictures off to his right.

Thud . . . thud . . . thud . . .

Jack pressed his fingers to his temples and rubbed in slow circles. As he passed the high-striker machine, Jack picked up the heavy mallet used to pound the block and send the metal puck upward to ring the bell.

The wood felt right in his hands.

The boy and his mother had covered significant ground on their way toward the woods. The woman pointed to the horizon, but Jack couldn't spot what she indicated. He glanced over his shoulder at the distant, glowing carnival lights. No one paid them any attention.

Jack quietly closed the distance. The woman may have sensed something, a presence, or maybe an energy, a disruption of air that sends our reptilian brain into overdrive, activating the hairs on the back of the neck and transmitting the icy signals along our spine. She peeked over her shoulder.

Jack balanced the mallet above his head.

The first blow went awry and caught the woman's shoulder, the crack sounding as if someone had stomped a heavy branch. A groan escaped her lips as she stumbled forward and faceplanted into the grass. The boy dashed to his mother's side, but she pushed him away with her good arm, gesturing toward the woods. The air came in ragged gasps, and she moaned like a wounded animal as she rolled onto her back to face her attacker. Jack waited until the boy had found his feet and hustled toward the woods.

He shouldn't see this.

She closed her eyes as the mallet's second blow hit paydirt, a strike so perfect Jack didn't even feel the impact in his hands. He swiped the blood spatter from his face and knelt beside the woman, pressing his hand against her forearm to calm the twitching extremity. As Jack gazed at what remained of her face, a glint of reflected moonlight beside her caught his attention. Jack gathered the horse-shaped pendant from her neck and stuffed it into his pocket. He glanced at the crying boy huffing and puffing toward the woods and the safety his mother had promised there. He followed, dragging the mallet through the grass.

He would have to break that promise.

The vision dimmed and then bloomed again, revealing Jack standing in the dark on a rocky clearing above a body of water, a quarry somewhere. Both bodies lay at his feet, wrapped in garbage bags and bound in duct tape. He had secured dumbbells to the corpses with nylon cords to add the necessary weight. Using his foot, Jack sent the larger parcel into the water with a distant slap. As he prepared to nudge the smaller one beyond the precipice, a fluttering stirred within the black plastic bag, as if a life-size butterfly found itself trapped inside. The bag rose and fell with a breath-like cadence, in and out, up and down. Jack dropped to his knees and urged the package over the edge, taking with it the writhing form inside.

As the vision faded to black, The Tar released Jack from his gaze. Breaking the linkage had the effect of cutting the rope in a tug of war, and Jack stumbled backward, hitting the floor.

He burst to his feet. "That's not real! You're showing me things that never happened."

"They happened, Jack. Why do you suppose I sent those two back to you?" He pointed at Jack's head. "Figured it might jog the old memory. But you've got a lot buttoned up in there, I guess."

Jack bolted for the screen door, nearly punching it off its hinges as he raced onto the porch. Leaning against the broken railing, he gazed out into the yard beside the gravel driveway.

Something wriggled upon the grass.

He squinted, blinking his eyes to focus on the writhing mass. Blood stains pooled under the squirming form, turning the grass into crimson mud.

Jack's father lay on his back. A handful of buzzards circled above the tattered body, but a determined delegation gathered closer. No longer perceiving any threat from their prey, they took their time. The scavengers plucked at the elder Rainne's eyes, tugging at gelatinous sclera and pulling out ropy tendons and bloody sinew from other tender parts of his body. His ears and cheeks lay in tatters, as if someone had sprayed the side of his head with buckshot, and squirming vermin amassed at his midsection, hollowing out his stomach. The man's mouth gasped at the air, and what remained of his tongue wagged as he grunted, attempting to formulate words. The birds pecked and plucked, eating Jack's father alive, piece by piece.

"Remember him?" The Tar joined him on the porch.

Jack's stomach clenched and he doubled over, the spasms ripping through his gut. He bit the back of his hand to keep whatever he had inside from coming up. "What did you do to him?"

The Tar waved his hand. "Come on, you hated your father. I figured you would enjoy watching what his hell was like. And what it will be during his eternity with me."

You did this to him, Jack.

"It's important to consider others as well, like your wife. I'd hate to see her undergo any unpleasantries while she's here."

Jack pictured Sam pinned to the ground as a buzzard throng wavered back and forth. He imagined her squirming beneath the scorching sunshine, the scavengers' bobbing heads casting her in brief shadow as their beaks pecked at her bleeding skin and penetrated her viscera. This is where Sam would end up if he didn't do The Tar's bidding. The beast had delivered a not-so-subtle message.

The Tar squeezed the back of Jack's neck. "I suggest you don't let me down."

Jack straightened, gaining his legs. "If I do what you ask, how can I be sure you'll let her go."

"You can't. But even if I do keep her around," The Tar said with a grin, "I'll make sure she won't end up like your father."

Jack raked fingers through his hair and paced the creaky porch floorboards, struggling to find a way out of the situation. He either killed for The Tar or Sam would be in agony for eternity. If he did kill for The Tar, he would lose his soul.

You've already lost it. Long ago.

"You've been killing for years, and you didn't even know it, ever since we met for the first time. But you've fought so hard against it. There could have been so many more. Why don't you just give in."

"What if I take over for Carver?"

The Tar turned, scrunching his eyebrows.

"You know, putting people on his carousel. I could do that for you."

"Why would you want to do that?"

Jack swallowed. "Because I'm not a killer."

"Oh, I see. You would leave it to *them* to choose their fate. Maybe they choose my horse, maybe they don't. Gets you off the hook, doesn't it? When the hell did you become squeamish?"

"You'll still get your souls. Why do you care how I get them for you? I could learn the ropes, maybe work with Carver for a while and get the hang of it. You told me he wasn't getting the job done anymore."

"It's true I have grown tired of Mr. Carver's services," The Tar said. "He's grown older and slower, and he's barely meeting his quota. I guess we could use some new blood." The beast chuckled as he pointed at Jack. "Pardon the pun."

You're a fucking riot.

The silence stretched as The Tar rubbed his chin, staring upward. Maybe this negotiation would buy Jack time to get out of this crazy mess.

"All right, Jack. Ride with Carver for the next few weeks and get up to speed, but you need to show me you're serious. Only one person can run the carousel. You get him on the coffee-colored horse, or you kill him. Either way, I get his soul."

"Wait a minute." Jack pivoted. "I thought if he honored his agreement, you would release his family."

"My negotiation with him is none of your concern."

"The hell it's not," Jack said, jamming his hands against his hips. "If I'm going to work for you, I need to be sure you'll honor our agreement. You're damn well not honoring the one you made with Carver!"

"Look who's complaining about honoring agreements? You were the one who started this whole thing by not honoring our agreement twenty-five years ago. If that isn't the pot calling the kettle black."

"Listen, Carver did his time. Let him go."

The Tar frowned and shook his head. "Just get him on the horse. And if he won't do it, you *will* kill him."

Jack sensed the bile erupting in his gut, imagining the choice The Tar was forcing him to make. Kill Carver or save Sam. It didn't leave Carver a chance in hell.

"Once he's out of the picture, you had better show me your chops. If you don't work quicker than Carver did, I'll shut down that damn carousel and have you focus on what you do best." The Tar grinned. "And it ain't writing. That's for damn sure."

Jack blew out a breath. *Fuck me.* "Okay. But I have one more request."

The Tar scratched under his arm, releasing a stench wave through the air. "You have cajónes on you, Jack. That I'll admit. What is it?"

"Let me see Sam. I came all the way to hell to see her. I can't go back without—"

"Oh, boo-hoo, Jack. Stop with the sappy shit. You are such a pansy!"

"If you let me see her, I'll do what you ask."

The Tar bobbed his head side-to-side as if deliberating. "You're gonna do what I ask regardless, but if it makes you a happier worker, why not?"

"Thank you. I—"

The Tar's eyes blazed as he squeezed his fist.

A familiar dull pulse amplified in Jack's skull—*thud . . . thud . . . thud*. He dropped to the floor, pressing his hands against his ears.

The Tar stomped about the living room, knocking lamps from tables and pictures from the wall. He folded his arms and waited until his breathing subsided. "What did I say about *please* and *thank you* down here, Jack?" He uncurled his fist.

Jack struggled to his feet as the thrumming in his head receded. The room swayed before him, and he staggered to maintain his balance. Leaning forward, he rested his hands against his knees. "When can I see her?"

The Tar pointed to the kitchen door. "She's right through there." He held out his other hand, fingers splayed. "You got five minutes."

The air caught in Jack's throat as he stumbled toward the kitchen.

I'm coming, Sam.

CHAPTER THIRTY-TWO

Jack pressed a hand against the kitchen door, but it wouldn't budge. He pushed harder, leaning his entire weight against the wood.

Motherfucker.

Jack took two steps backward and rocketed forward, slamming his shoulder into the door panel. The wood splintered and gave way, pitching him forward through the frame. He expected to tumble across the linoleum kitchen floor, but instead, he plunged into blackness. Weightlessness pulled at his core as he plummeted. Fire erupted around him, illuminating the stone walls whizzing past in an ember-orange blur.

The ground approached at an unimaginable rate of speed, and Jack closed his eyes, anticipating the bone-splintering impact. But instead, his body decelerated as if dropped into a net. When his momentum halted, Jack burst from the pitch blackness across a marble floor into excruciating light. Before him, a staircase curved upward to a second-floor landing.

Oh my God.

The place didn't look quite right. But then again, this was Sam's personal hell, not his. Jack rose to his feet in the entryway to his Martha's Vineyard house.

Sam's hell. The place we called home.

Jack hung his head, a dark pain festering in the pit of his stomach. Part of her hell must have been him, but he had a good idea what the other part might have been.

"Sam," Jack cried, cupping his hands around his mouth. "Are you here?"

He scoured the lower floor, searching for her in her favorite spots: the high-back chairs surrounding the kitchen island, the living room's deep sofa, and the sunroom's hidden reading nook. Sam didn't have all the dimensions imagined correctly or the furniture and wall hangings exact. In the entryway below the stairs, the mirror on the far wall hung a bit too low, and she had envisioned the floor's pattern a bit brighter than it was. Of course, Jack had picked the tile. Sam had chosen the chandelier above the front door, so that might have been accurate. What stood out to him was the pervasive sadness and gloom suspended in the air like fog. He could sense Sam's pain the way he could when he held her or heard her voice. But now he was inside her. No sunlight filtered through the overhead skylight or pierced the window panels lining the second-floor landing. Of course, Sam's world would be much darker on the second floor.

Jack mounted the steps two at a time.

He padded along the carpeted hallway and surveyed the family photos on the wall outside the bedrooms. Sam had recalled them with amazing accuracy, the Edgartown Harbor boats' vivid colors and the distance between the ice cream and T-shirt shops along Main Street—even the strangers' faces captured in a fleeting moment entering or exiting the frame. She had spent a lifetime gazing at these images. But something was different. The family's smiles had been reimagined, replaced with blank stares and indifferent glances. The images documented the uncertainty in Sam's life and the pain and suffering that had taken root.

Jack peeked into the main bedroom, but the room sat empty. The queen bed he had shared with his wife was now a twin, reviving the squeeze in the hollow pit of his stomach. He advanced along the hallway until he reached Morgan's room. A gentle voice carried along the narrow corridor. Nudging the door open, he found Sam on the bed, gently rocking Morgan's still body. She sang to her, telling her to sleep pretty darling, don't you cry, and she would sing a lullaby.

Whatever Sam held in her arms wasn't Morgan, and it had been dead for a while, judging from the body's state of decay. The thing in her arms resembled nothing more than a prop in the Underground's strange stage show, something Sam couldn't discern in her current state. Jack breathed a sigh of relief. His daughter hadn't suffered the indignity of this insidious hell hole. She resided in a better place. He had no doubt. His experience in the Underground all those years ago and his connection with Carver gave him clarity and understanding of this fact, which he couldn't explain.

"Sam." Jack crept into the room.

His wife lifted her head, her eyes glazed over and distant. "Jack?" The words came out flat, without emotion, as if the name meant nothing. "I'm getting Morgan ready for bed." The dead, doll-like thing lolled across her lap.

"You need to give her to me, Sam." Jack advanced and picked up the putrid corpse, placing her . . . *or it* . . . on the floor.

Sam pushed her fingers against her temples. "Why did you put her there? She can't sleep on the floor."

Jack gathered Sam and held her against him. Nothing felt more like life, her warm body and holding her close, in a world of the dead and missing. His wife's arms snaked around his waist. "I came here for you, Sam."

She leaned away from the embrace, scanning the room's walls and furniture. Her gaze fixed on the lifeless flesh resting on the floor. "This place . . . something's wrong with it."

"You're not at the Vineyard anymore." She moved as if under a spell, drugged on terror or an incomprehensible reality. He figured she wouldn't remember this, just as he hadn't after his first Underground visit. "This is like"—how would he explain it?— "a waiting room, sort of. You need to wait here for a while until I come back to get you."

"Where are you going?" She gazed into his eyes with a longing she hadn't revealed in a long time, bringing a flutter to his heart. "Are you leaving me here?"

"Never." Jack worked his jaw back and forth. "But I have things I need to do before I can get you home. I'll be back, I promise." He leaned forward and pressed his lips to her, sensing a reanimation in her waning spirit. She kissed him back.

"I love you, Jack," she said. Clarity had returned, as though the woman he had known forever had emerged from behind cloudy eyes. "I always have."

Jack expected a burst of emotion. But something had muffled his sensations, as if there could be no feelings in the Underground. Nothing beautiful. Nothing but misery. "When we get out of here, we'll start over again. I promise. We'll get the hell away from the Vineyard."

Sam grinned and squeezed his hand. "You'll never leave Massachusetts. You know it."

"I will for you. I'll do anything you want."

Her arms dropped from around his waist, and her eyes glossed over again. "You want me to just wait here?" Sam asked.

"That's the best idea, I think." He bent over and picked up the Morgan thing. "I'm going to take our girl with me. She'll be fine, and you won't need to worry about her."

"That's good because she doesn't seem well." She inspected the room. "And this place. I think it's killing her. Maybe it's killing me, too."

Jack's heart sank as he imagined the suffering she had endured here. "I'll take care of Morgan. You stay here and wait for me. Okay?"

"Don't be too long, Jack." Shuffling to the bed, Sam lay across Morgan's mattress. She closed her eyes and drifted into silence.

Jack fought the urge to pick her up and take her back to his personal hell in Spring Valley, but he didn't want her anywhere near The Tar. He didn't want to leave her alone, either. As he contemplated his options, a beckoning pull swelled in his gut, as if a rope had cinched itself around his waist and a powerful hand gave it a yank. Jack stumbled backward through the door, across the hallway, and down the steps. The pitch black enveloped him as he tumbled into freefall.

CHAPTER THIRTY-THREE

Excerpt from *The Following*, by Jack Rainne:

Malcolm Morris rested alone at the kitchen table. He had sorted his mother's possessions into piles, the task of boxing her life falling onto her only child's sagging shoulders. Her pocketbook's contents lay scattered before him: credit cards, reading glasses, an empty cigarette case, all useless remnants destined for a final resting place in a cardboard grave.

Mother, dead? It couldn't be. He never considered death an option for a woman who had grown up on her grampa's farm skinning rabbits and coyotes, who could outdrink a man twice her size and still hike a straight line in stiletto heels. Malcolm pitied the dark angel who drew the short straw to escort the hard-edged and gritty Lilly Morris to the afterlife. Until the day Malcolm had discovered her face down in a bowl of lentils, a smoldering cigarette still wedged between her gnarled fingers, he wasn't sure she could die.

He dragged a hand across his chin. Lilly's cell phone poked out of a zippered pocket inside her pocketbook. He fished it out and palmed the device, turning it over in his hands. He stroked the glass, illuminating the screen. Malcolm hadn't had the chance to say goodbye, but maybe if he could listen to her voice just once more, it would bring him peace. Placing her device on the table, he reached into his back pocket and extracted his battered cell, tapping on her name. Her phone buzzed, dancing across the wooden table—one ring, two rings, three rings—until her raspy, recorded voice broke the silence.

Malcolm pressed his eyes shut as he listened, her voice right there inside his head. His eyes rimmed with tears as he pressed a reluctant finger to disconnect. Tossing the cell into the box, he lined up the flaps and taped it shut.

———

"Dammit, Malcolm!" Eve Hunter glanced over her shoulder as she rummaged through the hall closet for her hat and gloves. "Can we not argue about this tonight?" Her heels clicked across the hardwood floor.

"I don't mind you inviting the firm's top brass to dinner, but why Frank Nichols?"

"Because he's my ticket to a promotion. You can appreciate that. I realize he's the guy who fired you, but let's not make this about you, okay? Could you at least try to make this work? I need the old Malcolm tonight."

I wonder if she's sleeping with him.

"Maybe we can prop the old Malcolm beside you two in the living room while this version watches TV upstairs?" He flashed a weak smile.

Eve lowered her sunglasses, fixing him with a laser glare. "TV? That's the only thing you're good at these days, and I mean the only thing."

She's definitely sleeping with him.

"Ever since Mummy died." She adopted a spot-on impression of Lilly's smoky voice. "Oh Malcolm, bring me some tea, will you? That's a good boy." She snapped her fingers twice before his face. "Wake up! She died three months ago . . . and not a minute too soon, I might add."

Eve threw open the front door and bounded onto the porch, her free hand releasing the long hair trapped beneath her jacket collar. "Now Malcolm, don't forget to call the restaurant and pick up the food. It needs to be hot and ready to serve when Frank and I arrive home. Make sure you get the oven going early."

Malcolm frowned. Ever since he lost his job, Eve had reduced him to little more than a houseboy. "You can count on me." He stepped forward to hug her, but her hand shot out and stopped him. She wrinkled her nose as she gave him the once-over.

"And for God's sake, take a shower today. You may be down and out, but you don't have to act like it. Try to maintain your dignity." She descended the front steps and marched along the sidewalk without glancing back.

Maybe Mother had been right about Eve. He recalled the night before the wedding, parked at the kitchen table as his mother circled the room in her bathrobe, bourbon sloshing across the tumbler's rim as she snarled at him.

"She's a whore, Malcolm." She sucked at the Pall Mall dangling from her lip. "You'll never be able to satisfy a gold-digging slut like her. She'll wring you out and leave you dry. What did I tell you about women?"

"You can't trust them," he repeated.

"Someone should skin that bitch."

If anyone could, it would be Lilly. Despite her rough edges, the past months without her had been more difficult than he had expected. He still hadn't canceled Lilly's phone service, the desire to hear her voice overpowering. Someday he would, of course, but for now, three rings and she was alive in his head once again.

You're going crazy. That's what Dr. Haskell would say.

Digging into his jacket pocket, he gripped the cell and scrolled through his recent calls list. Like an alcoholic's hesitation before twisting the cap and breaking the seal, Malcolm's finger hovered above the glass. He tapped her name as the morning sun spilled through the living room window, warming his face.

He just needed to hear her voice one more time.

One ring, two rings . . . then, silence. As he awaited a third ring, a gravelly voice echoed in his head. "Did you miss me, Malcolm?"

The air thickened in his lungs as the cell tumbled from his hand. He wavered on his feet, struggling to keep the world from pulling away. Dropping to all fours, he retrieved the cell and pressed it to his ear.

"Mother?"

"She's no good, Malcolm. She never was."

Malcolm disconnected, Lilly's words sending an electric surge through his rigid muscles. Bolting from the apartment, he stumbled along the sidewalk and filled his pleading lungs with fresh air. He mopped the sweat from his wispy scalp. Lowering the damp handkerchief, he swabbed the patchy fog forming on his glasses. When he returned home, he collapsed on the living room couch, playing the scene over in his head. Cell signals crossed, that's all, happens all the time. Just an elderly woman somewhere talking to the wrong Malcolm, and there must be thousands of Boston area older women with sons named Malcolm.

He gave a nervous chuckle as he headed to the basement, the knobby wood's squeals and groans marking his descent into the moldy darkness. He threw back the plastic tarp sheltering the boxes he had hauled from Lilly's house and searched for the one that would calm his irrational fear. Ripping open the package, he fished inside for the cell, shaking the box empty. Purse, wallet, and ID cards tumbled to the cement floor.

"It has to be here."

Sweat sprinkled his forehead. He tore open each remaining box, scattering Lilly's worldly belongings across the dusty floor. With each box turning up empty, Malcolm assured himself he had made a mistake and deposited the cell in the next box, or the next one. Malcolm dropped onto the floor, lost in his thoughts, the dimming light breaching the ground-level window and casting lengthening shadows across the room. When Eve and Frank Nichols' feet tapped across the hallway floor above, he still rested motionless amongst the scattered debris.

"Eve hasn't come home yet?" Stephanie Haskell glanced from her notepad, rolling a pen between her fingers.

Malcolm shook his head.

"She just needs time to get past her anger." Dr. Haskell checked her watch. "By the time you get home, I'm sure she'll be there."

Malcolm squirmed in his seat, digging his fingers into the decorative studs along the upholstered couch arm. "I spoke with her on the phone."

"Well, that's a start. Was she still upset about—"

"I didn't speak with Eve," he said. "I spoke with Mother."

Haskell shut her notepad. "You know that's not possible."

"I call her sometimes to listen to her voice. It rings three times, and her recorded greeting comes on. But yesterday, she picked up after the second ring."

Haskell leaned back and pocketed her glasses. "Malcolm, look at me."

He raised his head but could barely meet her gaze.

"Your mother's dead."

"She has her cell now." He stood and circled the room, pressing his fingertips into his sweaty palms. "She's back."

The doctor eyed Malcolm as he paced the office like a caged animal. "Death is the hardest thing we face in life. The sooner we accept it, the sooner we can move on."

He raked a hand through his thinning mane. "If I call her again, she's gonna pick up. I know it."

"Then let's do it."

"What?"

"Call her. So what if she picks up?" Haskell shrugged. "It will give us all a chance to talk together."

Malcolm swallowed. "Mother wouldn't like that. There's no telling what she'd do." He could sense the cell burning in his back pocket, scorching his skin through the trousers' thin fabric.

"Well, I'm not afraid of her." She grinned, reaching her hand out for the cell.

Maybe you should be.

"Come on," Haskell said, wiggling her fingers. "Give it here."

You have no idea what you're about to do.

She snatched the phone and scrolled through his contact list. "Let's see . . . Lilly Morris, where are you?" She tapped the name on the screen.

Mother's going to be very angry.

Haskell tapped the speaker icon and stood, holding the phone toward Malcolm—one ring, two rings, and then a click. Silence. She inspected the phone, tilting her head as she squinted at the screen.

Malcolm waited for the third ring he knew wouldn't come. Mother had already picked up. She was there . . . on the line. He could hear her strained breathing and the gentle clink of ice against glass as she swirled her drink. She remained silent, content to wait them out.

Malcolm stepped forward, shouting at the device. "We shouldn't have called, Mother! I'm . . . I'm sorry—"

"Mrs. Morris." Dr. Haskell raised her hand. "Are you there?"

Again, the breathing. The imperceptible clink of her ice-filled highball.

She gazed at Malcolm as the phone disconnected. His hands curled into fists behind his back. The heat spread through his veins until he sensed his whole body on fire.

"You really shouldn't have done that, Dr. Haskell."

———

Malcolm stood on the crowded subway platform, jostling for space, eyes peering toward the dark tunnel for the approaching train. The air squeezed from his lungs as the cell buzzed in his back pocket. He glanced at the screen. Lilly. The underground station's buzz filtered to silence, the sound muffled in his head. Grabbing a stranger's shoulder beside him, Malcolm steadied himself to keep from toppling to the floor. He stumbled through the crowd as the trolley squealed and rumbled to a stop. He accepted the call, pressing a finger to his opposite ear to drown out the dull roar.

"Surprised?" Lilly growled.

He slammed a fist over his mouth and squeezed his eyes shut. He teetered, leaning against the station's grimy tiled wall for support. The voice was unmistakable but wrong at the same time. It echoed in his ear as if from a great distance but seemed to originate within his brain's center lobes.

"Snap out of it, Malcolm!" the gruff voice spat.

"I'm sorry, Mother."

"So, you wanted to show me off to the doctor today. What do you think I am, some dog and pony show?"

"No, Mother, I didn't want to call. She took my phone, she made me—"

"You never had any backbone, Malcolm. And why did you hang up on me yesterday?"

"I wasn't sure if you were . . ."

"Spit it out! Not sure if I was what, real?"

"Dr. Haskell said you couldn't have picked up." He wrapped his arms around himself, doubling over at the waist. "She said you're . . ." He slid down the wall until his backside met the dusty cement floor. He pulled with his lungs, but he couldn't draw a breath.

"Dead?"

Malcolm nodded, oblivious to whether Lilly could gauge his silent response.

"Well, I may need to have a talk with her, show her just how real I am."

He sprang to his feet. "Please, don't do that, Mother!"

"You don't happen to have her number handy, do you?" She barked out a sharp laugh.

"She's helping me . . ."

"Helping you? By telling you I'm dead? How does that help you?"

"I don't know, but I think it does. I need to face up to—"

"You need to accept the fact you're nothing without me," Lilly said. "You never were. What did I tell you about women?"

"You can't trust them," he replied, lowering his head.

A sharp intake of breath rattled his ear, no doubt Lilly taking a throaty drag from her cigarette. The swirling ice plinked the side of her glass.

"You don't need to talk to any doctor. I'm back, and you're gonna do what I say now."

"Yes, Mother."

"You should've listened when I warned you about marrying that bitch Eve, as well. She's no good either."

"I know."

"All these women in your life, no good. Especially that scheming doctor trying to drive a wedge between us."

He nodded his head.

"Now, are you going to get rid of her, or am I?"

Ice fingers traipsed along his spine. "Get rid of her?"

"Cancel your appointments, Malcolm," she said with a chuckle. "That's all I meant."

He swiped the sheen from his forehead. "I'll go back right now, Mother."

"Good boy, Malcolm." A moment of silence. "Because that's one visit you don't want me to make."

———

He woke the following morning to a blizzard of dust motes dancing among the sunbeams pouring through the bedroom window. Rolling over, he reached to Eve's undisturbed bedside. Two nights and she hadn't bothered to call.

God knows living with her took a toll, but nighttime was the worst. Eve would wake him in the middle of the night checking a text, or she would pull out her laptop—*tap, tap, tap*—and keep him up for hours. Stretching his muscles from head to toe, Malcolm assembled the pillows behind him, propping himself against the headboard. He couldn't remember the last time he had awoken feeling so refreshed. If he could feel this rested after two nights without her, maybe a few days apart would do him good.

Throwing back the blankets, he padded into the kitchen. He wrinkled his nose at an odor wafting from the basement. He grasped the handle and cracked the door, his head snapping back at the stale darkness, as if it had reached out and slapped him with an open hand. Jamming the door closed, Malcolm swatted at the bad air.

Smells like a goddamn cesspool down there.

Malcolm strode to the hallway window, scanning the street. A Boston Water and Sewer vehicle rested against the curb beside an open manhole. Two men leaned against the truck, sipping coffee while a third descended a ladder into the city's bowels.

He unbolted the front door and pulled the chill winter air into his lungs to chase the stench from his sinuses. As he snatched the *Boston Globe* from the porch, two men emerged from a sedan parked across the street. Checking for traffic, they jogged across Beacon Street, suit jackets flapping in the breeze. They slowed as they reached the sidewalk, smoothing their ties and buttoning their coats.

"Are you Malcolm Morris?" The larger man flashed a gold shield. "I'm Detective Ray Harrington. My partner Paul Becker, Boston PD. Can we come in?"

Oh God, something happened to Eve. "Is she all right?" Malcolm squeezed the paper, newsprint staining his sweaty hands.

Harrington tilted his head. "Is who all right?"

"My wife, Eve." Malcolm's stomach dropped. "Eve Hunter?"

Harrington and Becker exchanged glances.

"We don't know anything about an Eve Hunter," Becker offered. "We're investigating the death of Dr. Stephanie Haskell. Someone murdered her in her office late yesterday afternoon. You were her last patient, so naturally…"

"I understand." Malcolm flexed his legs to keep his knees from buckling, shifting his weight from one foot to the other.

"What happened to your wife, Mr. Morris?" Harrington inquired.

Tremors slaked Malcolm's legs, and he dabbed at his forehead. "We got into a little disagreement, that's all. She hasn't come home since then. You guys had me thinking the worst, that's all. Please come in."

He led the detectives into the living room. The temperature had spiked, sending sweat beads trickling between his shoulder blades.

Harrington dropped onto the sofa and fished through his jacket pockets, removing a worn spiral notebook. "Sir, we'd like to ask you a few questions, if you don't mind."

"Sure, but I don't know anything."

Harrington checked his notebook. "Did you notice anything out of the ordinary during your visit with Dr. Haskell? Did she appear anxious? Distracted?"

She was scared. Malcolm squeezed his fingers against his palms. "I don't remember anything."

Harrington paused. "Aren't you at least curious?"

"About what?" Malcolm raised his head.

"How she died," Becker added.

Mother skinned her.

Malcolm swallowed. "I don't really want to know."

"What's that smell?" Harrington's nose creased as he drew a sharp inhale.

"Sewer lines, I think. There's a city truck across the street working on it."

Becker moved to the window and pulled the curtain. "Where?"

"Just down the street." Malcolm pointed, but Becker shook his head.

"I don't see anything."

Malcolm joined Becker at the window, gazing at the spot where he had observed the truck minutes earlier. "That's funny. It's like they vanished. They must have finished the job."

Malcolm's cell buzzed in his back pocket. He flicked away the sweat at his temple as his cell vibrated. *God, it's hot in here.*

"Expecting a call?" Harrington asked.

"I need to take this. It could be Eve." *You know it isn't, though, don't you?*

Clutching the cell, Malcolm stepped out of the living room. He swiped the screen and waited.

"Are those boys giving you a hard time, Malcolm?" Lilly's voice reached into his head.

"What the hell did you do?" Malcolm snapped.

"Time to find a new doctor . . ." She gave a soft chuckle.

"Why did you have to kill her?" he whispered, hand cupping the cell. "I went back and canceled my appointments like you told me to."

God, she was so scared.

"What makes you think I did it?"

"Mr. Morris." Harrington's voice boomed from the living room. "We have a few more questions."

Lilly's dead voice rattled in his skull. "Refreshing sleep last night?"

"How do you know?"

"Because Eve's gone now. You figured out that much, didn't you?"

Malcolm's heart hesitated in its rhythm as his face flushed with heat.

"Mr. Morris." Becker stepped into the foyer. "Tell them you'll call them back."

"Mother, I need to go now."

"Sir, the smell's overpowering," Becker said, waving a hand beneath his nose. "You mind if we take a look down there? I'm a bit of an amateur plumber myself. Maybe I could help figure out the problem."

Liar.

Malcolm stepped in front of the basement door. "I'd rather we keep the door closed. You know . . . the smell." The sweat beneath his armpits dripped along his sides.

"Odor coming from the basement?" Lilly paused as if for effect. "What could that be?"

"Mr. Morris." Harrington signaled his partner with a head nod. "Detective Becker's gonna take a look anyway. I need you to step away from the door and face the wall so I can search you, make sure you don't have a weapon."

He turned, leaning against the wall with one arm, the other pressing the cell to his ear. "Mother, what do I do?"

"We got a woman's body down here," Becker shouted from the darkness.

"They'll take my cell, Mother. How will I reach you?"

Harrington unholstered his sidearm. "Mr. Morris, you're under arrest. You have the right to remain silent. Anything you say can and will . . ."

The detective's words dissolved away, unable to penetrate Malcolm's ears as he strained to hear his mother.

"Don't you worry, Malcolm. We'll find a way."

Becker stumbled up the basement stairs. "There's a second body down there, Ray. Male."

"Mother?" Malcolm mumbled as Harrington cuffed him.

"What did you expect?" Lilly's words fizzled deep inside his head. "That's what Eve gets for bringing her boyfriend home and parading him around."

"Holy Jesus . . ." Becker leaned forward at the waist, hands resting against his thighs. "These bodies were peeled, too, Ray."

"What?" Harrington winced.

Becker raised his head. "Like the doctor. Skinned . . . alive."

PART FOUR

The Reckoning

CHAPTER THIRTY-FOUR

Spring Valley, Missouri

Jack awoke on the living room floor and maneuvered to a sitting position, his eyes adjusting to the sunlight pouring in through the broken windows. He shielded his face, unprepared for the piercing light stinging his retinas and igniting his rods and cones. The room blazed as if a wild hand had painted every wall, door frame, and floorboard in neon colors. Jack blinked, allowing his eyes to calibrate to the vivid surroundings. Compared to the muted hues he'd experienced over the past few hours—or had it been days, he didn't know—it appeared as if the sun had finally risen.

Struggling to his feet, he wandered across the room and gazed through the window.

No bloated livestock lay strewn about the farm, and the body odor and death scent had dissipated. A familiar manure aroma drifted through the holes in the crumbled walls and rotting window frames. Jack scanned the living room. Warped floorboards sagged under his weight, and water-stained tiles hung from the ceiling joists.

"Where the hell is all the furniture?" he mumbled. Jack's eyes widened as the gears turned in his mind and tumblers clicked into place.

He was home. Not stuck in some Underground stage set concocted to resemble his childhood home, but the real thing. Spring Valley, Missouri. The Tar had let him go.

Jack beamed, a quiet joy erupting from deep inside. He could sense his emotions again, The Tar's hellish environs no longer suppressing them. For a second time, he had escaped the beast's clutches. It should have been a time for celebration, but Jack's elation dimmed as he replayed his interactions with The Tar and what he had told him to do. Kill Carver, just as he had killed others over the years. Send him more souls and someday he would have Sam again—maybe. He would need to do what The Tar demanded, and still, he had no guarantees. He pictured Sam in her hideous personal hell, strung out on the Underground's numbing miasma and lamenting Morgan's loss for the rest of eternity. He had no choice. Jack never doubted he would give his life for Sam at a moment's notice if the situation arose. But his adventure in the Underground with The Tar revealed a greater depth to his love for her than he had ever imagined. He wouldn't just die for her; he would relinquish his soul for her.

Jack gave his living room the once over. *At least my house isn't a meth lab.* Departing the dying structure, Jack aimed his feet toward Prairie Road. He had no idea how long he had been in the Underground, but he had faith that Carver would await him in the cornfield beside Johnson Farm. The Tar would have instructed him to remain there.

As his feet crunched dirt and pebbles, a discordant tune fluttered along the breeze. Ahead, Carver leaned against the carousel's gear panel, pulling his silver hair back in a ponytail. Jack knifed through the knee-high grass, a rhythmic swish sounding against his pant legs with each step.

"Don't you have anywhere else to be?" he shouted.

"Didn't expect you to make it back, to tell you the truth." Carver pressed his hands against his hips. "I've been trying to get you back into the Underground for years and you're out again. You must have negotiated one hell of a deal."

You have no idea. "Well, I don't have my wife back." He gazed at the man he would double cross, either killing or sending him back to hell on his own carousel. "Not much of a deal, if you ask me."

"You're still bleeding." Carver pointed to Jack's nose.

Jack pressed a palm against his nostrils, reigniting the searing pain from his headlong crash into the carousel guide pole earlier. The stinging sensation lingered, filling his eyes with water. "Christ, that smarts. Why did you have to remind me?"

"I didn't remind you to jam your hand against it." Carver tossed him a handkerchief.

Jack dabbed gingerly at a new blood trickle above his upper lip. "Now that I'm back from that hell hole, I can get pissed at you about this."

Carver sighed. "Don't hold a grudge, mate. The way I see it, we're square now."

Jack scrunched his face. "How's that?"

"I dealt with The Tar's wrath for a quarter century, and you get a bloody nose. Even Steven."

"Whatever." Jack threw the bloody handkerchief onto the grass.

Carver stepped forward. "So, I need to ask you . . . how did you do it?"

"Do what?"

"How did you escape the Underground?"

The lie would need to be convincing. "I got you a reprieve, Carver." He gestured toward the carousel. "You're going to be done with this assignment and get your family back."

Carver's face changed, and Jack witnessed a hint of emotion—even hope—flicker in his eyes. "What's the catch?"

"No catch. I take over your operation. Now it's *me* who has the quota to meet."

"You . . . running the carousel?"

"All you need to do is show me the ropes. The sooner you get me up to speed, the sooner you get to join your family."

Carver folded his arms. "And how is this transition supposed to work?"

Jack traipsed through the field and hauled himself onto the platform. "Well, once I get the hang of things with this contraption, I send you back to The Tar." Jack forced a smile. "Your job is over. You leave the Underground with your family."

"Send me to The Tar, huh?" Carver gave Jack a sidelong glance, his gaze lingering as if searching for a tell. "I just step onto the carousel, mount the coffee-colored jumper, and let you send me to the Underground?"

Or I kill you. Jack struggled to keep his gaze fixed on Carver. "The Tar makes the rules, not me."

"You sure about that?"

Jack's insides twisted. *He's not buying it.* "I'm only doing what The Tar wanted."

The men stood in silence as the breeze rustled the grass. Carver grinned and eyed Jack with a slow nod. The man understood better than anyone that if you've visited the Underground, you'd sell your mother's soul to avoid another get-together with The Tar. Carver may have figured Jack's negotiation with The Tar wasn't as straightforward as it appeared.

"How long will it take?" Jack redirected, winding his way through the carousel horses. "You know, to get me up to speed?"

"We'll have to see." A slight change in Carver's body language. "There's much to learn."

As much as Jack wanted to get Sam out of the Underworld as soon as possible, he would need to be patient. Not only would the training be lengthy, but Carver might even slow the training, stall to find a way out of the new arrangement and save his own ass.

A familiar beat thrummed in Jack's head—*thud . . . thud . . . thud.* A signal from The Tar. Jack glanced at Carver, who lifted his fingers to his temple and rubbed circles. He sensed it, too.

"We have work to do, don't we?" Jack asked.

"It never ends," Carver said.

"How do we take this thing apart?" Jack stepped off the platform.

"We don't."

"What the hell does that mean?"

Carver blew out a breath. "When I worked for my former boss at the Kent Avenue factory in New York City, I spent sixteen-hour days on the factory floor. But at night, I would process the job in my dreams. Images would flood through me: wooden planks arranging to form the platform, steam-powered engine motors' spinning pulleys attaching to drive belts, and suspension rods assembling to support roof pieces. Now, all I have to do is press my eyes shut and the carousel parts find their way together, and apart, like they did in my dreams."

"A gift from The Tar?"

"Most likely. That's what I'll teach you: how to assemble and disassemble this thing without raising a finger. It'll take time. Once you picture it happening up here"—Carver pointed at his head—"it can happen automatically."

"Show me."

Carver pressed his eyes shut. The screech of metal on metal rose in Jack's ears as support poles disassembled from brass fittings, wooden planks rose off the platform, nuts twisted free from engine motor bolts, guide poles dis-impaled the horses, and suspension rods spun away from the roof. Carver hobbled to the pickup and threw back the tarp on the flatbed trailer. The materials organized themselves on the wooden surface as Carver secured the pieces beneath the tarp with bungee cords. Jack glanced at the spot on the Johnsons' cornfield where the carousel had rested, but not a single flattened stalk existed among the swaying corn.

"When we arrive at our destination, you'll put it together by hand and take it down the same way. We'll do it that way each time until your dreams fill with images of carousel pieces fitting together properly. Once that happens, the carousel will start doing all the heavy work for you."

"What if it doesn't?"

Carver scratched his ear. "Then I guess you'll put it together by hand."

Jeez, maybe The Tar was right. Killing people might be easier.

———

In the days following, Jack worked with Carver to get his clients through their journeys. Many never got close to The Tar's coffee-colored Uber. They took their ride and left the carousel, changed forever, born into a new world having glimpsed the glorious eternal. Others made a beeline for the hell-bound mare as if they had no other choice, bringing them everlasting suffering.

Those clients were the hardest to stomach.

Jack's gut wrenched before each client's fateful decision. He took to positioning himself in the client's line of sight as they approached a particular horse. He would give a slight head shake or nod if they made eye contact, depending on their choice. Only once did the communication appear to change a mind, one client redirecting her steps away from the sixth horse. But Jack had paid the price, suffering an extended pounding in his head until the sun rose the next day. The Tar had delivered his message. There could be no interference.

With each client, Jack had to construct and disassemble the carousel. The chore added considerable time to each appointment, but Carver didn't appear to mind. He would hover over Jack's shoulder as he laid out each piece in preparation for the assembly. He would encourage him despite his repeated mistakes. But Jack's limited mechanical skills frustrated the former engineer, who couldn't understand that a man who had lived more than forty years didn't know the difference between a socket wrench and a screwdriver. Jack reminded him every day that, as a writer, the only things he had ever assembled had been stories in his mind. Oh, and one baby crib.

Over time, Jack questioned whether Carver held back on the knowledge he relinquished to slow Jack's training, to delay his inevitable meeting with The Tar. Progress had been at a snail's pace, and if Jack didn't get a move on, he would never spring Sam from her prison hell.

Along with Carver, Jack sensed the pounding in his head with the approach of each new client. He could read it on Carver's face, the way an old married couple might perceive what one was thinking before the other spoke. They would glance at each other and get to work. But Jack sensed a different pounding that Carver was not privy to, The Tar's impatience signaling a change in his dealings with Jack. This pounding came as a direct message from The Tar to get moving, dispatch Carver, and start running the carousel himself.

Then the dreams came. Jack discovered he could assemble and disassemble the carousel in his sleep, just as Carver predicted. But when it came time for a client, Jack still had to put the machine together by hand. The pounding in his head continued. Stronger and stronger with each passing day. *Thud . . . thud . . . thud . . .*

One morning, as Carver slept, Jack guided the truck through the Ohio River Valley. They traveled south through the Midwest's dusty backroads to join a client who would meet his fate along the Cuyahoga's banks. Jack couldn't take another gut-twisting appointment like the four they had during the past week—just kids—who hadn't made the correct decision. Aware their new client was a bit longer in the tooth made things easier, but not much.

They jumped from the truck and threw back the tarp. Pressing his eyes shut, Jack tried to imagine the pieces fitting together. Nothing. Carver let out a groan and led Jack from the trailer.

"You need a break. Let's just get this one over with." The old man closed his eyes as calm descended over him. Within minutes, as if he had a team of men working for him, the carousel and its half-dozen horses spun slowly as the droning, hurdy-gurdy carnival jangle floated across the still air.

Carver slapped Jack on the back. "Why don't you let me do the assembly and disassembly for a while."

He's stalling. Jack sensed a twinge in his gut. *He knows I'm getting close.*

"Our client will be along soon." Carver checked his watch and gestured toward the stool beside the carousel. "You can do this one if you want." He handed Jack a wood chunk and tossed him his pocketknife. "Passes the time."

Jack dropped onto the seat and glanced upward. The sun had finally chased away the thick clouds, unraveling them into thin, white vapor trails across the sky. He stroked the knife blade along the wood's edge until he had removed the bark and blemishes. The warm timber heated his palm.

A man arrived on foot, wandering the riverbank before stopping a hundred yards from the carousel. Even from a distance, the man appeared as if he would dwarf the structure. But his imposing size wouldn't matter today. Large or small, rich or poor, everyone met their fate here. He would choose a horse and fulfill his destiny. Jack hoped it would be a good outcome for him. The man resumed his lumbering advance as if caught in the carousel's orbit and subject to its gravitational pull. He stopped before the machine and adjusted thick, horned-rimmed glasses.

Jack sheathed the knife in his front pocket and stood. "What's your name, friend?"

"Richard." The giant stood at least six-and-a-half feet tall and spoke with a hint of an accent, pronouncing his name *Ree-shar*. Maybe Canadian. "Richard Malik."

"Want to take a ride?" Jack yanked the lever and killed the engine, slowing the carousel to a halt.

Malik rested a hand on his chin as he surveyed the carousel. His mitts were as thick as hams. "It's been years since I've been on one of these things."

His grin revealed a pair of missing teeth on his upper palate, contributing to a raspy lisp. His arms hung several inches too low as if they hadn't known when to stop growing. If he wore skates, he could have passed for one of the Hanson brothers from that old hockey movie. The puck he must have taken to his teeth only solidified the image.

When the carousel stopped, Malik stepped onto the platform and inspected the different horses. "The craftsmanship on these," he said. "Simply amazing."

Jack gestured toward Carver. "This guy's the genius."

Malik glanced at the old man. "Beautiful work, sir. And you'll let me ride on one, eh?"

Carver shook his head. "Go ahead. Pick yourself a jumper."

"Oh, for sure." Malik lumbered from one horse to another. "You don't suppose I'll break them, do you?"

Carver chuckled. "Hasn't happened yet."

Malik continued to inspect the animals, stroking their manes. "How did you get the hair so fine? It's like a real horse."

Carver approached the man, grasping a support pole and pulling himself onto the platform. He pressed a hand against a horse's coat. "Indeed, this is genuine horsehair—"

Malik grabbed the old man, halting him in midsentence. He pressed his forearm against his neck. Carver's eyes bulged in their sockets and his face flushed purple as he struggled to pull in a breath. Jack pounced toward the platform and swung an off-balance fist at the giant, grazing his temple. The blow didn't have the intended effect but threw the man off just enough to make him stumble and drop Carver to the platform. In an instant, Malik had recovered and secured Jack in a headlock.

"That's enough, Jack." Malik tightened his grip.

Jack's vision narrowed as the giant squeezed off the oxygen. *He knows who I am.* Black and gray spots floated before Jack's vision, unconsciousness dropping like nightfall before his eyes. Jamming a hand into his front pocket, he palmed the whittling knife. With his grip weakening, Jack could only manage a superficial slice across Malik's thigh, but the blade did enough to relinquish the man's hold.

"Jesus fucking Murphy!" Malik shouted, pressing a hand against the dripping slice wound.

Jack sputtered and backpedaled, sucking in the precious oxygen as he put distance between himself and the giant. Carver remained motionless on the platform.

"Who the hell are you?" Jack held the knife at arm's length.

"I told you already. Richard."

Jack tilted his head, figuring Malik may have taken a few too many pucks to the head and didn't grasp his meaning. "If you want to tell me why you're here, I'm all ears."

"Oh, right. The Tar sent me, and he's pissed. Says you're not doing your job. Either you're not learning fast enough"—the man gestured to Carver—"or he isn't teaching you. So I'm taking one of you with me."

"Is this part of your . . . negotiation?"

"Not that it's any of your business, but yeah. Once the old man is back with The Tar, I'm one step closer to getting home."

If that's what you think, then you don't know The Tar. Jack's deep breaths eased his pounding heartbeat, but he kept his weapon raised. "Looks to me like you were hoping for a two-for-one deal."

Malik glanced at the blade. "How I do the job is at my discretion. Let's say I kill you. Well, I just enhance my opportunities with The Tar." The man scooped up Carver and laid him over the coffee-colored mare. "I can come back and finish this job another time."

Jack angled his neck to peek at Carver's face. "Is he . . . ?"

"Dead? Nah, just taking a nap." Malik chuckled as he grasped Carver's hair and lifted his head. "Hope he's having a nice dream because when he wakes, he'll be in a nightmare." Mounting the mare, Malik pressed a hand into Carver's back and grasped the guide pole. "Don't worry, we'll be seeing each other again."

Jack's stomach clenched.

"Well, what are you waiting for, Carousel Man? Do your job."

Jack advanced to the gearbox but hesitated. "I'm not sending you anywhere."

Malik shook his head. He dismounted his steed and limped off the platform, grimacing as he held his palm against his bloody wound.

Jack inspected the oozing gash on Malik's thigh. "Smarts a bit . . . eh?"

Malik grinned before lunging forward. His palm exploded into Jack's chest, sending him pinwheeling backward. Bounding off the carousel, Jack ended up flat on his back, the wind knocked from his lungs with an audible *whoosh*. Light flashes streaked across his vision. He held the knife in front of him as Malik strode to the gearbox without the faintest hitch in his step.

The giant flashed a toothless smile. "Never seen such a fast healer, eh?" He grasped the lever and eased it forward, but the carousel lurched in the reverse direction with a yawning screech. "What the . . . ? Why's this thing trying to go backward?"

Jack pushed himself to the seated position as the machine's shrill squeal rose in pitch, like nails across a chalkboard. The horses vibrated in place. "Maybe Carver can help you fix that." His eyes darted to the still form draped over the jumper.

"I'm getting tired of your chirping." Malik bounded toward Jack, sidestepping his slashing blade. He booted his ribcage, jackknifing him into the fetal position. A bloody mist escaped Jack's lips and speckled the dirt.

"You relax, I got this." Malik twisted knobs and flicked switches before gripping the lever and jamming it forward. After several tries and different combinations, he quelled the carousel's painful wail and resumed its counterclockwise direction. He leaped onto the platform and mounted the coffee-colored horse as the machine increased its tempo. "See you around."

Jack glanced at Carver. The old man's eyes fluttered open, and his gaze darted about as if taking in his dire circumstances. Locking gazes with Jack, he gave him a quick wink and squeezed his eyes shut. Support poles disengaged from their fittings, and suspension rods twisted from the roof's metallic insertions at breakneck speed. Wooden planks rumbled and burst off the carousel floor, and rivets shot out of the machine in all directions. Jack covered his head, protecting himself from Carver's last-ditch effort to dismantle the carousel and prevent Malik from making his delivery.

The carousel rotated in a blur as the skies dimmed, pieces flying from the machine and scattering across the field. The carousel shimmied and broke apart in a metallic explosion, but too late to halt the coffee-colored mare from bolting from the carousel. The sixth horse tromped across the meadow with its riders; its hooves thundered against the scorched earth as it picked up speed. Jack lay back in the dirt and closed his eyes. Following the hell-horse in his mind, the beast exploded through rocky canyons and into the earth's bowels until it disappeared into the burning abyss.

So long, Carver.

CHAPTER THIRTY-FIVE

South of Cleveland, Ohio (Ohio River Valley)

Jack lay on the ground, arms wrapped around his midsection, ribs cracked and maybe broken. Painful spasms ripped through his core and squeezed the air from his lungs each time he straightened. The sun balanced high in the sky, igniting the sweat beads burning a trail from hairline to chin as he struggled to a sitting position.

He rose to his feet and shuffled to the wooden stool beside the carousel's twisted wreckage. His midsection ached from the wrecking ball plowing into him. Dropping onto the seat, Jack closed his eyes, unsure what to do next. His tenure as carousel operator had lasted a brief fortnight, but it had proved far too long for The Tar's patience. Jack hadn't delivered Carver promptly, or killed him, which The Tar had expected, and he had pulled the plug on the experiment. Maybe he figured Jack didn't have the heart, or he had found his new killer in Malik and decided to cut his losses, Carver first, then Jack. He waited for a signal, a connection with that other world. But nothing happened—no visions, no thudding in his ears, only the wind rifling through the grass. He was on his own. Jack shuddered, recalling Malik's warning. He had a sinking feeling the giant would be back before long to finish his assignment. Not because he had to but because he wanted to.

Jack glanced at the empty space where the carousel had stood only moments before, the remnants strewn across the landscape. Carver had hit the self-destruct button, but his actions still couldn't save him from a one-way ticket to the Underground. Even with Carver, Jack would have no shot at putting together the mangled carousel. And with no carousel, he would never be able to rescue Sam. With Jack cut loose, the beast would no longer need his carrot, Sam, to dangle before him. A twisted

knot formed in the pit of his stomach. Not only had he become expend-
able, but Sam had as well.

Finding his feet, he limped to the truck and disconnected the flatbed
trailer. He gazed over his shoulder at the bits and pieces of carousel strewn
about the tall grass beside the Cuyahoga River. Cradling his ribs, Jack
eased himself into the front seat. He had one last shot at Sam, an outside
shot, another Hail Mary, but one he had to take. And he didn't have
much time. He fired the engine and threw the truck in gear, kicking up
pebbles as he floored it toward the highway. Glancing into the rearview
mirror, he watched as the remnants of the carousel that had haunted him
his entire life disappeared for the final time in a billowing dust cloud.

———

After falling into line with the cars on I-71, Jack grabbed his cell.
Wincing, he wrapped a tentative arm around his ribs, the slightest movement derailing the air in his throat. He scrolled through his favorites
list and tapped Dr. Lang's number, reciting the rundown of what had
transpired since they last saw each other in the Johnsons' cornfield. Jack
fielded the doctor's question barrage, one after another: Yes, he had made
another deal with The Tar. No, it didn't go well. Yes, it would be a problem. No, the whole ordeal wasn't over yet. Yes, Sam was still there.

"I should probably fill you in on what's happened while you've been
away," Lang began. "First, you're all over the news. I'm sure you've figured
that out already. Every law enforcement agency in the country is searching for you. They have you for at least three deaths, including your wife.
I don't understand how they think you could have killed anyone—"

"They're right, Doc," Jack said. "They're only wrong about Sam."

"What are you talking about?"

"I learned things about myself in the Underground. Things I've
done."

Jack pictured Lang processing this latest information. The man had
treated him for years and had been his friend for as many. Maybe he
finally recognized he had no idea who Jack Rainne really was.

"Are you sure what you learned was real? Could The Tar have put
false images in your head?"

"No, Doc. They were real."

"Do you want to tell me about them?"

Jack told him about his father, how he had *really* died. He explained about the boy, Jack Morgan, and his mother, Ellen. He described the pounding in his head, the rhythmic throbbing he had chalked up to tumors and migraines after his father's death. "Those were The Tar's way to urge me to kill. There are others, Doc. I'm sure of it."

"You must ask yourself something." Jack could tell Lang had put on his therapist hat, his words chosen carefully. "Is someone a killer if the circumstances around each killing were beyond his control? I've been in courtrooms where defendants insisted God or the devil drove them to kill. You're the only one I know of who could truly claim that defense."

"You can't let me off the hook for my sins, Doc. I'm gonna pay the price either here on earth or afterward."

"You already have paid the price. You've been to hell and back twice now. That's got to be some kind of record."

"Well, I'm going to make a third trip, Doc. Sam's in mortal danger now. The Tar doesn't need her anymore. He had her as leverage to keep me working for him. But now . . ."

"How are you planning to get back there without the carousel?"

"It's a long shot, but I have to find Graham Carver. He's the only person who can help me."

"Wait. I thought you said the giant took him back to the Underground?"

"He did, but there's another Graham Carver."

Lang remained silent as if waiting for Jack to explain this one.

"I know this will sound crazy—"

"I think we can stop with that qualifier from now on. I've seen enough to believe whatever you say."

"Well, this *other* Graham Carver lived on the Vineyard long ago." Jack imagined the younger version strolling through Cottage City with his family. "If I can find him again, he might be able to help me get into the Underground undetected."

"But how?"

"There's a replica carousel on the Vineyard. I visited Carver there once before, in a different century. There's no reason to believe I won't find him there again, but I don't know when he'll be there."

Lang assembled the pieces. "Let me get this straight. The two things you need to get to the Underground are a working carousel and Carver. The Tar has Carver and must know the carousel is gone. Sounds like he won't be expecting you."

"Exactly. I'm not even sure if The Tar is tracking me anymore. I don't sense him inside my head."

"To your advantage."

"The big question is, how do I get Sam and myself back out?" Jack switched his cell to the opposite ear. "If The Tar remains in the dark, I might have bought myself enough time to find Sam before he figures out I'm even there."

"Can Carver get you out?"

Jack hesitated. "I don't know." *Not a chance, Jack.*

"But you've gotten out twice, maybe the third time's a charm."

"It's my only chance to get her back, and I'm gonna take it." *It's a suicide mission, pal.*

Lang's silence on the line only reinforced the little voice whispering in Jack's ear.

"Well, I do have a bit of good news."

"You can't be serious."

Lang chuckled. "Your books have shot to the top of the New York Times best-seller list. I heard you have the top three spots and a couple more in the top ten. You know how America loves its mass murderers."

"Just what I need, a new fan base. Listen, Doc. I need to get back to the Vineyard, and I need you to meet me there. I'm driving, and I won't be able to get there until tomorrow."

"Whatever you need, Jack. But can I ask why? I'm not sure how I can help you. All this . . . it's way above my pay grade."

"It's not for me, Doc. I'm going back in for Sam, and I may not make it back. But I'll be damn sure I get her out. She's gonna need help and for a long time. Just like I did. I want you to stay at the house. Take care of her for a while."

"Whatever you need. Whatever she needs, I'll be there. I can catch a flight and be on the island before you even get there."

"Make sure you stay away from the house, Doc. If they're searching for me, I'm sure they'll have surveillance on the place. I imagine you'll run into more cops than at all the Massachusetts Dunkin' Donuts combined."

"I'll lay low and wait to hear from you. Good luck, my friend. I'll be praying for you."

"Thanks, Doc." *I'm gonna need it.*

CHAPTER THIRTY-SIX

Boston, Massachusetts

Jack drove along I-90 deep into the night, skirting the edge of Pennsylvania through Erie and into New York State. After seven hours of indistinguishable Empire State Highway, the sun peeked above the horizon as he hit the Massachusetts line, detonating the Berkshires sky in pink and orange hues. Jack savored the morning's offering, trying to recall how the atmosphere scattered light rays and produced such magnificent displays—something about particles, angles of light, shorter wavelength blue light, and longer wavelength reds. It never made sense to him, and maybe that was why he never lost each morning's inherent wonder. Dissect and dismantle the glorious, and fascination and awe disappear. Knowing what Jack understood about life, death, and existence, he kept his focus on the sky, reveling in one remaining fleeting mystery.

Two hours later, Jack battled the traffic on Storrow Drive and exited onto Commonwealth until he reached the Boston Public Gardens. He hung a right onto Arlington and then another into the public alley behind Hal's Newbury Street office. He slid from the seat and doubled over, wincing as the spasms forced the air from his lungs. He wrapped his arms across his aching ribs, a constant reminder of the beating the giant had delivered.

Stepping toward the building, he buried his head in his cell to check for an ancient text from Hal. He squinted at the screen and punched the access code to gain entry. Better for the FBI's most wanted to slip through the backdoor and surprise Hal in his office rather than burst into a waiting room full of clients.

Jack padded up the back stairs and gently tapped on Hal's rear office door.

"Hal, it's Jack."

A muted *Jesus Christ* reached Jack's ears as Hal threw open the door and ushered him inside. "What the fuck, Jack!"

"Good to see you too, Hal." Jack gave his friend an awkward embrace as he surveyed the familiar office. An oversized desk and plush leather chairs, framed photographs of his famed clients, and a wall of bestsellers displayed on his bookshelves. He gaped at the empty wall space that had housed his photo for more than a decade.

Hal pushed him away.

"Is that any way to treat your most famous client?"

Hal's fingers rubbed against his palms as he scampered to the window. "My most famous ex-client, that is. And for all the wrong reasons." He scanned the street before snapping the curtains closed. He faced Jack, his eyes blinking a mile a minute. "You shouldn't be here. I have detectives, cops, and the FBI stopping by every day, all hours. It's like they've made this place their unofficial headquarters. Do you have any idea what's going on?"

"I'm getting the sense I'm not wanted here."

Hal threw his hand up in a salute. "Welcome aboard, Captain Obvious. Where's your red fucking coat?"

"Jeez, I thought I was finally making you a few dollars."

"Very funny, smartass. It's blood money, and I'm donating every penny of it." Hal scooted to his desk, picked up the *Boston Globe*, and slapped it against Jack's chest. "Here you go. This is just *today's* story."

Jack winced as the impact jolted his ribs. He unfurled the newspaper. "'Rainne of Terror.' Now that's a clever headline."

"You should see the *Herald*."

"Listen." Jack held up his hands. "I know none of this can make any sense to you, but it's not what you think."

Hal circled behind his desk and pressed his palms against the oak top. "Tell me you didn't kill the boy and his mother?"

Jack hesitated, unable to explain himself. "All I can say, Hal, is I'm not fully responsible for my actions."

"But you did it, didn't you? Same with Sam and the others."

"Sam's alive."

"She's missing, Jack." Hal pointed. "People don't simply disappear."

"Actually, they do." Jack imagined Carver's carousel, in operation for over a century. He imagined the *others*, as Carver called them, using their talents to collect for The Tar. How many were out there? Jack waved his hand. "There's so much you don't know. I can't begin to explain—"

"Fuck!" Hal collapsed into his desk chair. "You've been my friend, Jack. You've been inside my home, played with my kids . . ." He rubbed his eyes. "How can it be I have no idea who you are?"

"You know who I am." He took a step toward the desk. "It's Jack."

"The Ripper, maybe." Hal stood and threw open a desk drawer. He grabbed a copy of *Double-Barrel Justice* and snapped it open, nearly breaking the binding. "Susan, out front, has been scanning and copying the murder scenes from your books for the past few days and sending them to law enforcement." He tossed the misshapen tome back into the drawer. "Those sections match a whole bunch of murders they're trying to pin on you." Hal interlaced his fingers on the top of his head. "God, how could I have not known?"

"Don't beat yourself up, Hal. You couldn't have known anything. I didn't even know anything."

"So, what, you have multiple personalities? You black out when you kill? The devil talks to you?" Hal counted off on his fingers.

Not a bad guess, that one.

"What is it, Jack? What fiction will the lawyers try to spin at your trial." He folded his arms. "They're going to hang you in front of the federal courthouse on Fan Pier, you know?"

"I know, Hal. But I have one chance to make things right. I can't undo the past, but there's one person I can save. Sam. But I need to get to the Flying Horses on the Vineyard. After that, everything will make sense."

Hal scrunched his eyebrows. "She's being held at a carousel? That's insane. Sounds like more of your bad fiction."

Ouch, Hal.

Three knocks echoed off the thick office door. "Mr. Bader? Your nine o'clock is still waiting."

"Tell him to sit tight, Susan. I'll be right out." Hal tossed a thumb toward the back entrance. "You gotta go, Jack. My livelihood is at stake here. Clients are dropping like flies. No one wants to be associated with anyone connected with public enemy number one. Including me."

Ouch again.

Hal held the door. "Now go."

"Wait. I came here for a reason. I need your help. Just one last time. Please, hear me out."

Hal blew out a breath and let the door swing shut. "Okay, what?"

"I'm heading out to the Vineyard. I'm gonna get Sam back. After that, I don't care what they do to me. She's all that matters right now. I need to hole up there for a day or so, maybe longer."

"What do you want from me?"

"I can't go to Edgartown; I'm sure they have surveillance on the place, and the entire Massachusetts law enforcement community is probably waiting for me in my driveway."

"Yeah, you don't want to go—" Hal stopped himself, his eyes lighting up like bulbs on a Christmas tree as recognition dawned across his face. "No way, don't even ask—"

"Let me lie low at your place," Jack said. He had been to Hal's tidy bungalow near Lake Tashmoo Harbor in Vineyard Haven countless times. With Hal's office cooperating with law enforcement, no one would be expecting him there. "I can keep out of sight for a while. Until I can get Sam back. I need a few days at most, I swear."

"Oh, sure!" Hal threw his arms out. "Aiding and abetting a fugitive. Well, that should only get me five to ten years."

"No one will ever know. I'll knock out a windowpane on the back door. It will look like a break-in." Jack fished through his pockets. "Here, I'll pay for the damage up front."

"Keep your money." Hal took off his glasses and tossed them on the desk. He slogged to the window, turning his back on his old friend. "Do what you gotta do."

Jack crossed the carpet. "Thanks, Hal. I can't tell you how—"

"Just go." Hal waved his hand. "And don't contact me again." He faced off against Jack. "This is where you leave, and we go our separate ways."

Jack dropped a hand on Hal's shoulder. "I won't forget this."

Hal swiped it away and spun to the window, his gaze directed across Newbury Street. He dragged the back of his hand across his eyes. "Just get the hell out of here."

———

Jack followed the stream of cars pouring off the ferry and clogging the tight Vineyard Haven streets. The late afternoon sun perched on the horizon, balanced on the pencil-thin line between sea and sky. Its dying light pierced his vision like a fiery blade. Snapping the visor into place, Jack drove with a palm in front of his face to offset the blinding assault. As he gazed at his familiar environs, it dawned on him that despite being back home on the island, he would never be home again. Best case scenario, he returns with Sam from the Underground. They would never share life together again. He would go to prison for what he had done. He would never see the light of day except for whatever stray remnants might stream through a narrow, barred window.

He took Beach Road over Lagoon Pond Bridge and past the hospital, winding the pickup through Oak Bluffs, conscious of staying at the speed limit. The Vineyard wasn't a place to worry much about the police pulling you over for speeding, but he was too close to his goal for missteps now. Pulling in front of the Flying Horses, Jack grabbed the John Deere cap he'd purchased at a Midwest Flying J. As a disguise, it left much to be desired, but he would make do with whatever he had to work with. He killed the engine and ventured from the truck, yanking his visor low and keeping his gaze aimed at the sidewalk. As he circled the ancient barn, he pressed a tentative hand against the wall. He expected the familiar electrical surge that had driven him to his knees during his last visit, but his hand met nothing but splintered clapboard.

Reaching the front door, Jack entered the crowded pavilion. He immediately questioned the decision, sensing every stray eye dart in his direction and each cursory gaze burn a hole through him. They must suspect the Vineyard's most notorious killer had returned. His heated blood settled in his face, and his heart hammered against his ribcage as he circled the twirling platform. Keeping his head bowed, Jack blended in with the crowd and scanned the room for his quarry. The Wurlitzer's discordant carnival sound rang in his ears as the carousel spun. Joyous cries and laughter sounded from the children grasping for the brass ring mounted against the wall with each revolution. Jack circled the carousel, but no Carver. He would need to wait. At some point, Oak Bluffs would morph into Cottage City, and the Flying Horses would transform into the gateway to hell. But when?

Jack exited the building and slunk toward the truck. He dropped into the front seat and leaned the seat back, waiting until the sun had set and Oak Bluffs went dark. The first time he had met the younger Carver in Cottage City, it had been in the dead of night. Maybe the town needed the cover of darkness to perform its mysterious retro make-over or conjure up the nineteenth-century carousel maker. In the vehicle's dim recesses, Jack closed his eyes and concentrated. He slowed his breathing, visualizing the extinct Cottage City and the youthful Graham Carver. He concentrated, willing them to appear. He snapped his eyes open, but Oak Bluffs hadn't gotten the memo. People in shorts and T-shirts continued to fill the streets, ice cream cones and large Starbucks lattes clutched in their hands. He couldn't wish Cottage City or Graham Carver into existence any more than he could wish The Tar out of it. Maybe he should have thought this crazy plan through more carefully. Slamming his palm on the steering wheel, he inadvertently hit the car horn and drew stares from the passersby. One by one, the curious shuffled past and peered into the vehicle's darkened interior as Jack pulled his cap further down his face.

Brilliant, Jack.

He fired the engine and aimed the pickup toward Vineyard Haven. When he reached Pond Road near the harbor, Jack drove past Hal's cottage, taking a slow-speed loop through the neighborhood and scanning for any hint of surveillance. He had written enough crime novels to know what to search for—a lone car or van parked along the street, utility or cable company workers fixing lines or ground cables, or someone walking their dog. Observing none, he wheeled the truck from the neighborhood and dumped it along a side street. He returned on foot and paced the quiet stretch of road behind Hal's home, thick woods separating the parallel streets. Attempting to guestimate the cottage's location, Jack strained to peer through the dense foliage. He crept through a tidy yard, careful to stay out of sight at the property's edge until he could slip into the woods. If he had guessed correctly, he would emerge straight into Hal's backyard.

As he escaped the underbrush, Jack frowned. Hal's cottage loomed several houses away, requiring a skulk through a line of spacious yards. Moving with stealth through the darkness, he made it undetected into Hal's yard and approached the rear door. He grabbed a stone from the flower bed and pressed it against the glass panel until it gave way with a muted crack. Knocking the glass shards inward onto the carpet, he reached through the pane and freed the lock. He stepped inside, advancing through the hallway and mounting the steps to the first floor.

In the darkness, Jack gave the main floor layout a quick scan. To his right, the living room. Ceiling-to-floor windows stretched along the wall and gave a glimpse of the backyard, but he could barely make out the vague tree line behind the house, the Vineyard night cloaking everything in a murky blanket. To his left, beside the front door, Hal's windbreaker hung from a hook above a pair of tennis shoes. A set of housekeys and loose change lay scattered upon the entryway table. Facing him was the kitchen. Jack hoped Hal had stored something in the pantry—canned soup, crackers, anything that could sustain him for a few days. After he struck out today at the carousel, Jack had no clue when he should next attempt a rendezvous with Carver. When would Cottage City once again appear to him? It could be tomorrow, the next day, next year, or maybe never. In the meantime, he would need sustenance.

Stepping into the kitchen, Jack did a cursory search of the pantry, fridge, and cupboards. His face fell. *Jesus Christ, Hal. Don't you ever cook?* He would live on Goldfish crackers and condiments for the foreseeable future. No way could he show his most-wanted mug at the local market.

Jack advanced to the living room, pausing to peruse the graduation and wedding photos along the mantel. He approached the built-in bookshelves and scanned the handful of titles. Jack's books, no others. A framed photo rested on the empty shelf below. It featured Jack, Hal, and Hal's wife, Sherry, before the divorce. He pictured Sam behind the camera that day, trying to get Jack and Hal to quit giggling like schoolboys. Hal had his arm around Jack's neck, and they had burst into laughter as

Sam snapped the shutter. Jack leaned forward, squinting at the inscription on the frame:

Friendship is Forever.

"Unless you're a killer." Jack pushed out a breath. He rubbed a finger across the inscription before slinking across the carpet and dropping onto the couch. Perched in the darkness, he had never felt more alone.

———

He jerked awake, lost for a moment in groggy consciousness. He had been drifting on the cusp of a dream with Sam beside him in his old bedroom and Morgan mere steps down the hall. But his wishful fantasy crumbled as his eyes adjusted to unfamiliar surroundings. A tingling sensation pulsed along his left leg as if he had slept on it wrong and it had fallen asleep. Rising from the living room sofa, he massaged the limb and shifted his weight from one foot to the other to get the blood flowing. The tingling bloomed, forcing Jack's hand to the rear of his upper thigh. As his kneading fingers worked the area, he felt Carver's whittling knife through his back pocket. He removed the blade, halting the tingling sensation. Jack tested the limb, bouncing on his left foot before giving it his full weight.

Jack squeezed the knife, its prickling warmth humming in his hands. He pictured his ponytailed partner, adversary, counterpart . . . pick one. Carver's words echoed in his head. *"You see, we're connected. That's why you see me sometimes . . . That's why I see you."* Both had suffered at The Tar's hands. Both had lost their families to the Underground. Both had negotiations they had to fulfill.

Connected.

Jack rolled the knife in his palm. An image flashed in his head, moving through him at lightning speed. His eyelids fluttered as the world went gray. The Flying Horses carousel spun before him, Sam and Morgan sharing a jumper and giggling along with the families spinning about the carousel's mirrored core in blissful ecstasy. His daughter's eighth birthday. Less than three years later, she would be dead. If he had known, what would he have done differently? Held her close every minute of the day and never let her out of his sight? He would have filled in that goddamn pool. But would that have changed the outcome? Did fate predetermine one's moment of death? Or was the moment and manner in which it occurred subject to setting and circumstance? Maybe Morgan would have sleepwalked into the ocean—he would never know. In the memory, he perused the crowd and glimpsed a long-haired man moving against the far wall. Jack shifted his feet, stepping to his right to get a better view across the twirling mass of bodies rotating on their horses. The man pulled his hair back into a ponytail and glanced through the crowd, meeting Jack's gaze. He couldn't tell if Carver had inserted himself into Jack's memory or if he had been there all along. Carver acknowledged him with a grin, and the dream fell away like rain along a windowpane. His eyes flipped open, and he stumbled backward, dropping the throbbing knife and steadying himself on the sofa arm.

The knife. The one physical link left between Jack and Carver. It had to be a sign. Could the carousel man have used the knife to reach out to Jack and tell him the time had come?

Would have been more convenient a few hours ago when I was in town . . . just saying.

From the corner of his eye, he caught movement. Glancing toward the front door, he understood the timing of Carver's urgent message. Red and blue strobes pierced the front door glass, a soundless light show deflecting off the entryway's ceiling and walls. Jack raced to the door and peered through the glass panes to find an army of police cars gathering along Pond Road, officers hustling into formation behind trees and patrol car doors.

Time to fly, Jack.

He could almost hear Carver's voice.

He snatched his cell phone and wallet off the end table. He juggled them in his hands as he grabbed his sneakers and hopped across the floor, securing them to his feet. The jostling dance sent his cell tumbling from his grip.

"Fuck!"

As Jack retrieved the device from the floor and inspected it, his hand froze. A text message from Hal appeared in his notifications, written hours ago.

Sorry, Jack. They're on their way

He flew down the basement stairs and burst through the back door. Patrol cars on the road behind the woods aimed their spotlights toward the house, backlighting a wall of uniformed shapes crunching through the underbrush. Roots and twigs snapped as the horde advanced.

Jack crouched as he accelerated in the opposite direction across the lawn and into the woods. If he could get to his car, he might have a chance to get to Oak Bluffs and the Flying Horses.

"Over there! He's running!" The shouts came from behind.

Jack stepped up his pace, his feet flying out of his untied sneakers and onto the craggy ground. His unprotected soles blistered raw as the vegetation and scrub ripped through his socks and skin. Twigs and branches lashed his face and hands as he flew headlong through the darkness. If he smashed into a knotty pine whipping past, the chase would be over. But the swirling blue and red lights behind him illuminated a path.

His lungs burned as his breathing labored. But the light had faded, and the voices behind him grew distant. Then the woods went dark and quiet. *Too many donuts for Martha's Vineyard's finest?* Jack slowed and rested his hands on his knees.

Pushing through the darkness, Jack held his arms out before him. He could still barely make out his hands through the murk. His gut sensed the police would flank him, and at some point, he would run directly into a wall of blinding spotlights, ending his journey. But if that was their plan, they moved with the stealth and silence of a well-oiled military SEAL team. Jack veered in a direction he assumed would free him from the woods. Anticipating cool asphalt to rescue his battered feet, he met only soft, earthy ground.

Where the hell am I?

Jack slowed, the darkness now all-encompassing. A slight ringing in his ears proved the only sound in the Vineyard's blanketing silence. He could find no main road, no footpath, and no side street concealing his vehicle, nothing to suggest he was still in Hal's neighborhood. But how had he wandered so far? Changing direction, he moved to the east, then the west, but he could not escape the thick woods. He checked his watch.

2:30 a.m.

He had lost all track of time. Unaware of when he fell asleep or awoke, he might have been plodding along for ten minutes or two hours. It must have been closer to the latter, as each step sent a numbing pain through the soles of his tattered feet. By now, he should have been able to detect the trees' shapes, but his eyes hadn't adjusted to the heavy darkness.

But soon, he could.

He sensed the foliage's outline and a light source ahead. Tree trunks aimed their shadows toward him as he advanced through the copse. Jack quickened his pace as the woods thinned. Ahead, streetlights flickered through the trees. Stepping from the shadows, Jack's worn feet pressed against the main road's cool cobblestones as he squinted at the street-lights. No electric buzz accompanied their shimmering glow. Open flames danced upon their oil-bathed wicks as they did more than a century ago.

Cottage City. Waking from its slumber.

Despite the pain, Jack hurried along Lake Avenue. His footfalls along the wood-planked walkways reverberated through the still night. Cottage City appeared abandoned, but Jack sensed someone else keeping vigil in the forgotten town. He spotted the Flying Horses ahead, the aged barn a perfect complement to the other wood and clapboard structures surrounding it.

Jack strode to the barn, the crisp, surrounding air fat with a sizzling charge pulsing toward him. The door sat open, barely enough room to slip through. As he entered, a fiery heat surged from the top of his head to his feet, providing a gentle reminder this place had forever been the epicenter, the true gateway to hell. The barn was empty, its carousel, floor, and windowsills covered in a dusty filth blanket.

"Carver, are you here?" Jack shouted.

From a darkened corner, footsteps scuffed across the floor's sawdust and grit.

"Well, look who's here." The words hissed through the huge man's missing front teeth. He straightened his thick, horn-rimmed glasses. "I told you we would meet again."

CHAPTER THIRTY-SEVEN

Cottage City, Massachusetts (Martha's Vineyard)

Malik stood between Jack and the door to Cottage City, ensuring he wouldn't escape unless he could find a way over, under, or through him.

"Glad to see me, eh? I figured you would show up eventually." Malik squeezed his fists and advanced toward Jack. "I'm sorry. But you know it had to end this way."

"Wait a minute!" Jack held up his hands. "You're here to take me back to the Underground, I get it. But I'm going anyway. You don't need to—"

"I'm not here to take you back." Malik shuffled closer. "I'm here to stop you from going."

Glancing into Malik's eyes, Jack understood the giant's mission. "The Tar is done with me?"

Malik tilted his head to the side. "The Tar still thinks you can be an asset to his operation, but not with a carousel."

"That's what I figured."

The giant revealed a toothless grin. "He says you're a killer. He likes that about you. He'd welcome you back, for sure. But he gave me . . . options."

Jack tilted his head. "Like . . . ?"

"Take you back if I can. Kill you if I can't. Truth is, I could take you back if I wanted to." He took another step in Jack's direction. "But after you stuck me with that blade . . ."

Jack noted the slight limp. "You lucked out. I was going for your balls."

"Luck, eh? That's something you're gonna need."

Jack spotted movement behind the carousel. A young, ponytailed Graham Carver crept toward the pair. He advanced out of Malik's line of sight, hugging the barn wall. Carver would flank Malik with no more than a few steps. But only if he continued his stealthy advance. Jack would need to keep the giant distracted.

"Sounds like you're the kind to hold a grudge."

Malik raised his shoulders slowly and let them drop. "Bummer for you, eh? And your city friend."

"My what?"

"I didn't catch the man's name, but he had a nice office. Lots of books on his shelves. He had your books, too, but he kept those in his desk."

Jack detected blood splattered across the front of Malik's shirt and pants.

Hal. Jack worked his jaw. "You sonofabitch!"

"Sorry." Malik frowned. "But he tipped off the cops today. I couldn't have that. I got my own plans for you."

Jack recalled the text message. *Sorry, Jack. They're on their way.* Was it a change of heart, Hal's last chance to give him a head's up? Jack chose to live with the idea that Hal had done what he did for his benefit, not to rub salt into the wound.

"You're gonna pay for that." Jack made eye contact with Carver, who gave him a nod. The carousel man flashed his whittling knife, the same one he would give Jack a hundred and fifty years from now. The same one Jack still had in his pocket.

"Oh, no. Today you're gonna pay for this." Malik put a finger into the stab wound in his legs, initiating a fresh blood rivulet along his leg. Stepping to the wall, he pried a wooden plank from the window frame. He tapped it twice against his massive hand. "I won't lie to you. This is gonna hurt."

"Not very sporting, Malik. You know, beating my brains out with a piece of lumber when I don't have anything to defend myself with."

"Feel free to tear something off the wall if you like." He flipped the wood over in his hands and advanced toward Jack. "They come off pretty easy."

As Malik raised the wood to strike, Carver launched himself at the giant, embedding the steel blade into Malik's back. The man stumbled forward with a howl, falling to the ground and dropping the timber. It skidded across the floor, inches from Jack's feet. Retrieving the weapon, Jack swung it like a golf club as Malik made it to all fours and raised his head. He caught Malik flush in the mouth with a sickening crack, the assassin's remaining teeth exploding from his kisser and scattering across the barn floor.

"Nice cut, Jack," Carver said, sidling beside him and dropping a hand on his shoulder. "You would have made a good stickball player."

Stickball? "You're dating yourself, Carver."

He squinted at him. "By the way, your nose looks better."

"My . . . oh, yeah." Jack pressed a finger to his tender schnoz. "No thanks to you."

Carver pointed at the giant moaning on the floor and reaching to gather his Chiclets. "What do we do with him?"

"We put him on the carousel and send him back where he belongs."

As the men advanced, Malik grasped the knife's hilt and slipped the blade from his back with a wet slurp. He sprung to his feet.

"I'm not finissed wiss you, you son of a biss," he slurred, his new-found dental status creating an indistinguishable word salad. Balancing the knife between his thumb and index finger, Malik drew his arm back and slung the dagger. Carver dove, knocking Jack to the floor as the shank sailed past his shoulder and flew toward the carousel. The whizzing blade pierced the coffee-colored horse's neck, embedded to the hilt.

The mare let loose an ear-splitting shriek as jet-black blood burst from the wound, bathing it in an inky paste. The enraged horse burst from its guide pole, lowering its head and raising its hindquarters as it bucked. Scissoring its rear legs like pistons, the horse snapped support struts like matchsticks as it escaped the damaged carousel platform and galloped about the barn. The possessed animal crashed into walls and shattered wooden planks with powerful hindquarters thrusts, a hellish yowl escaping its bloody throat.

Jack yanked Carver to the floor as the incensed beast thundered past. They rolled beneath the platform, but a loopy Malik stood watching. The horse focused its lifeless eyes on the giant as it charged him head-on, the collision leaving Malik sprawled across the floor. He raised a woozy head as the infuriated horse thundered past him and sent a powerful double-heeled kick to his face. The sound of hooves on bone resonated like an axe impacting wood. The powerful blow removed the lower half of Malik's jaw and snapped his head backward with a sickening crack. Malik's twitching body fell forward, but his partially severed head continued to gaze at the ceiling from between his shoulder blades. The giant's tongue lolled from a shattered maw as his eyelids fluttered shut.

The mare thrashed and whinnied as it fought for its life, blood spurting from the gaping neck wound. As the horse staggered and dropped to the floor, its underbelly ripped open with a wet slurp. An oily-black mass slipped to the floor, twisting and jerking in a slimy puddle.

"Jesus Christ." Carver's eyes glowed. "What the hell is that thing?"

The grotesque form flipped and writhed across the slick floor.

"I've seen it before. Or something like it." Jack pictured The Tar standing in his Underground living room and glimpsing the blackened husk behind the beast's human disguise. "I'm guessing the carousel just exorcised its demon."

The pair covered their ears as the twitching mutation let out a shrill wail. The sound grew in tenor and volume, as if the gates of hell had opened and released every burning soul's agony at once. Flames erupted from the writhing hell-thing, rising and swelling until the shrieks had subsided and the searing heat had reduced the blackened soul to ashes. The dusty remains swirled and dispersed into the air.

Jack and Carver slid from beneath the carousel platform. Behind them, the machine sprung to life, the hurdy-gurdy Wurlitzer offering a musical epilogue to the sixth horse's strange death dance. But the carousel struggled to spin, jerking and stalling like a bicycle wheel with a stick through its spokes.

"What's it doing?" Jack rubbed his chin. The machine bucked and hummed as though voicing its displeasure.

Carver hesitated. "I don't know."

"I think it's trying to go in reverse."

"Clockwise?" Carver mumbled. "It's not supposed to do that."

"I thought you said—"

"It *can* go clockwise," Carver said, tapping his nose. "You found that out the hard way. But only if it's set to go that way. Right now, the carousel is doing it on its own, and I'm not sure why."

Jack threw his arms up. "You're the guy that built this hunk of junk. Shouldn't you know?"

The carousel screeched as it labored to reverse direction.

Jack pivoted to face the struggling machine. He slapped a palm against his forehead and straightened as if every nerve in his body had fired at once. "Wait a minute."

Sprinting to the carousel's control panel, he examined its buttons and switches from every angle. "How do you make this hunk of junk go backward . . . or clockwise."

"There's a direction switch. Beneath the control panel." Carver joined Jack at the carousel and yanked the panel door from its hinges. "What are you thinking?"

Jack grabbed Carver by the shoulders. "When you built this thing, you could have designed a new motor, but you didn't. You used your old British design and just tweaked it a little." He pivoted and grabbed the lever. "You did it that way for a reason, and I think I know why."

"Look!" Carver pointed at the five remaining horses on the platform. "Now what the hell are they doing?"

The horses had spun on their guide poles and faced the opposite direction. Their hooves pelted the platform with a metallic ping as they attempted to gallop. Saliva foamed from their mouths, and mucus jetted from their snouts as they labored to reverse direction.

Jack gestured to the bucking steeds. "I learned about these horses when I rode the coffee-colored one all those years ago. Some kind of strange connection happened. These five never agreed with the sixth horse, but they couldn't do anything to oppose its power. They must have witnessed nothing but the sixth horse's evil for over a century, all those souls abducted and brought to the Underground. Now that the evil is dead, I suspect they want to do something about it. They want to help make things right."

The decibel level inside the barn escalated. The carousel's screech and horses' whinnying reached a fever pitch, reverberating off the floor and walls.

"Help them reverse direction!" Jack cried.

"I don't understand what that's gonna—"

"Just do it!" Jack shouted above the din.

Carver reached into the panel and flipped the directional switch as Jack threw the lever forward. The gears and cogs fell into place, reversing the carousel's counterclockwise course. The screeching sound halted as the carousel accelerated in the opposite direction.

The machine picked up speed as the horses galloped. They had escaped their guide poles and now thundered along the platform, their sleek muscles rippling beneath their taut coats. Their hooves clanged off the platform as they galloped in unison. The carousel spun in a vibrant, colorful blur, a whirling rainbow set to music.

Jack gazed in wonder through the swirling, iridescent glow. He glimpsed across the Earth's worldly gates to the other side, his retinas bombarded with a brilliant radiance in hues he had never beheld or could have imagined. All at once, everything made sense, and yet, he understood nothing, like a child viewing the world at the moment of its birth.

Jack now understood what Carver's clients experienced when they mounted one of the five horses and rode the carousel—they provided a glimpse of the eternal. But the horses hadn't been able to save everyone. Now they were working together to bring the eternal to those they couldn't save.

Advancing through the carousel's blur, the first figures arrived.

They stepped off the platform one at a time with the calm of those disembarking a train. They wandered through the barn to the exit, most holding hands but all gazing about with looks of wonder. They glowed, imbued with a deep-sea creature's phosphorescence. They proceeded in an orderly fashion, as though they understood each soul had its moment to progress to a new stage in the journey.

As they moved through the barn door and into Oak Bluffs, Jack followed. He gazed at the houses and buildings morphing and shifting before his eyes, from simple wood construction to post-war clapboard to steel and glass and back again. The horse-drawn carriages transformed into gas-powered vehicles, and the colors mutated with the different eras, as if viewing the transition through a photograph shifting from sepia tones, to black and white, to technicolor, and beyond.

"Who are these people?" Jack whispered.

"My clients. The souls I sent to The Tar for the past century-and-a-half." Carver gripped Jack's shoulder. "They're going home."

Others arrived, ambling from the carousel's spinning light show.

Jack's hands trembled, the vibration advancing through his arms, legs, and core. Jack Morgan and his mother, Ellen, gazed at him with sympathetic eyes, the boy grinning ear to ear and holding his mother's hand. Jack's other victims filed past, and he sensed nothing but love and forgiveness in their hearts. But Jack could only envision the terror on their faces and recount the screams and pleas for the lives he never spared. The horrific images from their final moments flew past him like a video played on fast-forward, a memory collage he had kept darkened projected on a wall in his mind. He dropped to his knees as the truth finally hit home. He was a killer, and he would pay for his sins in this life and the next.

Carver rested a gentle hand on the back of Jack's neck. "Don't be too hard on yourself. The man who did those things wasn't you." Carver gestured to the colorful figures filing through the Flying Horses barn. "You freed them and so many other souls."

"I don't understand." Jack pivoted to face Carver. "The carousel didn't take these people to hell. I did. Why are they coming back through it?"

"Each rode the carousel, but none chose the sixth horse. They made it. But still, The Tar made sure he acquired their souls. He used you to get them. I sense the carousel is trying to ease their pain. And yours. They're going to a better place now."

Jack stood in awe as the final glowing figures proceeded past them. The carousel continued to spin like a whirling dervish. The horses galloped in unison, the five sets of hooves striking the platform simultaneously with a staccato ping.

Jack sensed the vice-grip squeeze on his forearm. When he glanced at Carver, the man had appeared to stop breathing, his eyes fixed on the carousel. Jack directed his gaze at the three figures stepping from the kaleidoscope twirl.

Carver steadied himself against Jack's shoulder as his wife, Annabelle, and his children, Rebecca and Zachariah, strode toward them. Jack stepped away as they gathered beside the carousel operator. Carver dropped to a knee. Zachariah embraced him, snuggling his head into his chest while Rebecca wrapped her arms around his neck from behind. Annabelle peppered her husband's face with kisses before taking his hand and coaxing him to his feet. Rebecca remained attached to her father's neck, refusing to let go as he hoisted her off the ground. Wrapping his arms around his wife, Carver sandwiched young Zachariah between them.

The carousel's glow aroused Jack's attention. He spun his head toward the machine in time to witness the figure emerge, its familiar shape seared into his subconscious. Sam stepped from the platform and collapsed into his arms. Her body fit perfectly within his embrace as if their forms had originated from the same mold. The heat from her breath onto his cheek warmed him, body and soul.

"You saved me," Sam mumbled. "You got me out."

"I told you I would."

She glanced about the structure. "Am I really home?"

The way she uttered the final word sent a tingle deep into Jack's bones. He pulled her close. But he couldn't help imagining who or what would be waiting for them when they left the building and entered twenty-first-century Oak Bluffs. He had a debt to pay. He would be trading his home for another soon, one with bars over the windows. But right now, at this moment, he had Sam in his arms. He squeezed his eyes shut. He would worry about his future later. No matter what happened, she was here with him now in this special place. The place she called home. He could not only sense her love, but he witnessed it radiating from her soul in vivid hues. This was the moment of his life, right here, right now. He savored it, sensing he would draw upon it for the rest of his days.

Sam adjusted her position, burying her face into his neck.

"I missed you, Sam. I'm sorry I left you down there so long."

"I'm here, and nothing matters anymore."

Jack disengaged, holding her at arm's length while he inspected her. "Are you okay?"

"I think so. I don't remember much." She rubbed her forehead. "Just . . . isolation and despair, like a weight on my shoulders, and every emotion buried under the heaviness. The only thing reversing the crushing sadness was when you came for me. It gave me hope. It kept me going."

He pressed a hand against her cheek and brushed away a tear with his thumb.

"It made me realize how much I love you, Jack. How much I've always loved you. If there's one thing I've learned in all this, it's that I can't live without love. Or you."

"You don't have to." Jack melted into her arms. He didn't want to lie, but now wasn't the moment to tell her everything. He only hoped she would hold tight her emotions once the barn door opened onto Oak Bluffs, when reality set in and she learned about him and his past. She would need to recall this moment, when her memories faded and she questioned whether she had even been to the Underground or whether it had been one of those strange, recurring nightmares.

"Morgan came to me while I was away."

Jack pictured the shapeless carcass Sam had carried with her in the Underground. "I don't think that was her."

She pulled away from his embrace, eyes dancing. "No, she was there." The tears tumbled from her eyes. "You have to believe me. She came to see me. I got to say goodbye to her, Jack. I finally said goodbye."

A burning sensation grew inside his nose and behind his eyes, the precursor for one of his regular Morgan cries. He leaned in and kissed her forehead.

"She misses you, too. She has a lot to tell you."

Jack squished his eyebrows together. "What do you mean?"

"Jack." The voice came from inside his head like a whisper. Carver stood with his family beside the door to the Flying Horses, holding each other close. The man's eyes flickered to the carousel, still spinning in a chromatic blur.

"I think the carousel has one more gift for you." Carver grinned as he and his beloved Annabelle scooped up their children and stepped through the door into the night, disappearing into nineteenth-century Cottage City.

CHAPTER THIRTY-EIGHT

Cottage City, Massachusetts (Martha's Vineyard)

From within the carousel's whirling rainbow, her tiny form stepped into view. Morgan Rainne glowed with a brilliance the previous figures hadn't possessed, as if she had hijacked each drop of the twirling machine's flowing color and spun it around herself like a technicolor cloak.

In her pint-sized frame, Jack could picture the child she had been and the woman she would grow into all at once. Her life's entirety, her dreams and accomplishments, unveiled in one instantaneous moment. The carousel had granted Jack a glimpse of Morgan's essence in a way he couldn't comprehend during her brief time as his daughter. He immediately understood life on Earth could not encapsulate or define one's existence or come close to revealing what would come. The soul's complexity approached the infinite, and there was so much more.

Morgan glanced at her mother and smiled, touching Sam's hand as she passed. Jack fell to his knees as if Earth's gravity had tripled and yanked him downward.

Morgan knelt beside him. "What happened to your nose, Daddy?"

Jack grinned as the tears spilled from his eyes. He wrapped his arms around his daughter. "Does it look bad?"

"Just kinda funny, that's all."

"You came back to me." His chest hitched.

She glanced at the carousel. "Just for a little while."

Jack pulled her close and squeezed. He pressed his hands to her arms, back, and shoulders. "Are you even real?"

"Of course, you silly goose." She scrunched her face. "What do you think?"

"I'm not sure what to think anymore." He released her and swiped a sleeve across his eyes. "How did you get here? You weren't living where Mommy was, were you?"

She shook her head. "I live somewhere much better, and I try to stay away from bad places like that. I get to go where I can help people who need me."

Like an angel, Jack mused.

"But Mommy needed me." She pressed her palm against Jack's face. "And now *you* need me."

Jack sensed the sting in his nose as the tears renewed their descent along his cheeks. "I've needed you for a long time. I've missed you so much."

"Me, too." She stood and reached for his hand, drawing him to his feet. She guided him to the window. Oak Bluffs rose from its sleep as the dawn filled the skyline with pink and orange watercolor shades.

"It wasn't your fault, you know."

Jack opened his mouth but couldn't speak.

"And it didn't hurt at all."

For the first time since the accident, the images exploded inside his memory: the hook and eye closure outside her bedroom door, the hook dangling against the jamb; the basement door open to the backyard; the pitch black pool water as still as glass; the pajama-clad body floating in the shallow end. Jack tried to swallow but gagged on a mouthful of cotton.

"I always locked your door at night."

"To keep me from sleepwalking, I know."

Another teardrop fell from his cheek onto the dusty floorboards. "I must have forgotten."

"Some things are just meant to happen. They're not anybody's fault."

Jack lifted her, letting her peer through the window. "Can you come with Mommy and me for a little while? We could get you an ice cream across the street or walk along the pier."

Morgan glanced over her shoulder at the carousel. "I can't leave here. But we'll be together someday, Daddy." She grinned at Sam. "All of us."

Jack's lungs struggled for air. "I don't think so, Morgan. I'm not going to the place where you are. I've done things in this life. Things you don't know—"

"I know about those things," the little girl said. "Each one. I also know you saved all those innocent souls from a bad place . . . and a bad man. *You* did that, Daddy. No one else."

"But there are others—"

Morgan put her tiny fingers over his lips, silencing him. "You didn't do those bad things all by yourself, you know. You had the bad man inside you making you do those things. It's like when Mommy used to make hand puppets from our old socks, and they would sing songs."

Jack chuckled at the memory, curling a lock of hair behind her ear.

"The socks weren't really singing, Daddy—Mommy made them sing. That's kind of what happened to you."

She squirmed in his arms, the way she used to do, signaling she wanted down. He lowered her onto the floor.

She wandered to the carousel. "The bad man is still trying to make you do things for him. All you have to do is say 'no' in your mind. Then we'll see each other again."

"That's all?"

"Your head will hurt bad, but you'll have to sacrifice." She smiled and pushed her sleeve to her elbow. "You know what I miss most?"

Jack knelt on the floor beside her. He used his fingertips to caress the underside of her arm. The left one and then the right one, making her even. "That's why you *really* came back, isn't it?"

She giggled, inching toward the carousel as if an invisible force beckoned.

Jack followed her to the light, glancing at Sam. "Can Mommy and I come with you?"

She shook her head and grasped her father's hand. "I wish you could, but you're not ready yet."

"Are you happy where you are, Morgan?"

His daughter's eyes softened. "I am. It doesn't mean I don't miss you and Mommy every day, though."

Jack settled both hands on his daughter's head, stroking her curls, running his fingers along her ears, her cheeks, and her chin. He sensed this moment to be his last chance to touch her, hold her, and experience her presence in this world . . . or whatever world they found themselves in now.

"The place where I live is like a big carnival, Daddy. It's kinda like when we used to come here to ride the horses." She gazed about the barn as a wide grin spread across her cheeks. "And one day, we'll all be at the carnival together."

"I can't wait to get there."

"And you know what?" she whispered.

"What?"

"It's got the biggest, most beautiful carousel I've ever seen." She dropped her father's hand and sighed. "I love you, Daddy." She hugged Sam. "I love you, Mommy."

As Morgan neared the carousel, she faced her parents. Waving her hand, she stepped into the twirling rainbow and disappeared. The machine's clockwise spin slowed until the carousel ground to a halt. Sunshine pierced the building's windows, dust motes dancing in its beams. The five horses spun on their guide poles until they faced the opposite direction, ready for a new day undulating beneath Oak Bluffs' paying customers.

Jack reached for Sam and gathered her into his embrace. He pressed his lips against hers, electricity jetting through his core like it did when they first met. He grasped her hand and led her toward the exit.

"Are you ready?" Sam squeezed his hand.

As he threw the door open, flashing blue lights engulfed the pair in a blinding assault. Detectives Mike Stahl and Chris Daniels stood on the landing with weapons drawn, behind them a regiment of Massachusetts' finest, poised with rifles and handguns behind patrol car doors. Hundreds of citizens stood cordoned off on distant sidewalks, viewing the show with cellphones raised.

Daniels leveled his weapon at Jack's chest as Stahl fished the handcuffs from his belt. "Put your hands behind your back, Mr. Rainne. You're under arrest for the murder of Ellen and Jack Morgan."

CHAPTER THIRTY-NINE

Plymouth, Massachusetts (Plymouth County Correctional Facility)

In the days following, Jack learned additional murder charges would be forthcoming, including one for Hal Bader's death. Alleyway security cameras had captured him behind Bader's office and entering his building on the morning of the murder. After recording the incriminating images, the alley's camera systems somehow malfunctioned simultaneously. A power surge or something, according to Boston Edison. But Jack didn't buy it. Malik had made sure no one would find his hulking image on any tape and prevent him from carrying out his preferred *options* when it came to Jack. Malik had clearly gone rogue in his pursuit, ignoring his employer's wish to have Jack free and alive to conduct his soul-hunting for him. In the end, eyewitness accounts had Bader alive and well until his appointments ended and administrative staff bid him farewell. The working theory was Jack lay in wait until Bader was alone in the office. Not the definitive smoking gun the DA would prefer, but incriminating circumstantial evidence, nonetheless.

Stahl and Daniels' search of Jack's home had yielded Ellen Morgan's horsehead pendant and other evidence linking him to more than a half dozen murder victims. They had found a sharpened, bloody crucifix, a syringe, a breathalyzer and phony police badge, severed finger joints and body parts, a blood-stained antler, and several teeth with cracked, bloody roots attached as if wrenched from a skull. In a crawl space beneath the house, they had found at least two mutilated and partially skinned bodies. The detectives would have to connect the dots in these cases, but they had descriptions in each of his novels and the necessary time to gather evidence with Jack secured in Plymouth County Correctional Facility

north of Cape Cod. For Jack, they had him dead to rights on Ellen and
young Jack's murder, and each carried a life sentence without the possibility of parole. Any additional convictions would only add more post-mor-
tem years to his sentence. Truth was, Jack wasn't interested in putting
any murder victim's family through a trial. He agreed to plead guilty to
first-degree murder in Ellen and Jack Morgan's deaths and led police to
the quarry where he had dumped the bodies. As Jack learned about the
other victims—reviewing the case files and examining their images—the
full memories of what he had done returned. Jack's skill at the killing
game didn't just shock the country, but himself. He found comfort that
his victims had forgiven him as they passed through the Flying Horses
carousel to their better place, but their families never would. Nor could
they move on until they had closure. Jack chose to cooperate with the
district attorney and pleaded guilty to each charge. It had pained him to
confess to the murder of his friend Hal. But he agreed to do it and ease
the family's suffering.

According to Marcus Lang, Sam had exhibited signs of disorientation
and confusion following Jack's arrest. Stahl and Daniels had taken her to
the Behavioral Health Unit of Cape Cod Hospital, where doctors diag-
nosed her with post-traumatic stress disorder. Still, she could not account
for the events contributing to her condition. She repeatedly asked for her
husband and daughter. Soon after, the hospital released her under Lang's
supervision to continue her recovery at home. In time, Lang explained
to her that Jack had been right about everything. He had witnessed his
nightmare, and Sam had been a pawn in his chess match with The Tar.
The understanding that her intense daydreams and nightmares were
based in truth and not a twisted story in a confused mind helped accelerate her healing. She told Lang she drew strength from her remembrances
of Morgan's visits and remained confident she would reunite with her
beloved daughter someday.

For Jack, the confinement and distance from Sam proved excruciating at first. But she and Lang visited regularly, and Jack witnessed Sam's
incremental mental health improvements with each visit. Her friends
from LA had been her best support network. Sasha Kohl had flown out
and stayed with her, using her connections to help get her acting gigs

on the East Coast. Sam appeared in commercials and soon graduated to independent film productions. Sasha tried to convince her to move back to LA, but Sam refused. With Jack housed at Plymouth County Correctional, she had no desire to relocate to Tinseltown. She considered Martha's Vineyard home. Dr. Lang found he had no desire to return to Missouri, either. With Sam on the mend, he found a place in Falmouth, close to a mental health facility, where he could work part-time. The location kept him close enough to Jack and Sam, should they need him.

Jack paced the confines of his six-by-eight cell, unsure how he would spend the rest of his life in such a limited space. For the past twenty-five years, he had taken for granted freedom's endless borders and independence. But twenty-three hours a day in confinement stirred story ideas inside Jack's once dormant imagination, and he found himself writing effortlessly. Stories, characters, and plot twists poured from his active right brain faster than he could transfer them onto paper. He no longer desired to publish his work or spend time fretting about movie deals. With Sam doing well, such things no longer mattered. His burgeoning imagination took him outside the prison walls to places that freed his mind from the excruciating sameness of each day. But most importantly, writing helped him lose time. Afternoons and evenings passed effortlessly, and with time, the only asset he could claim in abundance, he embraced the chance to rid himself of it. The sooner it all went away, the sooner he, Sam, and Morgan would be together again.

When Lang visited, they spent time catching up on life, not revisiting the strange experiences they shared. The only thing reawakening the remembrances of his former life was the gradual reappearance of the headaches. They had crept in like an unwanted companion, becoming stronger and stronger with each passing day. At times, the blood pulsing against his skull forced him to bury his head between his hands.

THUD ... THUD ... THUD ...

Malik had mentioned—before the sixth horse removed his head—that The Tar thought Jack could still be a useful resource. The Underground king shit was reminding Jack of his unfulfilled responsibilities. Plus, he had cost The Tar too many freed souls for the beast to sit idly back and let Jack get the best of him. Jack pleaded for relief from the constant pounding, but he would need to find a stray, someone—a prisoner or staff member—who found themselves in the wrong place at the wrong time. One more soul for The Tar, and an instant respite from the pain. How difficult would that be?

One afternoon, Jack followed a newbie returning from the prison yard to the ward. For a moment, he had a chance. A wrong turn. Two men alone in a stairway corridor, the thudding in his head reaching a debilitating crescendo. But Morgan's words repeated in his head. *All you have to do is say 'no' in your mind. Then we'll see each other again.* He had the power to define his future. He could choose whether he and Morgan would be together or not. He just had to fight it. Jack had slunk back to his cell and crawled onto his cot, arms wrapped around his head to stop the throbbing. He wasn't sleeping anymore. He couldn't concentrate or write. Before long, he couldn't eat without vomiting. He had reached wit's end, unsure how long he could go on. *You'll have to sacrifice*, Morgan had said at the carousel. But she was wrong. He wasn't strong enough. Something would have to give.

On Tuesday, Jack shuffled into the chow hall, grabbed a tray, and dropped into his seat. Propping his elbows onto the table, he held a glass of ice water against his head to quell the agony. He glanced at the prison guard making his way from table to table and keeping tabs on the crowded galley. Danny Martin wasn't the typical Plymouth County Correctional guard. Picture a southern preacher in a bulging-at-the-seams uniform and you've got Officer Martin. He didn't just clock in for the eight-hour shifts and hide behind his Ray Bans. He cared about his flock, as he called them, and went out of his way for them. While most inmates took to him and his avocation, others weren't interested in his overt attempts to send them along the road to Jesusville.

Martin gave Jack the once over. "You don't look too good, partner."

"It's never a good idea to look too good in prison. Know what I mean?"

Martin chuckled. "You have a point. Not hungry?"

Jack had only pushed his food around his plate. "Not today."

"Not yesterday or the day before, either. How about we make a trip to the infirmary? You look like shit."

"They can't help me there, Danny."

From the corner of his eye, Jack spotted Billy Ray Bradley at the far table, gathered with a handful of his followers. Jack had stayed away from Bradley and his gang as much as he could since his incarceration. Although the man only weighed a buck fifty soaking wet, he was the leader of Satan's Army—more of a cult, really—that believed they had a direct line of communication with the devil. With triple sixes stenciled beneath their eyes, upside-down crosses tattooed to their faces, and goat heads etched along their arms and backs, they bore all the horror movie tropes associated with the demonic. Jack smirked.

If you guys only had a clue.

Martin put a hand on Jack's shoulder. "I know it's tough in here, Jack. But you gotta keep up your health. The predators in here can sense weakness."

Jack kept his attention focused across the room. Bradley's glare possessed a feral quality he hadn't witnessed before. "I appreciate the help, Danny. I think I'll pass. Go take care of the rest of your flock."

Martin grinned. "If you need anything, Jack, you know where to find me."

Bradley fixed his gaze on Jack, his eyes like black bottomless pits. Maybe Jack's indifference toward Bradley communicated his fearlessness of death, hell, or the devil himself, something the cult leader hadn't encountered before. Maybe Jack's boldness had convinced Bradley he *was* the real deal, or the man had seen far worse than some wannabe devil bootlicker. As for Martin, Bradley hated any God-fearing man. Martin had made it a personal mission to help convert Satan's Army and had lured a handful of Bradley's members to the chapel for his weekly Christian boot camp meetings. Martin would regularly take a seat with the Army at chow time and have them chanting *amen* right along with him. All but Bradley, and rumor had it he wanted to make the bastard pay. Danny Martin had thinned his ranks, and in prison, that made you vulnerable.

"Oh, and by the way," Martin added. "I know I've asked you before, but if you'd like to join us at boot camp this afternoon, we would love to have you. We're talking about sacrifice today, the things we can do for each other that make life better, even here in prison."

Sacrifice. Jack shook his head. "I don't know, Danny. I suspect it would take one hell of a sacrifice to redeem my soul."

Martin dropped a hand on Jack's shoulder. "You'd be surprised, my friend. Everyone has a shot at redemption." He squeezed his shoulder and wandered off to the next table of disciples.

Bradley whispered to a fellow Army member beside him as his gaze locked onto Jack's. The other man passed something to Bradley behind his back. Jack struggled to extricate his lower half from below the table as Bradley crossed the room in his direction. He advanced at a leisurely clip with his hand hidden from view. Jack had witnessed this kind of thing before, a slow approach to avoid drawing attention, a quick strike, two or three times to the chest, and problem solved.

Not good, Jack. Get your ass up.

When the distance had closed to no more than a few feet, Jack glimpsed the shank in Bradley's withdrawn grip. He stood as Bradley accelerated past him toward an unsuspecting Danny Martin, the guard's back turned to his assailant. *We're talking about sacrifice today.* Martin's words echoed in his ears. Jack reached out with his leg, sweeping Bradley's foot and knocking him off stride as he went in for the strike. As Bradley recovered his gait, Jack sprinted to the adjacent table.

"Danny!" Jack shouted.

Time slowed as Bradley closed the distance, knife raised. Disconnected thoughts swirled in Jack's mind. Morgan's face appeared at the carousel, illuminated with the rainbow colors of the eternal. The words she chose to leave him with repeated in his head. *You'll have to sacrifice.* Jack glanced at Danny Martin pivoting to face his attacker, hands raised in defense. Jack pictured the burly guard at his table only minutes earlier, palm on his shoulder, discussing the afternoon's boot camp on sacrifice. *Everyone has a shot at redemption.*

Bradley's steel-embedded fist thrust forward in a descending arc, but Jack bounced along a Missouri road in Carver's truck, picking up the old man's thoughts as he lamented about what drew his clients to the carousel. *Maybe the universe orchestrated happenstance and fate to intersect at some exact moment and time.* Jack considered whether Morgan and Danny Martin's message on sacrifice could be happenstance, or whether Carver could be telling Jack that happenstance and fate had intersected, and his moment and time had arrived. In the instant of Bradley's attack, Jack believed Morgan and Martin had reached out and reminded him that sacrifice was his only path to salvation.

Jack's recollections fell away, and the world around him accelerated into real time as Jack hurled his body before Danny Martin. Bradley buried the blade straight into Jack's chest through bone and soft tissue until it ripped through his heart. He lay on the prison floor in a rapidly growing blood pool as the seconds ticked off in an interminable cadence.

A dizzying calm blanketed him, and a cold sensation crept along his legs into his core. He fought to keep his eyes open as he took in the scene before him: blood gushing from a gaping hole in his chest; lockdown alarms and shouts filling the space as guards flooded the dining area and buried Bradley under a writhing, baton-wielding human mass; Danny Martin kneeling over him.

The pounding in Jack's head had stopped, rendering a comforting peace despite the chow hall's chaotic noise. Danny Martin pressed a hand against the dying man's cheek.

"What did you do that for, you dumbass writer?"

"You have a wife and kid, Danny," he whispered. "It's only right you get to go home to them tonight." *Maybe I get to go home to mine, too.*

Pictures and memories flooded Jack's mind one after another and all at once, pieces of his life flashing before his fading vision: wrapping his arms around his mother's leg in the backyard as she pinned the laundry on the clothesline against the buzzing backdrop of summer's choking heat; lounging on the porch swing with his first puppy, Fergus, a fuzzy head pressed against his thigh; holding hands with Mandy Laine on his first date, snug in the rusty old Ford's short bed under the stars at the Moberly drive-in; strolling the warm Cape Cod shoreline with Sam and Morgan, hands under his daughter's arms to hoist her above the incoming waves. The moving pictures and still frames grayed and blurred like an old UHF channel as they accelerated across his foggy vision, falling away in a gradually darkening and soundless void. Then nothing. His eyelids fluttered and fell shut.

Jack waited—for what, he didn't know. A spark of light? Oblivion? He waited in the indescribable pitch black for whichever would come first.

CHAPTER FORTY

Excerpt from *Untitled*, by Jack Rainne:

As the dead man lingered in the blinding darkness, a faint, familiar sound reached his ears. A boisterous carnival melody swirled from a calliope, ushering in a dim light behind his eyes–growing as if the sun chose to take its time rising from an eternal night. He found himself back at the carousel. The place where he had last held his daughter.

The little girl stood beside the twirling carnival ride. The man rose on shaky legs and stumbled forward, enveloping her in a desperate hug. "Oh, baby. I did it! I made it back to you."

He squeezed, expecting her tiny arms to fly around his neck and hold on tight. But they barely brushed his body before settling at her side. He released her and said, "I fought so hard to keep my promise to you, sweetie, and I did what you told me to do. And here I am. I can't wait for you to show me where you live." He stood, placing a hand on his daughter's shoulder. "I mean, where you and I are gonna live."

"The carousel will take us there soon," she said in a flat voice.

The man inspected his surroundings. The barn housing the carousel had finally shown signs of its age, the hint of sky peeking through the crumbling roof. The warped wooden wall planks littered the floor, leaving gaping holes in the building's sides. The curved, rotting floorboards left a mushy feel beneath his shoes.

What happened here?

"I trust you'll get us there." The man leaned forward and held his daughter's head between his palms. He kissed her forehead. "I can't wait."

As he pulled away, he glanced at the sticky black film coating his fingers. Raising a hand to his nose, he recoiled from the body odor and fecal matter stench and wiped the greasy filth on his pants.

He gazed at the black muck dripping from his daughter's ears. "Jesus, sweetie. Are you okay?"

An infernal heat wafted from her tiny frame. The man pivoted as the floorboards rattled, a pounding erupting from below. To his right, a hand pushed through the soft wood and dragged its tattered fingernails against the planks. To his left, a head and shoulders burst through the floor, the shattered skull sporting a blown-out exit wound through the crown. Other shapes broke through the surface, writhing to free themselves. They crawled toward the man.

"What's happening?" The man gaped at his daughter, eyes bulging in her head. Her legs shook like a fish caught on a line as black goo jetted from her ears and mouth. The convulsions cycled upward into her core and chest. An internal force pushed against her body's seams, stretching and pulling her fragile form to its breaking point. A dark shape burst from her body with a wet pop, shedding her outer core like snakeskin. Thick slime bathed the writhing form as heat billowed from its surface.

In an instant, the man understood.

He gazed at the beast before him, now revealed in its true form, the one he had imagined would greet him again when forced to account for his life's sins. His legs failed, dropping him to the floor. A bony hand grasped his ankle. The man kicked at it, locking eyes with the woman it belonged to. The naked body thrashed as her nails dug into his limb. Her grin revealed a mouth with broken and missing teeth, as if someone had wrenched them from her skull. The hands of a young boy and his mother clamped onto his wrist, their heads smashed to a frothy pulp. A horsehead pendant dangled from the woman's broken neck. In moments, a half dozen or more broken bodies—the man's victims—enveloped him, dragging him halfway through the floorboards.

"The carousel." His darting eyes locked onto the hell-creature as he fought to free himself. "I rescued them. I helped them escape to a better place."

The beast fixed the man with his gaze. "Their souls may have found a way out, but everything leaves a shadow. This is a place of shadows," he said, gesturing about the room, "and these souls have a score to settle."

The man pictured his father tethered to the ground, carrion picking at his eyes and innards for eternity. He reached a flailing hand toward the beast as the shadows dragged him further through the floor.

"Help me. Please." The pounding rose in his head.

Thud . . . Thud . . . Thud . . .

The beast shook, punching holes in the walls and raking grooves into the floorboards with razor-sharp talons. "What did I say about *please* and *thank you*?"

THUD . . . THUD . . . THUD . . .

The beast's chuckle rumbled through the ancient structure. "Welcome back, old friend. Or should I say, welcome home?"

EPILOGUE

Oak Bluffs, Massachusetts (Martha's Vineyard)
Present Day

If anyone could claim the record for breaking into haunted places and living to tell the tale, it would be Suzi-T.

If you've watched her YouTube channel—and who hasn't—you would know the Ghost Hunter Goth could gain access to any place, any time she wanted. Haunted houses, no sweat. Shuttered mental institutions. Please. And when she sprung the lock and hit 'em with her trademark wink and "Gotcha," forget about it. Cue the corporate sponsors. And how about the flirty banter between Suzi-T and her GHG sidekick, Mindi Marks? It never failed to stir social media into a frenzy. Were the two an item off camera, or did Mindi stay true to her spicy brush-offs during each episode's closing segment? Stay tuned for their next adventure to find out.

Truth was, Suzi-T's lifestyle appetites had grown too exotic for Mindi. The residue of instant fame, she figured. But she hoped that Suzi-T might one day remember she was Suzi Tindall, former Walmart associate from Schenectady, and return to her sweet, humble self. Maybe even return to Mindi's arms—but she wasn't holding her breath.

Suzi-T hadn't so much as broken a sweat picking the lock of the ancient barn housing the historic Flying Horses carousel. Mindi paced the wooden floorboards, fiddling with the GoPro as Suzi-T cased the square footage, searching for the best shots. The moon cast light through gaps in the aged building's clapboard walls, revealing lazy dust motes in no hurry to settle. The six horses stood frozen in mid-gallop above the carousel's metal platform, guide poles skewering their midsections to secure them in place.

"Get some closeups of the horses," Suzi-T barked, gesturing toward the carousel. "Make it spooky for the opening segment."

Mindi lowered the camera and checked the settings. "What do you want for the ISO?"

"Forty-six hundred for the closeups, but sixteen hundred for everything else."

"That's gonna make it pretty grainy, we'd be safer at—"

"Just do what I fucking tell you. When did you become Martin Scorsese?"

"Chill, Suze. Jeez." Mindi pointed at the camera. "Don't forget who makes you look good every week." *Fucking prima-donna.*

A metallic squeal rattled the old barn.

Mindi jumped, her head swiveling toward the sound.

"Relax, kiddo. Just this hunk of junk settling." Suzi-T grabbed a guide pole and hoisted herself onto the carousel platform. She inspected the nuts and bolts securing the worn suspension cables and struts. "These things probably jostle loose a little during the day. Don't tell me you're starting to believe all those crazy stories."

Ever since Mindi stumbled upon an old newspaper article describing unexplained disappearances near the Flying Horses carousel, Martha's Vineyard was on their radar for a GHG episode. Mindi and Suzi-T had spent the past week in Oak Bluffs, chasing the locals and picking their brains. Most spouted the company line about how the carousel has been the town's signature attraction since the nineteenth century, drawing tourists from around the country to ride the beautiful handmade gallopers. But in the pubs, pool halls, and dimly lit places, the locals whispered about what happens inside the shuttered building in the diminished light. They shared the rumors and cautionary tales their parents had passed along, trading stories with those who understood or had borne witness. Some even shared the story about the crime-writing serial killer—you remember, the Rainne of Terror guy who was obsessed with the carousel—how he might have been using the place to commune with the devil. They warned the girls to stay away from the carousel in the wee hours when terrible sounds rattled the building's timber frame and seeped through the walls, when the town itself appeared to shift and dance like a flickering mirage.

Suzi-T checked her watch. "Let's get filming or we're not gonna have a show. God, we should have focused on Plymouth instead." She pivoted to face Mindi. "What were you thinking? At least downtown Plymouth has electromagnetic fields to light up our K-IIs. We haven't gotten a god-damn blip around here yet."

A rattle pinged from the platform's opposite side.

"That doesn't sound like the machine settling," Mindi said, switching on the GoPro. "It came from one of the horses."

Suzi-T slalomed through the guide poles until she reached the far horse—the coffee-colored one. She gazed at the mare with its shimmering coat, lifelike eyes, and lush leather saddle. "Jesus, Mindi. Check this thing out."

"What is it?"

"It's just so . . . real."

"Probably made in some third-world sweatshop."

Suzi-T ran a hand across its coat.

Mindi fiddled with the GoPro. "What do you say, Suze? How about we get this done."

She didn't answer. She didn't move.

Mindi shifted her weight from one foot to the other and checked her watch. "Suzi?" She crept toward the carousel.

Suzi-T threw a Chuck Taylor into the stirrup and swung her leg across the horse's back.

"What are you doing?"

Settling into the saddle, Suzi-T gazed at Mindi. A line of drool escaped her gaping mouth.

Mindi mounted the platform. "You okay, hon?"

Suzi-T's eyeballs danced beneath their lids. Mindi leaned a hand against the horse as she grabbed her friend and gave her a shake. The mare's silky coat twitched, and a slithering shape squirmed beneath her fingers. Pulling her hand away, Mindi backpedaled as the scream escaped her lips. She stumbled from the carousel, landing hard on her backside. The GoPro shattered against the floor.

The carousel's antique steam organ blinked on, ringing out a discordant carnival melody. The carousel platform rotated with a screech, gaining momentum.

"Get off that thing," Mindi shouted.

Suzi-T's eyes rolled back in their sockets as the carousel picked up speed. The horse bucked its hindlimbs with fury, each explosive kick loosening the bolts that fastened the guide pole to its platform moorings. A high-pitched whinny urged from the mare's throat as Mindi sprinted for the barn door. The light dimmed as the music reached an ear-splitting crescendo, shaking the building's aged bones and sending barn mice scurrying through gaps in the floorboards and walls. The horse swished its tail, puffs of putrid air escaping its nostrils. In the corner of the building, a figure stepped from the shadows, shoulder-length hair waving in the carousel's spinning breeze. Mindi heard herself scream as she circled the room in a frenzy, pounding the wooden wall panels and searching for the building's exit. Dropping in a heap on the dusty floorboards, Mindi covered her ears with bloodied hands.

The doorway was gone.

ABOUT THE AUTHOR

STEPHEN PAUL SAYERS is the top-ten Amazon bestselling author of *The Caretakers horror trilogy: A Taker of Morrows, The Soul Dweller*, and *The Immortal Force*. As a college professor and research scientist, Stephen yields to the left-brain world of data analysis and statistics by day but releases the demons in his slightly twisted right-brain by night. It gets confusing around dusk when neither side is in control. Jet-setting between New England and the Midwest—well, more like driving back and forth in an RV—he divides his time between Columbia, Missouri, and Plymouth, Massachusetts, thinking up scary stories and watching classic horror films with his ill-behaved dog, Ollie. Visit Steve at stephenpaulsayers.com or reach out on Facebook: facebook.com/stephenpaulsayers; Twitter: twitter.com/SayersAuthor; or Instagram: instagram.com/stephenpaulsayers.

www.ingramcontent.com/pod-product-compliance
Lightning Source LLC
Chambersburg PA
CBHW011404010726
47495CB00009B/2776